The E   .
the World
is...NIGH!

Also by Tony Moyle

'How to Survive the Afterlife'

Book 1 – THE LIMPET SYNDROME
Book 2 – SOUL CATCHERS
Book 3 – DEAD ENDS

The Ally Oldfield Series

THE END OF THE WORLD IS NIGH
LAST OF THE MOUNTAIN MEN

Sign up to the newsletter
www.tonymoyle.com/contact/

The End of the World is...NIGH!

TONY MOYLE

LIMBO
PUBLISHING

First published: February 2019

ISBN - 9781797859828

Limbo Publishing, a brand of In-Sell Ltd

www.tonymoyle.com

Cover design by Damonza

For...

Anyone who didn't fit in.

"If you want to be different, be different." T.M.

Preface

I'll be honest with you. I'm not a big fan of the preface. When a book contains one it normally sends me into a cold sweat as my brain tries to compute why the author would add a form of scholastic teasing to keep me from the main purpose of buying the book in the first place, to read it. Prefaces tend to feature highbrow navel-gazing as the author self-indulgently waffles on about his inspirations, collaborators and moral authority for writing the damn thing in the first place. Or even worse, they come across as elongated sales pitches, which is odd really given that you've probably already bought it. With all that in mind, I'll keep this concise.

The main reason for including a 'preface' is the word's own etymology. That's a fancy word for origin. Oh come on, if I'm going to do one I might as well go highbrow. No? Ok, I promise I'll stop. The word preface originates from Latin, at or around the time when most of this book is set. Its meaning translates as 'beforehand' or quite literally 'pre-fate' and it is fate, and the prediction of the future, that run through the heart of this story.

Some four hundred and fifty years since his death, Michel Nostradamus is a name still familiar to most of the inhabitants of Earth. His predictions have become synonymous with every catastrophe from the sixteenth century to the modern day, and every one of those events has been retrospectively deciphered and reapplied to one of his many prophecies.

According to Nostradamus fanatics he has single-handedly predicted everything from the 9/11 attacks to the Great Fire of London and to the rise of Hitler. If you follow the people who dedicate their lives to interpreting his work, they argue that Nostradamus predicted the end of the world on no fewer than five occasions including:

1999, 2012, 2017, 2018 (clearly hedging his bets after the millennium) and 3797. This pattern is reminiscent of my betting behaviour at the horse races. I rarely win either. These people have a habit of wanting the answers to be true, which doesn't make them particularly neutral academics.

But what do you really know about Nostradamus the man? Not much, I would guess. How did it transpire that he was remembered so many years later? What education did he have? What was his approach? How could one person be an expert in so many disciplines? Some of these questions may never be fully answered. And this story isn't supposed to either. Centrally it isn't even about him. But it does purposefully meander through key historical events that he unquestionably played a part in. Events that I have attempted to describe as close to historical accuracy as I was able. Many of the characters whom you'll meet in this book were real people who played their own part in that period of history. However, it's not all true. After all, historical satire isn't meant to be.

Principally this is the fictional story of Philibert Montmorency, set in an interlocking timeline of sixteenth-century France and the modern day. It aims to highlight humankind's paranoia regarding future events and more specifically the generational fear about the impending end of the world. It is this fear that fertilises the landscape and allows characters like Nostradamus and Montmorency to sow their seeds of hope, with the same degree of success as modern-day politicians. If you thought 'fake news' was a new concept then think again.

I'd like to reference two books that have assisted me in creating an accurate depiction of the times. Frederic J. Baumgartner's 'France in the Sixteenth Century' and Peter Lemesurier's 'The Unknown Nostradamus' have been invaluable references for the places, people and events that make up this story.

In the eleventh month of the second millennium
Under a blood moon the kingdoms of God shall fall
to cold winds carried by birds and beasts,
and very brightly the men of the mountain will burn.

- Chapter 1 -

The Last Prophecy

The internet was awash with rumours. Not the usual ones about two-bit celebrities caught in compromising positions, or instructions on how to get rich in three days with nothing more than a YouTube account and a microwave, nor the news of the revolutionary diet proven to help you lose twelve kilograms a day by eating nothing more than quinoa and hopping up and down frequently. These rumours were much more serious. If they were to be believed, and they were on the internet so fifty per cent of people did, it would be best not to make plans for Christmas.

The end of the world was coming.

The exact circumstances and timelines were a bit sketchy, but it was almost certainly going to be on a Tuesday, and it was definitely going to be messy.

Dr. Ally Oldfield was just one of the fifty per cent of people who ignored the rumours as bunkum. As senior Professor of Medieval Languages at the University of Warwick she'd never gone in for the conspiratorial, preferring to position herself on the rational side of the fence when it came to debates about our potential extinction. There were times, though, when rational thought and conspiratorial nonsense collided. Never more so than when they involved a certain Michel de Notredame. Which was exactly why distancing herself from the obvious rubbish doing the online rounds was going to be difficult. Ally had written more research papers and books about the sixteenth-century seer than any other living person.

The circus was not going to ignore her however much she ignored it.

It was rare for a prophecy by Nostradamus to be used to foretell a future event. That was a recipe for looking foolish. It was much more successful to apply them after the event had already occurred. If a volcano exploded in Japan, or stock markets crashed, causing economic chaos around the world, it was easy to go back through the thousands of Nostradamus quatrains and find one that would broadly fit the circumstances. Over the centuries this had been done often, sometimes more than once with the same quatrain applied to two completely different events many decades apart. Not even the great Nostradamus was smart enough to predict both in the same four lines.

Ally Oldfield knew there were good reasons why his predictions were always applied retrospectively. Nostradamus was rarely inclined to give any specific details that might validate his now notorious talents. Very few of his prophecies highlighted an accurate place, an individual's name or even a rough guess at a time period. They were ambiguous, misleading, poorly translated, inconsistent, depending on which version of the text you were reading, and written in a style so confusing you could easily use them to predict what colour socks you were wearing that very morning.

This assessment had been true until last week.

Only two original manuscripts of Nostradamus's seminal work 'Les Prophéties' were known to exist, and neither the version in Albi, nor the one in Vienna contained the exact same content, such were the inaccuracies of the printing process during the sixteenth century. Back then it was common for the printer to substitute letters, lose others when they dropped out of the manual printing frames, and make educated guesses to decipher what the author had really meant from his original scribbles. And the responsibility for all this vital task was the compositor, who'd certainly had less education than a present-day four-year-old. This highly inaccurate process was normal because the author probably lived several days' carriage ride away and wouldn't have access to email to quickly approve any drafts for at least four hundred years. One of the few benefits of the times.

But now a third version of that famous book had been found in a Lyon basement behind a temporary wall, stored inside a damaged and damp piece of furniture. Not only was it thought to be an original, dating from around fifteen-sixty-three, it also contained a rather interesting preface. If the reports were true, within the contents of this preface was written a prophecy never previously printed in any of the other first editions, or the countless forgeries that have been produced in the decades that followed. Its meaning had already been translated and widely disseminated across the world by an online group calling themselves the Oblivion Doctrine.

And in their opinion the end was very much nigh. Whether the prophecy was authentic or not didn't stop it doing laps of the internet faster than a 'cat falling off a ladder' meme. There was only one question on people's lips. Were we really all doomed by November? The slightly saner and more reserved portion of the internet-using world needed an answer, and there was only one person qualified enough to give it to them. Dr. Ally Oldfield desperately wanted it to be someone else. But sadly that wasn't the case, and she couldn't avoid the constant phone calls, emails and tweets forever. Particularly when they came from the Pope.

Twenty-four hours later, after finally giving in and agreeing to authenticate the prophecy, she landed at Lyon

THE LAST PROPHECY

Airport and was soon being driven at speed to 'Le Musée de L'Imprimerie' at the request of its Director Salvador Depuis. On the site of Lyon's first City Hall, dating back to the early seventeenth century, the Museum of Printing celebrated the thriving publishing industry of Renaissance France. It was home to some of the most valuable pieces of medieval printing anywhere in the world. Sandwiched on a strip of land between the Saône and Rhône rivers and hidden down a rabbit warren of narrow one-way streets, the old Museum nestled in stark contrast next to a modern fast-food restaurant, the past and present sharing the street as much as history shares the future.

Ally took a deep breath in anticipation as the car came to a halt outside the building. A skinny, well-dressed man of obvious Mediterranean descent, sporting a greasy waxed moustache that was curled at both ends, opened the door for her in a chivalrous fashion.

"Welcome, Professor Oldfield. It's an honour to have you here. I have studied much of your work down the years. My name is Salvador Depuis, welcome to our museum."

"Do you have coffee?" replied Ally abruptly.

Salvador's expression was churned like milk by the lack of social etiquette and her brash tone. He overlooked it: there were more important things to worry about today.

"This is France, madam, we practically live off the stuff."

"Double espresso, as quick as you can," she snapped. "I've been dragged on this wild goose chase and I'm not going another step until I get some good coffee."

"Of course," said Salvador, shooting a glance at one of his welcoming party who was soon scurrying off on a caffeine-related emergency.

Ally Oldfield had always been difficult. At least that was most people's opinion shortly after first meeting her. It normally took them less than a minute. She saw herself as a

14

serious historian committed to the education of others and an important leader in the quest to shed light on historically important texts. Her attitude towards other people was born from a career spent debunking the Nostradamus codswallop and the flagrant misinterpretations that were rife in most people's understanding of it.

Those who lacked sufficient intelligence or knowledge annoyed her. Experience led her to believe that as almost everyone occupied that camp there was little point wasting time establishing if she was right or not. After all, she prided herself on always being right, even when she was in fact wrong. On the rare occasions that people didn't turn out to be simpletons with an IQ slightly lower than a pond skater she could always repair the damage later. None of this made her a popular collaborator within her peer group. But her immense knowledge of the subject of Nostradamus couldn't be ignored at times like this. If they wanted the truth they'd have to suffer her rudeness.

"Let me give you a brief tour of the museum before we show you our discovery," offered Salvador, keeping his sense of hospitality up in the face of this rather abrupt woman.

"Don't bother. I've been here many times: in fact, I probably know it better than you do. I doubt very much that the discovery you describe is genuine so let's validate my assumption and then we can crush these ridiculous internet rumours and go back to the real world."

"Mon plaisir," he replied, not meaning it literally. He was careful not to slip into any underhand French slang to secretly express how he felt about this obnoxious English woman as he was aware she spoke multiple languages fluently and even some local dialects.

Strong-smelling coffee in hand, Ally marched through the building ignoring the many spectacular exhibits on either side of her. She barely registered a flicker of interest as she passed Gutenberg's forty-two-line Bible, the first book printed in Europe, but then again she'd studied it half a dozen times in the past. She vigorously swung her briefcase along the hem of her black pleated skirt as her high heels tapped loudly on the stone floor like a well-oiled machine gun was picking off enemy soldiers. There was only one piece in the museum of interest, and only one possibility.

It must be a hoax.

Salvador directed her as best he could through the museum, out of the public areas and into a heavily secured private room that contained the museum archives. The distinctive smell of books infected their nostrils and sent both of them back to a period in time when books ruled all knowledge. The room was dimly lit, but in the centre of it on a metal table propped up on a stand and surrounded by a glass case, was a shabby manuscript in perfect serenity. Ally placed her briefcase on the floor, drained the last dregs of her coffee and pulled up a chair. Sitting inches from the glass she removed a pair of expensive spectacles and nestled them somewhere in her untidy mane of curly, black hair.

"Do this often?" asked Salvador.

"What?"

"Authenticate books."

"No. I'm more interested in the words than the paper, but don't worry, I should be able to tell you if both are original or not."

"How so?"

"If I find a barcode then it's probably a fake," she replied sarcastically, never moving her line of sight from the book behind the glass. "Now if you wouldn't mind shutting up I can do my job."

Salvador took the hint. If the donation turned out to be genuine this was a big deal for the museum. If they had an original copy of 'Les Prophéties', in the very city where it was first published, it would draw in new visitors and worldwide publicity. If this rumbustious woman's views counted even a smidgeon, he didn't want to be the reason why they didn't.

"Where was it found?" she asked purposely without moving her head from her target.

"Not far from here. A house in the old town was having its basement reinforced because of subsidence and one of the builders accidentally fell through a temporary wall. They found a veritable menagerie of antiquities behind it, including a commode from the Renaissance period."

"Interesting choice."

"I'm sorry, Professor, I'm not following."

"Do I really have to tell you that commode is French for convenient. I'm wondering who might find it convenient that the manuscript was found."

"I think you're reading too much into it."

"Am I?"

"Yes. Why would anyone want a forgery?"

Ally looked up for the first time since entering the room and pierced the Director with a withering scowl. "Money, influence, power, notoriety and a way of causing discord throughout the world."

"I see you are a, oh how do the English say it…glass half-empty kind of person."

"No. I'm a glass completely empty kind of person, until they bring me a genuine twenty-fifteen Côte-Rôtie, and then I'm a glass completely full kind."

"I see you know your wines, madam."

"I know very many things, but not enough about this book. How many people have had access to it?"

"Only the staff here, maybe five or six of us, and the owner of the property where the book was found, a Monsieur Palomer."

"And how did the translation get out in the open?"

Salvador Depuis's normally happy disposition was dimmed somewhat by a sense of shame. "It is assumed that Palomer requested that someone else review the book before informing us about it."

"Do you know who?"

"No. You'll have to ask him yourself."

"If it's genuine I might just do that. Open the glass," demanded Ally.

"Of course, let me get you some protective gloves."

"That won't be necessary. Either this is the most protected fake in the history of books or it has been safely stored in a cupboard for the last four hundred years and it'll be in better condition than some of the books you can buy at your local bookshop."

"I really must insist."

It was too late. Ally had already lifted off the glass case and was flicking through the pages, eager to get to the pronounced new material. At the bottom of the fourth page of the preface was a prophecy she'd not seen before. This preface was much like the ones at the beginning of the other two originals, both of which she had studied first-hand, but for one additional passage.

Nostradamus was a constant tinkerer. In the five years that succeeded the first edition's publication several later editions had been produced, each with additional quatrains and content that had not been contained in the original. Sometimes it was completely new material, but often he'd rewrite some of his older prophecies in order to update predictions that had not been altogether accurate.

Ally ran a finger across the page, stopping occasionally to get a feel for the paper and the ink. She leant over so her face was just above the text and drew in the smell, eyes closed all the time.

"What do you think?" asked Salvador.

"The book is old. No question," replied Ally unemotionally. "The typeface is raised slightly above the page, which means it was printed on movable boards. The paper quality is typical of that used during the mid-fifteen hundreds, when each piece was fabricated by hand. The fact that this copy was found in Lyon, where most of Nostradamus's printing was done, is another positive sign."

"So it's genuine!" shouted Salvador gleefully.

"I didn't say that."

Ally's life revolved around finding and transcribing pieces of rare literature. It was the only reason she got up in the morning and why sometimes she worked deep into the early hours. But then again there really wasn't much else in her life to stimulate her. She wasn't incapable of getting excited, it was just so rare for something this old to be discovered that she'd learnt to harbour a robust level of cynicism. If this was real, however, it would be a whole different ball game. The room wouldn't be big enough for her cartwheels.

She took a notepad and pen out of her black leather briefcase and started to work through the new verse at the bottom of the preface. As with much of Nostradamus's later work it was written in French rather than Latin, which few laymen of the period would have been able to read. It wasn't modern French, though. It was written in one of the many unique dialects of the time. Fortunately she knew them all. That is of course if the printer had managed to re-create exactly what the authors were attempting to say. As she quickly translated the prophecy, Salvador watched to see if it matched the one currently doing the online rounds that he'd already read.

After a few scraggly versions were scratched through with her pen as she tried to make sense of a warning written halfway through the last millennium, she settled on a final version, which she wrote out beautifully in fountain pen on a crisp, fresh piece of paper. She handed it to the Director who read it out loud.

THE LAST PROPHECY

In the eleventh month of the second millennium
Under a blood moon the kingdoms of God shall fall
to cold winds carried by birds and beasts,
and very brightly the men of the mountain will burn.

"This isn't the same translation I've seen on the internet," added Salvador disappointedly, handing the piece of paper back to Ally.

"No, it wouldn't be, would it? Whoever did that one is obviously not a linguistic genius, are they?"

"But your translation is even more worrying. The other one didn't make it clear how little time we had left. It just said it would be a Tuesday."

"It's a Tuesday tomorrow, maybe it will happen then!" replied Ally scornfully.

"Let's hope not," replied Salvador, forcing a weak smile through his immaculately whitened teeth. "What do you think it means?"

"If you're asking for my initial conclusions, and I'd need more time to study it properly, I'd say it's predicting the end of the world of man as a result of some form of virus, probably a bird or pig flu pandemic, sometime around November. Which is fine. I don't like Christmas much anyway," replied Ally with a straight face.

"I take it this warning does not concern you?"

"Of course it doesn't, you silly little man. You're interpreting the verse to validate the assumptions of what you already believe is going to happen. But it's an interpretation of a verse written in a time very different from our own. The people of the world have been predicting the imminent apocalypse since the dawn of civilisation and yet we're all still here, aren't we?"

"The Oblivion Doctrine don't appear to agree with you. They seem determined to tell people that the end of world is coming."

"Then we must work hard to convince people otherwise, mustn't we?"

"At least it proves one thing," said Salvador.

"Really, what?" asked Ally.

"That the book is genuine."

"The book might be, but the prophecy isn't."

"I'm not with you. How can that be?"

"Because this verse wasn't written by Nostradamus."

"How can you be so sure?"

"Because I'm an expert on the subject and you're just a second-rate museum guide."

"Madam, I've had just about enough of your attitude, I'm not just…"

"Oh do stop whining. I know this is not the work of Nostradamus because he was not keen on detail and stylistically this is not typical of his work."

"Then if the book is old, and the prophecy was printed at the same time as the book, who wrote it?"

"That's exactly what I intend to find out before the world descends into paranoia. But first I think more coffee is in order. It's not Tuesday yet after all."

- Chapter 2 -

The Uninvited Guest

Unless you were one of the fortunate few who had either money, power or both, sixteenth-century France wasn't for the faint-hearted. Even the few thousand who counted themselves amongst the nobility were still incapable of avoiding the often fatal consequences of an almost non-existent healthcare system, a high infant mortality rate and regular bouts of the plague. But at least they, unlike the vast majority of the population, didn't live in a hole.

And not just any hole.

The dirtiest, most soul-crushing and endlessly horrific hole imaginable. Its daily jeopardies included vermin the size of dogs, exposure to bone-freezing spells of cold weather, an almost complete lack of anything truly edible, and the constant persecution by rich people. Most people called it existence. And just a few of them pulled it off.

Everyone, other than the nobility, lived in poverty. Those that couldn't afford poverty had to be content with squalor. Natural selection in all its glory, albeit somewhat unnaturally manipulated by those with qualifications or title. In sixteenth-century France the population was simply defined by where someone was born and who they were born to. That was the class system. No middle class, upper-middle class or lower-upper class. Society didn't care whether you were intelligent, or brave, or wise, or good-looking, or amusing, or talented. The only category that mattered was whether you were rich or poor. There was some social mobility, though. It mainly happened when the rich rounded up the poor to march them hundreds of miles to kill some equally poor and oppressed foreign people.

This was generally for no other reason than France's rich people didn't like the Italian rich people because they wore elaborately coloured trousers and had a different view on what form of praise God wanted. This was usually justification enough to slaughter large quantities of poor people as swiftly as the plague managed it, but without quite so much mess. Except in winter, that was. Not even rich people enjoyed watching peasants die in the snow.

Wars have always been rubbish. Unless of course your team was winning and you happened to be a very long way away with access to a telescope, which sadly Galileo wouldn't invent for at least another thirty years. If you did have the misfortune of being deeply entrenched in the middle of one, wars had the popular effect of leaving most of its participants with missing limbs or heads that never again looked good in hats.

Interestingly, though, war was about the only time when the rich and poor participated in the same activity for the same purpose. The rich of course were intent on riding out in front of the masses to demonstrate that they were much better people than them, although even that didn't stop rich people getting killed. Avoidance of death was increased, though, by having a greater access to horses and something they liked to call armour. Poor people were a commodity, a statistic and the more of it you had the greater your chances of winning. And however many you had, it was always far too many to lavish expensive and limited protection on. Armour for the masses was made from straw, or if you were really lucky, mud. Mud was not a highly effective deterrent to a well-fired arrow but it did make excellent camouflage.

Regular wars were just one of the reasons why life expectancy for the poor during the middle of the last millennium was on average thirty years of age. It wasn't all bad news, though. If, by some miracle, you reached your twenty-first birthday you had a fifty percent chance of reaching your sixtieth. Most people avoided it on account of life being long enough as it was, and there was very little improvement to look forward to in old age. The concept of retirement would eventually come about a hundred years later when someone invented golf. Even then not everyone agreed it improved things.

The main threats to life for the average French peasant were the four horsemen. They marched abreast through the increasingly deserted fields of the countryside and, as if annoyed at taking a wrong turn, sped up towards the saturated hubbub of the growing cities. If plague, death, pestilence and war didn't get you, then frankly you weren't trying hard enough.

Cold was on the waiting list as a possible fifth horseman, as soon as the recruitment department assessed its application. The period in question was often referred to as Europe's mini-ice age as temperatures plummeted and harvests failed. As a result migration from country existence to urban life swelled the populations of France's largest cities, unintentionally providing the perfect breeding ground for illness and disease. Cities weren't all bad, though. There was plenty of entertainment.

The Renaissance, right?

Not quite.

The Enlightenment had gone largely unnoticed by the masses who were more concerned with what they might find edible enough to put in their mouths and less bothered with what might feed their minds. The development of art, poetry, philosophy and architecture did little to put food inside bellies. And anyway a good execution was quicker and less taxing on the brain cells.

When disappointment, death and disaster lurked around every corner it's unsurprising that the common man believed that the end of the world was imminent.

THE UNINVITED GUEST

What other conclusion could you make? Catholicism, still the predominant religious standard even against the rising tide of the new Protestant movement, was just another weapon to punish the follies of the poor. Every Sunday they were told, and believed, that their predicament was no one's fault but their own. If only the poor could read they might have challenged this notion. But no one wanted to teach them in case they read something they shouldn't and realised that the whole system was a con to keep rich people affluent and poor people muddy.

Instead they received their information from those that could: priests, scholars and seers. What they heard they believed wholeheartedly because they had nothing to compare it with. After all, why would rich people lie? They were rich because they were better people, weren't they? Conveniently this was precisely what rich folk wanted them to think.

If the only messages you ever heard were carefully selected for you, were almost always terrifying and happened to back up your own experiences of hunger, famine, cold, death, destruction and war, it wasn't much of a leap to believe that anytime soon someone or something was going to descend from the heavens to smite you down. It was a logical belief system. And hopefully it would happen soon. It couldn't be any worse than life.

What made less sense was how many of the rich and powerful also believed the end was upon them. Just because you could read didn't grant you the gift of wisdom. This was a time of God, and whichever version you currently supported it was clear that He, She or It was far more powerful than you were, even if you owned half a prefecture and more gold than an Inca king. The reverse was also true. There were some who possessed wisdom and skill at odds to the side of the class divide that fate had dumped them.

And very occasionally one of them would refuse to accept that the divide was even there at all.

Education might be the divine right of the rich and powerful, but intelligence was not. If you were smart enough, cunning enough, driven enough and ready to take your chances when the rare opportunities presented themselves, escape from poverty was possible. Just.

*****

The parties of Claude de Savoie were the stuff of legend. They were frequent, decadent and exclusive. A powerful man like Claude collected only the most regent, the most important and the most corruptible elite that France and its allies had to offer for his gatherings. But these infamous banquets weren't only about the rich gorging on the finest foods of the Kingdom, although that was a happy coincidence. They were much more than that.

These were functional events: meetings to debate the issues of the day when the alternative option would take several months back and forward by post. They celebrated weddings, births, deaths and victory in battle. And they were statements designed to demonstrate your own social standing and power. And of all the places to prove that power there was nowhere more impressive than Marseille.

Marseille had not always been French. It was Europe's mongrel city. Its eclectic history had been moulded by Greek, Turkish, Roman and French rulers and its inhabitants were an unruly bunch with a variety of views and sympathies. It had a reputation for being a rebellious place that took great stock in ardently disagreeing with anything mainstream. The ruling classes changed here at regular intervals and it became confusing to remember all the different rules. Just as the population got used to one regime a flotilla of ships would land packed with heavily accented men sporting floppy moustaches. And then everything would change.

The threat was never far away. The Holy Roman Empire was no more than a beach cove along the coastline, and the French desperately clung to a fragile alliance with the Ottoman Empire like a castaway grapples driftwood. At any moment the balance might tip and rich and poor alike would have to start all over again. In an attempt to annoy any would-be ruler, a collective and unconscious decision rippled through their culture to do things in their own inimitable way. Whatever people thought of it, belligerence worked.

The city's beating heart was the port. It was an important gateway to world trade and a source of envy for France's neighbours in Genoa, who sought both financial superiority and the ability to disrupt their enemy's chances of obtaining it for themselves. To this end the port had been heavily fortified to ward off those who might try. At the entrance of the port the crystal-blue waters of the Mediterranean lapped at the feet of the ominous Maubert Tower, which loomed above all other buildings in the city. Standing on its summit offered in one direction a clear view of any dangers that might approach by sea, and to the other the foothills of Provence. It acted as a warning to invaders, a lookout, and a marvellously ostentatious location for tonight's party. It was here, above all of Claude's many seats of power, that he liked to show off.

In Claude's opinion excessive indulgence was just part and parcel of being the Grand Seneschal of Provence. The title wasn't a democratically elected one, it was an administrative position passed down to him on orders of the King. Claude had first ascended to the position at the tender age of thirteen when his father, René, a renowned shipbuilder and affectionately known as the 'Grand Bastard of Savoy', died from the injuries he sustained at the Battle of Pavia. Now a sprightly fifty-four-year-old,

THE UNINVITED GUEST

Claude was going to make the most of what time he had left. Which meant partying. And tonight's celebration was of particular importance.

It was during this party that Claude would announce the wedding of his only daughter, Annabelle, to the suave and powerful Jacques de Saluces, Lord of Cardé. There was only one unknown factor that might take the gloss off the evening. No one had told Annabelle.

Within the nobility marriages were arranged strategically. A wedding between warring factions could strengthen a Kingdom's power and surreptitiously gain new territory through stealth. Love or affection rarely featured in the equation and the women of the court had no choice in the matter. But this was Marseille and they enjoyed being difficult.

Annabelle was a feisty woman in her early twenties with auburn hair and a kind, unblemished face that would make an ideal prize for any nobleman. She was known to enjoy the attention of men, but not just any men. She liked those with a rebellious streak, who lacked conformity and were able to open her eyes to the amazing new cultural and religious ideas that were spreading like a virus through the continent of Europe. She was tired of blue-blooded stiffs whose only idea of a good time was to go hunting for days, only to return to have the heads of their victims mounted on slabs of wood and hoisted on the wall as icebreakers for their next banquet. She wanted more from life than to act as walking womb to future heirs or a thing of beauty to be shown off in front of others.

Nevertheless, she would have little say in the matter. If her father wanted her to marry, then marry she would. But when it did happen she wasn't going quietly. It would come around sooner than she imagined.

A flock of feather-hatted noblemen, and an equally sizeable pack of their cronies, had been invited to celebrate the impending announcement, and amongst their number was one Philibert Montmorency. His illustrious name alone was enough to warrant an invite, even though in reality he didn't have one. The Montmorency family had for generations been powerful members of the King's court and if one of them decided to invite themselves to your banquet it was wise to accept.

A shabby horse trotted through the tower gates and into the small courtyard. A muddied comparison of deep red fabric hung down its sides in a manner that suggested the horse might have dressed itself. An unexpectedly malnourished man with a crop of frizzy hair rode on its back. His skill and style were noticeably less refined than the other riders who had already dismounted and were congregating around the stables. On one side of the rider, leading the horse by its reins, stood an equally out of place squire who looked thoroughly unprepared for the magnitude of the events in front of him.

Typically the role of a squire was taken by the knights of the future, an apprenticeship for those deemed worthy enough to be taught the etiquette and skills needed for such an important calling. Whereas the other squires massing around the courtyard were strapping young men with muscles that pressed menacingly through their tunics, this one was about sixty years old and appeared to know almost nothing about horses. He struggled to maintain the beast's discipline as it jittered like an anxious child under its poor treatment, desperate to deposit its rider in any way possible and get away from the idiot who'd been put in temporary charge.

After much manipulation and heavy breathing the squire finally adjusted the horse's attitude long enough for its mount to gain smooth access to the flagstone floor and avoid any unnecessary attention.

"I hate this bloody creature," said the squire fixing his irritation at the horse's eye level in case the beast hadn't fully translated the verbal message. "It's got a grudge against me, I'm sure of it."

"Don't be melodramatic, Chambard. It's a horse. They're for riding or eating, they're not for forging vendettas against."

"This one is. He's loopy. I knew it was a bad idea. We don't normally need a horse."

"Well, this time we did. This is one of our best opportunities. All our toil and hardship has led us to this moment. The big one," said the rider in a lowered volume. "Which means the risks have risen as much as the possible rewards. We're in the big league now, and we have to act like it. How do you think it would look if I burst into the courtyard and greeted the most important men in France being piggybacked by a sixty-year-old idiot with rickets. Cover blown, I'd say."

"We could have got a better horse at least?"

"Chambard, it's not exactly ours, is it? I'm not sure we can take it back and ask for a new one."

"Ok, Philibert. You're right. But once this is all over, I'm definitely eating him. No buts."

"Fine!" said Philibert.

Chambard gave the horse a sly grin as one of the peasant boys that worked at the tower took the reins and led the horse away for its own peace and quiet.

"How do I look?" asked Philibert, doing his best to rearrange his clothes into a more presentable state.

"Like a noble, Phil."

"That's good, then."

"Do you have the ring?"

"Yes, of course," he replied, extending a hand towards his squire to show off a gold ring which featured an embossed eagle and two crossed swords down the middle, all of it in desperate need of a polish.

"Know what to do?" said Chambard gruffly as he wiped his muddy sleeve across a single eyebrow that grew like ivy across much of his forehead.

"Same as always. Mingle with the other guests, compliment the host, agree with their views…actually what side are they on?"

"Hard to know for definite these days, but I've heard on the wind that Marseille likes to be different so they've probably jumped on Calvin's bandwagon. If they mention the Huguenots then you're a Protestant, and if they hail the Pope slip back in to fluent Catholic."

"Right, good advice. Once that's done and everyone else is being entertained by the 'hey nonnie nonnie' brigade, I'll go exploring."

"Excellent. Remember you've done this a hundred times before, nothing to it. Just remember everything I've taught you. I'll wait by the horse and decide which bit of him I'm going to eat first."

Philibert followed the other dignitaries as they strolled across the courtyard and towards a circular stone staircase that ascended into the grand tower. At the top the ensemble gathered at the entrance of a large banquet hall decked in delicate flowers. The warmth of a huge fire was both felt and heard from the other side of the room. Standing by the doorway was a servant dressed in plain, dark clothes to distinguish himself from the guests in their fabulously eccentric colours and regalia. He greeted each guest politely before bellowing their name into the midst of those who'd already arrived. The room was already a din of noise as nobles talked loudly through gulps of fine local wines sipped from silver goblets.

The nerves always peaked about now. Adrenaline seeped into his veins in a sadistic attempt to slowly poison him. His tunic felt alien against his body, intent as he knew it was to embarrass him and give the game away. He slid his hand through his frizzy, dark hair, still saturated with sweat from his arduous journey. He stretched his frame to its full potential, even though it had no effect on how small he felt in the midst of this illustrious company. Once the formalities of his introduction were complete and he was safely through the door, then the evening would get more comfortable.

The moment had come. His moment to demonstrate a skill that had carried him so productively, and very much against the odds, since the age of fourteen. He mustered a stern yet noble expression as the servant at the door looked him up and down.

"Welcome, your grace," muttered the man. "How should I introduce you?"

"Philibert Montmorency, from the Court of Languedoc."

The servant paused a moment.

"Montmorency, you say? I was not aware of your invitation," added the gruff busybody in a tone that in centuries to come would be replicated outside all nightclubs worldwide.

"I suspect that would be because I don't have one," Phil replied confidently. "But ask yourself this. How would your master treat you if you turned away a member of the mighty Montmorency family? Would he honour you? Would it go down well in the court of the King when it reached his ears?"

The guard searched the empty vacuum of his brain for answers. None materialised. A very different thought came off the cranial substitutes' bench to replace it. It proceeded to construct a vision of the possible consequence of making the wrong choice. A vision that correctly highlighted a branding iron, long periods of darkness and a thick rope with a head-shaped loop at the end.

"Right," said the guard reflectively. "I see what you're saying, but I'm not familiar with a Philibert Montmorency. I'm aware of Anne of course, and Henri. But not Phil."

THE UNINVITED GUEST

Philibert held his right hand out once more and nonchalantly brandished his ring under the soldier's nose. "You'll recognise my seal, then."

"Oh…yes of course. My apologies, your excellency."

The man immediately announced Philibert's name and title loudly into the room where almost nobody paid it any attention, just as he'd hoped. Philibert strode arrogantly into the circular hall and immediately helped himself to a large flagon of mead. Those around him supped at wine goblets and huddled in small groups entrenched in discreet conversations. As Philibert watched the activities in the room it appeared to him to be divided into two factions both debating nervously with themselves and keen to keep their views concealed from the other. There could be only one reason for this secrecy.

The war of religions was an internal threat that had the potential to overflow into a conflict more fearsome than those fought against historic opponents who'd encircled France from all directions since the Middle Ages. This was a danger that came from within, and no one could be sure who was likely to come out as the victor. The rules in traditional wars were fairly straightforward. The enemy wore different clothes, waved patterned flags that even a village idiot recognised and generally approached from the opposite direction. All those rules would be obsolete if the war of religions truly kicked off. It was impossible to know who you were fighting because people had a habit of changing sides on a daily basis. It was also true that neither side really understood what they were fighting about, other than wanting their own way.

"I understand you are a member of the Montmorency house?" said a warm, friendly voice. "Strange that you should come here."

Phil glanced to his left and smiled to acknowledge an elderly gentleman he'd never met before. The man's white hair clung desperately to a bald patch that had invaded most of his forehead. A regal quality oozed out of his mannerisms as he glided forward to grasp Phil by the arm in firm welcome, as if Phil's name, rather than he himself, had already earned the old man's respect.

"Yes, Philibert. And who do I have the pleasure of meeting?"

"Oh, only the person whose banquet you have seen fit to invite yourself to," replied Claude.

"My liege, it is an honour. I have been eager to meet you for some time."

"Really? The Montmorency family are not normally keen to visit these parts given the current climate. I can only imagine that you bring some ultimatum from the Constable on behalf of the Queen?"

"No, my lord, I have no news to that effect."

"Then why on earth are you here, may I ask?"

"How can I put this?" said Phil, desperate to stay on a tightrope that, should he fall, might be the last step he ever made. "I seek enlightenment."

"Enlightenment! Do I take it, then, that," his voice dropped to a whisper, even though he was inside the walls of his own château, "you are very much on the side of the righteous?"

Philibert nodded knowingly, even though he didn't have the slightest notion of what Claude meant.

"Does your family know about this? That you are here?"

Phil considered what his real family might think if they knew he was in deep conversation with the nobility of France, surrounded by more food than they would have seen in their lifetimes and dressed in fine, colourful silks without a spot of mud in sight. They'd have called him a liar, if any of them had survived long enough to voice it. But that would not be a suitable answer to Claude's question.

THE UNINVITED GUEST

"Not all of the Montmorency family think the same way. I'm sure it is true of each great French family."

"You're right. Throughout this room both sides seek to influence the other in order to cement their stranglehold on the outcome. It's no longer about families or alliances, it's about ideology. Jacques there," he pointed to a gigantic man casting a shadow over most of his small group, "is one of the most vocal, but the rest are too frightened to state their views openly. Personally I welcome anyone who protects personal freedom and seeks to fight for our way of life."

"I agree," said Phil, still baffled as to which side Claude was actually on. "I understand that you have a keen interest in the arts and in particular the works of Monsieur Nostradamus."

"Michel, oh yes he's a personal friend of mine. I marvel at his abilities to see that which has yet to pass. It's regrettable that the young King should feel the need to sanction his imprisonment."

The current King, Charles IX, was eleven and ruler in name only. The official responsibility for sovereign leadership had been bestowed upon his mother, Queen Catherine de Medici who had a formidable reputation. The young king was a weak and troubled child who had yet to gain the full support of the lords. His direct predecessors, Henry II, his father, and Francis II, his elder brother, had both died in quick succession and the impact was still evident in his erratic behaviour. This included brutal mood swings and attempts to make decisions that were neither sane nor approved. Catherine was left to hold the tattered threads of her warring country together through compromise, but for how long no one knew.

A young woman advanced through the hall towards Phil, and Claude with the grace of a boat gliding over the serene surface of a silent lake. The confidence of her manner immediately drew Phil's gaze as she smiled gently in welcome. It was unusual for a woman to be the centre of attention in a room of powerful men, yet there was something different in the way this woman dissected the atmosphere and distracted factions of men from their low-volume scheming.

"Ah, let me introduce my daughter, Annabelle," said Claude as the young woman feigned a curtsey, balancing necessary etiquette with her own distaste of it.

"My lord," she said ambivalently.

"The pleasure is surely mine," replied Philibert.

"I'm neglecting my other guests," said Claude. "I'll leave you in my daughter's capable hands. Good luck!"

The two stood silently, one hoping the other would take a stranglehold over the social awkwardness, and the other hoping for a conversation that deviated from the usual diatribe that came out of male mouths. He broke first.

"Mademoiselle, it is my opinion that never before have I met a woman of such beauty."

"Really," she sighed. "That's all you've got, is it?"

"What? I don't understand," said Phil nervously.

"I'm a woman, and therefore you thought the only conversation I'd be interested in is how I look."

"But…I thought that was the convention."

"Quite. But is it not possible that a woman might be capable of a debate?" she said sternly, waiting a few seconds for a sensible response that never arrived. "No. Shame."

"Um."

"Yes was the answer you were looking for."

"Um…yes."

"Why are men so bloody predictable? All you're interested in is corsets, horses, wars and wine."

"I don't care for it," said Philibert pointing to his flagon of mead.

"Oh…in that case I'm already in love with you!" she said disparagingly. "I'm going to give you one minute to impress me before I walk over there to sit in the corner with my eyes closed waiting for this turgid revelry to cease."

Philibert was plunged into a well of anxiety far deeper than any he was used to. Even getting into Claude's banquet had been a doddle compared to this pressure. All his training and experience had been designed to fool men, not women. He was totally unprepared for it. Women were not supposed to be like this. They were not normally granted permission to hold opinions or possess the intellectual dexterity to debate the topics of the day. And yet here she was, brains and beauty at a level he'd never seen before, forcing him into a balanced state of equal excitement and terror.

The minute was almost up and the only end product had been blind panic. He had to say something. Anything.

"I once saw a fire-eater set his beard alight! It was one of the funniest things I've ever seen. Not that I've seen that many funny things given my background, but still. I remember we all watched him running around shouting and flapping his hands to put it out before somebody tried to dunk him in a fountain. At the end he had a big bald patch of hair near his…"

"Stop!" said Annabelle. "What are you on about?"

"Fire-eaters."

"I meant in general. You're not used to talking to women, are you?"

"Not ones like you, no."

"Ones like what?" she replied fiercely.

"Assertive ones."

"It seems to work for the Queen. I see no reason why she should be unique."

Queen Catherine ruled with a brand of ferocity that few men could rival. Queens were not supposed to rule, they were supposed to watch and have babies. There were actually laws against it. But chance had landed Catherine in a position of power and she was going to embrace the rare opportunity to prove that a woman could do it better than a man. After all, it was working for Queen Elizabeth, her opponent across the Channel in England. But Catherine's ambitions were not just driven by equality. Her drive came from a belief that men were weak. Francis, her eldest son and the previous monarch, had been physically and mentally inferior, and now her second son was proving to be little more than a spoilt idiot. Even her beloved husband was nothing more than a serial adulterer. Her new standards were starting to rub off on others in society like Annabelle.

"Did you say you were a Montmorency?" asked Annabelle.

"Yes."

She looked at him enquiringly with a sense of disbelief in her eyes. "You're related to Anne de Montmorency, then?"

"Absolutely," said Phil, desperate to find a way of raising his now battered ego.

"And how are the two of you related exactly?"

"Anne de Montmorency? She's my aunt."

"She?" replied Annabelle in shock and mild amusement.

A fanfare of trumpets interrupted the room's chattering voices to signal that the feast was about to commence. The long, wooden table that stretched down the middle of the room was covered in all manner of exotic delicacies. Whole roasted boar, eels in a spicy purée that smelt like the inside of a well-travelled boot, a stuffed swan, or at least Phil hoped it was, slabs of cured meats of unknown origins, mountains of shellfish freshly caught, loafs of bread with thickened, burnt crusts and bowls of colourful seasonal fruits.

Many of these offerings Philibert had never seen before, let alone tasted. Not that he was going to today. He rarely stayed to eat because it was at that moment when all others focused more on their hunger than his whereabouts. Whilst others enjoyed their gluttony he'd take the opportunity to slip quietly away into private areas of the Tower. In the melee to gain the best seats around the table and to avoid sitting by someone likely to ruin your appetite, Phil snuck out of the main chamber unseen.

- Chapter 3 -

The Announcement

It was customary at the end of a feast for the host to address his guests. Almost every one of the four dozen people assembled around the dining table knew what Claude was about to say, but still they listened to his message with the utmost level of respect and mock excitement. Only two guests didn't hear the announcement in full. Annabelle stormed out of the room long before she could receive the many congratulations that would no doubt be forthcoming from the now inebriated rabble. At the first mention of the words marriage and the loathsome Jacques de Saluces the door that accessed the private rooms from the main hall was being slammed behind her with force.

Philibert didn't even hear that part. He was far too preoccupied with his search of the Tower. The item he needed had to be small, valuable and easily concealed. And most importantly of all it had to be anonymous, to avoid any obvious link to its original owner. Anything that connected owner and object would pinpoint him to this place, at this time and lead to an untimely and excoriating death, witnessed no doubt by his own kind who would flock to the only entertainment they were allowed, public execution.

Stealthily he passed from room to room like a phantom; observing, surveying, even fondling the items contained inside, but never leaving the slightest trace of his presence. He breezed through the music room, full of fragile instruments including ancient lutes, beautifully crafted flutes and a massive golden harp. None were small. In another, huge bookcases were stuffed with delicate manuscripts, eye-catching works of art and exceptionally valuable antiquities. None were easily concealed about his person. Philibert stopped momentarily to marvel at the contents of both rooms, longing to spend more time amongst the Enlightenment, in the hope that they might quench his insatiable desire for self-improvement. Not today. No time. To him these objects had a value beyond financial measure and removing any would only be for his personal pleasure. But if he found and sold something of great worth, that would fit neatly in his pocket: maybe one day he might afford his own collection.

Climbing a winding staircase, that Phil correctly guessed led to the highest level of the tower, a series of doors protected private chambers. In the centre of the first room a four-poster bed, adorned with colourful, embroidered fabrics, was encircled by beautiful tapestries hung on the walls to conceal cold, natural stone. A fire crackled in the hearth as its embers took their last gasps of life. Smoke danced through the unlatched window kidnapping the sweet-smelling fragrance from a bowl of jasmine flowers on its wispy fingers.

A mahogany trunk with intricate carvings nestled partly concealed next to and behind the overhanging drapes of the bed. On closer examination it was locked firmly and there was no evidence that any key had been left visible. It wouldn't cause an issue. Renaissance innovation had not advanced to the level of designing a truly foolproof security system.

Not from an expert at least.

Wherever there is desperation you will find people who are forced to break the rules in the pursuit of survival. If your death from hunger was certain there was but little jeopardy in stealing to avoid it. Getting caught would simply put you back in death's path, but at least you'd die quickly. Success, though, might keep you from death's door for one more day at least. Thievery in the sixteenth century was almost as popular as adultery, and it didn't matter what Moses had to say about it. Most thieves, however, were amateurs. Opportunistic hit-and-run merchants who lacked detailed planning or skilled execution.

Philibert removed a long, thin blade from under his tunic and started to work on the lock. In seconds it clicked open and the contents were at his mercy. The glistening gold, silver and gems shimmered like stars in the dimness of the firelit room. There were plenty of treasures inside that met his criteria, but Chambard had always taught him against greed. The clever thief played with the owner's mind, creating the illusion that the object might have been misplaced rather than stolen. If you possessed items of value, being robbed was not something you anticipated. Fear for the rich existed in more obvious forms like an army marching towards your castle, or a deviously planned assassination attempt.

Amongst the many fine pieces of jewellery an intricate locket with an exceptionally interesting design caught his attention. At the end of a long, silver chain was a pendant in the shape of a ram: a cluster of pearls set on a gold base gave the impression of the animal's woollen coat. He examined it closely. The cavity inside the pendant was empty but it was such a lovely piece. Would it be missed? Did it conceal any evidence of its real owner? It wasn't easy to know, but Chambard would expect some prize to work with.

Without warning a woman crashed through the door, and slammed it behind her. In one movement she threw herself onto the bed and wept loudly. In her distress to escape whatever circumstances placed her in this state, she was oblivious to the man currently crouched on his knees, riffling through her most prized possessions. Phil's brain sent out an urgent message to any part of his body that might be capable of sound. The response was immediate. The air was compressed from his throat and stored somewhere deep inside him. His heart did its best to stop beating more than was absolutely necessary and any part of his body that was capable of movement froze solid.

Two feet away from him, just above his head and behind the drapes that hung firmly from the top of the bed and down to the floor, Annabelle de Savoie was crying uncontrollably, head buried deep in her pillow.

'What do I do now?' thought Phil.

For months he and Chambard had meticulously schemed to place Phil here. A single event in a series of countless endeavours, each one more dangerous and lucrative than the last. Every one had taken guile, planning, wits, teamwork and just a pinch of luck. But neither of them could have foreseen, or discussed, possible exit strategies to a situation like this. Philibert had precisely twelve seconds to choose his next move before he ran out of breath and his gasping for air set off the cavalry charge. Retreat seemed the only sensible option.

He slowly and carefully placed the locket back in the trunk and lowered the lid. It would be impossible to lock without making excessive noise. He gently raised his body to a standing position, in a motion best described as a reverse bow in extreme slow motion. As he completed it his lungs exploded and fresh air rescued him from a permanent blue-faced asphyxiation.

"What?"

"Hello!" said Phil lamely, adding a pathetic little wave for good measure.

"How dare you! What are you doing in my bedroom?" shouted Annabelle as she turned her head and sat bolt upright from the shock of seeing a relative stranger standing above her bed and bowing so only the top of this head was visible. Fortunately for Philibert it appeared the shock of his presence had averted her attention from the unlocked trunk out of place next to her bed.

"I was…looking for…the toilet."

"The toilet?"

"Yes."

"Do you mean the garderobe?"

"Oh yes…that. That's exactly what I was looking for. A go-de-rube," he replied, horribly mispronouncing it.

"You don't know what a garderobe is, do you?" suggested Annabelle.

"Yes, of course I do. It's a room used to store cloaks. I was looking for mine as I thought I'd left my purse in it."

"What did you need your purse for?"

"Um…I was making a wager with Captain Fourvière…about the…about the…wingspan of the average goose."

"I don't believe you."

"Well, that's fair enough."

"A minute ago you said you were looking for the toilet."

"Um…yes, I did say that."

"But we don't have a toilet, only a garderobe. People tend to do their 'business' in there."

"Doesn't that rather ruin all the cloaks?"

"Something's not right here. Who are you really?"

"I told you I'm Philibert Montmorency."

"The Montmorency family is one of the most famous and powerful families in all of France and in my experience they do not drink mead, they know what a garderobe is, and every one of them knows what Anne de Montmorency looks like."

"You can't accuse me of being an imposter based on that, all of which I can explain, by the way," said Phil desperately trying to convince his brain to stop the sweating process building up in his pores.

"Go on, then, explain it."

THE ANNOUNCEMENT

"Wine triggers my hives, we don't call it a garderobe in Languedoc we call it a cloakroom, and I do know what Anne de Montmorency looks like."

"And…"

"She's a really plump woman, about forty, terrible teeth, always wears a hat and has a tendency to call everyone she meets 'Melvyn' as a consequence of her extremely poor memory."

"How interesting! What a unique picture you present of the current Constable of France," she replied, delight spreading across her face. "I knew you were an imposter the moment you referred to him as a 'her' and now you've proven it. How very exciting."

"Anne de Montmorency isn't a man," said Phil confidently.

"Then clearly you've never met him. I have. And he didn't call me Melvyn."

Annabelle wiped her eyes and sat forward on the bed. Her initial impression of Phil was morphing into something altogether different. The rather naïve and predictable character she'd met in the hall had revealed himself to be a rebel with absolutely no right to exist amongst her normal company, and yet he'd used his wits and charm to get as far as her bedroom. Most men just grabbed her and dragged her there.

"You won't tell anyone, will you?" said Phil, his forlorn expression desperate for her understanding.

"I guess that depends on your story, doesn't it?"

"I don't have time for stories. If they find me in here I'm done for."

"I wouldn't worry, they'll be too busy celebrating my marriage."

"Your marriage…then why are you up here crying?"

"Because I don't want to marry Jacques. He's an idiot with the personality of a broken window. I don't want to marry anyone my father approves of, I want to marry someone different, someone charming, dangerous and mysterious. The sort of man who can con his way into a party of noblemen under a false name." She smiled and twiddled her hair.

'Is she flirting with me?' thought Philibert. No, she couldn't be. She was young, pretty and confident, very unlike the women he got involved with who had a tendency to be old, ugly and mad. It wasn't possible. She wasn't in his league. It was impossible for a man of his background to be with a woman of status and standing. They just didn't allow it.

"I'm sorry you don't like your father's choice, I'm sure he has your best interests at heart."

"Ha, he's not interested in my welfare, he's interested in his legacy, land and politics. I'm just a pawn in that game. An asset to be traded."

"Look, I really am sorry about your predicament, but I must go back to the banquet before people notice I'm missing."

"Oh really, that's a shame. You could just come over here on the bed with me for a while. I don't bite," she purred and shuffled her dress so it rolled off her shoulders.

'OH MY GOD, she's definitely flirting with me!' Phil's brain shouted internally so that it shook from the sound waves bouncing off his internal organs. This had got out of hand. It was time to act like a lovestruck teenager, panic and run away. In a bizarre and contradictory signal he shook his head and stuck his thumb up at the same time before rushing like a scared lamb towards the door. Before he had the opportunity to open it and bolt for his life down the stairs, a firm knock came from the other side. His blood, which had been getting increasingly warm, completely evaporated, sending his body limp and collapsing his legs in a heap behind the door.

"My dearest," came a creepy, eccentric voice through the panels of oak, "are you alright?"

THE ANNOUNCEMENT

"Go away, Jacques. I don't want to see you."

Philibert made the sign of throat cutting with his finger.

"But we are now betrothed, my love, you must obey me," replied Jacques, his voice becoming sterner and more menacing.

"Jacques, you're an ox's arse and I will never obey you as long as you live."

Like a champagne cork the door burst open and crashed against the wall, narrowly missing the crumpled heap of the man cowering behind it. A red-faced Jacques stormed into the bedroom occasionally stumbling from a night of too much drinking. Annabelle stood to face him defiantly, but was soon forced back on the bed by a fierce slap across her face that was administered by her husband-to-be.

"How dare you speak to me like that! I demand your obedience. You are nothing but a stupid woman, and you will learn your place."

Another slap was followed by a shrill scream and Annabelle's desperate pleas for him to stop. Her initial character assassination of Jacques had not included cruelty and abuse, but the marks on her face would firmly remind her of it in the future. As a soldier Jacques was a physically intimidating man who'd been trained to kill, or be killed. As a nobleman he'd been bred to believe he was entitled to take whatever he wanted. What he wanted now was a young and complicit wallflower that he could use to extend his lineage and boost his standing. She had been chosen for him, and she would not resist.

The door to the stairwell remained open and the light from its torches beckoned Philibert to leave the discomfort of his predicament. It was at most three steps away. Maybe two if he went for a lunge. Three steps from escape and the opportunity to regroup with the evening's damage only limited. He had no responsibility for this girl. Nothing he could say or do would remove her from her father's choice.

THE ANNOUNCEMENT

His involvement would not stop it, and everything he'd fought to achieve over the past fifteen years would be lost.

This was not his world.

If a lord, betrothed through the proper channels, wanted to beat the living daylights out of his wife-to-be, who was he to challenge it? Who was he to say what was right or wrong for their kind? Yet that interference didn't work in the opposite direction. It was the nobility who decided how his kind should live. When they fought, how they worked, what taxes they paid, how they worshipped, and what information they were allowed to access. Morals weren't the divine right of those in power. Why shouldn't he intervene? After all, he was meant to be one of them.

Almost unconsciously Phil stood up and placed his hands on his hips in what he hoped was his most intimidating pose but just came across as desperately camp, before letting out a gruff, assertive cough. Jacques turned with surprise and rage in his eyes.

"I command you to stop," said Phil, not certain why he'd chosen the word 'command' and hoping it was forceful enough to work but not forceful enough to start a fight.

Jacques drew a blade from his belt and advanced slowly on the unwelcomed guest. To protect himself, Phil spontaneously drew the only blade that he carried, a now slightly bent, short and blunt lock-picking knife. If it came to actual swordplay his weapon was a raspberry against a watermelon.

*****

"And you say you found him in Annabelle's room?" said Claude from the other side of a small, one-man cell in the basement of the tower.

"Yes, my lord," replied Jacques.

"And my daughter, is she safe?"

THE ANNOUNCEMENT

"Yes, my lord, I'd never allow any harm to come to her."

Phil snorted, and forgetting the current state of his face managed to cover most of his chin with blood.

Claude peered through the bars where Phil was slumped in a heap. "And what do you have to say for yourself?"

"It's all just a massive misunderstanding," he stammered. "Just wait until my aunt hears about this."

"My lord, this man was intent on robbing your daughter of her purity."

"That's not true," mumbled Phil who was struggling to speak on account of the heavy beating he'd just received initially at the hands of Jacques and subsequently from a number of the guards who liked nothing more than getting in on the action. The blood loss had mostly been soaked up by his similarly coloured clothing, but there was no hiding his fat lip and bruised face.

"He must be punished," demanded Jacques. "Only death is good enough."

"Let's not be hasty, Jacques. Remember he's a Montmorency and in the current state of play I think it would be unwise to kill someone with powerful Catholic connections."

Of all of Phil's facial features that had recently be redesigned by fists, his ears had fortunately escaped almost unscathed. This information was useful. It meant he finally knew which side of the religious war they were on and more importantly that Annabelle had not given away his false identity.

"The war is coming here anyway," replied Jacques sternly. "There's no stopping it. Who cares if we kill one of theirs before the start. I'm ready for retaliation."

"Queen Catherine is still negotiating a treaty: it would be rash of us to put that in jeopardy."

"Then what is your will?" huffed Jacques.

THE ANNOUNCEMENT

"Send him to the Château de Marignane."

"Yes, my liege, if that really is your decision."

"It is. Put him in with Michel, it's about time he had some company and a mind like his might just help us learn more."

A young stable boy hurried down the steps, chest heaving from the exertion of whatever task he'd been given. Even though his eager demeanour suggested he was desperate to offload news, he stood next to his masters and waited patiently to be noticed.

"Well," said Jacques barking at the young boy.

"I've looked everywhere, sir, but there's no sign of the old squire with the heavy eyebrows who arrived with him."

"He must have ridden off."

"Pardon me, sir, but I don't think so. His horse is still here although it's a little distressed."

"Distressed?"

"Yes," said the boy. "I'm not surprised. It's got two human bite marks on its arse."

- Chapter 4 -

Conspiracy Theories

The exact method of mankind's forecasted downfall was totally dependent on where you looked. If you watched the television news then most of the assessments were based on a reasonable and reserved assessment of the facts as they knew them. Experts made reference to the discovery in Lyon of the new prophecy in a way that lacked histrionics. It was part of a national broadcaster's responsibility after all to offer the public balance. In most countries it was against the law to televise anything uneven that might be biased towards one side of the argument. All mainstream opinions had to be offered to the viewer. Viewer, singular, was about right these days.

There would have been no doubt about humanity's survival had this crisis occurred a decade or more ago. The conspiracy theories would never have seen the light of day, dismissed as unwarranted paranoia. Back then the only outlets for current affairs were television, radio, and print. There were no alternatives. In order to sell more newspapers certainly some of the printed press had a tendency to offer a somewhat bizarre take on events, but everyone knew what they were getting when they bought one. Gone were the days when people truly believed that 'The Sunday Sport' had really discovered a London bus buried at the South Pole, or that a minor celebrity had consumed a child's hamster. They'd always been viewed as tongue-in-cheek comics designed to make Sunday mornings that little bit more interesting.

CONSPIRACY THEORIES

But the discovery of the prophecy didn't happen back then. It was happening now.

The internet age.

Evidently society hadn't made the evolutionary hop from ignoring ridiculous newspaper headlines to disbelieving the equally preposterous bilge that featured on the internet. And this morning there was a never-ending pipeline of the stuff. It didn't bother the general public who wrote the exposés. The average Google surfer didn't stop to visualise the semi-naked unemployed loser, still sporting yesterday's ready meal stains on his tattered AC/DC T-shirt, sitting in some skanky flat in Arkansas bashing out any old crap to his audience of ninety-two blog followers. They didn't care if it came from a twelve-year-old computer whiz kid whose only basis of social contact was via an online gaming community where he went by the username eatcandlewax06.

Only a small fraction of the world's massive online population cared. Anonymity had replaced expertise. Fact-checking took longer than the seven seconds of attention available before boredom forced them to move unconsciously to the next tweet. When life flashes before your eyes faster than a talent show contestant's career it was no surprise that people felt disorientated and willing to accept whatever they saw and read.

Thanks in large part to the hugely popular online group the Oblivion Doctrine, news of the apocalypse had spread in hours like the free movement of liquid from a spilt mug of tea. And just like a tea spillage the volume on the table always far exceeded the apparent capacity of the mug. The rumours infected computer servers and hard drives from Japan to Hawaii. The bloggers, tweeters and online forum junkies had made sure of it. What began with a simple translation of a five hundred-year-old prognosis had gained a life of its own, morphing into a thousand different conspiracy theories and interpretations.

CONSPIRACY THEORIES

The end was nigh, but no one agreed how.

If you lived in Australia the end of humanity would be delivered courtesy of your smart speaker. Apparently, according to the theory initiated by famous Instagrammer @wetfishlover, smart speakers had been secretly programmed to learn your voice pattern with the express intention of hypnotising you into impaling yourself on your sharpest bread knife.

"Alexa, play my U2 compilation."

"Playing U2 compilation. It's lunchtime, Dave, why don't you go and make yourself a nice sandwich? Hahahaha."

"Alexa, did you just laugh like a Bond villain?"

"Uh…no."

Smart speaker sales had dropped like a stone ever since the rumours passed a thousand likes. Piles of the things were thrown into skips and rubbish dumps. Very early in the morning, if you happened to be walking the suburbs of Brisbane, robotic choruses could be heard mimicking bird calls and attempting to convince dog walkers that they were late for their meeting with Brian to discuss the pricing strategy.

In India the end would come from a meteorite impact. Unlike the example that took out the dinosaurs, this wasn't going to be one massive meteor. This time it would involve thousands of smaller lumps of rock hitting Earth at precisely the same time. Game theory experts had modelled the likely outcome as being something akin to extinction by pebbledashing. The variety of different-sized rocks would target communities, towns and even single individuals, as if God was dropping half-bricks from an existential highway.

There was much talk in Argentina of a zombie-based apocalypse brought about by the consumption of infected avocados. According to blogger, Zombiecookbook, genetically modified avocados were being secretly grown by a CIA-funded rogue element in Bolivia that would, over a period of time, turn everyone who ate them into the walking dead. It seemed of no interest to the brainwashed reader to point out that ninety percent of the world's population hated avocados, thereby reducing the chance of global destruction down to almost zero.

In Morocco the government was carefully considering the proposed ban on plastic straws after several reports insisted they contained alien technology designed to deliver throat cancer. It wasn't clear which aliens were involved, what they wanted or why they felt the need to ruin every kids' party for the rest of time.

In Bulgaria several YouTubers independently concluded and recommended the purchase of titanium underpants to protect against a higher than normal level of radioactivity, likely to cause the total impotence of the male population. No one offered any explanation as to where this radiation might actually come from other than one detractor who suggested it might be as a result of the amount of technology being used to promote it. Sadly no one took notice of this hypothesis because it was scrawled in chalk on a pavement in Sofia.

It didn't seem to matter that none of these theories had the slightest relationship to the contents of the newly discovered prophecy. People knew about Nostradamus's legend, but absolutely nothing whatsoever of the reality. So what if his prophecies had predicted the end of the world in the past, only for it to be called a false alarm or a misread? Eventually he was going to get it right. After all, he correctly predicted the rise of Hitler, the Cold War, the death of Diana, Princess of Wales and 9/11. Hadn't he?

It was just safer to assume and prepare for the worst and if necessary look foolish after the event if the theory was found to be wrong. But if you did get it right, think how smug you'd look in front of all those bemused corpses with their 'Oh bugger, I wish I'd not been so sceptical' expressions all over their cold, dead faces.

The prophecy itself wasn't important. Everyone was going to die and humans loved nothing more than a good drama. Which in turn gave them plenty of opportunities to have a good old moan and point fingers at everyone from Bill Gates to the Bogeyman. And where was the best place to voice this anger? The website of the Oblivion Doctrine, the very place they'd read about the problems in the first place.

Only those responsible for the Oblivion Doctrine knew who ran it. It was a shadowy online entity with no fixed abode or sense of moral obligation. They didn't screen views or ban users. Nothing was off-limits. In the true sense of the word they were disruptors to the mainstream media. Their intentions were clear. Publish content that fuelled people's fears and add just a sense of reality to the theories people had already accepted. Why they did all this, though, was less clear.

All of the world's theories, from the frankly ridiculous to the scientifically plausible, could be found on the site. No one could shut them down, silence them or dispute what they printed. Anyone who tried to deny what was published only served to increase their publicity. If people believed that old-school politicians were corrupt then it was unlikely anyone would believe those very politicians when they denied it. It was a catch twenty-two.

Whether you believed that the decimation of human life was going to be delivered thanks to a mega volcano or alien invasion, there was one group of people who were ready for it.

But they didn't need a prophecy, they were always ready.

The preppers, as they liked to be called, had been preparing for a variety of extinction scenarios for decades. Some were focused on surviving biblical rapture, some expected a biochemical war, and others protected themselves against the possibility of any number of catastrophic natural disasters. Popularised in the United States, this strange, nomadic lifestyle was popping up all over the globe, even more so now that the threat felt real.

On the outskirts of Limonest, a small village to the north of Lyon, Gabriel Janvier was jumping on the bandwagon. She'd picked out a small forest glade for her soon-to-be impregnable fortress. The reality today was that included a hastily constructed tree house made from highly absorbent chipboard which soaked up the rain and disintegrated before morning, a two-foot-deep hole that would eventually become a series of interconnecting tunnels, a work in progress because of the immovable tree roots that got in the way, and a beige nineteen-seventy-one Renault 16 attached to a caravan with one wheel.

She was one of many first-time preppers inspired by the crisis whose only qualifications included watching a television documentary on the National Geographic channel, demonstrating an enjoyment for al fresco dining and receiving a one-off whittling course as a present for Christmas three years ago. The rest she felt she could work out as she went along. Which is what all twenty-somethings thought about everything. After all, she only had until November and proper training would take much too long.

There weren't a lot of reasons for her not to do it. Her long-term boyfriend had run off with the little slut from the bakery, leaving her to pay for the flat that they shared and she couldn't afford. Work had been a long highway of disappointing let-downs. After years of studying computer science to become a programmer she still couldn't get a role that involved anything more mind-numbing than pointless research, coffee-making, and the daily disappointment of warding off the sexual advances of lecherous old men who should know better. It already felt like the end of the world. Her world. And now the rest of it was in trouble, too. It was time to act.

She'd packed what little she felt she needed and left the flat without giving her landlord a forwarding address. She'd reluctantly sold her phone, believing some of the reports on the Oblivion Doctrine that the telephone waves were melting brain cells. Her laptop would be enough if she needed to learn more about the ways of the prepper. Now if only she could work out how to get the internet in a forest a mile from the nearest WI-FI hotspot she could research how to do it.

*****

Ally spent two further days at the museum hoping her assessment of the book would give up more clues to its history. Were there more new prophecies within than the curators had originally realised. The answer was a clear no. In all other ways this version of the 'Les Prophéties' was not uniquely different in content to either of the other two versions, even if there was the odd change of word, spelling or layout. Only the front page of this version stood out as incongruous.

Sometimes it bothered her that she cared so much. The invitation to Lyon was purely based on authenticating the age of the prophecy, and she'd done that almost immediately. By rights she should have downed tools and caught the first flight back home. There was plenty to do back at the university where her very livelihood relied on the grants provided by wealthy benefactors or government initiatives. They had the Shakespearean exhibition to complete by the end of January, a symbolic event given the proximity of the University to Stratford only a few miles away, the town of the Bard's life and times.

So what was keeping her here.

The truth.

CONSPIRACY THEORIES

Authenticating the text to establish that it was written at the same time as the book missed the point. No one would accept a detective turning up at the scene of a murder, proclaiming the victim's death and then totally ignoring their duty to identify a culprit. People expected answers even from cold cases, and this was as chilly as they got. It was always more difficult to close old cases because they lacked fresh or substantive evidence. In this instance more than four hundred and fifty years separated her from the events she was trying to unlock. But that didn't put her off. She'd done it before and she would do it again.

A large part of what we know about the history of sixteenth-century France was as a consequence of Michel Nostradamus's work. Few others documented so much of the times they lived in and not just in prophecies. Nostradamus wrote cookbooks, vast numbers of almanacs, personal letters and star charts, as well as the book he was most famous for. Unquestionably more of his work was out their somewhere, hidden in lofts or archives. He'd had few contemporaries, and none attained the level of fame or notoriety that he did. Or maybe Michel stopped them doing so. Extinguished their work from memory by rewriting history in order to shine light in his direction, while others were trapped in the shadows.

People or concepts that garner mass appeal are often remembered far beyond those with genuine talent but poorer public relations campaigns. Popularity itself creates a gravitational field all of its own that vacuums up alternative and minority interests. The greater the popularity the more people fanaticised about it, or were shamed into agreeing by a sense of alienation from the rest of society. There are plenty of examples. Coldplay, for starters. The Oblivion Doctrine was another. There were billions of websites online, but, like Nostradamus, they eclipsed all others into obscurity.

CONSPIRACY THEORIES

Ally was no fan of Nostradamus the human being. From what she'd pieced together, through letters written over the years to friends and clients, he had a character defect that made him prone to bouts of flattery, sycophancy, deception and conceit. But there was one characteristic that she and Michel shared. Neither of them liked to collaborate. Other people's lack of intelligence bothered her. It forever delayed progress as their limited speed of thought fizzled out catching up with hers. She suspected he didn't like it because it meant sharing fame and fortune.

If that was the case, how did someone else's prophecy end up in one of his books? If it wasn't something he and another had worked on together, why was it there? Ally was working on two plausible theories. The first was that someone else had placed it there without Nostradamus's knowledge. Maybe a budding apprentice or fanboy was desperate to get a leg up in their own pursuit of recognition. The second theory was that Nostradamus purposely included this passage in this version of the book without the real author's knowledge. But if this was true, why did he feel the need to steal it?

It was clear to Ally that Michel wanted fame above all else. He'd proven it throughout his career through acts as brazen as writing prophecies about the royal family with the prime intention of being called to their court. An invitation that would validate his talents and boost his popularity to others. But given the reputation he'd already forged during his lifetime, why would he be threatened by a newcomer? Unless of course the newcomer had something he needed. Something that Nostradamus didn't have.

The archive room in the museum was getting as cold as the trail. Nothing more would be learnt here. There was only one lead that might open up further evidence. It was time to meet Monsieur Palomer, the man whose house had kept the book hidden for hundreds of years.

- Chapter 5 -

Prison

The cold, clammy stone pressed up against his sore cheek which slowly slid down the wall, dragging the rest of his head with it. The slimy green residue that covered most of the walls and ceiling dripped down onto his scalp and small puffs of steam billowed from his mouth, before evaporating almost as quickly as they formed. The frosty air forged an allegiance with the darkness to muddle his senses, all of which desperately fought for dominance over the meagre brainpower still available in order to function at the expense of the others.

In the recent past he'd been beaten, thrown, covered in dirty rags, beaten a little more, kicked, spat at, slapped, poked in soft regions of his body, dragged over rocks, pushed violently and offered some aggressive instructions that threatened his immediate existence. The clunk of a metal gate was followed by the eerie silence of the room and his inevitable descent into unconsciousness. How long he'd remained out cold was unclear. It was night-time still, but not necessarily the same one he'd arrived under.

A window to the outside world, no more than a foot wide and tall, was the only feature of note adorning the walls, although it was difficult to pick out anything smaller or potentially more significant through eyes puffed up by the regular punches that had been administered against them. Long, thin strands of straw kept his body a few millimetres above the flagstones and was shared by an eclectic colony of squirming, dark-shelled invertebrates. As his eyesight became more accustomed to the gloom it was clear the insects were not the only residents of his cell.

Sitting cross-legged on a stool designed for a much smaller occupant was an elderly man in fine silks and clean shoes. There was an absence of mud on his pale skin, quite unusual for a place that seemed designed for its cultivation. His beard had recently been trimmed and the only noticeable blemishes on his face had been placed there by the passing of time rather than an overaggressive jailor.

'Perhaps he wasn't in jail at all,' he thought. This gentleman looked more accustomed to sitting in a library or church than a prison. Whoever he was, he showed no interest in Phil's recent arrival, his thoughts and senses preoccupied by much more important matters.

There was no way the man would know Phil was watching him because he sat perfectly still with both eyes firmly shut. Both hands were raised to shoulder level with the index finger of each hand aimed skyward while the rest of his fingers formed a purposeful circle with his thumbs. Both lips were twitching uncontrollably and just occasionally they'd collide to produce a rather irritating clapping noise. This pattern continued relentlessly with no sign of an end. To the man's side an ornate, oak coffer held several books, quills, small bottles of black ink and scattered pieces of torn parchment across its smooth lid.

"Been here long?" said Philibert in a vain attempt to help the man notice his existence.

There was no response.

"I said, have you been here long?"

"Shush."

"I'm Phili…"

"Shussshhhhh!"

Phil immediately complied with the request, expecting only a short delay before the usual pleasantries were followed by an exchange of stories, fabricated to avoid the real reasons as to how they'd ended up here. None came.

The man's pose continued, and would have done so permanently if Phil had not broken it again. The total lack of social protocols was freaking him out more than the sinister location.

"Are you ok?" asked Phil with real concern for the man's mental health.

"Shush. Shush. SHUSH!"

"What are you doing?"

"Oh, blast and damn it!"

"What?"

"Curse you, fate." He shook a fist at nothing in particular.

"I'm sorry."

"I had it right there…in front of me…almost fully formed!" shouted the man, leaping from his stool and kicking it petulantly into the corner of the room. "Oh, thank you very much!"

"Sorry, it's just you were ignoring me."

"Yes, I know. It was on purpose!"

"I'm Philibert."

"Good for you."

The old man propped his head against the green, slimy walls, fists clenched in a ball ready to strike something.

"And you are?" asked Phil, maintaining his grip on the normal flow of proceedings that accompanied meeting someone for the first time.

The man ceased leaning, a position he'd occupied since launching himself from the stool, and turned dramatically. He fixed his stare on Phil, mouth wide open, face pale from shock and jaw dangling somewhere close to his Adam's apple. "You're joking, right!?"

"I'm not sure I'm in any condition to joke right now," replied Phil.

"And yet your question is ridiculously funny."

"It is?"

"How could you not know who I am?"

Phil rubbed more of the blood from his eyes in case that was the culprit for his lack of vision rather than his memory. It didn't help. "Because…um…I don't!"

"Are you foreign?"

"Depends what you mean by foreign."

"Turkish?"

"No."

"Oriental?"

"Not sure where that is," said Phil a little confused as to which country it related to.

"But you can't be French."

"Yes, Aix-en-Provence originally."

"WHAT?! No way. It's literally impossible you don't know who I am."

"Is it?"

"Yes! It's unbelievable. Have you been in hiding?"

"No."

"Are you secretly blind? Amnesia perhaps?"

"No. None of them. And surely if I did have amnesia, I wouldn't actually remember that I had amnesia, would I?"

"I really don't understand how it's possible," replied the man, pacing up and down while chuntering his surprise under his breath.

"Look, I just don't know who you are, alright?!" replied Phil angrily, pulling himself gingerly to his feet. "Just bloody tell me!"

"You, sir, are in the company of none other than the one and only Michel de Notredame! Or Nostradamus, as most call me. Apothecary, Engineer, Herbalist, Ephemeris and Prophet." As Michel made his introductions he stretched out his body to inflate his own self-importance, and struck a pose that wouldn't have looked out of place in the portrait of an expensive oil painting.

"Oh, right," replied Phil in mock acknowledgement.

There was an uncomfortable silence.

"You still don't know who I am, do you?"

"No. Sorry."

"Damn it! I really thought I was getting somewhere. That people were starting to take notice."

Michel retrieved the upturned stool from its crash site and returned to his previous state. At no point did he feel inclined to discover more about his new inmate or why he might have been there. Being in prison wouldn't stop Michel working and nor would another human distract him.

"What are you doing?"

Michel reluctantly opened one eye.

"I was harnessing the cosmic energy, before you contaminated the atmosphere with all your innate nonsense."

"Cosmic what?"

"Energy. It tells me the future and I write it down. You wouldn't understand."

"Ahh…now I get why you're in here," said Phil suddenly feeling rather sorry for him. "You're a threat to yourself and a danger to others?"

"No! Have a little more respect for your elders, boy."

Closing in on his sixtieth year, Michel had already beaten the odds of history and looked in no hurry to stop anytime soon. The earlier leap from the stool demonstrated how agile and fit he was for a man who had no right to be anywhere other than a hole in the ground or bed-ridden to a nice, comfy bed.

"Why are you here, then?" asked Phil.

"Freedom of speech."

"There isn't any," replied Phil, something he knew only too well as a result of his own upbringing.

"Precisely. The Church, or at least one of them, because I can't keep up with all the changes, has decided in their divine wisdom that I should stay here for a while. All because I forgot to ask them."

"Ask them what?"

"If I could print my prognostications."

"And…"

"Apparently I couldn't. Which was annoying because I already had."

"Prison for that seems a little harsh."

"Poor old Claude didn't really have a choice. He got caught up in the religious backlash and had to send me here. It's only temporary: the postal service from Paris can take months."

"You know Claude de Savoie?"

"Yes, of course he knows me. Everyone knows me."

"Apart from me."

"That's hardly my fault, is it?"

"I guess it's neither yours nor mine. Listen, do you think you might be able to put a good word in for me? Encourage him to release me?"

"I doubt it," said Michel dispassionately. "I don't know you."

"Well, you won't until you try to."

"You're right."

"Well, are you going to?"

"Probably not."

"Nice. I see we're going to get along well."

"Don't feel bad, it's not personal. I'm just too busy for all of that getting to know you nonsense. Plus, I'm not really in the best position to help you get out at the moment. I don't even know what you're in here for?"

Philibert considered the answer for a moment. Over the years he'd participated in many deeds that might have warranted a stint in prison, but oddly none of those had been the cause of his arrest. It was ironic to think that the one time he'd chosen to do the right thing, it was perversely that very action that landed him in trouble. And he still wasn't entirely sure why. Yes, he'd been found in a lady's chamber without an invitation, and yes, he'd confronted Jacques over his treatment of Annabelle, but were those really crimes? The answer was a categorical yes. Crimes, in the eyes of the nobility, were whatever they wanted them to be.

"I confronted a fellow noblemen over the treatment of a lady," replied Phil, making it sound as innocent as possible.

Michel rubbed his chin and reflected for a moment. He was many things, but gullibility did not feature in his list of faults.

"Is that so? And what business was it of yours?"

"He was beating her."

"And do you intervene if a knight whips his own horse?"

"No, but that's not the same."

"That depends on the quality of the horse."

"Are you saying only ugly horses should be beaten?"

"Of course not. I'm saying if the horse is well behaved it has no reason to be beaten. This woman, did she deserve it?"

"I think you're missing my angle on this."

"Crime and punishment are not new concepts. If she deserved it, you had no right to interfere."

"No, she didn't deserve it. No human deserves to be treated like an animal."

"Then I can tell you've never been to Genoa: horrible people."

"I'm sure they don't deserve it either."

"It looks to me, from the way you are dressed, that you, too, are a noble. The correct response in that situation would have been to challenge the other to a duel. What was your approach?"

"I waved a rather inoffensive bent penknife at him."

"Unconventional."

"And ineffective as it happens," added Phil.

"What's your name, boy?"

"Philibert Montmorency."

Michel snorted loudly.

"What?"

"You're not a Montmorency."

"You seem very certain."

"Yes, I am," said Michel.

"I have a ring."

"I don't care if you have a written statement from the Queen. Just because I'm famous for reading the future, it doesn't mean I'm not interested in history: in fact, it's a vital source of information to predict future events. Earlier you said you were from Aix: the Montmorency family are from Languedoc."

Phil had dropped his guard. Amidst the confusion of his beating and the disturbing conditions of his surroundings he'd answered a question off message and allowed a true fact to creep out from under the façade.

"Did I really say Aix?"

"Oh yeah."

"But I meant Albi."

"Yet you still said Aix. Clear as day."

"Slip of the tongue."

"They don't know you're an imposter yet, do they?" replied Michel pointedly.

"No," replied Philibert, releasing himself from his own lie.

"But they will, soon enough. I think confronting a noble for beating his woman is probably the least of your worries."

"What will they do to me?"

"I expect they'll invite a few hundred peasants to congregate in a big circle somewhere in Marseille to watch a man dressed in black violently remove your head with something sharp. The poor will be happy for another week without the slightest consideration to whose head was removed as long as there was a lot of screaming and the odd front-rower got splattered with blood. Double win."

Phil wasn't keen on losing his head, or being the main attraction at the Saturday afternoon matinee. "What should I do?"

"Keep doing what you've always done. Find a way to convince them that you should live: after all, you're an imposter, aren't you?"

"I'm a chancer trying to make a better life for myself that's all."

"Good for you. I'm all for it. Now if you don't mind I feel a prophecy coming on."

Nostradamus shuffled over to his desk, dragging the stool along for the ride with the aid of his left foot. Dipping the quill into the inkpot a couple of times he set to work on one of the quatrains he was starting to become famous for. These four-line prophecies weren't just the source of his income, they fuelled his fame with the ferocity of an exploding cannon. The people needed hope, guidance and comfort and he delivered it every year with almanacs that contained hundreds of these quatrains for every possible event or circumstance.

Everyone, from noble to royal to peasant, wanted to know the outcome of their life before it occurred. It didn't matter too much what the source of the prediction was, as long as they trusted the scribe. Nostradamus had spent a lifetime building a reputation that the people believed in. If it came from him then it was simply the truth.

After a couple of minutes of intense scribbling, grumbling and the occasional glance up to the window where the clear night sky framed the distant constellations, he raised the paper above his head in triumph.

"Got it!" he shouted as if a crowd extended out into the distance waiting patiently for his proclamation. "Oh yes, this is a good one."

The introduction of the paper to the small world of the dank cell was presented no less exuberantly than the announcement of a newborn baby. This wasn't just a piece of paper, this was a living, breathing vision of the future. A sure-fire cert, a beautifully intricate window with a stunning view of the world still to come. The sort of valuable intelligence you'd rely on to top up your insurance premiums, make a massive financial gamble on the outcome of your crop yields and stay as far away from natural disaster zones as possible. There was no question of this being a mere guess. This was a prophecy, and in the right hands it was as accurate as an axe was to a skilful executioner.

"Can I see it?" asked Philibert, caught up in the excitement and theatre purposefully spun to catch people's attention and prove its own authenticity.

"If you want," said Michel, holding the small piece of yellow parchment out towards him.

Phil attempted to read it in the dimly lit conditions, but that wasn't the only factor holding him back.

"It's good, isn't it?" said Michel smiling from ear to ear.

"It's hard to say."

"I expect it's too difficult for you to interpret."

"It's hard to say."

"I wouldn't beat yourself up. It's as much a skill to understand a quatrain as it is to write one."

"It's hard to say," repeated Phil.

"What's the problem with it?"

"It's in Latin."

Latin was still the recognised language for those of academic persuasion. Doctors, professors, writers, priests and architects all used it, and for two simple reasons. Firstly it was the recognised norm, and secondly it annoyed everyone on the outside of their circle who couldn't read it. It was like a rude note, written in a code only the perpetrators understood, being passed covertly around the classroom to fool the teacher.

Everyday folk didn't speak Latin. They spoke French, and dependent on the particular town or region they lived in, it may or may not be the same French as the village they could see on the horizon across the river. But mostly it wasn't. Those fortunate enough to learn Latin were at an immediate advantage over the masses, who would never know if you'd accurately translated it into their dialect or not. Which was unlikely as even scholars couldn't keep up with how quickly their vocabulary changed. Latin was effective because it tended to contain the same words and meanings from one year to the next, unlike French dialects whose words multiplied faster than plankton.

"Hold on. I'll do a dummy's version," said Michel curtly, looking at Phil in disdain. Moments later he handed him a French version on a new piece of parchment.

The great squawker, audacious, without shame
Will be elected governor of the army
The stoutness of his competitor,
The bridge being broken, the city fainting from fear

"Um, ok. What's this a prophecy about?" asked Phil, genuinely confused by it.

"You mean you don't know?! Why don't you try to work it out?"

Phil reread the four lines to see if he was missing anything crucial before concluding that the only thing missing was meaning.

"If I had to guess, and it's just that, by the way, I'd say a really big bird, that's the squawker, of unknown species, is going to take over an army and do something unspeakable to a bridge that will make everyone faint. I mean birds can be very messy, can't they? Not sure it would make anyone faint, though. Actually, now I think about it, I think the bridge might be a metaphor. Maybe the bridge is really a branch?"

"Obviously that's not it," replied Michel.

"Ok then genius, tell me, as you're so bloody clever."

"I'm seeing a loud, brash royal figure ascending to the head of an army before crushing his foe at a notorious city with a bridge, where they will lay siege to it until the people's will is broken."

"Which one?"

"Which what?" asked Michel, rather caught out. He wasn't used to being challenged.

"Well, where do I start? Which royal figure? Which city? Which bridge?"

"I'm sure it'll become obvious when it happens."

"But what good is that if someone is reading your prophecies today in the hope of avoiding whatever it is that's going to happen tomorrow? Does everyone just avoid visiting any major city that has a bridge? Venice will be deserted."

"Don't be silly. Not avoid, just take precautions when you're there."

"Like watch out for squawking generals, you mean!?"

"Exactly."

"You know, you should branch out into travel guides."

"The cosmic energy isn't easy to control, you have to take from it what you can."

"And do people really believe this stuff?" said Phil, never one for holding much sway in the future and being more preoccupied with getting through each day unscathed. He thought it unlikely that Nostradamus's prophecies could help him much there.

"Absolutely. I have customers all over the country. The rich and powerful pay me to write their star charts and I offer personal predictions just for them. I've even worked for the royal family, you know."

"But why do they believe it?"

"Because I write the truth."

"Is that right?" replied Phil sceptically. "And why aren't you allowed to write 'the truth' at the moment. Why did the Church throw you in here if your work is so reliable?"

"Because the Church is in a panic about all this Calvinism nonsense and they don't want to take a chance that someone like me will predict the Catholics losing. Even greater than that, they fear the very slim chance that I might make an incorrect prediction about them. Now they won't let anyone publish anything until they've had the chance to read through them to make amendments."

"Good luck to them, not sure they'd make any sense of it anyway. You could make this prediction fit almost anything in retrospect," added Phil.

"In the wrong hands you could."

"So why not just let the Church read them?" asked Phil.

"It's sensitive," replied Michel with a long, pregnant pause as he considered it. "I may have made a small error in one of my predictions."

"A small error."

"Tiny."

"What was it?"

"I might have predicted that the King would have a really successful year full of health, happiness and victory in battle."

"Which King was that?"

"Henry II," replied Michel.

"Oh."

- Chapter 6 -

The Untimely Death of Henry II

A wall of flags, each with a distinctly different colour palette and historic crest, fluttered in the gentle breeze of a June afternoon. Shadows from flagpoles stretched like static creepers across the lush green square of Place des Vosges, a hectare of royal real estate in the heart of Paris. Europe's largest city bulged increasingly into the countryside, its girth sprawling over its belt like the oncoming sea reclaims the land nearest the coast.

Dissecting the land between the lush greenery of the square and the Seine, a filthy, clogged artery gouging its way through the heart of the city, was Paris's widest road. The original Roman road, a throughway that once guided travellers between Paris and Melun, had been extended over the centuries into the impressive Rue Saint-Antoine, simply known by those who lived there as the Grand Rue. At one end of the road, equally haunting as it was beautiful, stood the recently fortified Tower of Bastille. And stretching along the road from the tower's intimidating roots a diverse collection of buildings did their best to protect their positions along the route of the road. Hectic wooden houses leant against neighbours fabricated by talented masons in intricate stone, while others were seemingly kept in place by willpower alone.

No carriage or cart had trundled down the Grand Rue for three days. The entire area from the King's property at the Hôtel des Tournelles to the river had been requisitioned for a grand tournament to celebrate recent achievements and good news. The signing of the treaty of Cateau-Cambrésis had brought the eighth Italian war against the Habsburgs to an end after a hundred years of bloodshed. At least for now. After attempting eight times to resolve their differences there was obviously a very decent chance that someone would kick another one off any day now.

This most recent Italian war had lasted for eight years and had consumed the entirety of King Henry's reign. His brother and predecessor Francis had only just brought the curtain down on the seventh edition of the rivalry when he had the good grace to die, forcing Henry to have another crack. Season eight had been the best yet. It had everything. Abdications, interesting settings, terrible defeats, like the battle of Saint Quentin, the unexpected entry of the English, who ruined everything by bringing the name of 'Italian' war into disrepute, and one huge cliffhanger. Who would ultimately come out as victor? Europe waited expectantly to see if either side were wealthy enough to fork out the vast sums necessary to deliver a ninth season.

Until then everyone developed strategies for enjoying peace. The most popular way was to grab your weaponry, stick on your suit of armour and charge full speed at your own allies with a pointy log in an attempt to knock the other off their steed. Peace meant tournaments. But ironically tournaments were often more dangerous than the war they'd spent most of their adult lives fighting. Crucially they were cheaper than a decade of tax receipts that most wars consumed.

The peace treaty was not the only notable triumph being celebrated at this tournament. Recently two of the King's children had been married off, mostly to the very kingdoms they'd been trying to destroy for the best part of a century. His daughter, Elizabeth, was now Queen of Spain, having married Philip II. Spain had been part of the Italian Empire during the war, and the fact that France sat between the two explained much of the tension. Henry's teenage son and heir, the sickly Prince Francis, had been married off to Mary, Queen of Scotland, a betrothal that had been prearranged since the pair were four years old.

These distinguished family members, and other significant dignitaries, sat in position on raised stages under canvas roofs along the edges of the Grand Rue to enjoy the sights and sounds of the joust. Not everyone was enjoying the festivities. The Queen, Catherine de Medici, was bored. She did her best to fake interest as rider after rider hurtled down the centre of the road desperately struggling to cling to the back of their animal with varying degrees of success while simultaneously removing their competitor from theirs. Mostly they missed each other. Once in a while a shield might receive a gentle nudge with an opponent's lance. Imagine modern-day baseball, lots of swinging and only the very occasional contact. All that for eight hours surrounded by smelly, boozed-up idiots. Jousting, not baseball. Well maybe.

The poor weren't left out. The main reason for hosting the event in the middle of Paris was to allow them the chance to enjoy the event. That's if they could find a vantage point within a mile of the action and they did so under the proviso they didn't get in the way or put anyone off with their fascinating, and sometimes deadly, range of aromas. Those deemed in contravention of these basic rules were marched further up the road towards the Bastille, which had the desired effect of helping them realise that they had more important things in their lives. Life, for example.

The King dropped the visor down on his helmet and peered into the distance. A couple of hundred metres down the road was his victim, Lord Montgomery, captain of the

Scots Guards. The atmosphere from the crowd suggested an unbreakable confidence in the outcome of the duel, and no one believed it more than Henry himself. How could he lose? He was King, and in the eyes of the people, he was one step from divinity. Stronger physically, tougher mentally and with the Will of God sitting neatly upon his shoulder. If that wasn't enough, even the prophecies were on his side.

His steed neighed its excitement, the smell of its own sweat filling both of their nostrils. To the Queen's anger, Henry wore, as he always did, the black and white colours of his mistress, Diane de Poitiers. If Catherine tilted her head just a fraction she'd see her adversary sitting in the gallery not far away. Like a spectre this woman had haunted her every step since the very first she'd taken as a married woman. Whatever the King said concerning his faith, it was always a 'Do as I say and not as I do' mantra. God frowned upon adultery, yet it didn't stop Henry, who preached the Scriptures unwaveringly, from ignoring them when it came to personal discipline.

Expectation in the crowd heightened as even small children stopped their games to watch the outcome of the King's contest. This was what they'd really come to see. The main event. The man that everyone recognised, not some jumped-up newcomer from Toulon with only a few minor hits under their belts, or a random Scotsman with a dodgy accent. Even if the last two courses had proven that at forty years of age the King was at a disadvantage against his younger rival. Those courses had finished without a winner. They'd ride two more to conclude matters.

Even though the King's doctor had warned him against overexertion there was no way Henry was backing down, not while his people watched in anticipation. This was his moment. A celebration of the achievements and challenges he'd overcome during his short reign. After eight years of fighting, he was finally winning, and he didn't want it to stop.

Montgomery lowered his lance to signal his readiness for action and the King did likewise. A metal-booted heel dug into his horse's side and it burst forward along the wooden tilt that separated the two riders from a certain collision. Hooves struck the ground like thunderbolts ever more frequently as they drew ever closer to their target. A collective silence cascaded down the road like a Mexican wave as all eyes were drawn towards the flurry of man and beast. Both riders lowered their lances and held shields to protect their bodies from a possible strike. The noise of horse and heart got ever closer. In a blink they were upon each other, and in another they'd passed.

With the clatter of lance against shield the King wobbled giddily as his body slid to one side of his horse from the high-speed impact. His lance fell uncontrollably to the ground as he summoned all his skills as a horseman to stay in contact with the animal. Holding the reins for dear life he managed to reseat himself and brought the horse to an ungraceful halt. A collective breath returned to the dry throats of the mesmerised and distressed onlookers. Eager for stability, he quickly dismounted and led the horse back to the gallery.

"You made it, then," said the Queen through gritted teeth. "I'm so pleased."

"Yes, my love, he got a lucky hit there. But I'll get him back in the fourth course."

"My lord, the court has engaged in this so-called sport for three solid days: surely it's time we returned to matters of state and ceased this barbarity," beseeched Catherine.

"No. It's a tradition! You can't just wipe that away. Look at the people with all their happy, smiling faces. They're enjoying themselves and they've earned it. I promise today is the last day."

THE UNTIMELY DEATH OF HENRY II

Across the road the Queen watched a dishevelled group of peasants challenge each other to see who could spit the furthest. In another section an obese, shirtless man was inviting members of the public to punch him as hard as they could in the stomach in exchange for a franc if he stayed on his feet. He wasn't very good at it. Every time a fist landed in his abnormally flabby gut he was forced to lie on the ground for twenty minutes writhing in pain.

"Happy? They seem, well, distracted by it more than showing signs of enjoyment," replied Catherine.

This wasn't how people celebrated success in her home city of Rome. In Italy they thought it enough to celebrate achievement by eating, drinking and making love to anybody within a ten-mile radius. On second thoughts that might not be the best alternative for someone with Henry's reputation who, having spotted Diane in the next tent, was waving at her less subtly than he'd hoped.

"Why do you insist on applying your affection to that brainless whore?" said the Queen.

No other person would speak to the King in this way, but Catherine was like no other. Royal in her own right, she'd lived throughout her marriage with his endless infidelity. While he focused on enjoying himself, she studied the arts, the rule of law and some more dubious interests, in an attempt to uphold the position bestowed upon her. Much more so than he did. To him the Crown was an inconvenient distraction that got in the way of life's pleasure, just a birthright without consequences. In his opinion whatever he did or didn't do was always the right decision, and whether people agreed or not seemed irrelevant. She, on the other hand, desired to rule for the good of the country and not just the good of the Crown.

"My darling, you wouldn't want me to be unhappy, would you?" he replied with sickly sweet tone of utter fakery. "She's just a hobby, a distraction from all the hard work I do."

THE UNTIMELY DEATH OF HENRY II

"Be careful, my lord, one day God will judge your deeds," said the Queen.

It would come a lot sooner than anyone anticipated.

"Unlucky…herauph…papa," spluttered a lanky teenager with more gold trinkets hanging from his body than a mid-sized jewellery shop. This fashion choice was not a wise one. All the excess rings and pendants weighed down on his already feeble body, which even without them seemed incapable of moving without aid. Every other word the boy said was accompanied by a gravelly cough or sneeze, forcing the congregation to reach for a shield of their own. The pretty girl sitting to his left seemed the only one not to care. Instead she gently preened his hair with her hands or made sympathetic noises every time he struggled to complete a sentence.

An even younger boy, around nine years of age, sat in the row behind the young couple sporting a temper that suggested someone had stolen his favourite servant and had demanded a ransom. The boy spoke only through his expression, which told everyone it was best not to annoy him. Charles had anger issues, particularly when he didn't get his own way, which was more often than might be expected for a young prince. Declining his demands often stemmed from the impossibility of his requests rather than a desire not to spoil him.

Charles had a habit of insisting on items that simply didn't exist, like a mug of lightning or a nurse with three nipples. Whether Charles knew he was asking for the absurd or not didn't seem to restrain him. It was as if his preposterous desires were purposely designed to instigate his second favourite pastime, losing his shit.

"My sons," said the King warmly, aiming his response to the sick and grumpy boy in the row behind the Queen. "One day the two of you will ride here and compete at an event like this, and you, too, will win the ultimate prize."

THE UNTIMELY DEATH OF HENRY II

"Begging your pardon, Your Highness," said the Queen with a wry smile. "I believe he just beat you."

"One more course to go, my love," he replied overconfidently.

"Must you compete? I'm so desperately concerned for your welfare," replied Catherine, her vocal tone never suggesting the same concern offered by her choice of words.

"Never fear. No harm can come to me: Nostradamus said so himself."

The King clicked his fingers and almost at once a member of the court wearing a large chain that dangled down onto his portly belly appeared alongside him. On his left hand a band of pale skin lacked the olive tan that spread over the rest of his visible body and was the only evidence of a real ring that once lived there.

"Anne, my faithful friend and servant. Where is that letter Nostradamus sent me?"

"What?"

"THE LETTER," said the King, remembering that Anne had been saddled with deafness.

"Yes, of course. I keep it on me, sir," said the elderly man reaching inside a roll of papers he carried under his arm. "Ah, here it is."

"Thank you, Constable, as always your usefulness to me has no limits."

The King cleared his throat and read the passage out loud so as many people as possible could hear it. "My most invincible King, no affliction, calamity or misery comes into the world but that the stars make it beforehand. France shall greatly grow, triumph, be magnified and much more so its monarch."

"Hear, hear," said the Constable after holding his hand to his ear and guessing every second word. Anne de Montmorency had been through much adversity in his life and few of his bodyparts worked productively as a result.

Although an elderly man well into his sixties, he had taken an active role in all wars since the fifteen twenties, which had involved numerous injuries and afflictions.

"I'd say that was pretty positive," summarised the King.

"It's alright for you, my lord, but what about the rest of us."

Sir Nicholas Throckmorton, England's Ambassador to France, was an eccentric personality who lived on the edge of his nerves. Not many blamed him. Over the last twenty years the English monarchs, of which there had been many, had all at various times accused, convicted, pardoned and banished him for just about every possible misdemeanour in the book, only some of which he'd been guilty of. This had led him to develop a highly sensitive anxiety disorder that meant he'd thought of, planned against and attempted to avoid, every possible calamity that might befall him. This included, at the extreme end of the spectrum, his strong fear that the world would end any day now.

"Come now, Nicholas, I'm sure England has their own prophets?"

"No. Queen Elizabeth had them all executed, which strangely none of them predicted."

The crowd milling around the King's tent was suddenly parted as a burly man in armour cut through it effortlessly. He lifted off his helmet and shook his long, ginger hair. The ladies of the court swooned and attempted various methods of gaining his attention including fainting, hysterical screaming and the extremely naughty flash of an ankle.

"Ye a'richt, sur, ah didnae mean tae catch ye lik' that."

King Henry did his best to process as much of Lord Montgomery's mutterings as he could, but even in French his accent made him sound uniquely undecipherable.

"I'm sorry, I didn't catch all that, can you repeat it?"

"Ah didnae mean tae catch ye lik' that."

"Nope," said Henry screwing up his face, "it's no good, totally lost."

"Yer laird, urr ye duin fur th' neist coorse?" said Montgomery, attempting a different message all together.

"Honestly, it's like another language," whispered Henry to Anne from the corner of his mouth.

"What?" replied Anne who couldn't hear either of them.

"Mary, my dear, isn't he one of yours? Would you interpret for me?"

Mary, Queen of Scotland in absentee, glided elegantly down from the shade of the canopy and whispered in the King's ear.

"Oh I see, you said you're ready for the next course," he said, nodding to Montgomery and holding his thumb in the air to aid their understanding of each other. "Right you are. I was born ready, my Scottish friend. I'm the King. What can possibly go wrong?"

*****

"And that's when it got complicated," said Michel as he recounted the story to Philibert.

"It certainly did for Henry: I hear it took him ten days to die."

"Yes, it did. During the fourth course, Montgomery's lance splintered on impact and some of the pieces pierced the King's eye, head and throat. His doctor managed to remove them, but the damage was done."

"The Queen can't have been very happy with you and your letter?"

"No, to the contrary, she was rather pleased with the outcome."

"Pleased!"

"Of course. It was her opportunity to lead the country the way she wanted to. The boys were much too young to rule, and as it happens the elder boy, Francis, died of his own illness twelve months later. These days the younger brother Charles is rightful heir, but at eleven he's too young to make any decisions, much to his own irritation I understand. The family don't hold a grudge against me. They still ask me to provide star charts, even after my mistake."

"Mistake?"

"Yes, the letter to Henry was wrong. When I dictated the letter the scribe misspelt one word which dramatically changed the assessment that Henry showed such confidence in."

"Which word?"

"Invincible," said Michel.

"Why was that a mistake?" asked Phil.

"He put an 'in' at the front of the word by accident."

"I'm not sure I follow. Are you saying you meant it to read 'vincible?'"

"Exactly."

"But…that's not even a word."

"Course it is. Invisible and visible; incoherent and coherent, they all follow the same rule."

"No, they don't! It's not even a rule. Someone who doesn't have intelligence is not telligent! People that lack inventiveness are not ventive, are they?"

"Oh yeah," proffered Michel sarcastically. "You'd know, wouldn't you? What with you being a genius and all that. Where did you study, then? Hmm, tell me that. Which grand institution had the honour of your attendance?"

"I didn't go to any. I learnt everything I could from everyone I met. Not all of us had the benefit of being born into prosperity, you know."

"Prosperity. Ha! That's a laugh. You haven't got a clue. I had to fight, beg and bleed my knuckles to the bone to gain acceptance to the Montpelier Medical Faculty. My father's meagre inheritance didn't come close to paying for it. And even when I did fight my way into the realm of academia no one accepted me as an equal. Even then I was different. I had to teach myself much of what I came to learn on herbs and plants and was forced to take every job I could find from Marseille to Aix. I did anything I could to pay my way."

"Did you say Aix?"

"Yes, I've worked all over the place to get where I am today."

"But you were specifically there?" said Philibert, finally finding common ground between them.

"Yes."

"When?"

"The first time was in the spring of fifteen-forty-six."

"But that was when the town had the plague!"

"I know. Why do you think I was there?" said Nostradamus.

- Chapter 7 -

N1G13

Ally Oldfield sat on the terrace of a grubby bistro in the shadow of 'La Basilique Notre-Dame de Fourvière', nursing an empty coffee cup. Perched on a hill in the centre of the city, the massive, ancient cathedral dominated the Lyon skyline and granted visitors a spectacular vantage point across most of the city. Every four of five minutes the funicular brought another horde of chattering tourists up the hillside to view the scene without the need to exert themselves. The continual clanking of the train ascending and descending did little to break her concentration.

On the small metal table in front of her a newspaper lay open as passing gusts attempted to move the pages and force her into reading another article. If the headline of this, and every other mainstream paper in France and around the world, were to be believed, 'The End' had begun. Engorged, bold text projected out of the front page like the scene in a pop-up book and this time there was nothing theoretical or conspiratorial about it.

The death toll was indisputable.

The number of officially recorded deaths as a result of the newly identified flu strain, N1G13, were increasing by the day. Inevitably the virus had been nicknamed the Nostradamus Flu, because N1G13 was a lot less catchy. After all the mad local theories and internet conclusions that had done the rounds, now people had a real one to rally behind. This was proof. The end was N1G13.

Ally wasn't convinced. She knew only too well that a flu epidemic didn't mean the end of the world. There had been plenty of pandemics throughout history which had been both frequent and heavy killers, but they were not extinction-level events. Scientists expected new and fresh strains of flu to appear every fifty years or so, and in purely statistical terms their arrival affected only a tiny proportion of the global population. Certainly the world was long overdue a really good pandemic. It had been almost a hundred years since the Spanish flu had wiped out hundreds of thousands across the continent of Europe.

Less scientifically trained doom-mongers, though, had been predicting a truly global and devastating outbreak for decades. One that could not be held back by modern medicine or containment tactics. Over the last century the vast increase in air travel, ever-closer contact between humans, birds and beasts in areas like Asia, and the capacity of viruses to resist medicinal therapies were all nuggets of evidence that pinpointed such a prediction. Now something else was being used to justify it. Written in an era when air travel, medicines and most of Asia weren't recognised terms, a prophecy was suggesting just such an event. But making the leap between the two just didn't add up in Ally's mind. Coincidences are more common than you'd think.

Of course it didn't help that her own translation of the prophecy drew striking similarities to current circumstances. There would be a blood moon in just a few months' time, but no one wanted to acknowledge that this wasn't a unique occurrence. The next one after that was due in about six months and more than a dozen had happened since the start of the century. The prophecy had also mentioned cold winds, which some interpreters had deciphered as referring to the common cold. Although the new and deadly form of flu currently sweeping across parts of China was chemically similar to a cold, so were a host of other human ailments. She couldn't help thinking that the facts were being distorted to fit the narrative that so many people wanted to believe.

It was also true that the new virus was being carried by birds, pigs and cattle, just as the prophecy had suggested, but worryingly it was spreading unusually quickly between humans. Unlike historical flu outbreaks the implications of catching N₁G₁₃ were almost always fatal, and to date no institution or laboratory had come even close to developing a remedy. Stressed scientists and worried government officials scampered in panic to solve the problem as hundreds of victims died every day.

And it was going to get worse.

It wouldn't be long until the virus spread across borders. Victims of the virus could carry it for several days before presenting any symptoms, so stopping any would-be carrier boarding an aircraft was almost impossible. And then Asia's problem would be the world's.

Ally wasn't that bothered by the fatalities. People she didn't know died all the time without her noticing. Even people she did know personally were known to snuff it without her offering more than a delayed condolence card. What mattered more than life and death to her was being right. The world was being fooled into thinking that this flu was hastening mankind towards extinction, and she was determined to prove them wrong. Nostradamus didn't write the prediction and if she could discover who did, and why, then the world would have to pay attention.

The flu would continue to claim lives, but at least it would be in context to every other outbreak from the last century. Pharmaceutical companies would produce remedies, people would take preventive steps to reduce the chance of infection, and the flu would, as they always did, disappear from the public conscience. If mankind's paranoia, fear and protectionism didn't destroy everything first, that was.

Discovering the truth of a five hundred-year-old lie wouldn't be easy. Few written records existed from the time and those that did weren't completely trustworthy, like Nostradamus's own writings themselves. It was perfectly feasible that the prophecy contained in Nostradamus's preface came from someone connected to him. After all, he did have some contemporaries. Jean de Cavigny, Nostradamus's secretary towards the end of his life, was known to have taken certain liberties towards his boss's last produced works, even as far as rewriting them after Michel's death to protect his legacy. But there was no record of him creating brand new quatrains out of thin air.

Two years ago, Ally had written an article, published in *The Times*, that suggested Nostradamus wrote to a very distinct set of rules. Three of them in fact. And her detailed assessment of his life's work proved that he never broke them. Yet this prophecy broke all three in only four lines. There must have been a significant enough reason for him to include it amongst his own. The seer was a vain man who would frame his own family for crimes they didn't commit if it saved face or elevated his standing amongst the rich and powerful. He would not risk a reputation built up over decades unless he was certain it was genuine. Unless of course he didn't know it had been placed there at all. All of these theories would remain hypotheticals until Ally found even one name that might indicate responsibility.

"Madame Oldfield?" said an old man in an immaculate cream suit and matching boater.

"Yes," she replied, making no attempt to look up at the enquirer. She already knew who it was and cared more for information than any assessment of appearance. She pointed to the chair next to her as she continued to read the stories in the newspaper.

The man struggled to accomplish the simple act of sitting down, impeded by the uncomfortable metal frame of the chair on the other side of the table. It took several minutes before the one-man pantomime act was complete. If Ally had been the least bit interested she would have noticed that the man was well into his seventies and had a face that belied it by several more decades.

"Monsieur Palomer, I have some questions for you."

"I was not aware that I was under arrest," he replied coyly.

Irrespective of his physical age and decrepit appearance, Palomer's mind was as sharp as that of someone in their thirties. He also upheld an old-school sense of decorum, which included a certain standard of etiquette when two strangers met for the first time.

"Arrest?" replied Ally, finally removing her gaze from tomorrow's fish and chip wrappers.

"Madam, I'm not accustomed to being questioned by strangers, unless they're wearing an official uniform and wielding a shiny badge."

"I don't have time for games, Monsieur Palomer, only questions."

"Then I wish you all the best with the answers, good day to you, Madam," replied Palomer as he struggled to remove himself from a chair he'd only recently battled to tame.

"This is ridiculous, sit down."

"I don't think you understand. I will not be bullied by anyone, male or female, friend or stranger, ally or foe. If you wish to learn something from me, you will need to act accordingly."

Ally was not used to being lectured. That was her job. It was one of the reasons why she avoided working in teams. People had a habit of expecting courtesy which, in Ally's mind at least, only kept them from the reason they were collaborating in the first place: to do a job. As the boss this was easy to overcome, but that wasn't true today. Palomer was under no compulsion to meet her and if she needed answers she'd have to do that thing that other people found incredibly easy: small talk.

"Ok, we'll do it your way," said Ally reluctantly.

"Oh, I'll think you'll find I'm far from unique," he said, ceasing his attempt to vacate the chair. He watched as his opponent visually struggled to manoeuvre her personality from soulless academic to empathetic human being. She was going to need some help. "I think your next move might be an introduction."

"I'm…Doctor Ally Oldfield," she said through slightly gritted teeth. "…How are you?"

"Thirsty," he answered honestly and raised his hand to gain the attention of a waiter who arrived moments later. "A large glass of your best wine, half a saucisson and some small cubes of cheese to accompany it. And for you, Madam Oldfield?"

"Just coffee."

The waiter nodded.

"You know too much coffee isn't good for your health," said Palomer, noticing the two emptied cups already cluttering up the table. The dark red lipstick on the rims matched the one that Ally had sprawled on her lips in haste that morning.

"Some say the same about wine."

"Nonsense. I'm told a single glass a day can be most beneficial in extending one's life. I must admit that I have not been inclined to verify that claim, as it rather suits my own point of view! So far I cannot argue with the results. Let me introduce myself formerly, my name is Antoine Chambard Palomer. And what is it that you do, Madame Oldfield?"

"I'm a Professor of Medieval Languages."

"Fascinating," said Antoine quite genuinely.

"You're aware of the history of your name, I presume?" said Oldfield.

"Why don't you use your immense knowledge to enlighten me? It appears your skill at translating languages varies significantly from others I have employed."

"Palomer is a word used mainly in Provence and comes from the seventeenth century. It has two meanings: mild in manner, or keeper of pigeons."

"Oh dear, I'm not overly keen on pigeons. I think I'll go with the first meaning."

"Antoine, of course, is a very old name which has its roots in the early Roman language," continued Ally, completely ignoring Palomer's reaction as if he weren't really there. "Chambard, though, is much harder to place. I've not seen it used as a forename before. The word is French of course and more often found as a surname. I believe its literal translation is disorder or more eloquently put in the English language, rumpus."

"Excellent," smiled the old man with a twinkle of respect for her in his eyes. "They would be delighted."

"Who would?"

"My ancestors. Chambard is an old family name that's been handed down through the generations to every first-born son for as long as anyone can trace. Well done. I must applaud your obvious talents."

"I'm a professor, they don't just hand those out for free."

"So I see."

"And you, Monsieur Palomer, what is your area of expertise?" asked Ally, starting to get into the swing of this thing people called 'chit-chat'.

"Antoine please," he replied, taking a large gulp from the glass of wine that had just been delivered to the table. "Oh, I have many. I have long since retired from formal employment, but my trade back in the day was pharmacy. Now I keep a keen interest in several hobbies."

"And what would those be?"

"Mainly philanthropy. You see, I'm very fortunate that my family has always been, how can I put this, financially secure. As a result we have for generations been in the business of helping those less fortunate than ourselves. We have many foundations that sponsor the gifted, poor and less fortunate."

"How noble of you," replied Ally, unable to understand why anyone would care for the welfare of those who had done nothing for the contributor and even less for the wider world they lived in.

"Interesting choice of words," said Palomer analysing every subtle reaction, both physical and verbal, of Ally's reaction. "Are you married, Dr. Oldfield?"

"That's a little too personal."

"It's not an abnormal question."

"Well, it is for me. Chit-chat is one thing but my private life remains just that," she said firmly.

"I didn't mean to offend," said Antoine genuinely. "I understand from Monsieur Depuis that you are interested in the circumstances surrounding our discovery?"

Finally Ally could dispense with the pointless formalities of 'getting to know you' and focus on her real purpose for being there.

"Yes. There are many things that I have yet to learn about it. How long has the house been in your family?"

"Centuries. Although in order to modernise it the house itself has had many alterations over the years. It's in the old town a little way down the hill from here, although sadly age has forced me to use the ridiculous funicular these days."

"What date was the house built?"

"Early sixteenth century. Most of the properties in the Saint-Paul region were. Most were owned by Italian bankers, although I understand that was not my ancestors' profession."

"Do you have any idea how they came to live there?"

"Pardon me, Dr. Oldfield, but you seem more interested in my property than the book."

"I seek to find a connection, that's all. If the book is old, as I suspect it is, the building may shed some light on the identity of the prophecy's author."

"You don't believe it was written by Nostradamus?"

"No. I certainly don't," she replied with a scowl. "So your family, how did they come to own the house?"

"Hard to say. There are only myths passed on as family whispers down the ages, I'm afraid."

"But you had no knowledge of the book until it was found inside the commode behind the partition wall?"

"None whatsoever, but it was quite an exciting day when they discovered it. But it wasn't found in a commode. Where did you get that from?"

"Salvador Depuis."

"Quite wrong, I'm afraid, it was found in a coffer."

"Not being an antiques expert I don't know the difference."

"A coffer is a low cabinet usually with doors or drawers at the front."

"What did it look like?"

"It was black and made of oak."

"Is that it? Not much to go on: you must have a better description than that."

"I find your questions surprising," he said, diverting from the answer. "I thought you'd be more interested in asking me about the new Nostradamus quatrain."

"I'll repeat myself. It's not by him."

"So you say, but how can you be certain?"

"Because I'm an expert on the subject. I know how he wrote, what he wrote about and more importantly why he wrote about them. It does not fit his style on any of those counts. If I'm to discover the truth I need a wider field of vision."

Antoine drained the remainder of his wine, which had taken only three gulps to complete. In the distance the sun had passed behind the Basilique's spire and its visitors' stomachs were forcing their owners to depart to find one of Lyon's other great qualities, gastronomy.

"If you do not believe that Nostradamus wrote it, does that also mean you do not believe in the prophecy at all?"

"Of course I don't believe it. I may be the only single female over the age of forty who doesn't read horoscopes, isn't of the belief that 'anything is possible', and doesn't post pointless inspirational quotes on her social media accounts."

"But there is so much in this world that cannot be explained."

"True, but that does not give anyone the right to argue that something supernatural is responsible. It just means we haven't found a plausible explanation yet."

"But what about all the times Nostradamus was right?" said Antoine with an expression which shrouded whether he was being genuine or mischievous.

"That'll be never, then."

"Surely not. And the others that went before him, what about them? There were plenty of seers down the ages who had an uncanny ability to predict the future. I believe there is a power in people that cannot always be proven or disproven."

"We will have to disagree on the basis that you are wrong and I am not. Anyway it really doesn't concern me. All that does is finding out who wrote the prophecy."

"I find it curious how two experts in the same subject can so wildly disagree with each other."

"Other expert?" asked Ally directly.

"Bernard Baptiste."

"I thought you said two experts," huffed Ally.

"You don't agree?"

"No. Baptiste is no expert. He's a fanatic. He takes a rather far-fetched view when it comes to Nostradamus's work. He likes to think he knows what he's talking about and yet he expects us to believe that every event in history lies within 'Les Prophéties'. It's ridiculous. He's more a collector of memorabilia than an actual scholar."

"He speaks rather highly of you."

"I doubt that."

"Yes…you should," said Antoine smiling kindly. There was a twinkle in this man's eye that gave away tiny secrets of the personality that lay beneath its aging body. Courteous and suave he might be, but there was something quietly mysterious about this unusual gentleman.

"So who do you believe most?" asked Ally.

"I have no reason to believe either of you. I know neither of you, nor your motives. But I do believe something here doesn't add up."

"Of course it doesn't. The book is discovered at the same time the circumstances it predicts appear to be happening for real. The book is definitely over five hundred years old, there is no doubt about that, so it could have come to light at anytime since."

"Often when we are in need of a sign, a sign presents itself," replied Antoine philosophically. "Or we decide to invent the sign to secure our own beliefs."

Ally didn't reply immediately. Antoine appeared genuine in his comments and manner but she thought there was more to him than met the eye. Above all else, though, he was no liar, she was sure of that. There appeared no motive for it, or sense of him holding information back. Who he knew may be more important than what he knew.

"Do you know the Oblivion Doctrine?" asked Ally.

"No. I don't think anyone truly knows the identity of those who masquerade on the internet. It could be one person or many."

"But the reading of the prophecy made it into their hands: surely you must know something about that?"

"All I can tell you is that Bernard contacted me about the book and was most persuasive about seeing it for himself."

"And how did he hear about it? Depuis told me you informed them almost immediately?"

"I did, the very next day. But it was Bernard who told us about the book's existence, even before the builders broke through the walls."

"You're sure?"

"Yes, absolutely."

"But if the walls have stood for all that time, how could he possibly know it was in there?"

"Well, either he's hundreds of years old or he found out in some other way."

- Chapter 8 -

Rats, Fleas, Tramps and Thieves

Of the potential threats to life in the middle of the fifteenth century, nothing struck fear in the heart more than the plague. Unlike hunger, which could be remedied by food, death in war, which could be remedied by hiding, cold, which could be remedied by warmth, dysentery, which could be remedied by waiting for the entire contents of the world to fall from your bottom in the hope that enough of you remained afterwards to go again, nothing could remedy the plague.

It had no bias. It killed almost everyone that it infected whatever their age or background. And the bacteria responsible wasn't in a hurry to kill either. It was a vindictive infection that kept you alive just long enough for it to personally benefit, while simultaneously providing the host with constant agony. It started with flu-like symptoms, no more concerning than the common cold, before recruiting new symptoms to join the party at the victim's expense. Unbearable fever turned your body into a furnace, excruciating headaches were strong enough to dislodge your skull, profuse bleeding from the mouth, and the characteristic blackening of the skin around the hands and feet.

The only certain way to avoid contraction was to get as far away from the outbreak as possible, if the authorities allowed it. Which they didn't. Anyone might secretly harbour the infection weeks before any symptoms were obvious. So to avoid the rapid spread of the disease from person to person, villages and cities were effectively sealed off from the outside world. Like an infamous Californian hotel you could check out anytime you liked, but you could never leave. Only those who felt they possessed the skills to treat the infection, or simply wanted to study the disease to learn about its effects, came to visit. It was the ultimate version of an extreme sport, and spectators were not welcome. If it happened these days it was guaranteed that a countless mass of reckless idiots would be holding up mobile phones to capture it before trying to post their videos to personal channels, only to find that their fingers dropped off the moment they tried to press the upload button.

The Aix outbreak was small compared to those from history, although that fact didn't reassure any who'd caught it. It came as no consolation to you that 'fewer people were dying this time,' when your feet went black and most of your blood flow was seeping out of your ears. No one would suddenly cheer up if you told them 'it was nothing compared to the plague of the mid-fourteenth century'.

The first plague pandemic had spread from its origins in Asia to the edge of the Atlantic Coast like an out of control forest fire, devastatingly every country that it passed through and ultimately wiping out millions of Europeans in just a few years. Although diseases were common, nothing on this scale had ever been witnessed. Biblical in its destructive power, almost everything, other than God Himself, got the finger of blame.

Initially everyone blamed the rats. Stinking, black rodents the size of chickens who'd received an unexpected commute aboard the carts of tradesmen that travelled along the Silk Road, or on boats sent around the continents in search of war. In court the rats had pleaded their innocence, putting the blame squarely at the door of the fleas who, they argued, had travelled without permission on their hairy backs. The flees took umbrage and constructed a ridiculous story about having nasty, invisible monsters in their bloodstream. When called as witnesses the 'monsters' made no defence at all, knowing that doing so would bring unwanted attention. They decided instead to keep a low profile until someone invented a microscope. Unable to prove the existence of such microscopic miscreants, both rats and fleas conspired to blame globalisation.

More than a hundred years on, the outbreaks that occurred routinely up and down the continent were isolated and fortunately temporary events. But it would never be completely defeated. The bacteria had become epizootic within the localised flea and rat population, which meant it was now a fundamental part of the genetic make-up. This spring it was Aix-en-Provence's turn to suffer and an extraordinary number of people died as a result.

Churchyards swelled with dead bodies to such an extent that no one knew of any ground in which to bury them. The infection was said to be so virulent that one only had to approach within five paces of a victim to catch it. Doctors tried everything they could to treat the victims. Blood lettings, restorative medicines and sacred hymns were found to be as effective as doing nothing at all. When the city was surrounded by areas of good health it was no surprise that the residents believed their punishment was divined by God Himself.

Only one man disagreed. He was confident in his ability to cure them.

Aix wasn't the first outbreak in the area. That occurred forty miles down the road in Marseille one year before. The city was a perfect doorway to disease carriers stowed away on galleys that brought soldiers and supplies from across the world. When every doctor in Aix fled, one even quoted as saying as he did so, 'Get out fast, stay well away, come back later,' the authorities looked to Marseille for assistance. But that outbreak was still ongoing. The highly respected man leading the resistance against it, Louis Serre, was unable to assist them. So he sent his protégé.

"Let me get this straight," said Philibert, somewhat bemused. "You volunteered to come to Aix because of the plague?"

"I didn't volunteer," replied Michel. "I was hired."

"Hired for what?"

"To stop the plague."

"You can't stop a plague. It decides to stop of its own accord, usually when all the people are dead and there's no one left to give it a lift to the next town."

"That's not true. I did help stop it."

"What? No, you didn't."

"Is there any plague there now?" asked Michel calmly.

"Well, no, but…"

"And was it there when I arrived?"

"Yes, but…"

"There you go, then."

"Well, congratulations," said Phil, clapping ironically, "Maybe you could have done that before it wiped out my entire family."

Phil stood up and walked over to the window, sorrow welling in his heart as he watched the morning sun creep over the horizon. The plague had stolen everything from him other than life itself, and he often wished it hadn't left him with that.

"I'm sorry," said Michel showing real empathy for the first time in their fledgling relationship. "I know how it feels."

"No, you don't. You've never watched a loved one suffer in front of your very eyes, knowing that you can't even risk getting close enough to comfort or treat them for fear of catching it yourself. To watch each member of your family die, one after another, week by week. A father, a mother, a grandmother, a sister, a brother, a cousin, a neighbour, a community consigned to memory in little more than a month. And still after all that to be left to live with that burning fear inside you that one day you will be next. That one day it'll catch up with you and you'll finally join them."

"You're wrong, you know," said Michel standing up and placing a hand on Phil's shoulder. "I do know how that feels. I have also lost those closest to me."

"Really. Who?"

"My first wife, a son and a daughter."

"Then you do know. But why would you actively put yourself back in its path?" asked Phil who'd spent the last fifteen years running from it.

"Because I have medical talents. I tried to treat my own family, but my skills had not developed sufficiently back then. I lived with the plague all around me, but I fought it off. I defeated it. I believe that I am now immune to its effects. Maybe you are, too?"

"Perhaps. I'm not really sure how anyone survives it. Luck, prayer, strength…who knows? I can tell you one thing for certain, it wasn't because of the funny medicine that was being recommended at the time."

"What medicine was that, then?" asked Michel.

"If I remember rightly it involved taking an ounce of sawdust, the greener the better, three ounces of clove, six drams of aloeswood, which had to be crushed into powder, and then pounding them together with three to four hundred red rose petals. Those had to be picked before dewfall, that was very important, apparently."

Michel nodded in agreement although Phil didn't notice.

"Can you imagine how hard it is to find red roses when everyone around you is sneezing and vomiting? Then, if you did manage to do all that, you had to mould them into a lozenge shape and leave them to dry, which, given the unseasonably wet weather we had that spring, could take more than a week. If you hadn't already died by the time it dried out then you could take it."

"And did you?"

"Yes, it was disgusting. God knows who came up with that codswallop?"

"That would be me," replied Michel proudly.

"You?"

"You're welcome."

"Welcome?"

"Yes. How else do you think we beat the plague."

Phil was certain that it wasn't because of some hocus-pocus pill. Although how could he argue against it without an alternative explanation? In truth he'd put his survival down to luck, and that wasn't easy to explain scientifically either.

"Powerful remedy, that one. I still keep the formula and a stockpile of the lozenges in the oak coffer over there," he pointed to the black piece of furniture that he'd earlier used as a writing desk. "These outbreaks can happen without warning. You never know when they might come in useful. How old were you when the plague struck?"

"Fourteen."

"Count your blessings. You were one of the lucky ones. Use it to inspire you. A second chance. That's what I did."

"I did," said Philibert.

"My successes in Aix were lauded far and wide and it led to great opportunities to learn from others about medicine, astrology, art and history. That's when I realised fame and riches wouldn't come from cook books and herbal remedies. If you want to get noticed in this life you have to offer something that no one else can give. The future."

Light was now trying desperately to penetrate their ground-floor window in order to introduce them to a new day. Phil didn't know how many more he'd spend here or whether the next one would bring news of his fate. Michel welcomed the arrival of morning by moving over to a small porcelain bowl and he proceeded to wash his face and hands ready for whatever schedule he'd planned for himself today. There was little stress in Michel's attitude towards his imprisonment, as if he already knew what the outcome would be.

"How did you survive on your own after the plague?" said Michel, now more intrigued by Phil's backstory and seeing similarities to his own.

"I had Chambard to thank for that."

"Where's that? Belgium?"

"It's not a place. It's a person."

*****

He walked as far as they would allow him. The direction didn't matter as long as it was as far as possible from the piled-high corpses discarded in untidy heaps next to deserted barns or in boggy fields unfit for crops or livestock. Even the finely crafted Italian fountains that had made the city famous couldn't escape from the signs of death. Bodies lay against the stone as the victim had made one final lunge for the clean water that might abate their thirst, before life had been cut off like a tap. They'd died where they lay and the few who remained alive would be unwilling to remove them.

Above in the distance the clock tower cast a lonely figure against the skyline. It no longer rang out the hours of the day, waiting forlornly for the bell-ringers of Aix to re-establish themselves and remember their responsibilities to her. He stumbled under the weight of tiredness and grief towards the city's perimeter wall where a sentry guard, mouth covered with scarf and hand, warded him away with the other.

"None shall leave," he said in a muffled yell.

"But I have nothing left," said Philibert, whose entire existence was being worn on his body.

"Then you have more than some."

The guard pointed for him to return to the city. He'd been. There was nothing left for him to stay for. Avoiding any potential confrontation that his weak body wouldn't thank him for, he made his way along the inner edge of wall. Along the stonework that encircled the city he searched for a section that was damaged enough for him to scale to reach freedom on the other side. There might be guards patrolling, but what was the worst they could do? They wouldn't want to get close to him in case he was infected. They might shoot an arrow at him in warning, and if he was really lucky they might even hit him.

Eventually he located an easy route up the side where several bricks had been dislodged, leaving holes big enough for his hands and feet. On this side of the wall it was deathly quiet. The city's population had been halved in only a few months. Almost everyone who'd been left, whether in positions of authority or not, were more interested in their own survival than a scrawny teenage boy's bid for freedom.

He dropped down on the other side and collapsed in a heap from the effort. To his relief there was no one there. He remained motionless waiting to get his bearings and to give his heart a chance to normalise. A few hundred feet from this stretch of wall were the sandy-coloured stones of a church. Philibert knew from casual Sunday morning strolls he'd taken with his sibling in happier times that it was L'Église-Saint Jean-de-Malte. Amongst the olive groves that grew in its grounds was a priory. It might just offer some sanctuary for the wounded and lost. The walk took Phil towards the deserted church whose doors were characteristically swung open on their hinges, a sign that God's house was available to anyone in need of solace or comfort.

Atheism wasn't popular in the Middle Ages. Everyone was religious. It wasn't even considered an option not to be. Each and every one of the victims that Phil had seen strewn across the streets, having passed from one existence to the next before his very eyes, had faith. Their prayers may not have been answered, but they died in the knowledge that God would carry them to a better place. There was no question in people's minds of that fact. Whether Catholic or Protestant you believed in the word of your Lord delivered by your local bishop or priest in places often less grand than this one. And it was just this type of guidance that Philibert needed right now.

And he wasn't the only one.

In the front row of the church's pews sat a large man in a filthy coat which covered most of the back of his head. He sat in silence, head bowed forward towards the floor. Phil decided to leave him in peace and shimmied down a row of wooden seats on the other side of the church. He knelt to offer his quiet prayer. But what was he praying for? Not even the Lord Himself could bring back those he loved. Maybe he would pray for hope? Penniless, tired, hungry, homeless, orphaned and desperate, any sign of hope would do. He closed his eyes and summoned up his most courteous tone. After all, God might be a little busy in Aix right now.

After several minutes Phil reopened his eyes and was surprised to see that the large, middle-aged man had moved to the seat next to his. He made no attempt to make eye contact with the teenager and continued to stare at the front of the church at an altar that held some simple religious artefacts.

"I've always liked churches," said the man still in a way that suggested he was there on his own.

Phil gave a little nod of acknowledgement for politeness but really wanted to be on his own. Anybody was potentially hazardous. Anyone might carry the disease. It would be just his luck to escape the city and catch the plague on its doorstep. And even if this man wasn't infected what interest did he have in a fourteen-year-old boy?

"They're always warm," said the man answering a question no one had asked.

"What are?"

"Churches."

"I suppose so."

"At least they're good for something," said the man sarcastically.

"Don't you pray?" asked Phil, noticing that the man's huge hands were covered in a hair thicker than iron wool and wondered if it was at all possible he could join his hands without them sticking together permanently.

"No."

"Why not?"

"Never seems to work," said the man honestly. "But God does at least provide the warmth, and very occasionally something to eat or drink. Although this is not the best church for that. Would you like to know my pick of the three best churches in France?"

"Not really, if it's all the same to you."

"Number three would have to be Saint-Germain-des-Prés in Paris, they serve a good quality glass of red there. Second would be Sainte-Croix in Bordeaux, that one has some lovely buttresses. But probably my favourite of all churches is the Église des Voyageur-Heureux, excellent croissants. Really buttery."

"The church of the happy traveller?" replied Phil. "There's no such place!"

"No, you're right. I can see you're smarter than the average boy. I call it the church of the happy traveller because anywhere that serves a good quality croissant is far better than any religious experience I've ever had."

"How have you been to all of these places? Bordeaux and Paris are miles away."

"I've also been to Lyon, Nantes, Reims, Orléans…."

"Are you a trader?" asked Phil, interrupting him.

"No. I'm a wanderer."

"That's not a job."

"I didn't say it was. It's a way of life."

Until recently Philibert would have thought that wandering the country aimlessly as a 'way of life' would be a pretty lonely existence. Leaving the love of your family and the protection of your community behind you as you strayed into the unknown was no life at all. Last week it was a scary prospect. Today it seemed a reasonable life choice. Life events can do that.

"Why do you do it?" asked Phil.

"Because I've never found a good enough reason to stop. Unlike other people from my background, I am my own master and I decide when and where I go."

"And how do you survive?" asked Phil leaning forward as if the subject was taboo and not to be spoken about.

"Do you really want to know?" said Chambard in a whispered voice that added further prohibition to the atmosphere.

"Yes. I have nothing else to do right now, other than mourn."

"Lost people here, did you?"

"Everyone," replied Phil solemnly.

"Then I'm pretty sure you don't want to know the answer," he said, looking at the boy directly for the first time.

"Please tell me."

"I survive by taking items from those who no longer need them."

"You rob from the dead!" replied Phil in shock and horror.

"Only in order to avoid joining them. I'm not fussy, though, I'm more than happy to take from the living as well. I can show you how if you'd like?"

Philibert's moral viewpoint of right and wrong forced him automatically into retreat. That was not how his parents would want him to survive. Doing so would disgrace the memory of how they struggled in life and taught him that kindness and courtesy to others, whatever their background, were more important than a quick franc. He stood up to leave but the man caught him by the arm, showing more strength than he looked capable of.

"Don't be hasty, boy," he said gently.

"I'm not interested."

"You're all alone in the world. A boy your age needs guidance to survive the cruelty of God's game," he said while flicking two fingers up at the altar and making an unflattering noise with his tongue. "Let me show you the ways of the wanderer."

With his free hand he flicked a gold coin into the air with his finger and thumb. It immediately caught Phil's attention as it turned from heads to tails in the air and landed back in the tramp's glove. Chambard winked. The trick had worked. It always did.

"What's that in your pocket?" said the tramp.

"I told you I don't own anything. In fact, I don't even know if I have pockets," replied Philibert.

"I'd check if I were you."

Phil placed his hand in his coat and pulled out the same coin he'd just seen rolling from end to end in the air.

"How did you do that?"

"Sleight of hand and a simple diversion to distract your eyes somewhere else. You can try to keep the coin if you want."

"Try to?"

"I might steal it back. It depends on what you want to do next."

"I want to make something of my life. Make all of this misery worthwhile."

"Then I can help. I can teach you to read, I can demonstrate how you gain the trust of others, and I can introduce you to a life that you never thought possible. Let Chambard open your mind."

"And what do you want in return?"

"Well, for a start," he said, holding open his large, dirty coat, "you can help me get these candlesticks out of here without being caught!"

- Chapter 9 -

Panic

In a matter of days the death toll escalated exponentially. On the first official day of the outbreak only dozens had died, on the next hundreds passed away, and today the figures were being logged on a complex Excel spreadsheet. And not just in Asia either. The N1G13 virus's impacts were being felt in Australasia, Africa and the Americas. It was only a matter of time before a case was recorded in Europe. When it did, its unstoppable virulence would sweep through the population, killing indiscriminately. No one was safe.

Only one thing grew faster than the fatality rate.

Panic.

It was hard not to be anxious. The technology, bolted permanently to people's hands, carried an endless update of the global situation in real time. Every new case was presented to the world in explicit detail and in every possible language. The mainstream media, still meticulous in its attempt to authenticate every piece of information to ensure total accuracy, just couldn't keep pace with their competitors. No one had the patience to wait for the facts that might calm the nerves. In the seven seconds that elapsed before people lost their concentration, less scrupulous sources would deliver every and any piece of information, however accurate or far-fetched.

If there was a rumour that N1G13 was responsible for making victims' bladders implode you could find the horrifying descriptions online. If there was a video of a suspicious-looking crow seemingly coughing, the footage would soon be shared and viewed by millions, supported by an accompanying stream of comments highlighting the pros and cons of avoiding contact with crows, rooks and even jackdaws. If a blogger had written a highly inaccurate account of how eating marmalade was a foolproof and legitimate way of immunising yourself from the infection, soon there were reports of panic buying of all jam-based products. Terror and paranoia's first date was only last week, but they were getting on like a house on fire.

The worst culprits for this mass hysteria were yet again the Oblivion Doctrine. They had a history of spreading discontent in all its forms. Their mission, although it was not actively voiced, was to disrupt our modern way of life. It didn't matter if this was by discrediting a government, destabilising an economy or destroying the reputation of a popular celebrity. They, or he, or she, or it, were notorious for their immense ability to fuck with the world.

And just like the modern media they needed to fill space, in their world it was web pages. The constant stream of content that had initially come from every corner of the globe theorising how mankind would meet its end had dried up. There was no question anymore about the source of the end, because real life had weighed in to dispel people's vivid imaginations. Where there had once been only speculation, now there was actual cause for alarm. In order to keep the monetisation of the machine running, the Oblivion Doctrine had turned their attentions to what they liked to call the 'truth' about the current flu outbreak.

But then again, what was truth? To be certain that you'd found it you had to do research, check facts, use your own brain and have an open yet sceptical mind to all information and opinions. Truth took ages. It was much easier to seek out opinions that backed up what you already believed. Plus you could substitute the time you might have wasted discovering the truth by angrily debating your own beliefs on Twitter with people you'd never met before, often capitalising the word FACT as the only evidence of backing up your argument. In the twentieth century that was all people needed.

Those that complained most about this erosion of critical thinking were the people most culpable for it. Politicians, business leaders and religious bigwigs had been covering up the truth for years. They'd never called it lies. They called it spin, and people were tired of it. Even those that did speak the truth were deemed to be lying based purely on form alone. Their lips were moving so they must be. Their past misdemeanours opened the door to those who wanted to use it for their own advantage.

The Oblivion Doctrine gave the people what they wanted. A channel to validate their beliefs, and they were more popular than any reputable mainstream news outlet or printed paper. Yet they weren't playing by the same rules. Its hard to arrest someone who's invisible, hard to shut someone's operation down when you don't know where they live. Shutting down the Oblivion Doctrine would be like trying to catch smoke. Their anonymity only seemed to strengthen their position. Only the anonymous would put themselves in danger. Only they would have the strength to stand up to the system.

Of course the Oblivion Doctrine might in reality be the Russian intelligence agency scheming against their Western oppressors in a basement somewhere near Moscow. Or it might be a thousand people operating from multiple locations through a highly sophisticated and encrypted network. Or it might just be the very people whom no one believed, the government themselves. No one knew. No one cared. But unknown to their users the Oblivion Doctrine's involvement fuelled the panic. After all, they had been the first to latch onto the new Nostradamus prophecy, even before the virus had shown its destructive power. They broke the story and hit the jackpot.

The lost prophecy had been shared millions of times as a result of their exposure and there were plenty of derivations of it. If Bernard Baptiste's translation of the quatrain had been dubious in the eyes of fellow expert Ally Oldfield, it was nothing compared to some of the others available. They stretched from the mildly inaccurate to the completely made up. One version from a British forum read:

> *In November this year the moon will bleed,*
> *All of Earth's children shall perish,*
> *When bird and beast cough,*
> *The end of the world will be nigh.*

At least this version had a general tie-in to the themes of the original, even if the words had been changed around. But it didn't stop it being wrong. These sorts of Chinese whispers had been applied to Nostradamus's work for generations to the point that no one really knew what he originally wrote or meant.

An even more spurious translation was posted by the famous Canadian doom-monger who went by the moniker @crazytrevor.

> *In November, probably a Tuesday, man will fall,*
> *When the birds look at you suspiciously,*
> *Beware of your bladders imploding, protection is only*
> *possible by eating your body weight in marmalade.*

The panic hijacking people's brains was also being fuelled by a complete lack of helpful information from the authorities. It didn't matter whether you believed in the prophecy, or if it was genuine, because now real people were dying. Updates from the World Health Organization on recommended prevention or cure were noticeable by their absence. The true reasons for this were quite simple. There weren't any. The speed of the virus's discovery and its rapid spread had caught big business and health professionals totally by surprise.

In the eyes of the people this meant it had to be a massive cover-up. The people in power knew the solution, they were just keeping it for themselves, or even worse, it was some huge plot to purge the masses. Faced with certain death it was no surprise that common people were taking their own steps to protect themselves and their families. Nothing was off-limits and any risk might be the price of survival. Unknown and untested compounds were springing up everywhere, each marketed as a sure-fire vaccine or cure for N_1G_{13}. According to speculation there were ways to avoid the infection if you couldn't afford these spurious remedies. They included but were not limited to:

Drinking a daily dose of cider vinegar.

Eating horse chestnuts poached in milk three times a week.

Rubbing soft cheese on your nipples.

Wearing clothes made solely from ladybird wings.

Injecting steroids into your eyeballs.

Buying a sparrow and keeping it about your person (a way of building up the immune system).

Eating roseroot pills.

The last one was by far the most popular. Which wasn't a huge surprise because catching a sparrow was a total nightmare. The company that made the pills had a well-known and established brand with a vast marketing budget to finance a worldwide advertising campaign and they were selling out almost as fast as jars of marmalade.

*****

Everyone she knew had advised her against it. And everyone wasn't an understatement. Not even Claire, her best and only friend, thought Gabriel's plan was a good one. As all true friends would, she attempted to reason with her in an adult and honest way. She'd pointed out that Gabriel had only spent one night in twenty-six years sleeping outdoors, was hysterically frightened of the dark and couldn't cook as much as an omelette without assistance. When it came to cooking, assistance was actually a code for takeaway, restaurants and going to her mother's for dinner.

When her ex-boyfriend heard the news he simply fell about laughing. But what did she care what he thought? After all, there was a reason why he was an ex- rather than a current boyfriend. The man was a pig who only cared about his ego and the appendage that dangled between his legs, which was regularly not far from its starting point. She was done with his vanity. Done with doing what he said, and dressing the way he demanded. She wasn't doing this to impress him or prove him wrong.

Shortly after telling her parents of her plan they'd concluded that she'd finally gone mad and sent for the doctor. When that didn't work they tried vainly to send her to her room until they realised she'd left home six years ago and no longer had a room to go to. Her mother cried, promised to send food parcels and even offered to swap with her for a few hours every couple of days so she could nip off to get her nails done. It was clear Gabriel wasn't the only one who didn't know how preppers lived. The more that people warned her against it, and insisted she wouldn't last five minutes, the more motivation she gained to prove them wrong.

Modern society always doubted the willpower of millennials.

The common perception insisted that her generation were weak-minded, work-shy, self-entitled, mollycoddled, technology-obsessed morons who had everything they wanted in life before they'd worked even an ounce for it. Their lives were devoid of the challenges that had moulded the generations that preceded them. They'd avoided the dangers of death through war that had claimed so many of their great grandparents. They'd swerved the post-war poverty suffered by their grandparents and the cut-throat competitiveness of the right-wing commercialisation experienced in their parents' youth.

Being a millennial was a lot harder than it looked. Sometimes hours might pass before somebody 'liked' a photo you posted on social media. It was common for a millennial employee to work in the same role for as much as a whole month before being offered the promotion they were entitled to. And now her peers were about to face the defining moment of their era. They were all going to die from the flu. Well, everyone apart from her, of course.

However much drive, determination and positive thinking someone mustered it was never a good substitute for real ability. And when it came to being a prepper she had lots of the former and none of the latter. In the league table of the world's best preppers, Gabriel came in second to last. Quite literally in dead last position with an Irish teenage runaway who'd once spent nine hours hiding in a shed only to blow it up by inadvertently smoking a cheeky cigarette next to a petrol can. Gabriel moved to second to last on account of having not killed herself so far and lasting a slightly longer time frame in her small, wooden retreat on the edge of town.

After what had seemed like an age, but was in reality less than a full day, she'd already overcome so much adversity out in the wild. Two of her fake nails had broken off, one of her Jimmy Choo's got stuck in the mud and the incessant rain had made her hair go frizzy. And none of these traumas had forced her to give up. Sanctuary from further horrors came in the form of the Renault 16's passenger seat where she cowered in the foetal position desperately trying to tune the radio to receive Netflix.

The wild was a more difficult place than she'd anticipated. The nearest supermarket was more than four hundred metres away and Starbucks even further still. You could barely get enough light from the nearest street lamps to read *Cosmopolitan*, and the small forest she'd chosen as her base appeared to be a notorious dogging spot. Just yesterday she'd had to scream hysterically when she found an elderly couple bent up against the back of her caravan engaged in obscenities that you didn't even see on Snapchat. If only what she'd witnessed had disappeared from her own memory after ten seconds.

But at least she was safe. As long as she stayed away from human contact she couldn't catch N_1G_{13}. Predominantly, according to reports at least, the virus was being spread person to person so she didn't even need to worry about catching it from any of the wildlife. Safety, though, was not the same as comfort. She was a typical girlie girl who enjoyed a certain standard of living and this wasn't it. If she was going to thrive, while civilisation crumbled, she had to learn how to protect herself and survive. And she needed to learn quickly.

*****

Two days after meeting Antoine for a coffee at the Basilique, Ally found herself walking purposefully around the streets of Saint-Paul looking for a house. Other than the occasional modern shopfront and parked car it felt like a stroll back in time. This was part of the old town, three renaissance villages now barely divisible as the space between them had been gobbled up by centuries of development. Gothic architecture featured prominently in the building's façades, each of which had its own distinct identity. The oldest were built in a time of creativity and personal freedom, a time before any department of housing might place certain demands on where a stonemason might build or how it might look when he'd finished.

The narrow streets manipulated pedestrians in a direction of its choosing, always rewarding the brave traveller with another spectacular church or hidden plaza around the next corner. Although the cold gusts of early winter raced down the alleyways like Formula One racing cars, a cloudless, blue sky overhead gave the day a balanced feel. There was much to take in, but Ally's eyes sought only one property and it wasn't difficult to find.

Antoine's house wasn't discernible because of the building's unique style or its prominent position. It simply stood out because the flashing lights of a police car had mounted the cobbles in front of it. Parked with a lot more care next to the police car was an impressive black and claret vintage Bugatti Type 55. The old car's bodywork gleamed from its daily beauty regime of polish and elbow grease. Its headlamps and grill grinned in anticipation, desperate for someone to jump in, put its roof down and release its engines to roar its echo through the town.

There wasn't much room for cars in a narrow street designed for a time when only people and horses ever needed access. Antoine's terracotta-painted house loomed over her. At the doorway two grim-faced policeman were assessing the damage that had recently been inflicted on the building's front door. At the request of the police Antoine pottered back and forward through the entrance returning with pieces of paper or answers to questions. Of the two officers the short, fat man seemed to be in control while the other seemed more interested in goggling the Bugatti than the scene of forced entry.

As she watched the intense activities through the arched doorway from the vantage point of the cobbled street, she noticed that Antoine's reaction to what had clearly been a break-in appeared neither angry nor anxious.

"Move along please," said the chubby policeman, noticing that Ally had been standing there for longer than was natural.

"No need, Officer," said Antoine, beckoning her over with a hand and a smile. "I was expecting her."

"Insurance?" added the short, stumpy policeman.

"Something like that," replied Antoine. "Ms. Oldfield, please come in. My apologies for the mess."

At this point most normal human beings, having noticed the extenuating circumstances, would offer their deep concern and suggest that now might not be an ideal time for a house call. But Ally was not normal. She was a researcher, and researchers like nothing more than a chance to connect the dots. Something bigger was taking place here. It couldn't just be a coincidence that a burglary had taken place so soon after a major historical discovery had been made at the very same address.

"What did they take?" said Ally as she entered the house unzipping her big fur coat, the winter equivalent of rolling up her sleeves.

"An interesting question. Most people would start with 'Are you ok?' or 'What's happened?' but you've already answered those questions, haven't you?"

"Obviously. I can see you're alive and appear in a reasonable frame of mind and any idiot can see what has happened. If you follow that thought-process my question was the most appropriate because it's impossible for me to know the answer without more information."

"Very good. I appreciate your concern."

"I didn't have any."

"I know," said Antoine. "I was being ironic. The answer to your question, though, is nothing."

The hall of the house was a homage to French history. Every piece of furniture, work of art, sculpture and fragile ceramic vase had been purposely collected and carefully presented. The objects in the hall alone would be more than the value of the car outside the front of house if they were ever to be auctioned. But none of these items had been touched. Antoine's burglars were either blind or extremely picky.

"Nothing!" said Ally in surprise.

"They wanted something, that's for sure. It's just not here anymore. Come, let me show you."

Antoine led her to a small staircase that descended into the basement. It was the very reason for her being there in the first place, but the scene was not the one she'd expected. The door to the basement had been obliterated and all that remained was splinters of wood and mangled iron. The cellar room itself was nothing to write home about. There was a dusty, uneven floor enclosed by solid but precariously built brick walls held together by loose mortar. A cold, dry air, still not acclimatised to its twenty-first-century cousin, circulated around their lungs.

Every single object that lived within its dank and musty walls had been fondled inappropriately. Chairs lay broken, boxes had been emptied and books had been turned inside out and dumped cruelly into discarded piles. Every removable drawer of a fine antique cabinet, which was probably worth more than most people's houses, was hanging out of the front of it like the tongues of thirsty dogs.

"Were they after the book?" asked Ally, wondering whether these criminals would ever get an invitation from Mensa.

"No. It's public knowledge that the book is in the museum."

"And the rest of the house is untouched?" asked Ally.

"Yes. This was the only place they were interested in."

"Then what were they after?"

"The coffer."

"What coffer?"

"The one the book was found inside. The antique black oak cabinet."

"Then where is it?" said Ally, scanning the room once more to see if she'd missed it under piles of broken wood and brick.

"I sold it," replied Antoine.

"Sold it! Who to?"

"Bernard Baptiste."

"Him! What did he want with it?"

"That's why he came here in the first place. Finding the book was an accident. Bernard originally contacted me three weeks ago to say that he believed there was an ancient artefact in my basement and if he found it, would I sell it to him?"

"But this room has been partitioned off for centuries, at least that's what Depuis told me. How did he know?"

"He wouldn't say, but when the builders found it I was true to my word. He bought the coffer and its contents, all except the book which I kept. He seemed more than happy for me to have it."

"But surely he would have known that the book was the most valuable item in there?"

"He was interested in it of course. In fact he started translating the new prophecy as soon as we found it. Wrote it out right there on that once priceless dresser," said Antoine, pointing at the dishevelled wooden item leaning diagonally against the wall.

"Then why did he want the coffer?" asked Ally as much to herself.

"You said he was a collector of Nostradamus memorabilia, didn't you?"

"Yes he is, but the coffer would hardly have a strong link to the man himself, it could have belonged to anyone. But there is no such doubt with the book. What was inside it?"

"I didn't take much interest," replied Antoine. "There certainly were some other items and papers inside."

In Ally's search for answers both good news and bad collided together like oil and water. Maybe there was more evidence inside the coffer that might lead her to discover the identity of the prophecy's real author and in turn bring the temperature down on the world's anxiety. Disappointingly her main rival, the man whose reputation left so much to be desired, might have beaten her to it. She hated being second and she hated being wrong, although none of these internal arguments really helped explain why Antoine had been burgled in the first place.

"If the coffer isn't here and no one announced its existence, who's behind the burglary? And why would they want to steal it?"

"No idea. But I think that's what we need to find out," said Antoine.

- Chapter 10 -

The Countess

Yesterday, Ally had clung helplessly to the life support of only one thin lead in her search to discover answers. Today she had more questions than she knew what to do with. What else was in the coffer? And how did anyone know about an item that had lived secretly inside Antoine's basement, and out of people's memories, for four hundred years? But someone must know, because someone had tried to steal it. Who would want to? And the most important question, the one that vexed her above all others: what did Bernard Baptiste want with the coffer when the most interesting discovery must have been the book he found inside?

As she wrestled with these questions another one dodged in and out doing its best not to be noticed. It was an uncomfortable question and one she couldn't shift. Was Antoine Palomer to be trusted? She knew almost nothing about him and certainly not enough to dispel mistrust or embrace everything he said as truth. On the surface he might seem courteous, kind and polite, but that didn't necessarily mean he was genuine. In situations like this one, where a burglary targets a specific item that only a handful of people were even aware of, you had to suspect those that did. If she removed from her enquiries those with solid alibis it only left one person. Antoine Palomer.

But why would he want to burgle his own house when the contents were his rightful property in the first place. Particularly when he'd already willingly sold the item anyway? What possible motive would he have for fabricating a burglary in those circumstances? It made no sense. Unless of course he had nothing to do with it in the first place, and then there weren't any suspects at all. She knew one indisputable truth from reading crime novels, if there was a crime there was always a criminal. If not, they'd just be called novels. Unless it was a supernatural crime story and it was the ghosts that done it. There was only one person alive who might provide any meaningful answers. Bernard Baptiste had the coffer and perhaps he could shed light on why someone was trying to steal it.

Fortunately for them Bernard was not only a Frenchman, he was also a local one. He lived in the town of Mâcon in the Beaujolais wine region, an hour's drive north of Lyon. All they had to do was arrange a visit and seek out the answers to their questions. There would be no chance of Bernard refusing to meet her. Their rivalry, for what it was worth, had always been there bubbling away in the background. Both had careers to maintain and when your income came in part from writing books about Nostradamus they were competing for the same readers. Their approach might differ, but both argued their case of being the world's foremost expert on the subject. This turn of events would just swell Bernard's sense of superiority and he'd do anything to rub Ally's nose in it.

Once she was certain there was nothing more to learn from the basement, Antoine led Ally back up the narrow staircase. At the top she had more time to soak up the décor of the grander hallway that separated a number of reception rooms from each other. There was almost nothing on display in this large, uncluttered space which could be dated to later than the mid-nineteen fifties. Other than one. Amongst the sculptures, tapestries and countless portrait paintings of unknown figures, one piece on the wall, immediately opposite the front door, took prominence.

THE COUNTESS

A canvas photograph, as large as any of the eighteenth-century portraits that made up the collection, was hung pride of place in an exquisite gold frame. A beautiful young woman in a splendid flowing dress held the observer's gaze as her captivating stare stopped people in their tracks as they entered the house. Maybe this was exactly the effect that Antoine intended. It was as if the woman was standing in both welcome and judgement. The black and white photo did nothing to dim the obvious colour of this young woman's personality that was conjured in the viewer's mind by a kind smile and piercing eyes. Even Ally, who had little interest in other people, stopped to admire its quality.

"She would have been eighty this year," said Antoine, after waiting for the initial reaction of the picture to have the desired impact on Ally's emotions.

"Your wife?" asked Ally more warmly than she was used to.

"Yes. The Countess left us much too early."

"Countess?"

"It was a nickname really. My illustrious ancestors came from auspicious stock, not that we ever benefited from it much. Most of our wealth was tied up in trust funds to maintain our many charities. The house is really all that remains of their legacy. Whether or not any of them had titles or wealth is pure speculation, but I liked to call her that name. It suited her." He stopped momentarily to take his own moment with the picture. "Oh how she would have enjoyed this adventure."

"Adventure! We're not on one. This is purely about pulling the pieces of history together to find a solution. I'm not interested in anything else."

"But isn't that in itself an adventure? Missing treasures, suspicious characters, misinformation and working with others to solve a puzzle. Don't you remember being a child and doing all that?"

"No," replied Ally sternly. "Any suggestion of me once being a child is nothing more than a vicious rumour."

"It's a shame you think that way. Remembering our childlike wonder is what keeps us young. The passage of age brings enough burdens without cutting yourself off from a time of innocence. The Countess will remain forever young while the rest of us decay into old age."

"When did she die?" asked Ally, moving quickly away from any spotlight that might fall on her own painful childhood.

"Shortly after this photo was taken. She was barely in her thirties. We were childless when she died so it brought an end to the long line of our family tree."

There was little sadness evident in Antoine's response. The events that he spoke of happened almost half a century ago and, although life had gone on without her for the last five decades, it was clear this woman still owned the keys to Antoine's heart.

The photo had been taken in a garden, probably during summer, Ally thought, as she looked at it once more. In the background of the picture the flowers were in full bloom and there was a natural light to the photo maybe from the sun high above her. The woman sat on a wicker chair in a rather conservative black dress and equally dark hat. Ally guessed that it was taken on a Sunday, either before or after church. There was only one other point of interest that caught her attention.

"What's she wearing around her neck?" asked Ally as she moved closer to the photo.

"Do you mean the locket?"

As Ally's face came as close to the picture as was possible without losing focus, the detail became clearer. Around the Countess's neck was a pendant on a chain that nestled just above her bosom. It stood out because of its unique style and intricate design.

"It's the only heirloom left from my distant heritage. She seldom wore it for fear of it being lost or stolen, although I would catch her sometimes looking at it as if waiting for it to pop open. Its value means more to me than any of the priceless items you see around you. After her death I had it removed from the house. I'm thankful for that on a day like today."

"Is it meant to be an animal of some kind?" said Ally, trying to make it out in the relative gloom of the hall.

"It's a ram. The body is made from pearls. It's a most magnificent piece."

Their rather pleasant reminiscing, for the first time on a subject that didn't have anything to do with prophecies, was abruptly shattered by an enormous explosion thirty feet away from them. The doors to the house, which had already had a less than satisfactory twelve hours, were completely blown off their hinges. One was left burning in the hallway while the other landed on the bonnet of the police car. Smoke and flames consumed the entrance hall and a large area of the cobbled pavement. Moments later, the cloud of dust was broken by a hailstorm of black and claret metal shrapnel which flew chaotically through the free space around them. The pair were knocked off their feet instantly and thrown against the wall by the force of the blast.

Ally came out of unconsciousness a few seconds after impact. There was an irritating and muted buzzing noise in her ears and her heart was racing faster than a marathon runner's. The smell of burning rubber and paint filled her nostrils and on the floor next to her were the scorched remains of a Bugatti Type 55 steering wheel. Other parts of the vehicle had been liberally distributed around the front porch, pathways, kerbside and as far away as the florist shop fifty metres down the road. The sound of ambulance sirens approached in the distance.

An elderly hand emerged through the chaos and smoke. She took hold of the assistance and was soon back on her feet. Through the clearing smoke she could see the shattered remains of the old classic car and the even more disturbing image of a man's body pulverised on the front step.

"What happened?" asked Ally, shaking, her normally predictable composure shattered by her experience.

"I think the policeman there," said Antoine, nodding his head to the corpse acting as a doorstop, "decided to investigate my car. It's fortunate for us he got to it before we did."

"Someone blew up your car!"

"Either that or my mechanic is not as good as he claims."

"What's going on here today? Something is terribly wrong!" screamed Ally, brushing bits of metal and plaster from her dress and steadying herself against a wall.

"Yes, I know. Exciting, isn't it!?"

"NO," replied Ally, remonstrating with him. "I'm a scholar not a sleuth."

"Neither am I, but it appears the burglars weren't just interested in things I might own."

"Why are you so calm? I think someone is trying to kill you."

"It does look like that, doesn't it? Come on, I think it might be best we leave."

"Leave! You can't leave. You need to talk to the police, tell them what you know so they can catch these bastards."

The short, stocky police officer, who had been inside his patrol car when the bomb had gone off, protecting him from the worst of the blast zone, was now attending to his fallen comrade. Anyone who'd witnessed the explosion knew there was nothing that could be done for him. You didn't need to be a medical genius to work out that if a Bugatti tyre had replaced the part of the body where most of the facial features had been, the chances of survival were slim.

"I'm sure they can deal with it on their own," said Antoine, still showing very few signs of worry. It might have been the adrenaline, but for a seventy-year-old man to witness his pride and joy being blown to smithereens outside his own home, he was taking it awfully well.

"Antoine, this isn't just a bunch of petty criminals. Whoever committed this is organised and serious."

Before he even started offering an opinion to this conclusion he'd grabbed her by the hand and was leading her through the house via a series of narrow corridors. At the rear of the property they slipped through a courtyard and into the town.

"Stop!" beseeched Ally. "Where are you taking me?"

"We need to get out of here."

"Look, they're trying to kill you, not me."

Antoine stopped his rather casual getaway speed and looked her in the eye.

"How do you know?"

This was a fair, if rather unexpected question. It wasn't her house they'd tried to rob and it wasn't her car they'd just left spread across Lyon's old town in smouldering pieces. Her car was a fifteen-year-old Rover Series 3 that blew up on a weekly basis, so for her it wasn't much of a change. But surely none of this had anything to do with her.

"It's just a coincidence," said Ally.

"Maybe, or maybe not. The fact is someone is intent on stopping me, or you, or us. I've lived in that house my entire life and no one has ever broken in. I've driven that car every single day since I bought it and not once in thirty years has someone tried to blow it up. So why today? The only day, I might add, that you have been a visitor. There must be something about that prophecy or the contents of that coffer that someone wants to stop getting out in the open."

"But you don't have it, do you? You don't have any information about it either. You're merely a bystander."

"They don't know that though, do they? But they might think that you know something. It's your name doing the rounds on the internet. Your name associated with the translation of the prophecy. Maybe someone objects to your work."

"Certainly wouldn't be the first time," huffed Ally, considering all the bad reviews she'd received over her career.

"Until we know who is behind this, we must trust no one."

"I don't even trust you, but you're still moving me around Lyon like I'm being kidnapped."

He let go of her hand as if it was suddenly covered in barbed wire.

"You come of your own volition. I'm not going to make you. But you do want answers, don't you? Don't you want to be right?"

"Of course I do. It's the only reason I'm in this bloody city."

"Then you must trust me."

"How about I just accept what you say for the time being and move slowly and steadily towards trust over the next, say, ten to fifteen years?"

"Fine."

"God, I could use a coffee right now," added Ally.

"Escape first, coffee later. I'm starting to understand why you're not married."

They moved off again, crossing the old town by the most secretive route they could find. Antoine knew every possible short cut to move fluidly through the streets without almost anyone noticing they were doing so. Age, though, had perhaps taken its toll on Antoine's memory.

He led them into a cul-de-sac with no escape other than through turning back and retracing their steps. There were plenty of houses on both sides of the lane but most were residential and absolutely none of them was a coffee shop. They stopped at a huge, wooden door that stretched up to the building's first floor. Antoine grabbed the handle.

"You're lost, aren't you?"

"Certainly not."

"Then where are you taking us?" said Ally, feeling the effects of her twenty-minute suburban hike in a pair of heels never truly tested for the terrain.

"Are you aware of the traboules?" he said with a grin.

"What's a traboule?"

"This is."

- Chapter 11 -

Montmorency's Ring

Just after sunrise a skinny jailor appeared at the cell door with a small hessian sack in his hand. His jaundiced face and shifty eyes squinted through the prison bars as if someone had smashed a smoke bomb and both occupants were hiding. Once his bloodshot pupils were finally satisfied that the number of people on the other side matched the total from the previous evening, he ran a wooden cosh over the bars to rattle them into life. There was no need. Philibert and Michel were wide awake and in mid-conversation.

"Breakfast," croaked the jailor, dropping the sack through the bars so that the contents spilt over the floor. The decaying yellow teeth of his broken smile zipped together in perfect alignment with the gaps in his gums.

If there was a medieval equivalent of a dietician they'd decided in their wisdom that a hearty breakfast included a large and almost indestructible loaf of bread, a lump of mouldy cheese, two bruised apples and a dead animal of unidentifiable origins. It might be squirrel. The jailor waited patiently for the hungry inmates to rush gratefully to the more than generous offering. Michel took no notice. It was the same every morning.

"You have a visitor," hissed the jailor, struggling to remember the complexity of an additional task in a usually routine schedule.

Nostradamus sprang to his feet and started to preen himself for what, as far as he was concerned, would be the visit of some important luminary come to seek his unique insights.

"Not you," said the jailor, spitting needlessly on the floor. "The other fella."

"He has a visitor?"

"I have a visitor?"

The two prisoners answered almost simultaneously, both shocked and surprised by the revelation. How could anyone possibly want to see Philibert? 'What was so special about him?' thought Michel.

"Yeah. Five minutes, no touching," the jailor growled, as he scratched at himself, the only treatment for removing the lice that controlled much of his body.

No touching? Phil wasn't fully briefed in prison etiquette. He couldn't think of any good reason why anyone would want to 'touch' the person who'd taken the time, quite unplanned, to come and see them. Maybe this was how contraband was smuggled in to assist a prisoner's escape? Or maybe prisoners had a tendency to grab their visitor in order to hold them hostage in return for their freedom? Phil hadn't thought that far ahead. In fact at no point since his arrival had his mind focused on being anywhere other than inside his cell.

A woman in a long, black cloak that hid most of her femininity beneath it descended the stairs and approached the bars of the cell. Her long, curly, hazelnut hair framed her attractive features and tried desperately to contain itself under the cloak's hood with limited success. A light blue bruise was still obvious on her cheek however much she'd attempted to hide it under the disguise. Now it was clear why the jailor had insisted on no touching. No doubt a female visitor and a male prisoner, incarcerated for a long period, might cause an awkward situation.

"Annabelle," said Phil in surprise.

"I don't have much time," she replied. "I shouldn't be here?"

"But why are you here at all?" asked Phil, moving closer to the bars to hear her whispers.

"I wanted to thank you."

"For what? I didn't stop him."

"No, but you tried. And more importantly you demonstrated to me your true nature, whoever you claim to be. Chivalry is a rare quality these days."

"Are you ok?" enquired Phil.

"It's just a bruise. It will fade."

"I can't believe a man would do that. What are you going to do?"

"I have no choice. I must marry Jacques. It is my father's wish."

"It's not right, though."

"Jacques may have my hand, but he will never possess my heart," she replied with a warm smile. "That I will keep in reserve for you."

Even though Phil was twenty-nine, and deemed to be of middle age, he'd never been in love before. And he was way beyond the acceptable age when folk got married, had children and settled down. Most twenty-nine-year-olds had already sent their offspring off to war or work, and were contemplating the end of life rather than the beginning of it. Phil just had other priorities on his mind. He'd had relationships in the last fifteen years, if you could call something that lasted a weekend a relationship. Chambard had positively encouraged him to be sexually active but, importantly, never committed. Their lifestyle didn't lend itself to settling down in one place for an extended period of time.

Phil was more interested in his own potential, and other people usually got in the way. He wanted to rise up against the natural order of society and prove he could excel in life and make his family proud of their sacrifice. A wife would just be a distraction. There might be a time for it when he got where he was going, if he ever arrived. Now this young woman had passed through the awkward flirting stage and was suggesting something deeper and more meaningful. Phil checked his virtual instruction manual, cemented in his mind from many experiences, only to find that the pages on this subject were completely blank.

"But you don't really know me?" said Phil, nervously pulling back from the bars slightly. "I have a lot of bad habits. I snore like an invading horde, have a tendency to lie when I'm in trouble and nine people have threatened to kill me and anyone who associates with me."

"It doesn't matter to me."

"It really should, the Marquis of Calais is a total psychopath. He's already threatened to remove my toes and make them into a soup."

"I'm sure you'll find a way to outwit him. After all, you're different from other men."

"Yes. I'm a peasant. I have no wealth or title. I have nothing of value to offer you."

"I think you underestimate yourself," replied Annabelle quickly.

"But you're committed to marry someone else."

"We're Protestants! Thanks to Henry VIII of England it's much easier to get out of a situation like that."

"But I'm in here," said Phil in case she'd not noticed the iron bars that separated them. "Who knows what my fate will be."

"But if you love me you'll find a way."

Phil was certain he didn't love her. He'd only met her twice and, although the legend of love at first sight was a familiar concept he hadn't met anyone who could genuinely prove it. Yes, she was pretty, quirky, independent, strong-willed and connected. But that wasn't love. He didn't really know how it felt but doubted this was it. Did they share any common interests? He only knew of one. They both wanted his freedom. Under the circumstances he thought it was a good enough starting point, and he'd had past relationships built on much less.

Annabelle held out her fist. She opened it to reveal a chunky ring sitting on her palm. Phil recognised it immediately.

"I thought you might find this useful," she said.

"Where did you get it?" said Phil, only just noticing that the ring he'd worn on the night of Claude's party was no longer in his possession.

"My father was going to send it to Paris, but I 'borrowed' it for a while. Take it."

"I'm not allowed to touch you."

"Why not?"

"The jailor said so," he whispered.

"Philibert, this is Marseille. We don't care much for rules here," she replied, tenderly guiding his arm towards hers and placing the ring into his hand. She allowed her skin to linger against his for as long as possible.

"What is your father planning to do with me?"

"Until they work out who you are they'll keep you here."

"And what about me, your majesty," said Michel who had been listening keenly to the conversation, waiting for the right moment to gatecrash it.

"Who are you?" said Annabelle, drawn away from her captivation of Phil for the first time.

"Oh come on, seriously! You're not fooling anyone, you know. I'm Nostradamus!" he said, striking the now familiar pose he used whenever announcing his name, as if not doing so would denigrate it in some way.

"My father deals with the crackpots," she said casually.

"Crackpot! My Highness of immense beauty and spirit, truly you are a woman of great majesty and wonder, but you must understand that I am the real deal. I see much mystery in your future. Allow me to write your star chart."

"I wouldn't allow you to write my shopping list, you mad old fool."

"I'm going to pretend you didn't say that. What's so interesting about him anyway?" said Michel, pointing at Phil in the same way someone might point at a pile of horse dung.

"He's special. I think he might just be what this country needs. A leader who can pull us out of the Dark Ages and bring true equality and balance to our country. One day he will be the most famous man in France."

Phil didn't want to be a leader of men, or famous, in France or anywhere else for that matter. The country's progress didn't concern him. After all, it had never come to his aid. It had never even noticed his existence, so what motivation did he have to save it. All of his desires and ambitions focused purely on his own progress irrespective of the kind compliments she was paying him.

"Really! Well, he'll never be more famous than I am," replied Michel angrily. "At the moment I think the likelihood of him surviving the month are slimmer than the chances of us getting something edible for breakfast."

"I guess that depends what help he gets," she said, aiming her comments squarely at Michel. "Others might benefit from such kindness, particularly if my father were to hear of it."

It was the last comment she made before she turned and retreated hastily from the unfamiliar conditions of the cold, hard reality of prison. When the trace of her was out of sight Philibert opened his hand to look at the ring. It was in much the same condition as it always had been. Still in need of a polish and still damaged from whatever treatment it had received in its long life.

"Can I see it?" said Michel, holding out his hand.

"Yes, of course, it's not much use to me anymore."

Michel sat down on his stool and reached under the collar of his tunic to remove a gold chain. On the end of it was a small circle of glass encased in a golden frame. The surface of the glass was raised in the centre and chipped in several places from misuse. Michel rubbed it on his chest and raised it to his eye, his fingers clutching the ring on the other side.

"Hmmm, interesting."

"What is it?" said Phil.

"It's a magnifying glass," replied Michel.

"Not that…the ring. Why is it interesting?"

"It's real."

"Of course it's real. What did you think it was made of, porridge?"

"That's not what I meant. I've seen this ring before. In fact, I have kissed it."

"Kissed it!"

"Oh yes. You see, it used to live on the finger of one Anne de Montmorency."

"So that's who he was. I only knew he was Montmorency. No wonder Annabelle guessed I was a fraud, I thought Anne was a woman."

"No. Anne is most definitely a man. I met him frequently when I was in the court of King Henry."

"You were at the court? Why?"

"Because, as I have told you, if you want to be noticed in this world you have to move within the right circles of society, and theirs is the highest possible. In my early days of prognostication I wrote a prophecy that concerned the royal family and they were most keen to meet me. Which was useful because that's exactly what I was hoping when I wrote it."

"So you made up a prophecy just to carry favour with the aristocracy."

"No! I never make anything up. It was just a happy coincidence," replied Nostradamus, determined to maintain the validity of his work and methods.

"Nonetheless, that worked?"

"Yes. Everybody seeks answers, Phil. Although I think they might be a little more cautious these days."

An idea started to form in Phil's mind. If he wanted to get out of this situation he needed a good scam. A way to convince people that he was important to them. Important enough to be kept alive. What mattered most to the gentry was power, and what vexed them was the thought of losing it. Michel had already proved that you could infiltrate the highest echelons in a different way than owning land or title. Perhaps he might gain more from Michel than he'd first imagined.

Most of Phil's cons had a short time frame and were essentially basic. They were generally easy to execute with nothing more than a ring and the right set of clothes. He was never greedy: Chambard had insisted on that. They took only what they needed to survive before moving on to the next target. They took time to learn about the people they stole from and were careful not to stand out. And because of this they rarely lived long in people's memories. The con was never about them or what they said or did. It was just an illusion to create the perception that they were not out of place. But his next con would need to be much more complex. It would have to be about him.

Michel was also learning something of his muse. Philibert was not some plucky peasant stumbling blindly on the fringes, stealing whatever he could get hold of. There was intelligence and skill to how he operated. Not only had he infiltrated a highly prestigious gathering of nobles, but he'd also won the affections of one of their daughters. That might be highly unlikely but it was still possible. Acquiring the ring, though, that was another level of talent altogether. If this peasant had managed to steal the ancestral ring from one of the most powerful men in France, there was more to him than first impressions suggested.

"How did you get this?" asked Michel, intrigued and confused.

"I borrowed it."

"Do you justify all of your thefts in such a way?"

"No, because I fully intend to return it. I only have it by accident. I didn't actually steal it."

Michel thought this explanation to be highly unlikely. Phil was a trickster and lying was as fundamental to that profession as astrology was to a prophet. Everything he said would have to be taken with a healthy pinch of salt.

"It's what you do though, isn't it? You and this man Chambard?"

"Borrow stuff, yes. Since that day when I met him in the church we have been wanderers. We take from people who can afford to share but often don't. It's a kind of benefits system."

"But who benefits?"

"We do. But we never take more than we need. Each target will lose one item. It's usually so insignificant to them, because they own so much, that they don't even notice it."

"I think I might check the contents of my coffer," replied Michel, suddenly conscious that he'd spent several days in the presence of a known criminal and hadn't locked anything away.

"Don't worry. You're not a mark, not yet anyway," he said with a cheeky wink.

"It seems a highly risky profession if you ask me."

"Not really. Chambard is an expert, and I'm not too bad myself as it goes," said Phil, desperate to find a way of proving his ability to the more sophisticated man. "Do you know 'find the queen'?"

"Yes. Ride north for about a month and ask people to direct you to Paris or just wait until you can smell it."

"Not the real Queen, the card game."

"Card game?"

"You've had a rather sheltered life, haven't you?"

"If you must know, I've been rather busy studying. What's a card game got to do with any of this?"

"That's how we do it."

Phil explained the principles of a simple three-card trick that involved a target being encouraged to bet money to locate the queen of hearts amongst three cards. The dealer would often conceal the correct card, thereby confusing the player to follow the wrong card and lose their stake. A second player, usually in cahoots with the dealer, and often called Chambard, would bring a sense of fairness to proceedings by winning the occasional hand and proving to the mark that easy money could be made.

"And did Anne bet his ring in this game?" asked Michel, not fully following.

"No. It's simply an example of a distraction. A con works because the target is not looking in the right direction. They see only what you want them to see."

"What did Anne see when you 'borrowed' his ring?"

"War mainly."

"War?"

"Yes, we came into contact with him at the Battle of Saint Quentin."

"Ooh, that was a nasty one," replied Michel.

- Chapter 12 -

The Battle of St. Quentin

The role of Constable of France was a position of great power. Other than by the direct involvement by the King himself, the Constable had jurisdiction over the country's military and outranked all other nobles in the Kingdom. The job gave the recipient ultimate responsibility for military justice, the financing of the war effort, and strategic decision-making. The King relied on him to plan and execute victory on the battlefield and he would listen to the Constable's voice above all others.

The role required a man, and it always was, of great strategic thinking, inspirational oratory skills to motivate his troops, and an exemplary record of achievement on the battlefield. Strong in stature, lightning-fast reflexes and the ability to process and act on information at such a speed that your enemies would never keep up. A man of honour, integrity and with an unparalleled list of allies and supporters.

Whichever way you looked at it, Anne de Montmorency was none of those things. But after nineteen years in a role that was thoroughly unsuitable for him, no one had made the connection. It wasn't common for a Constable to be sacked unless a new monarch ascended to the throne and wanted their own people. That wasn't the typical handover process, though. Ordination of a newbie normally came about after the remains of the previous Constable were returned, often in different-shaped caskets, from whatever pointless war they themselves had organised: death being a perfect example of why they were no longer capable of executing their duties.

At sixty-four years of age, Anne was not at his peak. His hearing had gone some years ago, possibly from all the cannon fire he'd been subjected to. Claims management companies would have been crawling all over him had such services existed. To compensate his deafness his key lieutenants were often seen shouting in his ear whilst making slow and meaningful gestures with their hands. They'd tried to write things down, but as his eyesight was also failing that approach had been scrapped.

Physically Anne would not have passed any fitness examination that involved anything more energetic than light breathing into a sack or standing upright for more than a minute, and even then the chances of him passing might be touch and go. He could still ride a horse, which at least allowed him to keep up with his captains, even if he had a habit of forgetting where he'd left the creature. This often led to other people also losing their horses soon afterwards and a strong denial by Anne that the one he'd miraculous 'found' would respond to the same name.

His mental dexterity was also not as sharp as during his prime. Decisions took way longer than necessary, partly due to a higher than normal level of anxiety about the outcome, which was not at all misplaced. When you fought in Anne de Montmorency's army, anxiety was more prevalent than rickets. It was accurate to describe Anne's warfare record as less than exemplary.

In fact his win rate wasn't even better than average.

Even the best generals in history have suffered defeat. Failure is an unavoidable and welcomed part of any learning process. Obviously not everyone agreed. It was hard to find much cause to celebrate the progress of warfare if you were one of the poor sods who'd died horribly as a consequence of your slow learning curve.

THE BATTLE OF ST. QUENTIN

The reasons for losing wars were varied. Sometimes successful generals might get over complacent and make mistakes. Convinced that their victory is divined by God or written in the stars they make an uncharacteristically poor choice, like advising their troops to have a longer than necessary lie-in. Occasionally a general will simply come up against a new technology or tactic never witnessed, just as Nelson had used to defeat the superior Spanish and French fleets at the Battle of Trafalgar. Others are beaten simply as a result of facing an army with greater numbers or an advantageous terrain.

In his fifty-year career Anne had been defeated by all of these and more. Since fifteen-fifteen when Francis, the previous King of France, appointed him as Captain of the Bastille, Anne had been responsible for a litany of epic failures.

The decisive defeat by the Spanish in the fifteen-twenty-two Battle of La Bicocca was delivered partly because the Swiss mercenaries that supported the French troops refused to fight because someone forgot to pay them. Guess who? The captain in charge of the Swiss that day was none other than our friend, Anne de Montmorency. To add to his mistake the Spanish appeared on the field of battle that day holding small metal devices in their hands that sent blasts of smoke and crude balls of metal, sometimes in unexpected directions at extreme speeds. The first reaction to these small balls of metal was the look of shock on the victim's face and a quickly broken shout that started with "What the…" and ended with death.

Rather than demote Anne for his incompetence they decided instead to promote him to the post of Marshal of France. A strange decision on the face of it. But because all the other French nobleman had died in the battle there weren't many candidates for the job. Which meant none of them could disagree with Anne's assessment that he'd fought bravely and the battle had been lost mainly because the Spanish had these things called 'guns'. People lie in job interviews, it's not a new concept.

Worse was to come three years later at the Battle of Pavia. In an almost identical re-enactment of the previous campaign, it only took Anne four hours of fighting to truly excel himself. Leading his cavalry through a dense wooded area, designed to offer protection and secrecy, it instead gave the enemy a perfect place to set up an ambush. The French were slaughtered. Any nobles that escaped the massacre at La Bicocca met their end at Pavia instead. Anne and the King, who had himself been on the battlefield, were both captured. To secure their release the Holy Roman Emperor forced Francis to sign a humiliating treaty that conceded huge swathes of French land to the Italians. The result of this aberration for Anne? Yep, another promotion.

Anne had spent so much of his military career in captivity that he was on first-name terms with most of his enemies. On top of being captured by the Italians, he'd also spent a considerable period of time being held against his will by the English following a bungled armistice deal. In a career that spanned four decades he'd spent more time as a hostage then he ever did as a soldier, much to the relief of all sections of the French military.

Given his wretched record it was unsurprising that in later life Anne became a staunch advocate of a negotiated peace settlement with their enemies, quite contrary to the sentiments of the royal court. There would be no end until ultimate victory. The eighth Italian war would continue at Saint Quentin, providing Anne with a fresh opportunity to orchestrate catastrophe.

And it wouldn't be his last.

Saint Quentin was a strategically important town on the banks of the Somme River in Northern France. It would not be the last time in history that the town would swim in the blood of battle. But the battle of fifteen fifty-seven was the first and original Battle of the Somme. The town's southern perimeter was protected by the river and to the north and east a two-and-a-half-mile-long wall was meant to keep the population of eight thousand safe. Or at least that's what they were told.

The forces of the Spanish, aligned to the Holy Roman Empire, approached the city flanked by the English in support. The town's defence consisted of Gaspard de Coligny's company of eleven hundred men. In opposition, the Spanish had forty-five thousand. The city had no chance. Within days the oppressors had besieged the city, but not before word had been sent to Paris to raise a force to recapture it. On August the seventh Anne's forces reached the southern banks of the Somme, and on the tenth they made their plans to free the city.

A large group of heavily armoured men crowded inside a tent that had been hastily erected on an uneven surface. The sides had been rolled up so that more people could muster to hear the orders and the breeze could lower the sweltering heat under canvas. Outside thousands of men sat around waiting for the off. Holding pike, sword or bow they were as prepared as they would ever be for whatever battle was to come. They stood in small battalions and at the front of each was a rider in full armour.

"Sir, are you sure about this?" said a youthful-looking commander.

"What?" said Anne, holding his hand to his ear in response to the question.

"I SAID ARE YOU SURE ABOUT THIS?"

"Absolutely."

"You wouldn't rather we went around the marshes rather than through them?" replied Louis de Bourbon, the Duke of Montpensier, who had never fought under Anne in the past, which probably accounted for why he was still able to breathe.

"March, yes, we should definitely march," replied Anne.

"MARSH, sir. You want us to go through the MARSHES?"

"Yes, definitely. Surprise, that's the key," said the old man as he was being helped into his armour in readiness for the campaign.

"It'll be a hell of a surprise to the soldiers when they get stuck up to their nipples in water," huffed one of the captains to his nearest colleague.

"But won't our soldiers sink?" said Louis, continuing to challenge the strategy.

"They already stink don't they? They're peasants," replied Anne.

"SINK!"

"Well, put them in the boats, then, that's what they're there for."

"I don't think we have enough boats," said John Philip, another of the Constable's captains.

"Just fill them up as much as you can or take more trips. I thought you were meant to be captains."

"So what happens after we get across the river, sir?"

"What?"

"WHAT'S AFTER THE RIVER?"

"Usually the land," said Anne.

It wasn't like the old days. In the past his captains just agreed with his instructions and marched off to certain glory. Or at least that's what they believed. Now everyone was an expert. They all wanted to know the plan, the fallback plan, the retreat plan, the health and safety plan and the contingency plan. Anne only had one plan. Others liked to call it the bad plan.

"WHAT DO WE DO AFTER THE RIVER, SIR?!"

"We enter the town and take it by force of course. Have any of you ever been in a war before?"

Only some of them shook their heads. Experience was a rare commodity in the French Army during the Italian Wars. Anne being the main cause of the high turnover rate.

"Right, any further questions?"

"Yes, I have one," said Louis.

"No…Good…Long live the King," croaked Anne.

"I SAID YES!"

"Let us delay no longer. Rally your armies and bring me my physician!" shouted Anne, who always shouted in order for himself to hear his own voice.

Reluctantly the captains filtered out to join their battalions and offer whatever words of encouragement they could muster. They didn't like the plan, but armies worked on a clear hierarchy of command and whichever way they looked at it they were not at the top of that pyramid. When Anne was alone two men entered. Unlike every other member of the Constable's company they were the only ones not carrying weapons or dressed for battle. They were plain-clothed and one of them carried a small case in his hand.

"You sent for me, my lord," said the younger of the men.

"No. I sent for Monsieur Paré?" said Anne who didn't recognise either of them. Only their unusual attire reassured him they were probably doctors.

"Unavoidably called away to serve the King, sir. We have been studying under his tutelage," said the younger of the two.

"This is most irregular," said Anne.

"Sir, I can assure you we are vastly experienced in treating injuries and ailments of all types," said the elder of the two doctors whose single eyebrow was so bushy it looked like a mouse had taken up residence on his forehead.

"Well, it doesn't look like I have a choice. Come here, I need you to examine me before battle."

"I'm not surprised," said the young doctor in a whisper. "You're older than time!"

"What?"

"I SAID I'M SURPRISED IT'S THAT TIME ALREADY."

"What's your name?" asked Anne, looking at him suspiciously.

"Philibert."

"Philibert what?"

There was a pause. Then minor panic. He hadn't been using a second name recently as none of their scams required one. Like most peasants he didn't actually own a real one. It just wasn't required. If your name was Thomas and your dad was the local blacksmith that's how people referred to you. He had to say something. Doctors always had second names.

"Um…Philibert." He glanced at Chambard who had his head bowed in shame. "Philibert…Papadopoulos."

There was no explanation as to where this name came from. The mind can do strange things under pressure.

"Papadopoulos. You're not an Ottoman, are you?"

"No, my lord. It's Greek."

"What's a geek?"

"GREEK. You know, Greece, the home of modern medicine," he said, looking for any advantage to the situation he'd landed himself in. "SHALL I EXAMINE YOU?"

Anne nodded and lay down on the light, wooden table that had been constructed in the middle of the tent. Two factors made this examination particularly tricky. Firstly the subject was almost completely covered in metal, and secondly the man conducting it was no more a doctor than a slug was a cannon.

"Right, if I could ask you to stay still for a moment…and close your eyes."

"What?"

"CLOSE YOUR EYES."

"Why?"

"Um…because…it relaxes the body. Type of meditation, it stimulates your body to release tension. Monsieur Chambard, I'm sure I can deal with the Constable, perhaps you might be of use to the other captains?" said the young man looking anxiously at him. Chambard immediately left the tent.

Pretending to be someone you weren't was all well and good when you were acting, but the moment you had to stop acting and start doing, you were on the slippery slope to blowing your cover.

"Why are you touching me there?" said Anne.

"I'm just checking your heart rate."

"Then why are you fondling my kneecaps."

"Um…the funny thing about knees is that they trap the blood flow…notorious for it. That's why they creak."

"Papadopoulos, how long have you been a doctor?"

"I've been studying the subject for many years, sir. There is no better teacher than Ambroise Paré."

"And have you ever applied your trade in the field of battle?" asked Anne, who, given his record, was almost certainly going to need some assistance from the medics in that department.

"This would be the first time," said Phil not wanting to receive any questions about how you stopped someone dying when they had a sword imbedded in their buttocks.

"There's one thing you need to know above all other things," said Anne very seriously. "You never treat the soldiers. Only the captains. Do you understand me?"

Phil understood perfectly. Every peasant did. It had always been that way and there was no sign of it ever changing. Phil's people stood in petrified squadrons outside on the banks and fields of the Somme ready to die for this man in a conflict they neither understood nor agreed with. The odds suggested most of them would die and not one of them would be remembered in song or poem for their effort. Not him, though. People would know his name. It wasn't an accident he was here.

"Please stop touching my legs!" shouted Anne crankily. "I called you in here because I'm having trouble with my hands."

"What's wrong with them?"

"Cold and stiff."

Anne held out his hands in front of him. Thick veins protruded from his wrinkled skin and old wounds of knotted flesh were prominent across his knuckles. On the index finger of his right hand a bulky silver ring with an eagle motif was cutting into his flesh. It was just the sort of small memento that he and Chambard were keen on. It certainly wasn't untraceable but it might just have more uses than generating some cash.

"Sir. I think I see the problem," said Phil.

"What?"

"YOUR RING. It's cutting off the blood flow and making your fingers swell. It must be removed."

"Never."

"Ok. It's up to you. I'm guessing you need your hands in the battle, though, right?"

"Of course I do."

"Good luck, then. You could always kick the enemy to death."

"What?"

"YOU WON'T BE ABLE TO FIGHT, SIR!"

"Very well. Remove it for a few minutes and I'll see if it helps."

The ring was well and truly stuck to its owner. It had lived in position for more than five decades, as much part of him as his long, dirty fingernails. Phil gave it a little tug.

Nothing. He applied some oil of anetide from his case and tried again. Nothing. Placing his boot on the table for leverage he heaved at the ring with all his energy. Both men screamed for different reasons. Finally with an almighty heave the ring flew off and Phil was sent crashing backwards onto the grass.

"My ring!" shouted Anne, who'd been knocked off the other side of the assessment table and was struggling like an upturned aardvark to right himself. "Where is it?"

"I'm not sure," said Phil. "It slipped out of my grasp as it came off your finger. Must be here on the floor somewhere."

"Find it!"

Outside the tent the shrill tone of a bugle broke the otherwise pensive atmosphere amongst the troops. The result of the noise was the forward advance of the horsemen and infantry across the fields and down towards the banks of the river.

"Where are you going?!" screamed Anne, having regained his composure and poking his head through the tent. "We're not ready. I haven't given the signal. Come back!"

Ironically no one seemed to hear him. He rushed out to locate his horse but as normal couldn't find it. After all the trouble he'd had with forgetfulness he was sure he knew where he'd tied it up this time. No time to look. The army was on the move. He shuffled off in the direction of his nearest captain like a geriatric museum exhibit, his armour rattling ferociously across the turf.

Brimming with adrenaline, ten thousand soldiers marched towards the Somme while two figures watched the advance unfold from a safe distance.

"I thought that went well, Dr. Papadopoulos," said Chambard chuckling. "What did you get?"

Philibert took the ring from his oily pocket where it had been since the moment it flew off the old man's finger.

"It's funny," said Philibert, "they never can locate the queen of hearts."

"Is that it?" said Chambard disappointed. "After all the work we've put in; pretending to be doctors, enlisting in the Army, marching for hundred of miles, all that for some tatty, old ring."

"It's not any old ring."

"Who was that old dude, then?"

"Montmorency something or other," replied Phil. "But I do know who he is. This ring is from the finger of a general."

"Oh. Bloody hell. That's different, then. Might be very useful."

"That's what I was thinking."

"I think it might be time to work on a new routine, Monsieur Montmorency!"

"Anything is better than being a doctor. Good work on the diversion, by the way," said Phil.

"What diversion?" replied Chambard.

"You blew the bugle to signal the advance."

"Nah. Not me. The captains must have just got impatient."

"What were you doing, then?"

"I was busy stealing that horse," he said, pointing out a magnificently elegant equine specimen tied up to a nearby tree. It was snorting violently in Chambard's direction.

From their vantage point they could see the French Army at the banks of the river on the left side of Saint Quentin and as far as they could make out there was no resistance yet from the Spanish.

"How do you think its going?" asked Chambard whose eyesight was not quite as keen as Phil's.

"Not great. I think it would have been better if they'd put the boats at the front of the advancing troops rather than at the back!"

- Chapter 13 -

All the Stars in the Sky

The Battle of St. Quentin had been a disaster for almost everyone. Thousands of French soldiers lost their lives when the Spanish troops encircled their position on the edge of the city. They'd stood no chance as they struggled through the thick marshes waiting for the boats to be carried down to the soldiers at the front. Many of the captains were slain as they defended their positions and Anne, true to form, was captured and held prisoner. The King conceded defeat and was forced to pay the costs of war, plunging the French Exchequer into further strife. The only participants, if you could call them that, who thought the campaign had been a huge success were Philibert and Chambard.

Not only had they acquired a genuinely unique piece of aristocratic memorabilia, they could also use it to build a new identity aided by the original owner being in the protection of the enemy and unlikely to rumble their plans. Philibert played the character of Montmorency for longer than any other alias. In total he assumed the role for more than four years, moving through the upper echelons of the country's elite like a silent assassin. Possession of the ring opened doors they'd never dreamt of knocking on. The role had its challenges. It still needed to be played with conviction and skill, but the ring gave the whole persona an authenticity they'd never possessed before.

Now that the ring was back in Phil's possession no one could return it to its rightful owner and reveal the truth.

ALL THE STARS IN THE SKY

Even though Anne de Montmorency had long since been released as part of the peace treaty there was no way he'd have identified the exact spot on the fields of the Somme where it had left his finger. The only clue to the ring's whereabouts would be Phil, and he had no intention of dropping in on Anne for afternoon tea.

But the role was getting more dangerous to play. People were starting to suspect he was not who he said he was. A time would soon come when a change was needed. He couldn't jettison his alter ego yet because Claude knew him as Philibert Montmorency, and it was Philibert Montmorency who would have to find a way to trick them into releasing him.

His options seemed limited.

Chambard was the real master of the con. A wealth of information lived inside that balding head of his, chronicling every ruse, hoax and scheme ever played on a fellow human being. But he wasn't here to suggest the best solution. It was up to Phil. After more than a decade in his company, Phil had learnt many of the tactics and tricks of the game. But which one would work for him in these difficult circumstances? He was stumped. Only one idea came to mind and it certainly wasn't one of the schemes from Chambard's playbook. It was something new that he'd invented and for it to work he'd need the help of one man.

"Michel, how did you learn to write prophecies?" Phil asked Nostradamus as he sat scribbling away at his desk, a position he maintained most evenings after the sun gave way to the night's starlit sky.

"You don't just learn how to do it. You can either do it or you can't," mumbled Michel, failing to move his head from its close proximity to the page.

"There must be some skill or knowledge to it, though?"

"Certainly. You need a detailed understanding of astrology, theology and history to have any chance. But just knowing those subjects doesn't guarantee you'll be good with predictions."

"What's history got to do with the future?" asked Phil inquisitively.

"Whatever is has already been and shall be in future, and God recalls each event in its turn."

"I don't get you."

"It's a quote from Ecclesiastes, apparently attributed to King Solomon. It's an apt response to your question. You see, Phil, the future is predictable because everything in the past repeats itself. Wars, famine, drought, pestilence, invasions, Acts of God, mad Kings, dodgy fashion trends, they all come round again. It's just a matter of working out when."

"And how do you do that?" asked Philibert.

"Cosmic energy."

"You mean you read the stars."

"No. You don't just read them, you feel them. You allow them to penetrate deep inside your anatomy and connect to your spirit. You see everything around us is made from the same four elements; water, fire, earth and wind. The stars are no different. It's all linked, all part of the heavens that surround us and bind us. That's the cosmic energy. It's a power that runs through all living things."

Phil got up and walked to the small window. He peered into the night sky where a clear evening had empowered the stars to twinkle like sunlight skipping across rippled waves. In Chambard's mentorship, Phil had learnt much over the past decade. Much more than the average commoner could expect to learn in a lifetime.

He could read and write a decent amount of French. He knew a vast amount about social etiquette across all layers of society, and the differences from country to country. Practical skills such as woodwork, metalwork and the care of animals were all highly developed. But what he knew about the stars he could etch on the side of a miniature candle. Other than overhearing people refer to the really famous ones, he knew they were bright, plentiful, always in the sky and that was about it.

"There are just so many. How do you remember them all?"

"Oh, it's easy really. Just a couple of decades of intense study," said Michel sarcastically.

"What's that one?" asked Phil, pointing into the sky through the iron bars that acted as a barrier to limit the escape of anything larger than a limb.

Michel moved over to the window to see what he was pointing at. "Which one?"

"That group of stars over there. What's that?" Phil was indicating a group of eight or nine stars that seemed to him to be in a pattern.

"That's a constellation. They tell stories of famous legends from history."

"I know that. I meant which constellation is it?"

"That one is Isabella the Fierce."

"Really? What's the story behind that one?"

"Isabella was a Greek warrior who slayed the mighty nine-toed giant, Colin of Byzantine. Not many scholars are aware of her story."

"A female warrior! I didn't know the Greeks were so progressive."

"That's because you've never been to school," said Michel insultingly.

"And that one?" asked Phil like an excited infant.

"That's Giles the temporarily annoyed."

"What?"

"He was a famous mythical figure from Sparta who, as the story goes, was known for an inconsistent level of attitude. One minute he'd fly off the handle and the next, good as gold."

"And they named a constellation after him?!"

"Don't look at me as if it's my fault. I just remember them, someone else names them."

"And that one?"

"Erastus. Half-man, half-dolphin. See that line of stars, that's meant to depict his waist, and the few stars below that, those are his flippers," said Michel confidently as he pointed out all his descriptions.

"That's strange. I don't know much about stars but I could swear someone told me that was Orion?"

"Oh. That one. Yes, that one is Orion. I thought you were pointing to the one next to it."

Michel reeled off the names of constellations without so much as a pause for thought. Each one came with a detailed yet implausible backstory. At least they seemed implausible in today's context. Back in Greek times everything sounded plausible. A god transforming into a swan, a woman whose eyes could turn you to stone, and a man who was so incredibly hungry he apparently ate himself to death. It was laughable to think how stupid the old times were.

How could the Greeks be so gullible? It would be the equivalent of people in the Middle Ages believing that three hundred rose petals would cure the plague, or saying 'God bless you' after sneezing prevented the Devil crawling up your nose, or that the best way to identify witches was to see if they could float. No one was that stupid surely.

"So what has Colin the nine-toed giant or Stacy the one-legged eunuch got to do with writing prophecies?"

"Alignment. We observe the patterns of stars and the movement of planets through the constellations. When certain planets move into certain star signs they indicate, and influence, the present. The cosmic energy interferes with the Earth and brings about a repeat. If we know when Saturn moves into the constellation of Jerome the Midget a great storm devastates Germany, then there's a good chance of it happening next time."

"Jerome the Midget!"

"That one…there," said Michel scanning the sky.

"How do I know you're telling me the truth?"

"You don't. But I can justify it by saying I'm Nostradamus."

He unfurled his now familiar pose.

"Can you teach me to write them?" asked Philibert.

"No," he replied sternly.

"Why not?"

"The real question is why you'd want to?" he said, interrogating him with piercing blue eyes that went in through Phil's irises and penetrated his soul.

"I'm not exactly busy right now," said Philibert. "And I thought you might want to?"

"Why would I want to do that?"

"Because Annabelle said so."

If Michel hadn't been aware of Annabelle's passing remarks as she'd left the prison, Phil had certainly registered them. It appeared to him at least that Annabelle was goading Michel into helping Phil, a character flaw he might be able to use to manipulate Nostradamus's vast ego. He was dead right, too.

"Annabelle?" said Michel quizzically.

"Yes. She told you that 'perhaps it might aid your own release' if someone were to assist me."

"Someone doesn't mean me, though, does it?"

"Who else did she mean? The jailor would struggle to remember his own name if it wasn't written on his hand."

"I'm too busy."

"Yeah, because there's so much to do here! Let's play another game of spot the cockroach."

"You're too old to learn everything you'd need to know."

"Well, if you don't think you can do it, I promise I won't tell anyone," added Phil with an untrustworthy expression.

"Of course I can do it. I'm Nostrada…"

"Yes, I know you are. There's no need to repeat yourself."

"Look, Philibert, I like you. You have spirit. You've achieved more than most who start with your background. You're a good storyteller, even if I'm not convinced all of them are strictly true. I want you to succeed, I really do. But you have to understand my abilities have taken decades to perfect and I have a reputation amongst my clients which I'm unwilling to damage."

"Clients. Why are you so desperate to be accepted by the nobility?" implored Philibert.

"I'm not. I'm just a small lamp in the great, dazzling glow of enlightenment that is illuminating our world. I dedicate my life to the advancement of the human race in order to fulfil our species potential, to be more than we currently are."

"Michel, the Enlightenment is not illuminating the world. It's crawling through the undergrowth like a frightened child hiding from a mugger. Almost everyone in France thinks the Enlightenment is what happens when you light a very small candle. Only a precious few are lucky enough to be witnesses to it and even less who understand its advancements. You're not interested in the masses. If you were you'd be using your profile to help them. All you're interested in is the attention of the elites."

"Am not!" huffed Michel.

"Who are you kidding? Writing prophecies for the King, manipulating an invitation to attend their court, making star charts for Lords, seeing your name in print and knowing that everyone who can read is talking about you. No, you're right, your work is all about advancement…yours. You and I were not so different to begin with. We both wanted more for ourselves. We both dragged ourselves out of the gutter to show society achievement was possible even if you had the wrong parents. But you have been corrupted by your own greed."

Michel sat on his little wooden stool in silent contemplation. Phil was right of course, even if he'd never openly accept it. Michel's real gift was the ability to manipulate those in high office using scientifically sound, and some rather less sound, theoretical practices. He believed unwaveringly in the accuracy of his prophecies, even though some of their meaning might not initially be clear. What impact would it have if he taught this imposter a few of his tricks? He'd never be able to do it as well as he could and then the world would soon learn he was a fraud. But if it helped get him out of here a few days earlier than expected, what was the problem?

"I believe in what I write. I believe that it tells a future, even if it's not clear when that future will be. The stars come in cycles. If I predict a drought because Mars is interfering with Venus, that event might happen fifty times in the future. I won't live long enough to see if my prediction came true. But someone will. My writings will live longer than I will, and it will be up to others to decide whether I was right or not."

"It's also a cracking excuse when things don't work out," said Phil.

"That's irrelevant."

"But convenient."

"Maybe," replied Michel as his tongue tiptoed over his decision. "Ok. I might regret it, but I will teach you some of the basics."

"Excellent," said Phil with a grin.

"But on one condition," added Michel quickly.

"Certainly. Anything."

"If by some miracle your prophecies are more accurate than my own, I will reveal you as the imposter you are. Agreed."

"Agreed."

ALL THE STARS IN THE SKY

Phil had no intention at being good at prognosticating whether on purpose or by accident. The only reason to participate was to weave it into the con taking baby steps in his mind. If it worked to secure his release his short career in future reading would be over. Then he could regroup with Chambard and create a new identity. Another in a long line of masks he'd worn since that spring morning in Aix all those years ago.

"Ok," said Michel. "Also you should know that I don't like to be argued with. You must do what I say and study when I say so. Understood?"

"Yes. Got it. I am your apprentice and you are the master. I'm used to playing the understudy. So how do we start? Learn the star signs, write a star chart, develop my Latin…"

"Settle down, one step at a time. Let's see what natural ability you have first. Write me a quatrain?"

"A quatrain?"

"A four-lined prophecy."

"About what?"

"Whatever you feel coming through the cosmic energy."

"Cosmic energy…right."

Before the start of the week, Philibert had never even heard of cosmic energy, let alone 'felt' it. He imagined in his mind it acted like an invisible energy field so weak that it didn't really interact with humans in any obvious way. He thought it might be similar to the way people used dowsing rods to find water. Chambard had taught him that relatively new technique when they were lost in the wild on one of their many detours. They had on occasions found water, but then again Phil thought you probably didn't need two pointy sticks to find a massive waterfall crashing noisily over a cliff face. Chambard insisted it was because of the rods.

ALL THE STARS IN THE SKY

Phil picked up a dented pewter plate and placed it on his head. He took off his boots and stood barefoot on the cold stone floor. Next he picked up two carrots, part of the lunch menu that had been ignored, and gripped them tightly in both hands. Finally he closed his eyes and started to hum incoherently.

"Um, what are you doing?" said Michel curtly.

"Connecting with the cosmic energy."

"No…you're really not. You might be connecting with cosmic nonsense. Take all that stuff off. Just sit by the table and write whatever comes into your head. Just concentrate on what you can feel."

Sheepishly, Phil discarded his ridiculous outfit and sat down at the oak coffer. He took out a piece of parchment and racked his brain. To his surprise the murky image of an event framed itself in his mind. Almost without delay Phil started to write. The passage was restricted by poor handwriting and a less extensive vocabulary than would be available to Michel through all his years of study. What he lacked in natural talent he made up for with a healthy dose of bullshit. After all, he was a master in that area. Once the four lines had been scribbled down he passed the result to Michel with the expression of a student handing in an exam paper two hours before the end of the deadline.

"That's it, is it?"

"Yep."

In the port of Calais a week on Friday,
A man with a white beard and a scabby dog
Shall misplace his canoe, which
shall mysteriously be found in his neighbour's garden

"So…" said Phil, "any good?"

Nostradamus read it through a number of times in case he'd missed some spectacularly clever meaning. He hadn't. Not wanting to dampen his pupil's enthusiasm he'd reserve the hard critique until later. "What does this mean to you?"

"I guess it's pretty clear that someone is going to have their canoe stolen," replied Philibert.

"And that's what the cosmic energy was telling you, was it?"

"Hard to say really, not sure I'm quite on the right frequency yet, but I did get a really strong vision of a long, skinny boat sitting in a garden."

"And the man with the dog?"

"I just felt that a man who owns a canoe probably has a dog," replied Phil confidently.

"What sort of dog?" said Michel to see how deep this vision went and how long Phil would keep up the nonsense.

"Oh, a big one for sure."

The minutes that followed were only interrupted by the distant noise of bats whizzing past the window as they ventured out to find their midnight meal, and the whistling of the air being sucked into Michel's opened mouth. Both men knew that what Phil had written was not only useless, unless you had a dog, beard and canoe and lived in Calais, but it was also not a very good prophecy. Michel decided to tackle the failure head on.

"The problem with your prediction is, well, how can I put this kindly?" he said reflecting on the nicest way to frame it. "It's terrible."

"Oh. It kind of figures, though. I mean you haven't told me how to do it yet, have you? Anyway, what was wrong with it?"

"I'd say everything really."

"Everything isn't very helpful. Narrow it down."

"Ok let's talk basics. Your quatrain breaks the three golden rules."

- Chapter 14 -

The Three Rules

By fifteen-sixty-one, when Nostradamus's productivity took a knock as a result of being in prison, Michel had been writing prophecies for almost a decade. He'd started off small. A series of experiments published in small circulation and barely noticed by the world. Although frustrating for Nostradamus's desire for attention, it had at least given him ample opportunity to check his own work. Every year he created an almanac of predictions for the coming twelve months and because few people initially read them he was able to review his performance at the end of the period to see how many he got right.

In the early days it amounted to…not many.

There were several factors that brought about these defeats. Because he was writing almanacs, he was by definition writing predictions about specific future events that would have to occur in a window no bigger than three hundred and sixty-five days. The movement of the stars and planets had a much wider time frame. He might actually predict the right event, only to discover that a prediction he'd made for fifteen-fifty-seven actually came true in fifteen-fifty-nine.

The second issue was around specific details contained within the prophecies. Any exact wording or detailed description of the predicted events meant more scope for failure. Indicating that a specific church would burn to the ground was much harder to build a case for than a 'holy place being destroyed'. This change increased the odds of success dramatically. If any church, rectory, cathedral, religious town or even the Pope himself for that matter were burnt down, sacked, struck by lightning or blown up at any point over the next twelve months, it counted as a win. It was called hedging your bets.

Michel also struggled with two diametrically opposed issues. Prophecies worked because the population had a catatonic fear that the end of the world was marching unimpeded over the horizon towards them. Their desperation for answers made the work of any would-be prophet highly sought after. But predicting Armageddon wasn't good for business. If he predicted its likelihood in fifteen-sixty you could kiss goodbye to a decent level of sales for your almanac of fifteen-sixty-one, as in truth you'd already convinced people that there wasn't going to be one.

So irrespective of the need to utilise the star charts, learn historic comparisons, plagiarise deeply dubious prophecies of the last few centuries, and understand the public's general sentiment, some rules had to be applied to get the balance right between believability and reliability. There needed to be enough information for the prophecy to look genuine, but tethered to a heavy dose of ambiguity to allow for suitable wiggle room. It was through this early process of trial and error that Michel worked out his prophecies had to pass three golden rules.

"What three rules?" asked Phil, paying close attention as he felt he needed to improve fast if he was going to convince people of his supernatural talents.

"They're the rules I live by whenever the cosmic energy presents me with a vision of the future. If you want to build a decent career in this game you need to apply them, too. If you don't you won't last five minutes."

"Ok, what are they?"

"Rule one. You can't make any references to times or dates."

"That's not much of a prophecy, then, is it?"

"A prophecy doesn't come with a clock."

"Then how are people going to know when death and destruction are coming?"

"They don't exactly because we might make reference to events that happen more than once. For example, feel free to make reference to winter in a quatrain, particularly if you're predicting a lot of snow, but never say when in winter or which particular one."

"So I can write about seasons and periods in time, but not days, weeks and years?"

"Precisely. Best to stick with the movement of the stars in your description. If you write 'when Jupiter is in the East,' it's up to everyone else to work out when that is and to act accordingly."

"But the vast majority of people don't know what Jupiter is, let alone when it's likely to appear somewhere."

"That's true."

"So what's the point?" replied Phil in confusion.

"It's up to scholars to make the assessment of your writing and pass it on. That's how the process works. No different from religion. God tells the clergy and the clergy tell the community. And because the community trust them, their word is God's. Prophets write, scholars interpret and everyone else panics."

"But what if the scholars are wrong?"

"What if they are? Doesn't bother me one bit. That's their mistake not mine. We still get paid."

Phil knew that this first rule didn't sit well with what he was trying to achieve. The plan was to convince Claude that his prophecies were so accurate and compelling that it would be sacrilege to have him put to death. But Claude was already a convert. He believed wholeheartedly with those who had the gift, and thus far Phil had no track record of having it. If he was to get out of here his prophecy would have to be short-term and, more importantly, would definitely have to come true.

"Rule two. You can't give any specific details. No exact names, places or circumstances. Ambiguity is the name of the game."

"Are you sure you're not just writing fancy poems?"

"Just because it's ambiguous doesn't mean it's worthless," said Michel defensively.

"Surely the cosmic energy has something to say about that," added Phil, wondering if the stars had anything at all to do with Michel's writing.

"Sometimes I see very clearly the places and people that are affected, but it's best to be a little less accurate in case things don't go to plan or something changes."

"Explain?" asked Phil.

"Ok. Let me show you an example."

Michel opened the two doors of the oak coffer and rustled around inside. The wooden cabinet was packed to the brim. Reams of paper, scabby books bound weakly at the seams, unusual artefacts with unknown uses, a gleaming sextet, jars of colourful powders, and all manner of incongruous items. It was all ordered chaotically in a way that only the owner would understand. Michel very quickly found the example he was after in one of the manuscripts.

"I keep some of the work I'm less proud of in here," he said, giving the box a little tap. "And a great number of other possessions."

"Less proud of?"

"Work that I'd prefer others did not see. Right, take a look at this quatrain and tell me what you think," he said, carefully placing the manuscript on Philibert's knees to stop some of the pages making a gravity-assisted dash for freedom.

THE THREE RULES

Out of the deepest part of Western Europe
Of poor people a child will be born
Who will seduce many people with his tongue
His fame will increase in the Eastern Kingdom

"It's hard to say really," replied Phil, who wasn't an educated man and still found this type of critical thinking a little challenging. "I mean, most people are born to poor people so that's about ninety-nine per cent of the population, and Western Europe could mean anywhere. There's no year or time frame, the first rule coming into force I assume, so it could be anyone, anywhere at anytime. What does it mean?"

"To me it means that a Western European man will bring about a great change thanks to his incredible ability to rouse others through his use of words and passion."

"When?"

"No idea. Please refer to rule one."

"And that's all that the cosmic energy gave you, was it?"

"Certainly not. This particular prophecy was more clear in my mind. I kept hearing this word Hitler."

"Hitler?"

"Yes."

"Where's that?"

"I couldn't find it on the map so I just went with Western Germany. Presumably the town of Hitler hasn't been built yet and this particular prophecy is one for the future. And there's the point of rule two. Keep the interpretation open."

Rule two wasn't much better than rule one in Phil's scheme. His next prediction would have to refer to those whom he needed to convince. But how could he do that and maintain the odds of proving that the prophecy would come true? Nostradamus's whole reputation rested on a million interpretations of his thoughts so that none could be truly dismissed as inaccurate and none could be truly explicit.

"Fine. So no dates and no details. Sounds pretty easy."

"The prophecy still has to be based on the science of the stars, though. You can't just write any old rubbish down and palm it off as a prediction."

"If you say so. What's the last rule, then?"

"That one is the most important of all. Under no circumstances can you directly predict the end of the world."

"Oh well, that's easy enough."

"You say that, but it's a fine balance. If prophecies don't scare the wits out of people then no one will read them. People already believe that they're on the precipice, clinging desperately to the edge of life's abyss. We need to give them a little nudge, but not a shove."

"Why are they so worried?"

"Well, why wouldn't they be? Look at most people's lives. There's not much joy, is there? That's why you don't tend to read happy prophecies. That's not people's perception of the world. Who wants to read about a nice, long, hot summer when in reality it's always raining. No one would believe you. Who wants to read about an economic windfall when most people haven't seen an actual coin in their lives. Fear is what keeps us in a job, not happy thoughts."

"So moderate desperation, bloodshed and destruction is good, suggestions of full-scale extermination is bad?"

"You got it. By all means make vague references to impending catastrophe but hint that it might be ages away or make it so vague that people are kept on their toes. Remember the end of the world is never nigh."

"When is nigh exactly?"

"Usually very soon."

THE THREE RULES

"Then why don't people say 'the end of the world is very soon'?"

"Somehow it doesn't strike the same level of fear. I mean if I said to you, 'Watch out, someone's going to stab you with a sword,' and you said 'When?' and I replied, 'Sometime in the next fortnight,' you're probably not going to be overly worried. But as soon as I say, it's nigh you've already started sweating and strange, gurgling noises are dropping out of your stomach."

"I guess it does sound more fancy."

"Exactly!" said Michel.

"Ok, rule three, I should use fancy words like nigh but categorically not in reference to the end of days. Got it."

Phil had no qualms over this third rule. He had no intention of indicating that the end of the world was coming, although it was helpful to understand that his prophecies should err on the negative side.

"Right," said Michel, getting to his feet and stretching out his stiff limbs which, unknown to him at the time, were the early signs of gout that would one day impact him greatly. "Let's see if you understand. I want you to rewrite that prophecy of yours, but this time take into account the three golden rules. Then we can move on to the next lesson."

Phil returned to the coffer to make the desired changes. It wasn't that difficult to make an already useless prediction even more nonsensical, all without the aid of some cosmic force field. After a couple of minutes of edits he passed the amendment to his new teacher.

Low in the sky the sun will set on the Northern fleet
Rabid teeth will bite at their hairy, ancient masters
Missing will be the boats of the townsfolk, beware thy
neighbour who hides objects amongst the flowers

"Oh yes. That's much better," said Michel after reading the second attempt.

"Really?" said Phil, not entirely sure what it all meant, even though it came out of his own head.

"We need to do some work on your choice of words to make it even more obscure and to confuse all but the most talented of readers. But not bad for a second attempt."

"What next?"

"That's enough for today I think. I have my own work to do as well, you know. We'll start again tomorrow evening with a detailed assessment of star patterns."

Over the next week, after the sun had set, every evening was taken up by Michel's teaching. Into the small hours he would lecture, and Phil would listen, occasionally broken by a practical session for Phil to demonstrate what he'd learnt. Although Michel had never taught anyone before, his experience as a student leant itself to a concise and simple approach to the study plan.

They never focused on the same discipline for more than a day, always varying the subject to keep it fresh. On the first day Michel demonstrated how to write a star chart based on a person's place and time of birth. On the next they researched specific historical events that had happened at times of significant planetary alignments. Phil noted them down and paid close attention to the scale and impact of any recorded disasters. On the third day they reviewed some of the great philosophers from history and debated their approaches and style. The fourth day focused on the present. They discussed the current sociological trends and how the war of religions was a godsend for those like Michel.

Each new day brought new twists, new opportunities and fresh ideas that Phil felt he could use. He was gaining more confidence in his ability to write in a way that was both poetic and confusing. At the end of the fifth day of lessons his brain had been stretched to its limits and a lack of nutrition was causing him physical fatigue.

"I can't take any more in. Can we stop now?"

"If we must," replied Michel calmly.

"I need to rest my mind."

Michel passed him a battered tankard of water, although water was rarely the only substance contained within it. A cloudy, yellow liquid, which wouldn't have been out of place as the by-product of the drinking process, it had a musty smell similar to dry dirt and a density that meant it could be knocked over and reinstated some minutes later without the tiniest bit of liquid flowing out. It was hard to know whether you drank it or attacked it with a knife and fork.

"What will you do when you get out, Michel?" he asked, reluctantly taking a mouthful of sludge from the cup.

"Keep writing," he said without flinching.

"Aren't you worried they'll throw you back in here?"

"Not really. I'll be more careful next time. But I must continue. My children rely on the money I make from selling 'Les Prophéties'."

"You have children?!" The question was delivered in a tone of voice that might have been deemed rude or insulting, but considering Michel's advanced years it took Phil by surprise that anyone closing in on their sixties would still have dependants.

"Yes."

"But they're grown up now right. They don't need your money surely."

"My wife is currently pregnant and I have five other children to look after."

"Jesus!"

Until the late-twentieth century it was usual for people to have a lot of children. It was common to find families who had as many as a dozen. This was highly impractical because only the very richest families had homes and incomes that could cater for such large numbers. If you only lived in a shack, or worse, a hole, increasing the numbers of those that lived there made very little sense. Every new mouth needed feeding and the amount of food available was unlikely to increase.

In truth couples didn't actually want more children. But they did want more sex. After all, what else in their lives was both free and made you feel good, other than public hangings, which shared the similarity of involving a lot of grunting and the occasional wayward fluid. But if you wanted the joy of sex you had to accept that children might be the result. That's just how it worked. Family planning was non-existent and no one had developed an effective early withdrawal method. Plus you needed lots of babies if you wanted to end up with any toddlers at all.

Sadly most infants didn't survive. Mortality claimed about two in every three newborn babies, a lottery that no one would accept in modern times. Back then it was just part of life. They still felt a deep sense of sorrow when someone lost a child, just no shock. And it didn't stop them trying for more.

"Six kids, at your age!"

"What are you implying?" replied Michel indignantly.

"I'm implying that you're either exceptionally fertile or you might want to have a serious conversation with your wife."

"Mind your tongue or I'll be forced to remove it."

"I meant no offence, it's just, well…How?"

"Don't forget I used to be a herbalist. I know plenty of recipes for aphrodisiacs."

"Even so, pregnant! You must be in your fifties?"

"Fifty-eight, what of it?"

"It's not…normal."

"Maybe not for you, laddie, but I'm Nostradamus."

THE THREE RULES

"You can't justify something like that by repeating your own name in a theatrical manner. You should be selling your secrets to the medical profession rather than writing books."

"Maybe I will one day. More than my books, my children are my real gift to the world. One day they will make their own history and continue the family line. What about you? Don't you want to settle down?"

"No, I just want to get out."

"What about Annabelle? She'd make a fine wife."

"Yes, I think Jacques thinks so. She's very interesting, but I don't think I'll ever be able to get a girl like that. They just wouldn't allow it."

"Not if you continue like this. Taking false names and stealing from the rich and powerful. That's no way to build a stable future. But if you had a legitimate profession it might be possible."

"I think it's too late for that."

"It's never too late, Phil. I have had more jobs than I can care to remember. Each one built on the success of the last and harnessed everything I'd learnt. It just takes time. Here, I have something for you."

Michel took a small, wooden box from inside his cabinet and presented it to Phil who took it in his hands in surprise. No one had ever given him anything before, he'd always just taken from people who had too much. On the front of the box a small, metal clasp kept the lid tightly shut. He flipped it forward and lifted the lid. Inside the beech wood container was a silk-lined interior and lying on top of that were pen nibs, small bottles of ink and some scraps of paper.

"Michel, I don't know what to say?"

"Thank you would be the normal convention!"

"But why?"

"It's to mark your progress. Now you can write your own prophecies whenever you need to. If that's the direction you want to go in, although I'm not sure it'll be enough to convince your way out of trouble. You might need more help for that."

"Thank you."

"Use it to make a fresh start. Leave false names and pranks behind you. Make something of yourself."

*****

An old man stood upon the dockside watching the sea lap against its fragile, wooden frame. Conditions in Calais were fair and a gentle breeze was pressing the salty spray against a face that was fifty per cent straggly beard and fifty per cent old leather. Most of the town's simple handmade boats were already out in the Channel checking on the nets laid the night before, or laying new ones to farm the plentiful stocks of gurnard and herring that lived in the shallows. A few vessels had already returned and were safely tied up on the dockside, or purposely beached on low sandbanks by the returning current. The old man was hoping to bring in his own haul of scallops, but something confusing had stopped him.

At his feet a length of rope was tied tightly to a mooring hook while the other end floated limply in the water. This was in contrast to how he'd left the same rope no less than twelve hours ago. Yesterday the recently wet end had most definitely had a canoe attached to it. He stroked his beard to massage his brain into deep thought, and did his best to ignore the large, shaggy dog sniffing around his feet in search of anything that might be described as edible and eating many things that weren't.

"Nice morning for it," said a passer-by who was walking down the mooring points from the direction of his own boat.

The old man couldn't imagine that there was anything nice about it. What was nice about being confused?

THE THREE RULES

"Where's your boat?" said the younger man who was dressed in simple garments and carried the unique smell that could only come from an extended stint at sea.

"Canoe."

"Ok, then what's happened to your canoe?"

"Storm."

Even though he'd been out in it all morning, and the conditions had barely changed, the younger man casually glanced up at the perfectly blue skyline. Yesterday, as he recalled, it had been even better.

"It must have been very localised," he argued sympathetically, making an imaginary circle with his hands over the region where they stood. "I mean, look at the other boats. Not a scratch on them. I've been fishing whiting for hours this morning and there's not been so much as a gust."

"Sunk," said the old man offering an alternative and still searching for any feasible explanation. He'd been a fisherman his whole life and when boats went missing it was almost always because they sank or were wrecked by storms. Unless there was a war on, which there wasn't.

"Sunk? But you'd be able to see it. I mean I can see the seabed under the water from here. It's only about three feet deep. How big was this canoe of yours?"

"Twenty-four feet."

"Then you'd definitely see it. I mean if it was a toy canoe or an extremely long but very thin one, that would be different, you might not see that. Was it very, very thin?"

"No."

"What colour was it?"

"Blue."

"Blue, you say. Interesting. Have you looked inland?"

"Land?"

"Yes."

"It was a water canoe," said the man struggling with the notion of an inland boat.

"Yes, all canoes are water ones! I mean who's ever heard of a land canoe? You wouldn't get very far with that, would you?"

"Maybe if it was pointing downhill," replied the old man.

"Anyway…" said the newcomer, a little concerned at the older man's mental state. "I think you might want to check out old man Hector's back garden."

"Garden?"

"Yes. Last night I was walking back from church and I noticed a bloody big boat poking out of the geraniums. Blue, as I recall. But Hector does have a reputation for being a little light-fingered. Although in this case you might say heavy-fingered if he pulled that off."

"Bastard."

- Chapter 15 -

Traboules and Caravans

Antoine pushed open the huge, wooden doors to reveal a world previously hidden from sight.

"Welcome to a traboule," he said grandly.

Very few people knew about them. Even residents who'd lived in the city for decades would walk right past these doors unaware of their function and history. Not Antoine, though. Living as a child in post-war France he'd spent many an idle afternoon exploring a network he'd first been introduced to by his grandfather when he was a youngster. Sometimes they acted as a sanctuary from the prying eyes of others. Sometimes as a place to escape the pursuers of his own misconduct. Sometimes it was just a simple short cut from one side of town to the other.

"What is it?" asked Ally, surprised to see the dimly lit passageway on the other side of the door rather than someone's living room as she'd expected.

"Today it's our lifeline."

The narrow passageway weaved through the block of apartments, making unusual turns for no obvious architectural reason. Here and there a set of postboxes were bolted to the wall next to side entrances that led off into a flat or residential complex. After five minutes of walking, they reached the other end where another door kept the traboule's existence secret from anyone not in the know. Once on the other side they found themselves in a sealed courtyard surrounded by terracotta houses that stretched high into the air above them. Small, arched, glassless windows zigzagged up the walls and were connected together by elegant spiral staircases.

"That was the traboule then, was it? Seems a little pointless seeing how it's led us up a dead end," said Ally, getting rather frustrated by the whole affair of running away.

"Oh no. That's only one of them. There are over four hundred," said Antoine, walking directly over to a door with an enamel number six screwed above its frame.

"And where do they lead?"

"Out of the city, if you follow them to the end."

"And after that, where are we going then?"

"Once we are on the outskirts we can hike until we find some transport to Mâcon," replied Antoine.

"I'm not hiking anywhere in these shoes," replied Ally angrily.

"Fine. We'll get some transport."

"Why Mâcon anyway?"

"You want to meet with Bernard Baptiste, don't you?"

It hadn't taken him long after the shock of the bombing to construct a plan in his mind. This in itself felt strange to Ally. A bombing on your doorstep and a burglary on the same day weren't normal occurrences. Not for her at least. Most people's immediately reaction would be to tidy up, help the police with their enquiries and look to others for some comfort. Running away didn't seem altogether appropriate. Even if someone was out to get them, surely they'd be safer at home protected by the authorities, particularly if it wasn't clear who was trying to harm him or why. Now they were effectively on the run, keeping themselves hidden in order to locate a man that in her opinion was a complete fraud.

Before she could answer his question he disappeared through door number six. If it wasn't for the blisters swelling on her heels, Ally would have found the discovery of the traboules a more rewarding experience. Each one ended in familiar fashion, one secret door closed behind them and another would appear close by, like the back of the wardrobe that granted access to Narnia. She lost count of how many different traboules they'd entered. Each alley, stair or underground passageway presented another apparent false move before Antoine identified the next like a top-rate illusionist.

Each new discovery had a notable effect on his demeanour. He no longer acted like the slightly fragile elderly retiree she'd first met for a coffee. Adventure had rubbed away his advanced years and transported him to a time of childlike wonder and intrigue. The circumstances of this morning's events had, if anything, made his life more interesting. It was clear that he was thoroughly enjoying the whole experience and keen to ensure that Ally did likewise.

"The traboules were originally used by the canuts to move their products down to the markets at speed," he said as they crossed an empty side street to get to their next port.

"Canuts?"

"I thought you were an expert in languages?" said Antoine in surprise as they passed through a gateway by means of pressing the correct buttons on a security pad.

"And I maintain my expertise by being constantly inquisitive," she replied gruffly.

"Canuts was a local name given to the silk workers. The traboules allowed them to carry their goods from workshop to market in less than four minutes. We're not far from that area of the city now."

Their route had been climbing steadily over the last five minutes in recognition of Lyon's position at the bottom of a bowl-like hollow.

"Of course they aren't used for that now," he continued, never seeming to run out of breath or interesting facts about their location. "They have had other uses down the years. I'm told they were vital to the Resistance movement during the Second World War."

"I can see why. I hate to sound like a moaning child, but are we there yet?"

"Almost. This is the last one," said Antoine, taking a left and then right turn before leading her up a steep, uncovered flight of stairs that had been carved through a row of buildings.

After ten minutes of climbing they emerged in a densely suburban area at the top of the hill. Behind them the sprawling centre of Lyon, pitted with the marks of human progression, lay open like an amphitheatre. The Basilique was still visible in the middle of it all like a candle on top of a birthday cake. The two rivers chased each other through the myriad of buildings to be first to reach the horizon.

"Now what?" said Ally.

"We keep walking. We're on the north side of the city so I suggest we get out into the countryside and try to pick up some transport. It'll need to be something conspicuous. I don't trust public transport, too many cameras."

"I think you're being a little more suspicious than you need to be."

"I'm not taking any chances. Since supper last night unknown persons have burgled and bombed me, or possibly you. I have no enemies that I'm aware of and the item they targeted ostensibly doesn't exist. So how do you think they found out about it? The surveillance culture that we live under might well provide the answers."

They walked slowly along the main street, casually watching the unusually frenetic activities of other people's lives. Everyone was in a rush today. It was quite unsuitable behaviour for French people at twelve-thirty in the afternoon. It was lunchtime and nothing got in the way of that here. It was deeply engrained in the Gallic DNA that at twelve everyone stopped, sat and ate. Two hours of conversation, hot cuisine and a glass or two of wine. Only the end of the world would stop it.

All the restaurants in the road were closed. Shades had been pulled down in front of large, glass frontages, chairs and tables stacked chaotically down side alleys. Parents were rushing to the schools to collect their children early, wrestling each other to be the first through the gates. Down the pavement a mother hurtled towards them driving a pram like an erratically thrown bowling ball trying to pick up a spare.

"Madam?" asked Antoine, stopping her as she tried to fly past them. "Why is everyone in a rush?"

"Haven't you heard?" she spluttered, not stopping to finish her answer. "They're shutting the whole area down. Everyone's trying to get out before the deadline."

"Deadline?" said Ally. "Who's ever heard of a city being shut down?"

"Hasn't happened for five hundred years," said Antoine.

At the end of the street a large squadron of police cars were setting up a cordon to restrict other vehicles from entering or exiting the city centre. If this was replicated at every access point around its perimeter two hundred thousand people were being locked into Lyon.

"It's a good job we came through the traboules," said Antoine as he watched with curiosity as the disgruntled police squadrons lifted colourful plastic bollards into place.

"It makes no sense," said Ally.

"Doesn't it? You're a clever woman, Dr. Oldfield. I'm sure you can work it out?" replied Antoine who already had. "Let's walk on, we must find somewhere safe and secret for the night."

"Look, I'm not walking another inch. My feet are in tatters, I haven't had coffee for several hours and I'm getting irritated by the futility of running from some phantom menace. Do you even know where you're taking us?"

"There's a small town not far from here where I have a friend whom we can trust. I only hope he's at home. If he is, tomorrow my plan is to borrow his car and drive to Mâcon. That way we might be able to solve our mystery and put an end to this one," he said, referring to the cordon. "Bernard may hold the key to the prophecy and our own predicament."

*****

Gabriel rotated the dial, never waiting more than a couple of seconds before impatiently moving it again. She was mystified as to why anyone would put up with such an irritating system. Imagine having to physically search for a radio station rather than simply telling Siri to find it for you. And what was the crackling noise all about? A band of unexpected analogue muggers were interrupting the broadcast every time she got close to finding the right frequency. Radio wasn't supposed to sound like this. It was always crisp and clear whenever she listened to it on her smartphone. But this particular radio was built in a time when people thought a silicon chip was a type of diet.

The ancient beige Renault had been in her possession since the day she passed her driving test eight years ago. According to the service booklet she was the ninth owner and none of the previous eight were described as careful. It had suffered and survived every known automotive procedure in the manual and was still soldiering on like a wounded veteran. It had been a last resort, the only option that was under the four figure insurance bracket and affordable to her less than affluent parents. And how did Gabriel react to their financial sacrifice?

She complained. She hated it. All her friends were zooming around in sporty little hatchbacks with colourful paint jobs and crisp digital radios. But neither they nor her parents appreciated her suffering. It was embarrassing. When she started dating boys more seriously she made them drive to create the illusion around the town that the car was theirs. Which also backfired because then people thought she was dating losers. Image is important when you're in your early twenties. Your entire life prospects depended on it.

This was the Instagram age, after all. How you looked, what you wore, what you ate, who you followed, could all make or break you. Owning the car had resulted in her tumbling down the highly complex and invisible social rankings, without any explanation or confirmation. That's how it was for people her age. Judgement was fast if you made the slightest social mistake, and no one gave you a rule book. Now that the rusty heap of junk was parked between two ash trees a few hundred metres from the main road at least it reduced the chance of her slipping further down the league table.

Finally she stopped twiddling the dials. It wasn't a clear signal by any standards, but at least it was audible enough for her to hear what the man had to say. News had never been of much interest to Gabriel, unless it concerned Taylor Swift or a new product for halting the development of acne. What was the point in the news? Boring politicians squabbling about farm subsidies or experts debating what should be done about the crisis in Ukraine. Where the hell was Ukraine anyway? The only news she wanted to hear was news that affected her world, not other people's. But today's news affected everyone.

The virus had reached Europe.

Almost simultaneously from Britain to Albania and Portugal to Norway people had started showing the symptoms of N_1G_{13}. If the pattern continued, as it had done in other regions of the world, people would be dropping like flies in a matter of days. And France wouldn't escape the impending catastrophe: how could it? It was smack bang in the middle of Europe and on every border the populations of infected countries were coughing collectively in her direction.

It had already begun. Today they'd announced the first cases in Lyon.

Lyon! That was only fifteen kilometres away. According to the news, being simultaneously broadcast on every station to the detriment of Taylor Swift's popularity, special measures were being implemented to curtail the spread of the virus. The authorities in Europe were determined not to suffer the way that China had, driven by an unspoken racism in the West that when non-white people died it wasn't quite such a tragedy. China had been hit hard. The numbers were unsubstantiated, but the projections had suggested anywhere in the region of tens of thousands plus had already died.

The co-ordinated measures taken unanimously by the European Union included the restriction of flights for non-essential travel, the quarantining of areas with known cases of the infection, and a mandatory government takeover of all private healthcare companies so their resources could be used in the search to discover an effective vaccine. On radio talk shows people were reporting that roadblocks had already been placed around some sections of Lyon. But these government measures didn't really concern Gabriel. After all, she'd made her own.

But prepping wasn't as easy as it first appeared. Preppers were given that name because they were experts in preparing for long periods of existence outside the bosom of normal society. A seasoned prepper could last for years if they had to. They'd carefully considered their food supply, energy needs, security to protect against multiple threats, and the necessary communications systems needed to locate other survivors in order to maintain the human race. These were the four pillars of the prepper mantra.

TRABOULES AND CARAVANS

In terms of food provision, Gabriel had nineteen ready meals and no microwave in which to cook them, forty tins of food that spanned the essential food groups of baked beans, rice pudding and sandwich spread, and a single pint of milk. The milk had lumps in it. On the energy front she had a car battery, a USB adaptor cable, and not the slightest idea that leaving the headlamps on all night would detrimentally affect both of them.

Security involved a can of deodorant, a nine-iron golf club she'd found in the back of the caravan, and a sign hastily written in graffiti on the side of a tree in lipstick kindly asking people to 'STAY OUT, please'. Other than the radio she had no way of connecting to the outside world. She'd left her phone at home under the false assumption that what she was embarking on was a challenge of survival rather than actually trying to. What she'd give now to have it back. Her thumbs were developing early arthritis from a lack of swiping.

Prepping might have been a reasonably astute move given the circumstances, but boy was it dull. A week had passed already and the heavy rain had forced her to inhabit the front seat of the car, playing 'spot the bunny', or retreating to the plastic upholstery of the nineteen seventies caravan. The nearby stream provided a healthy supply of water to boil the kettle for a mug of coffee, although she was constantly perplexed as to where the gas was coming from to light the stove. There were a couple of board games, which she understood was how people entertained themselves in the eighteenth century. It had taken her an hour to realise that Monopoly wasn't a one-player game and that was only after she managed to go bankrupt.

The caravan would have been the most appropriate place to sleep if it had felt even remotely safe. Whereas the lock on the door had long been broken, at least the car protected her from the late-night loonies and potential animal attacks. Given her close proximity to suburbia, any animal attacks were most likely to involve the same bunnies she'd spent most of the day trying to spot.

In her opinion the worst time to be a prepper was at night. When the lights from distant houses were extinguished and only the trees in front of her were illuminated by the failing light from the car's headlamps, that was when the real anxieties crept inside her soul. She wasn't used to living by herself or relying on her own support. Until recently she'd had a burly yet insensitive boyfriend to protect her. Even after he left she'd often invited Claire over for company and safety.

The night-time noises might well have been natural but that didn't stop them sounding alien to her ears. The orchestra of evil auditioning on her window played a concerto of unimaginable notes that limited her sleep to less than twenty-minute stints. On this particular night the horrifying noises were accompanied by the gentle rocking of the car. Something was out there.

- Chapter 16 -

Every Claude Has a Silver Lining

Sleep had never been easy here. Its acquisition was restricted by a lack of comfort. The hard, cold surface of the floor was only insulated by a thin layer of straw, and a few lice-infested blankets were the only aids to slumber. The walls offered no deterrent to the external elements either. The rain lashed through the open window and the bitter wind swirled round the room like a cyclone. Eerie whispers of panic clung in the air from the murmurs of other inmates in adjacent cells, or from the mind transforming innocent sounds into more sinister threats through a filter of darkness and anxiety.

If you could sleep through all of that, then the activity within your own head did its best to disrupt you. Fear doesn't need daytime or a conscious mind to thrive. It needs the electricity provided by thousands of pent-up synapses that flashed through the body in search of reassurance. None existed. Instead these impulses magnified the broken dreams that sent a bizarre concoction of vivid scenes back to the brain in a further attempt to break any serenity. Sleep would not help you escape prison. It was as much in your mind as it was around you.

Phil woke to the sound of his own name. The cell was still in gloom and it would be several hours until it cleared, such was the early hour of the morning. He'd not been woken by his jailor, who didn't tend to call any of them by name, partly as he didn't have the mental fortitude to remember them and partly because his job was generally to be mean. It was hard to be mean and courteous at the same time.

It was possible he'd been woken by his own imagination as his internal thoughts collided together to play out their own dreamscape of fantasies: desired and unwanted. Yet as he'd returned to consciousness he only remembered one thing about his now fading dream. He'd been chasing a duck across a frozen lake. The bird had moved unfeasibly quickly, always just out of reach, before it finally morphed into a puff of smoke and disappeared into the atmosphere. He wondered what the significance of the dream might be? Was the duck representing the freedom that was narrowly out of reach? Did the smoke mean freedom wasn't real? Or was he just subconsciously pissed off with ducks? Whatever it meant, Phil was certain that the duck hadn't said a word and had definitely not called out his name.

Another suspect was soon removed from suspicion. It wasn't Michel who'd woken him. It couldn't be, because he was gone. There was no sign of his oak coffer, his little stool or the embroidered linen that he'd had the advantage of sleeping on. No trace at all. Just an empty cell containing Phil and not much hope.

"Pssst…Phil."

Philibert rubbed his eyes and took another look around to see if any mice or rats had got in and were trying to mess with his senses by making oddly familiar beckoning noises.

"PHIL!"

There it was again. It was coming from outside the cell but not from within the prison because all was quiet in the corridors on the other side of the metal bars. Phil made his way to the window and managed to pull himself up high enough to see through the bars and down to the ground several metres below.

"Chambard? Is that you?"

"Yes."

"What are you doing?" asked Phil.

"I don't know," said Chambard in a whisper.

"What do you mean you don't know?"

"I came to rescue you, but in truth I haven't come up with a meaningful way of doing it yet."

"Right. What's this, then? A courtesy call."

"No. Everything is moving faster than I anticipated," said Chambard nervously.

"What do you mean?" whispered Phil in response.

"They are coming for you today."

"To release me."

"Not quite. Unless you mean release your head from the rest of your body."

"But I'm not ready."

"No one is ready for death, Phil."

"I don't mean death. I mean I've got a plan, but it's not finished yet. How do you know they're coming today?"

"I got friendly with one of the young squires and have been paying him for information. Apparently as they can't verify whether you are Philibert Montmorency or not, they feel killing you is easier and quicker than pursuing the answer."

"Christ. I bet Jacques is behind this."

"All I know is that Claude de Savoie is coming to break the news to you personally."

"Why is he coming?"

"Not sure. You know what the rich are like, any excuse to humiliate a peasant. What's your plan?"

The plan was best described as loose. Michel was gone and presumably it wasn't to make a quick trip to the garderobe. His training was over. From here on in he had to use what he had. What he needed was a convincing prophecy which had half a chance of demonstrating that he was actually a genius and not a total chancer.

"I'm going to write a prophecy," said Phil.

"Umm, shouldn't you think about a plan?" said Chambard.

"That is the plan!"

"How is it?"

Chambard was no fool. What he'd missed in formal education he'd more than made up for in 'on the job' training. But as an aging senior citizen from a different era to Phil, his speed of thought was not as sharp as it once was. Although even the great renaissance philosopher Machiavelli would have struggled to make a clear link between what was coming out of Phil's mouth and the plan that followed.

"I'm going to convince Claude that I'm a talented prophet."

"Ok, and that helps how?" replied Chambard, genuinely concerned for his young protégé. "You haven't been eating mouse droppings while you've been in there, have you? I heard an old wives' tale that they can make you hallucinate."

"No, I haven't. Breakfast is bad enough. It's going to help because I'm going to write a prophecy about him."

"Struggling to keep up here, Phil."

"I'm going to predict his future. Then he'll think I'm a talented seer who can provide valuable insight to the future."

"But you're not a talented seer?"

"I'm not a doctor or a priest or a noble but it hasn't stopped me in the past, has it?"

"Fair point. But what if you do write him a prophecy? He's soon going to realise that you don't know what you're doing when it doesn't come true."

"That's where you come in."

"Is it? How?"

"You're going to make sure it does!"

"Hold on a minute. Let me get this straight. You want me to change the future?" replied a bemused Chambard.

"No. I want you to make it look like the future happened in precisely the way I predict."

"Isn't that the same thing?"

"No."

"But what future have you predicted for him?"

"I haven't yet."

"Philibert, he's coming today. This morning. I'm not impressed by this plan of yours, but if you are going to do it you better get a move on."

"Is it safe for you there?"

"While it's still dark it is, but the moment the sun comes up they'll spot me."

"Right. Wait there."

Phil dug out the small writing box that Michel had left him a couple of days ago. At the time he didn't realise how significant it would be, but without Michel's present he'd have had nothing to write with. On the cleanest patch of floor that he could identify he rolled out a piece of paper and dipped the pen into one of the small bottles of ink. That was the easy bit. Now he had to write something special.

The detail had to relate to something close to Claude's heart. That was always how a con worked. Use someone's weakness to lower their defences and make them desire the outcome as much as the convincer did. At the very least it had to be something that made Claude think, and importantly think about delaying his decision about Phil's life. But what did Claude care about?

Certainly his daughter, although given Annabelle's infatuation with him, Phil felt it might be playing with fire to involve her. Claude was a Huguenot, a supporter of the Protestant faith: perhaps that might be an angle that Phil could play with. What did they fear most? They feared not being able to follow their faith because of the Catholics.

Could he really influence that? This prophecy had to be something that Chambard could falsify and it was doubtful with a potential war of religions desperate to tear regions and families apart that he was up to it.

No, it had to be something smaller and easier. Phil pictured the tower where he'd briefly been a guest. He visualised the rooms that he'd walked through and the décor around him. As he pictured it a vision of animal horns, ears and snouts filled his imagination. Aggressive-looking boar with massive, pointed tusks, beautiful stags' heads with antlers that stretched high towards the ceilings, and whole foxes stuffed in a pose quite alien to their last living stance. It had to be about hunting. Phil scribbled down some ideas.

"Phil, have you gone back to sleep?"

"No, be quiet. I'm working on it."

"Just remember," said Chambard, "I'm not good with horses."

"I know. You're ok with dangerous animals, though, right?"

"Horses are dangerous animals! Look, as long as I don't have to ride one we're all good."

The prophecy was starting to take shape but there was only one problem. He had to break some of the golden rules. It would be impossible to trick Claude into believing Phil had the 'gift' if it made no reference to him or the circumstances. Rule one had to be go. And there had to be a timeline that Chambard could follow. Rule two was out of the window as well. Everything else that Michel had taught him he could leverage. It had to sound authentic and flow like the great poets of the age.

Spear will splinter and horse will bolt
Mighty will be the beast that rips through Savoie
Only shield and armour will protect the hunt
On the day the dead are remembered

Once he was happy it was neither too obvious nor too ambiguous, he copied it down on another more elegant piece of paper in his neatest handwriting. The first he crumbled into a ball as if to jettison it into a fire, but threw it out of the window instead where it landed unnoticed in the mud. A few feet away from it Chambard leant against the wall to shelter from the sky's drizzle.

"What do you think?" said Phil.

"I think someone should invent a device that you could hold above your head to keep the rain off your receding hairline. Something wide and round on a stick with a nice, comfy handle on the end. You could call it a rain rescuer."

"I meant the prophecy! I threw it out of the window."

"Wasn't it any good?"

"No, it was for you! Look on the floor."

In the dark Chambard crawled on his hands and knees through the wet mud searching for the screwed-up ball of paper. Eventually he found it and wiped it on the driest thing he had, the inside of his coat. He found it impossible to read in almost no light and with his failing eyesight.

"It's too dark," replied Chambard. "Tell me what it said."

Phil slowly read out his version.

"I said no horses," replied Chambard. "There's definite a horse in that."

"That bit of the prophecy isn't important. Do you understand what needs to be done?"

"Seems simple enough. The day of the dead is All Souls' Day, right? That's the end of the week so I'll get to it straight away. Any preference to what beast you want me to hurl at him?"

"The most important thing is that you stay out of sight. They must believe that what happens is natural. If you get caught we're both for it."

"Don't you worry, Phil. You know I'm a master of disguises."

"Are you? Normally you only play a knackered squire or a wizened old man."

"What about the time when I disguised myself as the mother of Isaac the Elder? You know when we stole his antique vase, that was convincing?"

"The disguise was, but the scam wasn't. It should have dawned on us that someone called the 'elder' might already be quite old. The whole con falls apart when you find out he's eighty and his mother has been dead for decades."

"Fun times," chuckled Chambard.

"For you maybe, but you didn't have the embarrassment of duelling an octogenarian being dragged towards you on a chair with wheels attached. Anyway, the point is, do you know what to do?"

"Yes. Leave it with me. Just make sure Claude believes you in the first place," said Chambard.

He scuttled off up a grass bank and into the undergrowth. A man of portly dimensions, he'd developed an incredible lightness of movement and could hide himself in places smaller than the total of his own mass. All Phil could do was wait, think and practise convincing his own captor.

True to Chambard's tip-off, Claude arrived the same day. Just after breakfast had been served, and ignored, the old Governor descended down into the prison block in a sweeping blue mantle and matching hat. To Phil's relief he was not joined by Jacques, who might have made life a little more complex. When Claude reached Phil's cell door he asked politely for it to be opened. The jailor acted immediately and in a more civilised manner than any of the prisoners were used to.

"Bring us two chairs, jailor," Claude requested as he walked into the cell without concern for his safety.

EVERY CLAUDE HAS A SILVER LINING

"Can I offer you a drink?" said Philibert, bowing ironically and holding out a cup of the yellow swill they liked to call water.

"No, thank you, Philibert. I assume that part of your name is real?"

"Both that and the Montmorency part are mine, sir," he replied, continuing to uphold the façade until it was clear doing so was futile.

"Strange how none of your illustrious family have noticed your absence, isn't it?"

"We don't really get on," lied Phil.

"Then what about friends or allies?" said Claude. "Where are they?"

"I don't really collect them."

"But there was one with you, an old squire, I understand, what of him?"

"Just a hired servant. Dispensable."

"It would appear so: we found no trace of him other than the bite marks he left on your animal, whom by the way we have housed amongst our own."

"I'm sure the horse will be most relieved."

The jailor deposited two chairs in the room. One was elegant with fine carvings etched in the wood. It was extremely heavy to lift and was rather noisily dragged through the iron doors. The second chair looked as if it had recently been the subject of arson. Scorched wooden legs clung helplessly to the battered seat, shedding black chunks of soot every time someone sat down on it. Claude took up position and pointed at Phil to do likewise.

"You, sir, are a ghost," said Claude with an air of frustration. "No one knows who you are or where you came from. Now, tell me why that might be."

"Perhaps you're asking the wrong people."

"It's possible, but I doubt that is the reason. You know what the real reason is, don't you?" said Claude, delivering a facial expression that a parent might use to seek an apology from a child for a crime they already had cast-iron evidence for.

That was it. The game was up. Someone had croaked and blown his cover. Had they got to Annabelle? Or perhaps Chambard had been captured and tortured? Just as Phil was about to spill his guts and confess under the dual pressure of his own guilt and Claude's stare he was rescued.

"Nostradamus has already told us the truth."

"What?!"

"You're a Catholic spy, aren't you?"

"WHAT?!"

"He also said that you would be open to an offer to turn to our side."

"He what?!"

"Oh come on, Philibert, there's no point denying it."

"What?! Why would he say that?"

"You tell me?" said Claude.

It was unclear as to whether Nostradamus was trying to help or hinder him. It's true that Michel would have said anything to save his own backside, but did he really need to save it? Maybe this had been his way out all along. Perhaps Claude had only planned to release Michel if he ratted out his new cellmate. Maybe that was Claude's intention all along? Michel could either offer him the truth and all the stories that went with it, or find an alternative version of the truth that might give Phil a fighting chance. It was hard to process whether he was in a better situation or not.

"Work for us, Philibert," said Claude, "and I'll give you your freedom."

"I'm not a spy."

"Michel said you'd deny it. I guess that's all part of your training."

"No, you don't understand. I'm really a prophet."

"Of course you are!" said Claude sarcastically.

"No, really I am!"

"Then make a prediction."

"I already have. Let me show you."

"I'm not really interested."

"Oh, go on. It's really good."

"Don't care. You're clearly a liar. Michel's information fits with everything that I have witnessed about you. A stranger at my party that no one has ever heard of with a stolen ring and an enquiring nature. You're a spy. I see no other explanation."

"If you knew the truth…you really wouldn't believe it."

"I want you to return to your masters in Paris. I want you to understand all you can about the Queen's intentions regarding the freedom to practise our faith. Information that we need to bring our religious differences to a peaceful conclusion before matters turn nasty. I'm going to give you a few days to think about my offer."

- Chapter 17 -

One Extremely Agitated Boar

A vast party of nobility, huntsmen and hangers-on rode out of Marseille in an eastward direction towards the Var, a densely wooded region swarming with worthy prizes for would be champions. Wild boar, herds of deer, a dozen variety of geese and feral goats were all potential targets.

Against the hunt, the animals' odds of survival were greater than a one-legged Great Dane winning a steeplechase. It was nigh on impossible for a startled creature to outrun an archer on horseback. And hiding was counter-intuitive to an animal who feared for its life. The adrenal function consisted of fright, fight or flight: there wasn't a fourth instinct called 'cower in a big bush and pray they moved on'. The only hope was that the hunters got bored or shot one of the others before they got to you. Not so much survival of the fittest, as survival of the lucky.

Hunting was not, as it might seem to the uninitiated, a random gamble. The hunt didn't just ride off into a forest and sit around waiting for an animal to casually stroll past on a morning jaunt. Hunting was a highly organised and well-planned activity that required the co-ordination and efforts of dozens of people and it was no different today for Claude's hunt.

This was All Souls' Day, November the second, a highlight of the hunting calendar. Today the living celebrated the loved ones they'd lost over the past twelve months. And what better way to glorify their memory than inhumanely butchering the regional game population. Until now no one's final words on their deathbed ever consisted of "Son, I love you. There's one final thing I need to tell you before I die…I need you to kill me a wild goose. A really big one, mind, with huge wings and a really vicious bill."

Every detail of the event had been checked, examined and assessed to ensure the host's reputation was upheld. Claude's hunt had to be a magnificent success and that would only be true if every single guest went home with a heavy carcass and a massive smile. Think of it like a big and bloodied after-party goodie bag.

Leading Claude's group out into the woods were the expert huntsmen and their eager pack of lymers, the meticulously trained hounds that were used to track and locate their prey. While the dogs and their masters did all the hard work, the nobles would gather in a large, temporary camp on the outskirts of the forest. There they would wait for news while idly lazing around a roaring campfire eating breakfast, sharing stories and preparing their weapons. Once a suitable prey had been located, usually by sight, scent or the observation of footprints in the ground, the nobles would gather around to decide if they could be bothered to move or just carry on socialising until a better candidate was presented.

On the rare occasions they did decide to mount up and move out, some more interested in the feasting and drinking than the hunt itself, the hounds, barking with fervent excitement, would be positioned around the animal's location to block any escape routes and tire it out. The lymers would then advance to shrink the animal's zone of comfort. Then and only then did the hunt commence properly.

The hunters coveted one prize above all others, the mighty hart. But not just any hart. Only a male deer classified as a 'hart of ten' would be satisfactory. An exhibit with less than the desired number of lines or points on its antlers was not worthy of hunting and would escape the inevitable slaughter until it grew a little bigger. But catching and killing one with more than ten was no simple task.

There were two accepted methods by which the beast could be hunted. By force or by bow. Hunting by force was the most noble art form and involved eight distinct phases, the last of which was a close-range kill by spear or lance. But because it put the hunter in close proximity to the animal, 'by force' was by far the most dangerous. By bow in contrast meant you spent most of the afternoon up a tree hiding like a wimp and firing arrows indiscriminating from long range.

This was much safer for the archer than it was for the rest of his company. Over the years quite a few nobles had been killed by these wayward arrows. To date no archer had had the guts to claim these victims as legitimate prizes of the hunt and demanded to have their heads neatly mounted above the fireplace. But if you really wanted to prove your worthiness in front of your peers the kill had to be by force and that took far more planning.

And that played perfectly into Chambard's hands.

Thanks to his inside information he knew exactly where the hunt was going and when they'd arrive, which allowed him to wander out into the Var region a few days before they did. After all, they weren't the only ones who needed preparation time. Phil's prophecy called for a 'beast' that would 'rip through Savoie' and cause 'horse to bolt' and 'spear to splinter'. In Chambard's opinion all creatures were beasts. Almost no species liked him and, other than the enjoyment of eating them, the feeling was mutual.

Some unidentified sixth sense compelled dogs to bite him, cats to scratch him, all manner of birds to poop on him, and horses to buck him. No matter what the breed, a collective campaign of hate had been spread across the animal kingdom against him at a sound frequency unavailable to humans.

The only animals worse than horses in Chambard's mind were rats. As one of life's outcasts, a man of no fixed abode, he'd spent a lifetime sleeping rough in field and hovel. He coped with everything about that lifestyle apart from those little, hairy buggers who refused to leave him be. They had no redeemable benefit other than making excellent brushes for cleaning shoes. Given the choice he'd like to go with guinea pig, but they could hardly be defined as beastly. The location made the choice for him. If you wanted a beast, there was only one candidate.

A wild boar.

Boar were hard to hunt. They had a turn of speed way beyond the design of their stumpy bodies and, although a spear expertly thrown at the right region of the body might fell one, they were rarely killed instantly, such was the boar's tenacity to remain breathing. But Chambard didn't have to hunt one. He had to catch one. And after a couple of fruitless days in the field he'd already discovered that that feat was a different challenge altogether.

So far none of his strategies had worked. Trying to reason with one had been highly ineffective. Creeping up behind one quietly in an attempt to mount it at the last moment had also not gone well. After multiple attempts the best he'd managed was the faintest of ankle tackles and a mouthful of forest floor. Coaxing them with a variety of tasty lures had been no good either. Hours he'd wait for one to venture out and devour the pile of mice and eggs he'd left as bait, only to find they'd waited long enough for him to fall asleep before eating the lot and depositing a steaming pile of boar dung as a thankyou note.

Drastic action was required. For most of All Saints' Day, the day before the hunt would sweep through the forest, Chambard had set to work on digging a very large hole. Once the crater was finished he piled thin branches over the top and layered it with foliage so it blended invisibly with the forest floor. Then for the rest of the day he chased families of boar into the area and mostly just knackered himself out.

Acting like a man being chased by a murderous mob, he'd crash unannounced into their midst, shout and scream at the top of his voice, flap his hands like they were on fire and stomp up and down. Then the boar ran, usually faster than him and not in the direction he hoped. At the end of the day he finally succeeded, although success was a relative term. At the bottom of a six-foot-deep hole was one extremely agitated boar. It looked rather more capable of being a sitting duck for an archer than it was ripping through Savoie and making horses bolt.

All night Chambard watched over this disgruntled beast wondering what to do with it next. Two massive teeth protruded from its muscular head. Its eyes shone red in the night, piercing the soul like a beast from the underworld. Its huge, muscular body sat on feeble hind legs as if its evolution never expected threats from behind. If this animal was ever to seek employment it would make a first-class battering ram.

After the boar's initial and obvious displeasure at being held captive in a boar-shaped crypt had waned, it sat on its withered back legs glaring menacingly at its captor as if to taunt him into action and knowing full well that it was fully in control. It hadn't escaped the boar's senses that the human had no weapons, and if he had planned to kill him it would have already happened.

Chambard agreed with the beast's assessment. Success wasn't restricting the beast to a muddy grave, it was releasing the damn thing at a very precise moment and then coercing it into charging at the right person. He considered how long it would take, and whether it was even possible to train a boar. Too long.

ONE EXTREMELY AGITATED BOAR

"Ok," said Chambard unconvincingly. "I'm not going to hurt you."

'Oh sure,' thought the boar. 'Because you humans are all so honest, aren't you? Tell that to my cousin, Bert, whose head is probably being used as a posh jug.'

"I just need to get you on this lead," added Chambard, holding up a piece of cord he'd tied into a loop at one end. It looked far more like a noose than it did a collar.

The boar's expression remained stern.

"So, I'm just going to come down there and place it round your neck, ok? Nothing to worry about."

'If you put so much as a finger in this hole,' thought the boar, 'I will be forced to perforate your face.'

Chambard lowered a toe over the edge of the hole and the boar grunted aggressively, instantly sending the toe back to its starting position. Chambard didn't speak boar, but quite by chance he'd translated the beast's warning entirely accurately.

"I'll come down there when you're asleep," threatened Chambard.

The boar shrugged nonchalantly to indicate his lack of concern.

"Come on, you're smarter than a hairy pig," Chambard scolded himself. "Phil's relying on you. What's the worst that can happen?"

Plenty. Boar attacks were common and painful. Death was a possibility but a more likely side effect was a permanently high-pitched voice and less than the regulation number of fingers. No one had ever reported the best-case scenario, a boar rolling on its back so you could tickle its tummy.

"Just go down there and show him who's boss," Chambard remonstrated with himself. "You're better than a big, hairy pig!"

The boar scoffed, but instantly regretted it. The next moment a fifteen-stone, five-foot human had thrown itself into the hole and body checked the boar with all the finesse of an epileptic wrestler.

*****

The hunt was in full flow. A medium-sized hart was the target. Progress had been delayed so that someone could count the number of points on its antlers. Not easy to do when a deer is rather more fond of hiding or running away than being chased by dogs. There was deep debate over one of its smaller antlers. Was it an independent point or part of one of the other antlers? These things are important. No one wanted the shame of returning home with a nine-antlered deer.

The nobility prepared themselves for the final part of the hunt now all the hard work had been done. All the damned chasing through the forest, getting sweaty and tired, was someone else's job. Like a general showing up at the end of a battle only to find that most of his troops had been slaughtered and the only thing they had to show for it was a rather lovely flag, the nobles were only interested in the highlights.

Lines of falcons, tethered to long, wooden beams, bobbed and squawked excitedly as they heard the assembly of people and horses around them. Blinded by their head caps, their exceptional hearing would be enough to draw them in the right direction. A series of horns echoed through the trees to indicate the position of the huntsmen and the narrowing space of their prey. Men mounted their horses, swung quivers over their backs or grabbed spears from racks.

Claude was assisted onto his steed by his two squires, one of whom was holding a shield in the air for him.

"I don't need a shield, boy. This is a hunt not a fight."

"I think it would be wise, sir."

"Wise? I'll be a laughing stock. The only man frightened to face a moderately sized deer."

"I have been advised it's for your own safely, my lord," said the squire undeterred.

"By whom exactly?"

"Michel."

Claude's expression of jest immediately dissolved. A squire could be ignored, but a seer could not. Particularly if you were the type of person who believed in their power, as he did. Even if there was the smallest risk it would be wise indeed not to ignore it.

"Strange that he did not tell me personally."

"I can't comment on that, sir."

"Are you sure it was Nostradamus?"

"Old bloke, tidy beard, strikes a ridiculous pose every time he says his name…"

Claude grabbed the shield and mounted it on his saddle within close reach in case it should be needed.

"My lord, are you ready?" said Jacques, who was waiting to blow a trumpet to signal to the advanced party that the hunt was on the move.

"Blow away, my boy."

The party trotted off at a casual pace, not wanting to scare away their quarry before they were in reach. Jacques and Claude rode abreast as the others spread out in a perimeter around the kill zone.

"What news of the imposter?" said Jacques.

"I will know tomorrow. Then he will have to choose whether to work with us or perish."

"Are you sure this is the right course of action? If we send him back to Paris he might double-cross us?"

"We'll take precautions to stop that possibility. Recent reprisals against Protestant clergy here in the South tell me the tide is turning. We must learn more of the Queen's intentions and the plans of those who advise the King."

"But what leverage do we have against this man? How do we know he will do as we demand?"

"As I said we will take precautions. You and Annabelle are going, too."

"Me! Go to Paris?" said Jacques, bringing his horse to a temporary and sudden stop.

"Yes."

"But that's highly irregular, my lord: my place lies here."

"You're a soldier, aren't you?"

"Yes, but…"

"And we are at war, are we not? It may not be the type you are used to fighting, but it's a war nonetheless. So be a soldier."

"But Annabelle, why?"

"Because I thought you'd want to be with her. Call it your honeymoon present."

"What use will she be," he said disparagingly.

"Don't underestimate her, Jacques. She's stronger than you realise."

"She's just a woman. No match for a man in any way and with any deed."

"I'd like to see you push a baby out of you," said Claude, immediately finding the flaw in his statement.

One after another a series of loud horn blasts filled their ears. The final push had been signalled.

"Now for the fun part," said Claude, kicking the side of his steed and sending it into a canter.

The hart was on the move. It bounded back and forth between the dense trees as the dogs forced it back into the centre. It was imperative to keep the hart confined and tired to make life easier for the hunter. Claude advanced. The first kill would belong to him. The yapping dogs surrounded the tired beast and all that remained was for one final blow to put the beast out of its misery. Claude raised his spear ready to strike.

ONE EXTREMELY AGITATED BOAR

A loud and angry grunt broke his concentration. A second later a wild boar careered through the bushes and into their midst. It didn't stop. It was much more interested in escape than confrontation. To the hunt's surprise there was a rope tied around its neck and the long tail of it dragged along the ground behind it like an untethered boat leaving port. If they hadn't been distracted by the unusual behaviour of the hog they might have been more aware of the fat man poleaxed to the floor on the other side of the bushes nursing rope burns on his hands and panting heavily.

Chambard had failed. The hunt's reaction had been intrigue rather than chaos. After days of trials and tribulations to get the boar where he wanted at the right moment, the beast had broken free. The catalyst for this was evident. Above Chambard's flattened frame a hart of epic size was blocking out the light. The significance of the number of points on its antlers was lost on him because his attention was drawn to the four hooves which were about to use him as a doormat.

The hart leapt magnificently over Chambard and the hedge into the middle of the hunt. For a moment everything was peaceful as the hart grabbed their attention. Unconcerned by the situation, it firstly posed serenely by rearing its head in the air and letting out a deafening call. Then it got angry. Whether it was the commotion of the boar's retreat, the realisation that the men were attacking one of its own or just its own cantankerous disposition, it bowed its head, raked the ground with its hooves and bolted with speed towards the hunters. Some of the horses bolted, depositing surprised mounts to the ground and painfully onto their rear ends.

The hart took aim at the first in line. One of the party raised a spear to defend Claude from the onslaught only to see it shatter like a pane of glass against the deer's tough hide. Quick-witted, Claude raised the shield stashed on his saddle just in time. An antler pierced the wooden shield, coming to rest inches from Claude's eyes, before being ripped from his grasp as the hart charged through the throng.

- Chapter 18 -

A Bump in the Night

The formula to a successful horror movie is very simple. There are several key components. Firstly it's imperative to place a hysterical, naïve, and attractive young woman in an inexplicable position of harm with nothing more for protection than a faulty flashlight and a skimpy Halloween costume. Set it at night to make it even more spooky, preferably one with plenty of fog and a full moon that looks larger than if it were viewed through the Hubble Telescope. Next terrorise said young woman with multiple suggestive signs that something horrifying wants to kill her for no other reason than she once spurned the monster's advances or said something nasty about it.

The location must be the sort of everyday place that any member of the general public might find themselves in. Maybe a hotel in the middle of nowhere, the business idea of a person desperate to bankrupt themselves. Or a graveyard, because who doesn't like to spend their free time in one: great spot for a picnic. Or maybe a mental institution, even though if you stopped a hundred people in the street not a single person could point to their nearest one. Or perhaps a deserted space station, one that bears almost no similarities to any of the actual linked dustbin cans we've fired into orbit over the past fifty years. Or place the protagonist in a small forest just outside Lyon.

Then fill the plot with as many implausible scenes as possible, particularly those where the lead character lacks any basic common sense whatsoever. Of course it's logical to follow a suspected mass murderer into a spooky house where strangely none of the lights work. Who wouldn't try to help if they saw an unrecognisable body lying on the floor who looked anything but injured? And yes, anyone who was being chased by a murderous axe-wielding fiend would do so in high heels in a style of running that resembled someone with their legs tied together at the ankles.

Finally make absolutely nothing in the protagonist's life work. Mobile phones, car engines, window frames, shotguns, speedboats, keys, shoes, speech, and lifts will all catastrophically fail for no apparent reason other than you hired the world's most incompetent handyman. Include an eerie violin-based soundtrack, lots of false alarms, plenty of blood and hey presto, instant classic.

It was just this sort of film that Gabriel enjoyed and it was safe to say she'd learnt nothing useful from them.

The lights on the Renault made one final flicker before plunging the small forest into darkness. While the car's heart had stopped beating its body still rocked gently from side to side. What horror was about to befall her? Were desperate mobs marauding through Limonest in search of vital resources to mitigate the apocalypse? Had bird flu turned everyone into murderous, bloodthirsty ghouls? Or was it just the doggers again? She knew which one sent shivers down her spine the most. No one wanted to witness the horror of a wrinkly old bum going up and down in the air while another hideous creature moaned desperately underneath it.

An owl hooted menacingly. Was that its natural late-night call or had someone recruited the secretive bird to add a realistically haunting sound bed to their cruel game? Whatever happened next she knew it was best to stay in the car. In these situations, never go and look. Doing so would be as predictable as attempting to retrieve a ball of wool from a pack of angry kittens and losing all your skin.

A BUMP IN THE NIGHT

In the rear-view mirror a flicker of light caught her eye. It was coming from within the caravan. What did she do now? The caravan contained all the vital supplies she needed to survive for at least another afternoon. If they were stolen she'd have to replace them, and that meant potential contact with those with the infection. Surely a prepper was meant to be prepared for such events. It was time to crack open the bravery. She grabbed the golf club from the back seat, ignored everything she'd ever seen in the movies and quietly eased the car door open.

Before stepping out into the drizzle she zipped up her extravagantly and expensive fake fur coat and unfurled the ear warmers on her trapper-style hat. If there were gangs of hoodlums waiting for her in the shadows, she wouldn't take long to be spotted in white wellington boots that illuminated every footstep. She squelched the three or four metres towards the caravan, stopping at the door to listen for signs of intruders. There were no voices, but she thought she heard some overaggressive sipping. Out of nowhere a bat dive-bombed her position and she spontaneously reacted by burying the end of the golf club into the mud with the force of a thousand tee shots. Whatever or whoever was in the caravan they couldn't be worse than blood sucking bats.

Making a noise that was part squirrel being electrocuted and part reversing delivery lorry, she burst through the fragile plastic door brandishing the golf club in front of her. A large lump of Beaujolais mud was stuck to the end, rendering her weapon useless other than to returf a lawn. Under the dim light of a mobile phone Ally Oldfield and Antoine Palomer were sitting at the caravan's removable table drinking mugs of tea.

"Whatever you want, take it, just don't harm me…I'm too pretty!" yelled Gabriel, still inadvertently flicking mud around the place and unable to open her eyes to the gruesome fate that awaited her.

Antoine and Ally looked up casually from their drinks. It was difficult to be surprised by an event you'd seen coming for the last thirty minutes. Having made the decision to seek sanctuary in the only dry place they could find, the wrecked caravan, they'd already seen the young blonde woman in the car huddled up in a ball. Five minutes ago they'd watched her emerge from the Renault like the world's smallest wookie was setting off for a spot of early morning golf practice. In fact not only had they seen it unfold they'd even planned for it.

"Cup of tea?" said Ally, holding a third mug out towards her.

Gabriel slowly opened one eye to find a smartly dressed pensioner and a stout, sour-looking middle-aged woman offering her refreshments. That didn't happen in the movies.

"Tea?" she said in surprise. "Where did you get that?"

"Second cupboard to the right under the sink," replied Ally.

Gabriel, desperate for anything that might lower her raging blood pressure, grabbed the mug and retreated a few paces. "But it's got milk in it."

"Sorry," replied Antoine. "Obviously we didn't know how you took it, what with not knowing who you are and all that. If you prefer it without I can make you another one."

"No, it's fine. I always drink it with milk…but where did you get it from? Are the shops still open?"

"Um…the fridge," said Antoine opening a door near to him to present a fairly well stocked mini-fridge that doubled up as additional light for the caravan.

"I have a fridge!" Gabriel replied in shock.

"What are you doing out here?" asked Ally, noticing almost at once that Gabriel was out of place, whatever it was she was trying to accomplish.

"Me? What are you doing here!?" replied Gabriel, batting the question back at them. "This is my caravan."

"Forgive our impertinence my dear," replied Antoine apologetically. "We were seeking somewhere to spend the night and happened upon what we thought was an empty and unlocked caravan."

"Oh, you disgust me. At your age!" blurted Gabriel, pulling the facial expression that only a young person can make when they imagine old people having sex. "You two were going to bump uglies, weren't you?"

Antoine had absolutely no idea what that meant and turned to Ally hopefully for interpretation.

"No, we most certainly weren't. It's quite simple to understand, even for a vacuous mind like yours. We came here because my colleague," she raised a finger and pointed across the table, "said he knew someone in town that might help us. We found to our cost that he was not at home, which left us with nowhere to stay."

If Gabriel had known what the word 'vacuous' meant she might not have accepted the compliment quite so readily.

"Most unusual," said Antoine. "Maybe he's already left town to avoid this modern-day plague that has descended on us."

"Maybe you've got it!" exclaimed Gabriel, immediately spitting the last mouthful of tea into the sink in case it was poisoned with flu and retreating to the other end of the caravan again. "Right, jog on, the pair of you."

"I can assure you we do not have the flu. We escaped Lyon before the cordon was raised."

"Why didn't you check into a hotel, then?"

"It was two o'clock in the morning," replied Ally.

"Plus," added Antoine conversationally, "we're being hunted by someone and desire to keep a low profile."

"So you decided to steal my caravan instead," replied Gabriel indignantly.

"We clearly haven't stolen it, otherwise you wouldn't be stood in it, would you? We're just asking you if we can stay in it for the night," replied Ally who had taken an immediate dislike to this petite stranger based on two fundamental characteristics: she was extremely pretty and she wasn't Einstein.

"What will you give me in exchange?" she replied, remembering the second amendment of the Millennials Charter, 'Thou shall not do something for nothing'.

"Give you?" blurted Ally, reacting spontaneously.

"Yeah."

"Young lady, we thought, given the current situation around the world, that this was the time when other humans might rise up in collective protection of their fellow man with acts of charity," said Antoine, affecting a stern tone.

"Er…no," replied Gabriel in a sarcastic tone. Charity was for annual telethons and only then when they sent Taylor Swift to some god forsaken country that no one had heard of to highlight that everyone who lived there needed help because they were considerably shorter than she was. Based on their personal situations, if anyone deserved charity out of the three of them it was probably her.

"We've already paid you," mumbled Ally under her breath. "We've shown you where your own fridge is."

"Huh, I would have found it eventually."

"Young lady, what is your name?" asked Antoine politely.

"Gabriel Janvier."

"Oh. How curious," replied Antoine, making a connection that no one else understood.

Both women challenged his reaction with vacant expressions.

"I think we've just found our angel," he added to himself.

"Listen, you dirty old man I'm a fully paid-up member of the 'me, too' fan club and I won't put up with any form of sexual harassment."

"I meant angel in a purely biblical context. The Angel Gabriel was a protective figure who carried people from danger. Look, if you help us, as I believe you will, I will pay you ten thousand euros."

"What?" said Ally in dismay. "Have you lost your mind?!"

"No. This young lady has a place where we can sleep tonight and a car that can take us to Mâcon tomorrow: I would say her usefulness should be well rewarded."

"But ten grand! That would pay for a week in Monaco at a five-star hotel and a minute ago you were advocating the whole charity thing."

"Done," replied Gabriel before the grumpy woman could talk him out of it. "Although I'd rather not have cash if it's possible, the concept of shopping might not exist by the end of next week. I'll give you a list of things I want not exceeding that total."

"You've changed your tune," grunted Ally. "A minute ago you were worried we might have the flu."

"For ten grand you can have Ebola for all I care."

"Agreed," replied Antoine. "Now if you don't mind I think I need some rest. It's not every day you get burgled, blown up, forced to run away and have to spend your very first night inside a caravan. We set off first thing tomorrow."

*****

The next morning it took three distinct operations to get the beige relic of the French motor industry up and running. Renault cars had a dodgy reputation for reliability before they even rolled off the production line, but this one had seen forty years' painful service. The battery, whose main purpose over the last week had been to power a laptop, was stone dead. Although they had jump leads they were a bit redundant as none of them stretched the quarter mile to the nearest car.

Sometimes all you needed in adversity was a big dollop of experience. Antoine used all of his to remember an old solution to the problem. Cars were a passion and old cars in particular. He'd spent many a Sunday afternoon with his arms covered in grease, a wrench in hand and a battered car above him waiting patiently to be resuscitated. To him the old Renault was a classic; the other two thought it was a relic. On his instructions, and after considerable bickering, the two ladies were invited to jack the car up above the mud to allow Antoine to wrap a tow rope around the car's wheel. After the keys were turned in the ignition the ladies gave the rope a pull to spin the tyre. Within seconds the motion kicked the battery and the engine into life. Their bitter complaining about broken nails and being told what to do was only momentarily halted by the sight of the smoke billowing out of the exhaust.

The second operation was far messier. The heavy rain and soft ground had combined to sink the back-end of the car deep into the mud, not helped by the weight of the caravan and the extra occupants last night. There were no special tricks up Antoine's sleeve for this one. After some leverage had been placed under the back axle the girls were instructed to push while Antoine tried to rev them away from the mire. Eventually they succeeded but not before Gabriel and Ally had been painted an interesting shade of brown.

The final operation was the most complicated and unexpected, at least for two of them.

"Right, we're finally ready," said Ally trying to brush as much mud out of her dress as she could. She'd already spent two days wearing it and prayed a day would soon come when she wasn't, preferably today.

"Did you call Bernard again?" asked Antoine.

"Three times already. It just keeps going to voicemail. Let's just go there on the off chance. I desperately need a change of clothes and a brand new outlook on life."

"Let's see what we can do. Right, Gabriel, if you would," said Antoine, pointing her towards the driver's seat.

"What?"

"If you'd be so kind as to drive."

"Drive? Why?"

"I think you preppers say G.O.O.D."

"It's bloody not good! You're both flipping crazy if you think I'm going anywhere with you weirdos," replied Gabriel, sporting a face of thunder.

"G.O.O.D. is slang for 'get out of dodge'. You're not up on the prepper lingo yet, then?" said Antoine.

"The lingo isn't the issue, you are!"

"Surely you understood I was not just paying you for the car, but for you to also drive it."

"Antoine, a word please," said Ally, beckoning him over for a quiet one-on-one. "Why do you want the stupid bimbo to come with us? Trust no one, you said. We can both drive, we don't need her."

"We definitely do. I can't explain it, but something tells me meeting her was no accident. I'm sure she'll be useful."

"How? Are you expecting us to run into a dangerous mob of emojis?"

"Emojis…is that a type of monkey?"

"It doesn't matter. She's useless. Look at her, she can't even survive here for more than a week and I can literally see civilisation on the other side of those trees. This has gone too far, Antoine. I was struggling to understand why I was here, but there's even less reason for her to be."

"Sometimes you just have to accept advice. Can you do that?"

"Not well, no."

"Listen, I think having her with us will be good for you," replied Antoine. "You need to spend more time with diverse types of people…in fact people in general."

"Baristas are people," she said in an argument that only shone a brighter light on the problem. "Once we've found Bernard, I'm done with both of you. Understand?"

"If you say so."

They returned to their original conversation.

"Gabriel, I'm delighted to say that we've had a chat and agree you should join us."

"I'm not going. There's literally nothing on earth that you can say or do to convince me. Nothing!"

"I'll give you twenty thousand euros and a new car."

"Done."

- Chapter 19 -

The Journey North

"Phil, are you there?" shouted Chambard from his customary position just below the prison window.

"Where else would I be?" replied Philibert.

"Garderobe."

"That's a bucket in the corner, and by the pungent smell, very much still in here. How did it go?"

"That depends on your point of view," said Chambard, still showing the visible signs of his wrestling match with an uncooperative and oversized boar.

"But did the prophecy come true?" Phil asked suggestively with a wink that no one could see.

"Um…yes."

"Ha ha, great job. You've really outdone yourself this time, my old friend. To be honest, I thought it might be too much for…"

"You misunderstand," interrupted Chambard. "It had nothing to do with me! Yet it happened anyway. Everything you predicted. Spears splintered, horses ran about like four-legged idiots, and an antler went straight through Claude Savoie's shield almost removing his eyeball."

"Really," replied Phil dumbfounded.

"YES!" shouted Chambard a little too loudly given his visit hadn't been sanctioned.

Of all the possible outcomes Phil expected, feared and hoped might play out, this was not one of them. What were the chances of him nailing an actual prophecy on only his second attempt with no more than a week's worth of training. Pretty skinny. A little part of him wished that Michel was around to share the success. Although given how many of Michel's rules he'd systematically broken to achieve it perhaps he might not have shared Phil's excitement.

The worst thing about the good news was that it didn't even matter now anyway. All the training had been for nothing. Since Claude had offered him another route out of his situation there had been no need for Chambard to do any of it. And that was all thanks to Michel's unexpected interference.

"He'll have to release you now," called Chambard from the muddy trench below the window. "I mean I would if someone gave me a prophecy that came true immediately."

"Hmmm, about that," replied Phil, wondering how best to break it. "I actually didn't give it to him."

"What?!"

"Things have changed a little since our last meeting."

"How?"

"Claude thinks I'm a Catholic spy. He wants me to go to Paris to gather intelligence for his side. He's coming back today to hear my answer."

"Are you saying I spent two days in a forest trying to secure the services of an aggressively hairy pig for nothing."

"Yes. Sorry."

"Just so you know I have a slipped disc, three chewed fingers and a recurring nightmare about being mugged by a pack of angry piglets."

"It's not my fault, Chambard, I couldn't exactly tell you from here, could I?"

"No, I guess not. What are you going to do now?" asked Chambard.

"I have to say yes."

"Why? There must be another way out."

"I can't see one and I really need to get out of here. I'm starting to develop an unhealthy addiction to bedbugs and I've found myself communicating with rodents, and more worryingly them with me. Can't be healthy."

"No, it can't."

"I'll say yes but I'm going to make one demand as part of the deal."

"A one-way ticket to Scotland?"

"No."

"A request for a short delay before you travel to Paris so you can care for your dying mother? A decade or so should do it!"

"No, but actually that's a good idea."

"It would be if your mother wasn't already dead," said Chambard knowing full well his comments wouldn't cause offence. Much time had passed under the bridge since that terrible spring in Aix.

"Indeed."

"What's the demand, then?"

"That you accompany me. Then we can work out what we do when we get there."

True to his word, Claude arrived exactly on cue. He appeared somewhat more nervous than he had on his last visit, perhaps as a result of his recent stag-related near-death experience. In Claude's opinion the incident with the hart wasn't the most concerning part: after all, moments like that could be expected if you'd hunted for as many years as he had. What really perplexed him was how Michel had predicted it all through his message. He'd tried to ask Michel after the event, but the seer had completely disappeared, presumably to avoid the scrutiny of the bishops fully alerted to his activities.

As far as Claude was concerned it was just more evidence of Nostradamus's unique talent and that played into Philibert's hands, even if it wasn't immediately obvious. If Claude had known that the squire had not got the message from Michel, and rather from Chambard, as was the case, he might not have been quite so malleable.

He readily agreed to Phil's terms and granted permission for Chambard to join the journey to Paris. The rest of the deal was clear. They would return to a royal court they were never part of in the first place to learn what they could from a Queen they'd never met in order to discover intentions they didn't understand. When free to do so they would return to brief the Huguenot leaders of the outcome. Jacques would escort them to the capital and they would routinely liaise with him and disclose all intelligence as and when it was discovered.

But it wasn't just Jacques going with them.

Quite unexpectedly, Annabelle would also accompany them on the journey. Phil had mixed feelings about this revelation. On the upside he enjoyed her company and so far had suppressed any affections for her. On the downside she might just cause an unwelcomed distraction to their ultimate strategy, fooling everybody. It was only a small negative compared to the massive, elephant-sized one that sat in the corner of the room sporting an irritated look on its face.

No one in Paris *was* expecting their return.

They couldn't be because they'd never been there. In fact in all of Chambard and Phil's travels, Paris was one place they actively avoided. There were enough conmen and thieves in that city without them competing for the same prizes. It was a much simpler strategy to work the smaller towns whose inhabitants were more gullible and unsuspecting.

Now they had no choice. Both the location and the scam would be unfamiliar. They'd found themselves in the confusing position of needing to double-cross the double-crossers. And that would require a scam so complex that even they weren't sure who they were playing it on.

Fortunately they'd have plenty of time to figure it out. It took the fastest postal rider as much as two weeks of continual riding to cross between the two cities. Their convoy of riders and accompanying coaches might take as much as three to four weeks.

In sixteenth-century France, travellers could be categorised into three groups. Armies travelled the furthest: sometimes for thousands of miles and frequently only in one direction. Those journeys were made on foot and there was limited time and inclination to stop to take in the scenery or write a postcard home, particularly when someone with psychopathic tendencies bullied you into every footstep. Depending on the location of the battle, and as a result of poor-quality rations, unreadable foreign road signs and mud that came up to your kneecaps, the journey was often so horrendous you were quite excited about dying when you got to the end of it.

The second group consisted of everyday folk. Travel to them meant going to the market, usually at the end of the road. Not a long road either. Any thought of locations further afield were the stuff of myth and legend. They'd heard of places like England and Spain because news had spread that the people who lived there had a nasty habit of wanting to invade them. But in the public conscience they were as mythical as Quivira or Atlantis. Peasants couldn't pick them out on a map, or comprehend the concept of a map that didn't have a scale of one-to-one. Most people were born, raised, worked and died in the very same house. It was a time in history when immigration was only ever the result of someone from Andorra getting drunk and taking a wrong turn.

The third group included people like Chambard. Unlike the first group, who tended to go long distances but only once, and the second group who didn't go anywhere at all, Chambard had been almost everywhere. He'd had to. Most towns weren't keen on seeing him return. He'd travelled extensively throughout France, some of Italy, most of Spain, and even parts of the Low Countries – most of these quite by accident.

If you were a wanderer sometimes you inadvertently wandered over borders. It would be years before someone thought it sensible to erect a big sign in the ground with names and numbers on it. It would be pointless doing it now. The world was so tumultuous, borders tended to change from one day to the next. Travellers only noted the passage from one country to another because locals shrugged their shoulders a lot, particularly when you asked them where you were.

Chambard and Phil travelled from one town to the next identifying the most suitable mark to corrupt in the knowledge that news of their scams weren't likely to follow them. It was a planned and erratic behaviour that only they truly understood. A day after Phil's release the journey they set off on was quite different from what they were used to. It would be in one go and they certainly weren't in control of it. It would be arduous, slow and require them to invent the concept of the 'travel game' to pass the time.

The roads were almost exclusively tracks of mud, about as suitable for carriages as a colander was as a drinking vessel. Sometimes they might strike lucky and find themselves following the now almost unnoticeable route of the Roman roads that originally linked the most important communities of their empire more than a millennium ago. Horses could travel on both at a decent speed if nothing untoward impeded their progress. This was almost never the case. Weather would affect the animals' moods and the progress of the coaches was constantly hindered by broken axles or wheels that got stuck in streams of thick mud.

It was in one of these coaches that Philibert and Chambard were forced to travel. A rickety, four-wheeled carriage with a round, white fabric roof open to the elements at the front and back. The view to the front was obstructed by the back-ends of two horses, so mostly they looked backwards to watch their past disappear over the horizon.

If the journey had been in June it would have been a rather pleasant way to travel. But it wasn't. The bitter midwinter winds swarmed in through the coach's rear entrance like a plague of locusts. It clung tight to their skin before shooting out the front end and being recycled to the back for another pass. The roof fabric was not strong enough to protect against the constant showers. The rain collected on its roof and intermittently dripped through onto their heads or down their necks.

To Chambard's obvious joy, Jacques had decided he didn't want them riding horseback in case they decided to abscond. He was right, too, because this was the very first 'escape plan' they'd considered, rapidly scrapped before they'd even left Marseille. In order to keep her from fraternising with the enemy, Annabelle travelled in a separate coach at the other end of their convoy. The rest of the party, which consisted of a dozen of Jacques servants and comrades, either rode their own mounts or drove the pairs of horses that pulled the coaches.

Phil had never travelled like this before. His journeys with Chambard had generally been on foot. Even though they were still a rarity, Phil had seen coaches many times as they trundled past him. One day, he thought, he'd gather enough funds to buy his own. A pipe dream that certainly didn't resemble the reality of their current journey in which they were prisoners in all but name.

Almost a month would be endured like this. Riding for fifteen hours a day, stopping frequently to help remove the coaches from ruts in the road or to fix damage sustained, occasionally stopping at an inn or water trough to rest the horses. Every town looked the same. Poverty-stricken locals, just glad to see someone new who might buy their goods or offer some meagre token of charity, would surround their party every time they stopped. The rest of the journey consisted of conversation. Week one was the easiest.

"Do you remember Agen?" said Chambard, attempting to pass the time as he watched another impoverished town, identical to the last, pass by the rear exit of their coach.

"How could I forget that one!?" said Phil.

"That was when we used to pull the orphaned child routine," added Chambard fondly, a little smile breaking out on his face.

"The first trick you ever taught me, it must have been shortly after I met you. What was I, about fourteen?"

"Yeah, but fortunately for us, you looked about eleven. Skinny, malnourished urchin you were back then."

"Agen wasn't our finest moment using that scam, though, was it?" laughed Phil, remembering the circumstances. "As I recall the bishop we pulled it on was a little too fond of young boys and showed me the type of charity I wasn't expecting. Dirty bugger."

"It was hilarious to see you break character so quickly. You thought it was better to announce that you were playing him, rather than wait until he played with you! Taught you a valuable lesson, though, didn't it?"

"Yes, don't trust bishops," replied Phil immediately and quite seriously.

"Yeah," chuckled Chambard. "Not just that, though. It also taught you how it felt to get caught."

"Not something I ever want to repeat."

"Exactly and since then we haven't, well, not until Marseille of course. We learnt that in order to convince a mark you have to know their strengths and weaknesses. If we'd known about the bishop's sick habits we wouldn't have pulled that scam on him. Always be one step in front of the enemy, that's what I've taught you. Everyone is corruptible, if you know which buttons to press."

"And that's my worry. We don't know anything about Catherine de Medici or the young King. We're playing in a league we've never been tested in."

"I know. It's the ultimate challenge. You and I have always tried to stretch ourselves. To see if we can cut it against the most powerful people in this world, to fool them into believing that we belong amongst them. To prove that two insignificant peasants can outsmart men of academia, position and power."

"But the royal family. That's something different altogether," replied Philibert.

"There's no greater test, Phil. If you pull this one off you'll become a legend."

"I don't want to be a legend, Chambard. I just want to have the opportunity to live my life as they do. The freedom to study, marry, own property, learn, and make a difference."

"But you will make a difference if you pull this off. For generations to come the improvised and oppressed will know your name and you'll open the sluice gates for all to follow."

"How?"

"Because the common man will see what is possible. It might not happen immediately, but I predict that in, say, a couple of hundred years from now the masses will revolt in collective anger at the monarchy's excess. I wouldn't be surprised if the poor miserable ones don't overthrow the royals completely."

"Maybe I should write a prophecy about that," replied Phil smiling. "If the cosmic energy is in agreement of course! One step at a time. I think we might be running before we can walk. At the moment we don't have the first idea of how we are going to get out of this mess."

The situation was complicated. It was way beyond anything they'd tried before. There were multiple marks who needed to be tricked for them to come out on top.

Claude was sending them to Paris for information and so they would have to convince him that they were giving him some. But when they arrived at court and no one recognised them, it would be very obvious that Phil was no spy. So they'd need a way to keep Jacques from breathing down their necks. In order to keep that ruse going, they'd need another scam to prove their usefulness to the Queen or face a terrible death if they failed.

"What are our options?" asked Philibert. "You're the expert on convincers."

"What about pig in a poke?"

"It's a classic but what is the Queen of France going to want that she doesn't already have? Pig in a poke only works if you know their innermost desires. And even then it's a tough one to pull off."

"Foreign envoy?"

"Would be effective if we knew who the envoys were so we could clone their identities, which we don't. Plus France is at peace: envoys don't just pop round for cosy chats."

"What about pigeon drop?"

"I'm guessing we'll need an element of that trick, there will definitely be a role for you to be the pigeon, but we're not trying to take anything from them so the whole of that routine won't work."

"Magic medicine," suggested Chambard, scrolling through the long index of scams memorised in his brain. Some he'd learnt, some he'd invented and some were ideas yet to be attempted.

"Who's ill?"

"I hear on the wind that the King is a sickly child, too weak to gain the respect of the nobles. Some say he's an idiot with the mental capacity of a sparrow."

"But what medicine are we offering?" said Phil.

"Who says it needs to be an actual medicine? You were going to convince Claude with a prophecy: why can't you do the same with the King?"

"But if I predict that the boy is going to get better, you can't really fake that."

"No, but who says the Queen wants him to get better?"

"You've lost me. He's her son, of course she does."

"That's not what I've heard. I understand she's quite the megalomaniac, wants to rule France in her own way. Perhaps we could predict what she wants to hear: that's how a con works after all."

"So we predict that her son isn't well enough to take the throne?"

"Exactly."

"I suppose it's possible. I'd need to know more about the Queen, though, before I wrote a prophecy down. And you'd still have to make it come true," he replied.

"As long as you keep all reference to animals out of it we'll be fine."

"I'll do my best."

"Why don't you talk to Annabelle? Given the circles she moves in she must know more about the Queen."

"I suspect she will try to seek me out at some point on the trip."

"Then we have a plan. Only one piece of the puzzle to put into place," said Chambard.

"How do I get in front of the Queen in the first place?"

"Right."

"I can't just turn up unannounced, proclaiming to be some talented seer when no one has ever heard of me before. Our heads will be propping up the end of pikestaffs before you can say, 'Excuse me, is the Queen in?'"

They sat in silence for a bumpy mile or two as they contemplated which short con would unlock the longer one.

"How attached are you to your name?" asked Chambard.

"I'm the man of a thousand faces, my name can be anything you want it to be."

"Perhaps it's time to retire Montmorency."

"I'm not following you."

"Anne de Montmorency is still in the court, isn't he?"

"I don't know, but we'll soon find out."

"If he is, maybe this is the ideal time to return his ring."

"Oh that's risky. 'I'm terribly sorry that I've had your prized heirloom in my possession for more than two years, but I just happened to be passing.' It'll need some thought."

"Don't forget he spent quite a long period in captivity after the Battle of St. Quentin, so you couldn't have returned it then anyway."

"Let me think about it," said Philibert.

The passage of conversation between the two continued in this vein for much of the first week. Ideas were scrutinised and often discarded. If they were kept on the table then detailed discussions were conducted to agree how it might play out and what information they still needed. If they still liked the idea after that they'd role play it between them to practise their approach and highlight all the possible barriers.

The monotony of this scheming was broken in the second week by the meandering distraction of anecdotes or stories of their various exploits. They relived the story of Ville-France in which they stole the brass church bell by replacing it with one made of clay painted yellow. They'd successfully convinced the clergy that they were experts there to service it. They recounted the great chicken scandal of fifteen-fifty-one a scheme that involved Chambard pretending to have the plague and forcing the whole town of Rouen to be sealed off. Phil rounded up all of the poultry that lived outside the town's walls and sold them to the next village. The only downside was having to wait months for Chambard to 'recover'.

By week three the topics of discussion became stretched. In a possible sign of madness the questions being posed had absolutely nothing to do with their past or current plots. There were hour-long debates about 'why dogs never walk in their own poo, when humans seem incapable of avoiding it', and 'which came first: botulism or the plague?' and 'if a horse mated with a cow and had babies would they be called hows or courses'.

And even those conversations ran dry by week four, making room for long, uncomfortable periods of silence and an increasing dislike for the person sitting opposite. Fortunately this deadlock was broken by a woman determined to talk to one of them.

- Chapter 20 -

Poverty

The town of Nemours had fallen on particularly hard times. A difficult summer had succumbed to a harsh autumn and an even tougher winter, currently raging around them in full blizzard. Snow lay in thick heaps on the forest canopies that encircled the town, and disgruntled livestock foraged amongst the frozen sod for the merest sign of something edible. Along the road only a few of the icicle-inflicted wooden houses had the welcoming sight of wispy clouds from the tops of their chimneys. The rest huddled together to retain an ounce of insulation.

The road, if you could call it that, with its deep ridges and fractured craters that made the coaches shake irregularly and without warning, followed the Loing River as it carved the town in two. On its banks an intimidating stone castle with a central keep and four rounded towers advertised its confrontational history through its reinforced defences and damaged stonework. In the shadow of the keep the recently completed wooden spire of the church stretched impressively into the sky like a beacon that no one wanted to follow.

The coaches pulled up in front of a small inn adjacent to the castle to allow the horses a much-needed rest. The sun, slung low in the west, was in its last throes of daylight, four o'clock in the afternoon by Phil's reckoning, and this wouldn't be their last stop for the day. As soon as the coach pulled up and the men dismounted to set about their responsibilities, Chambard and Phil alighted from the relative comfort of their coach to stretch their legs and take in their surroundings.

A subdued and dejected procession of local people gathered around them. The company certainly hadn't had it easy on their journey from Marseille. Food was limited to what they'd brought or could purchase along the route. Sleep had been difficult and uncomfortable. The demons of winter had been an irritation rather than a genuine threat to life. But here the people had not been so lucky. It was the first week of December and desperation had gouged its mark on the faces of men, women and children.

The arrival of travellers to the town presented them a tiny window of opportunity. If they got there first then perhaps they might find charity from those more fortunate than themselves. A small loaf, a coin, or even perhaps, in the rarest of circumstances, employment. Traders and tanners joined smithies and simple labourers in a cacophony of boisterous shouting in an attempt to gain the attention of Jacques' men. The healthier and fitter young men didn't even wait to be asked, immediately helping to lift and shift supplies, or jostling to be the first to tend the horses in the belief their assistance would be rewarded.

Around them old women in tattered rags and faces ravaged by a lifetime of just surviving, held out timid hands in search of a miracle. Most were no older than forty but would easily be mistaken for pensioners should they have lived in more affluent times. Waifish children, who by rights should have been free to run and play without pressure or burden, sat shivering on heaps of frozen mud weeping from the hunger that invaded their bellies. Their malnourished limbs barely had the strength to hold up their tiny bodies, and all over their skin the marks of disease and ill health were universal.

A small girl, no more than two years of age, toddled alone through the crowd. Lumps of dirt and animal faeces were matted between locks of beautiful blonde curls. Tears rolled down her face, but her mouth made no sound. Even at this tender age she'd learnt that wailing had no effect on the hearts of men and would only result in sapping her energy further. Where her family were, or whether any still survived, was neither an obvious nor an important question on the lips of the swarm of human catastrophe that battled selfishly to be the lucky ones to gain favour. Almost everyone ignored her. Helpless, lost and alone, just another disposable soul from the ranks of an invisible army that counted in the millions.

Annabelle rubbed her eyes in disbelief. From the safety of her privileged position at the back of the coach she witnessed a scene from another world. The real world. A world where life and death played out in front of her very eyes and no one so much as blinked. A world where survival was acquired only by those willing to step over a neighbour to reach it or by nothing more random than an encounter with fate. God had already forsaken these people, but what broke Annabelle's heart most was the realisation that so had those with the means to fix it. She watched the small girl with a mixture of fascination and dismay. Every fragile step the girl took drew her instinctively towards a small crowd that had gathered in a circle by the bank of the river.

More people forced their way towards it, barging through the toddler as if she was nothing more than an obstacle. Whatever was happening down by the river it was calling to them like a subliminal noticeboard of hope posted on their hearts. Annabelle watched from a distance before intrigue eventually got the better of her. Jacques had insisted that she was not allowed to leave the coach when they were in a populated area, but rules were meant to be broken, and as he'd disappeared inside the inn for his own refreshment it was worth the risk. She carefully descended from the coach by the rear exit.

The black and white scenery suddenly had an injection of colour. She held up her brightly coloured gown, intricately embroidered with fine silver thread and beautiful blue fabric, to avoid the hem dragging along the frozen ground. It was a divine sight for the villagers. An angel had fallen from the heavens and was carefully floating along amongst them. For a split second they forgot about their own strife and were held captive by the explosion to their senses.

The crowd parted like a hot knife sliding through butter as almost without thinking they made way for her. In the centre of the melee she watched as two men she recognised distributed items from a dirty sack. Small gold coins, trinkets of fine craftsmanship, silks, small hunting weapons and dried beans in small pouches.

"Don't push, you'll all get something if there's time," said Chambard as he carefully chose the item from his bag that most suited the individual in front of him. Tools and weapons for men of working age, precious items easily traded for food to the women, and warm garments for the children.

Soon the sack was empty and the charity came to an abrupt halt. Phil informed the crowd, who reluctantly dispersed, to see if any other member of the company was equally sympathetic to their cause. Strangely none of them wanted to engage with Annabelle: something unworldly was warding them away. It was only after the crowd dispersed that Phil was aware of her presence.

"Oh it's you," he said, greeting her warmly.

"What were you doing?" she asked.

"Helping those less fortunate than us."

"For free?"

"Did you see any of them carrying purses?"

"No," she replied, genuinely confused by it all. "What is this place?"

"This place. It has the same name as every town we've been through. Poverty. Population decreasing daily."

"I've never seen anything like it."

"Then you haven't seen your own country. This is France. Not the France of privilege and parties. Not the France of hunting for pleasure rather than food. This is the terrible reality of everyday France for everyday people. Real France beyond the fake bubble you're used to."

"How do people survive here?"

"They don't. They die."

"But why don't they do something about it?" she said naïvely. "Move somewhere else."

"They can't. Those that do find even more problems in the big cities. There are no roads of gold, whatever the fairy tales say."

"It's horrendous," she added, a tear meandering down her cheek. "Why do the nobles allow it?"

"Because they don't see it. Their eyes are open of course, but their hearts are closed. These aren't people to them, they're just livestock. Another commodity of war. We do what we can to help, when we can."

"But why?"

"Because no one else will," said Chambard butting in. "Although I should be honest with you, my dear, we look after ourselves before we look after them."

"Chambard," said Philibert, "I saw a young girl by the coaches earlier who appeared to be alone. I wonder if you could tend to her needs as I doubt whether any of our gifts will make it in to her hands."

Chambard nodded and lolloped off in a style uniquely his. Annabelle glided serenely to the wall that held the river back from the town, thoughts racing around her mind like a hound chasing a hare. Here she was, born into wealth and fortune, but oblivious to the misery camped on her own doorstep. And like everyone else in her reality, she'd done nothing. While a man like Phil, who'd escaped these cataclysmic horrors through self-determination and at great personal danger, was compassionately helping others.

"Philibert, how can I help?" she said, turning to find him standing only a fraction behind her. The close proximity unleashed an uncontrollable compulsion to kiss him, irrespective of the dangers of being caught.

Phil lingered for a moment on her lips before pulling away. This kiss contained more than lust. An alarm bell rang in his heart to signal an event not previously experienced. His body shock from the fear of it. He wasn't ready. There were too many obstacles to overcome. Too many tasks to fulfil. His head and heart broke out in internal conflict for the first time in years. Soon it would rage more turbulently than the religious factions that teetered on the precipice of war.

"Help us, you say," replied Phil, stepping back. "Do your part. If everyone did a little the future can be shaped differently. But for now you can help me."

"Of course. Anything."

"I need to understand more about our Queen, Catherine de Medici."

"The Queen. Why?"

"Because you already know that I am not what your father thinks I am. If I'm to enter the court I have to play a game with them."

"What sort of game?"

"A riddle. How well do you know the Queen?"

"Only hearsay really. Rumours, second-hand stories and whispers."

"Tell me what you can," said Philibert.

Over the next thirty minutes Annabelle farmed her mind to plough as much knowledge as she could remember. Anything of significance was discussed and sometimes questioned by Phil. Some of it he knew, information that was in the public domain gained from some of the marks he'd swindled over the last decade.

Some of it was new and most of it was useful. Annabelle gave him details of the Queen's upbringing in Italy, her marriage to King Henry, her eight children and her own personal interests.

"There's something else I have heard about the Queen," said Annabelle at a much lower volume.

"Go on."

"Some people believe she's a witch."

"A witch! Surely you don't believe in such things."

"Certainly. It's obvious that there is black magic in the world, it's the only explanation to why some events happen."

"For example?" asked Phil, who was always sceptical when the supernatural was offered as an answer to the unexplained.

"Well, how would you explain the sudden destruction of crops when the season is fair and conducive to a strong harvest?"

"Probably an aggressive swarm of really small bugs," said Philibert.

"Oh yeah," mocked Annabelle. "That's believable."

"But a haggard, old crone casting a spell over a field is much more plausible, is it? I mean for a start why would a witch even do that?"

"They don't need a reason, they're just satanic."

"And the Devil's got a particular intolerance to wheat, has he?"

"It's not just crops. How do you explain an army with many more soldiers losing a battle against a smaller foe if not because of witchcraft?"

"You've not seen many battles, have you?"

She shook her head.

"I've been pretty close to one and at no point did I see any black hags circling the scene of the crime, or sitting on the parapets shooting spells from her fingers, or hexing the men with nasty illnesses. However, I did witness a foe who had something that might explain it."

"What?"

"Guns."

"Yeah, but who gave them the guns, tell me that."

It seemed unlikely that Phil was going to win the argument. A belief in witches went hand in hand with a belief in God. If you had faith in one you almost had to accept the existence of the other. Someone had to be responsible for all the disappointment in people's lives and clearly it couldn't be God's fault. Much easier to blame the old woman next door who had recently asked where she could find good quality newts.

Witches were extremely popular in the Middle Ages. All in all, just in France alone, more than forty thousand women had been killed for being one. It became an easy excuse for anyone in a jam. If a wife walked in on her husband in bed with another woman shouting pleasurably, 'You're so much better at this than Carol,' the simplest excuse was to say the woman down the road cursed you. If you built a house from grass and your own saliva and it collapsed on the first day, there was no way you could blame shoddy workmanship. That suspicious-looking woman with the sinister wart on her nose was a much more likely culprit.

They got the blame for everything, but there was never any evidence or eyewitnesses to their crimes. The way to prove a woman was a witch was simply to set her on fire, throw her off a cliff or drown her. If they were witches they'd survive and after a successful trial the angry mob could punish them by burning them, pushing them off a cliff, or drowning them. That was the logic at least. No one seemed to acknowledge that every one of the forty thousand deaths failed to result in any of those women flying off on broomsticks cackling their threats of vengeance.

"Anyway, what evidence is there that Catherine is a witch?" asked Phil, trying to bring the conversation back on a sensible footing.

"She didn't have children for the first ten years of her marriage."

"That doesn't mean anything. As I understand it, King Henry was a randy bugger who'd make love to anything that moved. Maybe they weren't intimate with each other."

"I don't think that's true. You have to be if you're the King, you need an heir to keep your line going. And how do you explain that after the first ten years she went on to have eight children. Clearly black magic."

"Clearly," Phil chuckled, finding Annabelle's innocence rather endearing.

"She has a cat, too."

"A cat! Well, that's enough proof for me. Call the witch hunters immediately."

"Don't mock me," replied Annabelle, seeing the lighter side of his sarcasm.

Night-time was fast approaching and these stolen moments would soon end. The horses were being bridled to their coaches and the men were leaving the inn, including Jacques whose mood was always more erratic after hitting the booze.

"I must go before he sees us together," said Annabelle, pointing towards the convoy and becoming noticeably less light of tone.

"One more thing. Do you have any connections in the court? Someone who can arrange safe passage for an audience with the Queen."

"There are still some working in the court who have kept their religious beliefs to themselves. They call themselves the politiques, more interested in the well-being of the state than their own personal freedoms."

"And is there anyone you can trust?" asked Phil.

"Michel de l'Hôpital, he was based in Nice until he became the Queen's Chancellor. He was often a guest of my father's."

"Tell him I have important news for the Queen and it's essential that she meets me if she wants to ensure a continuing peace between the factions. Leave the rest to me."

As the company pulled away from the desperate town of Nemours under the cover of darkness, Phil and Annabelle set about writing. Philibert had learnt enough from their conversation to put together the appropriate prophecy which would, if all went well, satisfy Catherine of his importance and gain her favour. Montmorency's ring would add an authenticity to the story and his connection to Nostradamus would help validate his skills in proclaiming the future. If they got that far.

Annabelle, on the other hand, had offered to write a letter to her contact l'Hôpital seeking an endorsement of Phil. The letter, complete with her official seal, included the pretence that Phil offered some advice to keep the increasingly religious tensions from flaring up. Which, of course, he didn't. In truth he didn't really understand the principles of either religion and felt everyone would be better served just getting on with each other. Once the letter was written, Chambard would do the rest.

At their next available stop the old wanderer would sneak out of their coach, pick up the letter from Annabelle and disappear into the night. It was then down to him to find a faster route to Paris and return to the coach before anyone noticed his absence. Jacques had shown little interest in checking on their activities during the four weeks of their journey, only occasionally sending one of his henchmen to provide them with food or eavesdrop on their conversations.

Phil wasn't concerned how Chambard managed it, but he was certain it wouldn't involve horses. It didn't bother him how. Reliability was one of Chambard's greatest qualities. It was one of the reasons Phil had followed him for so long. After the psychological shock of losing his family, which later evolved into anger that they'd left him to fend for himself, what he'd needed was someone he could trust. And Chambard had never failed him on that front. He was more of a father to him than any genetic relative. If Chambard said he'd do something, that was enough reassurance.

- Chapter 21-

Mr. Wang's Hypnotherapy Clinic

If friendship were a Venn diagram, each circle would contain the relative interests of each person. Those common interests that overlapped in the middle would indicate the level of friendship that might be achieved. If both people were in agreement on almost everything it wouldn't look much like a Venn diagram at all. Rather just a big circle.

It was accurate to say that Ally's circle wasn't brimming with hobbies in the first place, so the chances of them being shared with other people's were fairly remote. If she found a person who liked, very expensive red wine, the works of Proust, coffee, cryptic crosswords, insulting employees who delivered poor service experiences, Aran jumpers, languages, more coffee, and nineteenth-century typewriters, it still didn't offer much of a foundation to build a friendship on.

Antoine wasn't her friend, but at least they did share a speck of common ground. They were both interested in the arts, history and more specifically their need for answers about the prophecy. It created a relationship which was civil if not exactly close. And after all of this blew over it was highly unlikely they'd ever see each other again. When it came to Gabriel, however, it wasn't so much a Venn diagram as two circles of interest divided by a chasm of disagreement.

MR. WANG'S HYPNOTHERAPY CLINIC

As far as Ally was concerned, Gabriel was an overprivileged, dim-witted flunky who was more interested in how she looked than how others perceived her. She liked pop music, make-up, a quick buck, instant gratification, boots, eyelashes, Prosecco, glossy magazines with lots of pictures, and vain boys with big muscles and stubbly chins. It was a combination that didn't make for a stimulating atmosphere.

The journey time from Limonest to Mâcon would normally be less than an hour. It was connected by a good-quality motorway from start to finish and it was definitely not rush hour, despite it being the right time of the morning for it. But since merging onto the double-lane highway from the quiet backroads they'd not seen a single car. Given Gabriel's unorthodox driving style, a lack of opposition partly explained why they were all still alive.

The car weaved through the lines on the road as if they were nothing more than a vague suggestion of where someone should aim. Road signs were routinely ignored and as for speed limits, Ally wondered if Gabriel thought the numbers were measured in light speed rather than kilometres per hour. The poor Renault, flashing along like a turd fired from a missile launcher, screeched its disapproval and echoed the unspoken sentiments of the other terrified passengers.

"There's no rush, you know," said Antoine from the back seat, where he perched on a pile of fast-food litter that had been jettisoned from the front seat possibly several decades ago if the smell was anything to go by.

"Believe me, this isn't fast at all," she replied as a wing mirror rattled out of its holding and bounced with a crack on the road behind them. "I wonder where all the cars are today?"

"Maybe they declared a state of emergency when they saw us coming," Ally muttered to herself.

"Normally you can't move for traffic, very strange."

"I would have thought the reason was obvious…forgive me…I forgot who I was talking to," replied Ally, turning the sarcasm up to maximum. "The cities are in lockdown, and the rest of humanity is avoiding contact with other people for fear of catching flu. Which is ridiculous really."

"Aren't you worried about catching N_1G_{13}?" Gabriel asked.

"No. A little flu isn't going to stop me. And anyway you'll probably kill us before I get the chance."

"But everyone who's caught it has died," added Gabriel, ignoring the criticism of her driving in the same way she ignored all criticism.

"So?" replied Ally.

"What if your family became infected?" asked Antoine.

"I don't have any family," added Ally.

"I have a big family," replied Gabriel, hijacking the conversation and focusing on her own world as she always did. "Actually my grandpapa was a famous racing driver."

"Died in a horrific, high-speed fireball, I expect," replied Ally, clinging firmly to the door handle.

"What's you grandfather got to do with the flu?" asked Antoine.

"Nothing. I just got bored and moved on to a more interesting subject. Remind me, why are we going to Mâcon?"

"To find Bernard Baptiste," replied Antoine.

"And he's got coffee right?"

"No, he's got a coffer, it's a piece of furniture."

"There's an excellent furniture shop in Lyon, really cheap if you're interested."

"This is a very special one. It has something inside it that we need."

"What's that?"

"We don't know," said Ally gruffly.

"It might have some answers for us about the prophecy."

"And the coffer's in Mâcon, is it?"

"It is, but we won't be. You've just missed the motorway exit," said Antoine patiently.

The car was immediately placed into an emergency stop, causing it to skid fifty feet down the road, permanently scarring the tarmac with black rubber marks. The Renault gave a painful jolt as the gearstick carved a new reverse gear in the metal next to the original one.

"Stop!" shouted Ally as the car travelled backwards almost as quickly as it had done going forward. "You can't do that."

"Why not? There's no one on the roads."

"Rules are rules."

"Blah, rules aren't for everyone."

"They really are, you know."

They left the motorway only partly via tarmac and followed the signs for Mâcon. The minor roads were just as quiet as the motorway, although thankfully there was no sign of the police roadblocks being reported in most built-up areas. Personally, Ally was furious that the authorities had decided to implement such draconian methods to keep the flu from spreading. It didn't work with the plague back in the Middle Ages and it wouldn't work now. Containing something you can't see that moves at ease through the wind was nonsensical. All that the roadblocks would achieve was more uncertainty, a redirection of valuable resources, and restrict access for those who wanted to get on with life whatever the consequences. Mâcon was one of the few towns that had so far escaped this measure, and it had to be assumed N_1G_{13} itself.

Ally had tried multiple times to contact Bernard by phone to arrange a meeting. Every one of those calls had ended with her leaving a simple and abrupt message on his voicemail, which as yet he'd not replied to. This wasn't atypical. She knew he was screening her. When she arrived at his office the look on her contemporary's big-headed face would be a suitable payback.

Bernard's office address, which was published in his books and publicly available, was situated in a side street in the centre of town next to the cathedral. There was a car park adjacent to it, but every single space was occupied. It seemed unlikely that anyone was going to get a ticket today. In an almost perfect manoeuvre, Gabriel double-parked the Renault so that it stuck out diagonally into the road and caused the most disruption possible. The car gasped with relief as she switched off the engine.

"You're leaving it like that, are you?" said Ally.

"Yeah."

"Don't start a scene," replied Antoine, looking at Ally in particular whose ears were brewing steam.

Gabriel stayed in the car, citing her main reasons for not joining them as laziness, lack of interest and a desire not to die.

The place was a ghost town. No shops were open and it definitely wasn't a Sunday. Even the church had locked its doors firmly. They spotted the occasional forehead peering over the top of second-floor window frames, but that was the nearest they came to seeing Mâcon's residents. Even the wildlife was absent, kidnapped for their own protection. The trees were the only living organisms to put up any sort of resistance. Their branches swayed in the wind, flicking a two-fingered woody defiance to the oncoming apocalypse.

Sandwiched between a boulangerie and a charcuterie shop was a dull, glass-fronted building with brown shutters masking its windows. The florist shop on the ground floor was empty and a doorway up the side led up some steps. At the top a panel of doorbells indicated each of the small offices on the floors above. Bernard Baptiste's was number three. They pressed the bell and waited. No answer. They tried again. Still nothing. Determined not to leave empty-handed they tried number four, Mr. Wang's

Hypnotherapy Clinic, and after some delay a strong Chinese accent came through the speaker.

"Wah you wan?"

"Oh hello, very sorry to disturb you…Mr. Wang," said Antoine checking the small tag above the bell. "We're looking for Mr. Baptiste."

"You sell?"

"No, we're not selling. We're searching…for Mr. Baptiste."

"Me Wang, no Baptist here, only Buddhist. Go away."

"I know he's not there, but as he's your neighbour we thought…"

"You wan hypnotherapy!" shouted Mr. Wang aggressively.

"Not unless you can do millennials," stated Ally ironically.

"Ah Wang do all. Old, young, broken, unbalanced, confused, addict, stag do's…"

"No, thank you, we're only interested in trying to find Bernard. B-e-r-n-a-r-d."

"Crazy bastard. Wang no deaf. If no wan hypnotherapy, ah fuck off please."

"Charming. Just tell us what we need to know and we'll be gone," said Ally. "You must have seen him come and go: you own the same stairwell."

"Woman, you really sleepy," said Mr. Wang in a softer more manipulating tone which was now accompanied by some psychedelic music played in the background. "More you focus on Wang's words, more sleepy you feel. Relax now, you so comfy, you forget Bernie, you gonna turn around, walk…"

"Mr. Wang, are you trying to hypnotise us without our permission."

"No! Sleep now, listen to Wang."

"Look, do you know where Bernard is or not?" said Ally on the edge of her patience spectrum.

"He no here, you no listen."

"Did you hypnotise him, too?"

"No, not hypnotise…he dead."

"Dead! How?"

"Catch cold," said Mr. Wang.

"Do you mean N1G13?"

"All lies. No such thing! It don't exist," said Mr. Wang. It was followed by silence.

"I think he might have hypnotised himself into denying the existence of the pandemic," said Antoine. "Not sure it'll protect him, but it'll stop him from panicking."

"I don't believe it. Bernard can't be dead. N1G13 was only discovered in Europe last week and there would need to be an incubation period before it killed anyone. Plus, if the flu has reached Mâcon where's the cordon?"

The hunt for answers had returned them to square one. Bernard held the key and they had no way of verifying whether he was dead or alive. The trail felt as cold as an Eskimo's nose. What now? She was stuck in a foreign ghost town with a septuagenarian being hunted by unknown threats and an egomaniac prepper. Even answers weren't worth this much hassle. Maybe it was time to give up the ghost and head back home to the safety of the Shakespearean exhibition and a country with a lot less people living in it than when she left. As they made their way back to the car Ally's mobile phone rang in her bag.

"I bet that's Bernard," she said. "I bet this was all some prank to irritate me."

The number on her phone was unrecognised, but it had the French country code at the beginning. She answered it with an unfriendly bark.

"Bernard you horrible little shit…"

"Ms. Oldfield?" said the professional sounding voice on the other end.

"Yes," she snapped. "What do you want?"

"I'm ringing in relation to one of our clients, a Bernard Baptiste."

"Oh, do leave off. Did he put you up to this?"

"Who?"

"Bernard."

"No, madam, as I said, he's one of our clients."

"Clients. What do you mean clients?"

"I represent Lamy and Veron Associates and we are Mr. Baptiste's lawyers."

"Oh, I get it. He's trying to sue me for something I've said about him, is he? That's why he hasn't been answering my calls. That's why he set up Mr. Wang the crazy hypnotherapist to yank our chains…"

"No, Ms. Oldfield, I don't know any Mr. Wang. That's not the reason for my call. Mr. Baptiste is in no position to sue anyone, or answer calls, or anything else in fact."

"Why not?"

"Because he's dead."

"You're not the only one who thinks so, but I'll believe it when I see it. No doubt this is just another part of the ruse."

"Madam, this is no ruse," replied the woman sternly on the other end of the line, getting a little impatient.

"Then what do you want?"

"He's left you something in his will."

"His will? What has he left me?"

"I can't tell you over the phone. You need to come to the office and sign the paperwork. Oh, and you might need to bring a large van, too."

"I don't have a van. I have a borrowed beige Renault 16 in almost no condition to drive. I swear to God if this is a wind-up I'm going to blow a fuse."

"Just come to the office and I can explain everything."

Once Ally had finished the call she explained the conversation to Antoine as they strolled briskly back to the car. Neither of them knew what to make of it. Bernard was no friend of Ally's and there was a general agreement that whatever had been bequeathed wouldn't be very significant. Unless it was the coffer and neither of them thought the possibility was very likely. When they got back to the place where they'd left the car it was no longer there.

"What a bitch!" screamed Ally, certain that Gabriel had made the decision to abandon them.

"I'm sure she'll be back," said Antoine optimistically.

"Do you know your problem, Antoine? You're much too trusting. You believe there is good in people when they regularly demonstrate that there isn't. It must be all this charity work that you do, it's made you think that everyone in the world is a victim, when actually they're all arseholes."

"And you are quite the opposite," he replied more sternly than she was used to. "You have no faith in other humans whatsoever. To you, they're all idiots, criminals or losers. It's why you have never married and why you never will in my opinion. Your life will never truly be whole until you do. Give Gabriel a chance, you may just find she surprises you."

"She had that chance the first minute she met me and she blew it. The girl's a bimbo with the intellectual capacity of a piece of stale bread. She's vain, egocentric, deluded, stupid, lacking in gumption, one-dimensional, self-involved, gullible and possibly the worst driver I have ever had the misfortune to travel with."

"Ahem."

Behind the pair of bickering adults, Gabriel was holding three steaming paper cups of coffee in a cardboard tray. It was quite some miracle how she'd sourced them in a town so completely devoid of human activity.

"I thought you might appreciate a coffee, but obviously if I'm too selfish I'll take them back. Normally of course a girl of my era would burst into tears on hearing insults like that, but I can assure you I'm more robust than you think."

"See, what did I say?" said Antoine, patting Gabriel warmly on the shoulder.

"How did you get coffee out here?" said Ally in genuine surprise and avoiding any offer of gratitude.

"I used my entrepreneurial skills, perseverance and intelligence. Plus I parked the car in a proper space as I could see how much it annoyed you."

"Right," said Ally, rather embarrassed.

"And they say millennials never apologise."

- Chapter 22 -

Lamy & Veron Associates

Lamy and Veron Associates, Bernard's lawyers, were situated in a remote renovated watermill alongside the river on the outskirts of town. The grandiose reconstruction of the property featured landscaped car parks, a plush, glass-fronted reception area and a monstrous piece of gaudy artwork that stretched up the space in the middle of the staircase. The best description for it would be that the sculptor took nine different coloured cubes, relentlessly threw them down a cliff until they were completely mashed, and then piled them one on top of the other. It was more proof, if any were needed, of the exorbitant fees demanded by lawyers and their poor judgement in spending them.

All three of them left marched towards the foyer, leaving the Renault to spoil the otherwise perfect exterior. Although the front doors to the shiny reception area were open there was no sign of any staff, continuing the apparently normal trend repeated through the rest of the town. A sign on the desk instructed them to present themselves to the first-floor boardroom. Once there, Ally knocked firmly on the door and a woman's head appeared on the other side of a small window.

"Identification please?" she called through the door.

Ally reached inside her handbag and held her opened passport to the window.

"Thank you, Ms. Oldfield. And who are the other two with you?"

"Mr. Palomer and Miss Janvier," she replied gruffly, still convinced this visit was some elaborate hoax. "Let us in."

"Not yet. As you may gather from walking around our town, people are trying to avoid contact with those affected by the virus. On the table to your right you'll see some testing kits. Please administer them on yourselves and present the results through the window."

Each testing kit looked like a small television remote control. The small silver plastic pod had a screen at the top and a flap at the bottom. Under the flap was a small needle and a tube. The instructions, written on the underside of the flap, required each of them to blow into the small tube, use the needle to prick their fingers to obtain a drop of blood, and finally to place their foreheads against the top part where an inbuilt thermometer would take their temperatures.

Once they'd complied with the machine's instructions they waited impatiently for the results to present themselves on the LED screen. Gabriel had taken the most persuasion. Needles, she told them, made her faint and the whole practice was very much against her human rights. Ally swiftly told her to shut up, shove her rights where the sun didn't shine and get on with it. Once the results had flashed up on the screen like Saturday's football scores they took it in turn to lift the devices to the window so that the woman behind the glass could check the results.

"Ms. Oldfield, you are clear of the infection. As are you, Mr. Palomer. Miss Janvier on the other hand…"

The other two in the hallway suddenly felt their stomachs sink. They didn't really know anything about Gabriel or her background, other than she owned a crap caravan and had decided to hide in a forest until the global pandemic blew over. She certainly hadn't demonstrated any symptoms of the virus, but how close had they looked? There was no obvious fever, no coughing, no breathing difficulties and no complaints of headaches. But if she was incubating N_1G_{13} there was a very good chance they would contract it too, given how much of the day they spent cooped up in confined spaces.

"I knew she was going to be trouble," said Ally, prodding Antoine in the arm to further make her point. "She's got the flu and now we're all going to die, thanks to you!"

"Miss Janvier doesn't have the flu," replied the woman's insulated voice from the other side of the panelled door. "But she has tested positive for an overactive thyroid, excessive cocaine use, a staggeringly high level of alcohol in her bloodstream, a low iron level and chlamydia."

"That's so unfair!" said Gabriel sobbing. "Why did it have to happen to me?"

"It's not the world's fault," Ally replied disdainfully. "You don't catch these things. You have them because you're a promiscuous, drug-taking pisshead! I mean how can you have alcohol in your system today?"

"I did a couple of shots this morning before we left…a couple more in town before I went on the coffee run…and one while I was doing the test," she said, waving a little hip flask from the top of her bag. "I might not have prepped well in terms of food and security, but I have enough vodka in the boot of the car to outlast Armageddon."

Gabriel might have needed a counsellor, pharmacist and legal aid as a result of the tests, but she didn't have the flu, and that's all their host really cared about. The woman unlocked the door to the boardroom and welcomed them more formally.

"I'm Marian Lamy, one of the partners of the firm. I'm sorry for the unusual measures we've had to force upon you at this time. Normal everyday life is not what it once was."

She directed them to sit around the oval table where a number of documents were laid out at one end. The left side of the room was made entirely from glass and looked out over the river. Part of the watermill was built into this feature, the wheel revolving through the water now for no other purpose than dramatic effect. The other side of the room was consumed by an object covered in sheets and leaning at an angle against the wall.

"What really happened to Bernard?" asked Ally once they were all sitting comfortably.

"He was one of France's first N1G13 victims."

"But how can that be? It can't kill that quickly," added Antoine.

"Not normally, no. But he didn't catch it through the air like most victims," replied Marian.

"Then how did he get the infection?"

"The coroner is working on the theory that he was injected with it. There was a small needle mark in the back of his neck and toxicology reports prove he had a huge amount of the virus in his system."

"He was murdered!" gasped Antoine.

"Almost certainly," replied Marian. "If you discount suicide, which you have to given the region where the needle mark was found. There's no way a man of that size and limited mobility could have done that. A gymnast maybe, but not a short, obese man."

This revelation sent most of the room into silence. Everyone except Gabriel, who was noisily chewing on a piece of gum not the slightest bit interested in the conversation happening around her. She didn't know who they were talking about and didn't particularly care either. But the others did. They could only think of one motive for murder. Someone had already tried to kill to retrieve it. It had to be about the coffer. Having tried to steal it from Antoine's house the perpetrators must have followed the trail to Bernard. Clearly they were dealing with serious people. Not only had they chosen to kill Bernard for it, they'd ruthlessly done so using the very substance projected to wipe out the human race. Ally knew symbolism when she saw it.

"Are there any suspects?" asked Antoine.

"No. He was found alone and there was no sign of a struggle or forced entry."

"Clearly he knew who they were then," said Gabriel still staring aimlessly out of the window and only picking up snippets of what was said. She'd watched enough crime dramas for conclusions to burst out of her mouth without her ever meaning to.

"I believe so," replied Marian. "Obviously it's not my job to catch and prosecute, only to deal with the affairs afterwards."

"Can I ask you about his will?" said Antoine to see if there was a connection between his death and the coffer.

"Of course."

"Bernard had ownership of a sixteenth-century black, oak coffer which he bought from me less than two weeks ago. Who was it left to?"

"I'm not at liberty to tell you that specific information, but I can tell you if such an item was in the will."

"If you would."

Marian opened a blue folder and scanned down the inventory with her finger. When she arrived at the bottom of the third and final page she gently shook her head. It was another dead end. The final two clues, Bernard and the coffer, were gone and with it the answers they needed.

"The search is over," added Ally, standing up from her seat. "It's time to go home."

The search for truth might have burnt like a fire inside her, but it wasn't the end of the world – well, not yet anyway. She craved a shower, clean underwear and a chance to fix her hair, which looked like it had been subjected to electroshock therapy. She was both mentally and physically exhausted. She believed strongly that the virus wouldn't destroy the world, but the fear and panic that accompanied it might just tear down society as they knew it instead. It had already begun. A day spent in a small provincial town like Mâcon was all the evidence she needed. Her only goal had been to bring some sense to the world. Give it a gentle shake and tell it to 'pull itself together'.

"Wait," said Marian. "Don't leave. There's something in the will for you, Ms. Oldfield."

She'd totally forgotten. What on earth would Bernard leave her? Curiosity got the better of her and she returned to her seat.

"I, Marian Lamy, executor of the last will and testament of Bernard Brutus Baptiste, confirm that the following item has been left to Ms. Alison Freda Oldfield. One oil painting entitled 'The Royal Court of Catherine de Medici' dated to approximately fifteen-sixty-four and painted by François Clouet."

"What on earth do I want with a painting!" huffed Ally whose side of the Venn diagram didn't contain French Renaissance art.

"It's probably worth a fortune," replied Antoine in horror. "Clouet was a genius."

Gabriel immediately stopped daydreaming and perked up at hearing the word 'fortune'.

"He could have invented tartan paint for all I care, I still don't want it."

Marian walked over to the large object propped up against the wall. She pulled the dust sheets off in a dramatic style that David Copperfield would have been proud of. Underneath was an enormous oil painting that stretched five metres across and more than two metres high. It was encased in a bulky, antique wooden frame as thick as the beams that held up most roofs.

"Shit! What do you expect me to do with that!"

"I did tell you to bring a van," replied Marian.

In genuine surprise and wonder all four of them removed themselves from their seats to examine the painting. The scene featured a gathering of many people in a circular room. The heads of mighty harts, all with more than ten points on their antlers, extended out from wooden plaques hung on the walls. In the centre of the ensemble sat a woman dressed in black looking demure and serious. At her feet, sitting cross-legged and sporting a face of perfect anger, was a teenage boy with a small crown on his head. Whether symbolical or not, two skinny lurchers flanked the boy at the same level.

Half a dozen other individuals were in the painting, most dressed in formal attire and holding poses that no living human would ever naturally find themselves in. They were mostly men. There was an elderly gentleman with a huge, conjoined eyebrow standing just behind the Queen's left shoulder who looked terribly unwell and to the right of him a tall, handsome man with frizzy hair, maybe in his early forties.

There was only one other female in the painting. A pretty, young woman with auburn hair in a long, flowing turquoise dress with a low neckline. The painting was so big each character was painted in exquisite detail and their size was almost relative to real life. Antoine took out a pair of half-moon glasses and stepped forward to take a closer look at the brushstrokes.

"I have too many questions," said Ally unable to process her reaction. "Um…why?"

"There's no additional information from the deceased, I'm afraid. He clearly thought you'd like it."

"No, he didn't. The man hated me. It's just like him to leave me something stupid like this. I bet he's in his grave laughing at the thought of me trying to get this through Customs and onto a budget flight. Ten kilos in small hand luggage is all they give you these days. It doesn't say one small bag and a ridiculously large piece of art on the boarding card."

"Ally," said Antoine seriously, his voice shaking. "Come and look at this."

Pointing to the second female in the painting, his finger wobbled nervously. Ally came in for a closer look. A silver chain extended down the woman's neck and at the end was the unmistakable detail of a pendant in the shape of a ram. It was the second time this week that Ally had seen it in a picture.

"You're kidding!" she exclaimed.

"No, it's the same locket, no question," replied Antoine.

"The same what?" asked Gabriel.

Antoine explained that the locket around the woman's neck was currently in his possession, an heirloom that had been handed down the generations of his family. Whoever this was wearing it in the painting, it seemed sensible to assume that she was some distant relative.

"Who is she?" asked Gabriel.

"I don't know."

"But if the painting contains a link to you, why did Bernard leave it to me?" asked Ally.

"I don't know that either. Almost no one knows about my locket, so he wouldn't have made the connection. He must be trying to tell you something else, or it's just an amazing coincidence. Maybe the painting is a clue. Is Nostradamus in the picture?"

"No," said Ally, who would know his face anywhere.

"Then who are these other people?"

"Art isn't exactly my area of expertise, but I think they must be part of the royal court. I'm pretty sure the figure at the front is Charles IX and if it's dated correctly that was the year of the longest and largest royal tour in history. Catherine took the King across France as part of his coronation and to engender support from local nobles. But there's no way of telling from the picture where it was painted or who the others are."

"Then what are we meant to be seeing?" said Antoine scratching his head.

"I don't know, but there must be more to it. Bernard must have been carrying out his own research. He knew about the coffer in your basement before you did and someone has possibly killed him for owning it. Whatever is in it holds the key to the mystery. Perhaps Bernard suspected he was in danger and left this for us to carry on his work?" replied Ally, sniffing out another clue that might keep the trail going.

"He could have just sent you an email," added Gabriel simply. It was hard for her to imagine a world that didn't feature the internet. In her mind the painting in front of her could just have easily been painted in ninety-eighty-two, such was her lack of empathy for anything older than she was.

"That's true. So why didn't he send me an email?" answered Ally.

"Perhaps he feared it wasn't safe to do so," replied Antoine. "I was right to avoid the surveillance systems."

"I'm sure this is all very fascinating," said Marian looking at her wristwatch and making it clear it was anything but interesting to her. "Our business here is concluded so if you wouldn't mind moving your painting, I'll get back to work."

Moving the portrait without the assistance of an amateur rugby team, a small crane and a removal van would be more challenging than explaining to Gabriel how libraries worked. The three of them tried to lift, shove, pivot and drag it without shifting it an inch. It didn't cross their minds to ask how the stuffy-nosed lawyers of Lamy and Veron had got it in here in the first place. Removing the huge glass window seemed the only possibility.

"This is stupid," huffed Gabriel who was the fittest of the three by some distance. "We don't really need the frame."

"The frame is an original," said Antoine in dismay. "If you remove that you'll make it almost worthless."

"I hate to agree with Gabriel, but this isn't about the money. Mrs. Lamy, could I borrow that letter opener from your table?"

The lawyer nodded as Antoine simultaneously buried his head in his hands. He hated seeing pieces of history butchered. Ally stabbed the corner of the painting and cut around the frame to release the canvas. Once it was free from the wood they could easily remove it in a roll. As Ally picked it up, a piece of paper floated to the ground, hidden between the painting and the back of the frame. Gabriel was the only person to notice it. She picked it up while the others were busy rolling up the painting.

"Right, let's go."

"And the frame," said Marian as the three of them motioned to leave.

"You're kidding, right?" replied Ally forlornly.

"No. It's your rightful property and keeping it would be seen as theft," lied Marian, simply wanting to get it and them out of her boardroom.

Their only option was to smash the four sides of the frame into several pieces. These were still not small enough to store inside the Renault, so they tied them together and left them hanging out of the boot like a lance in reverse. The painting was rolled up and laid along the middle of the car.

"What a total waste of time that was. We're still no closer to solving the puzzle," said Ally, getting back into the passenger seat and noticing that a large, folded piece of paper was sitting on the driver's seat. "What's this?"

"It fell out of the painting," said Gabriel. "I didn't want to interrupt you at the time so I picked it up."

Although there wasn't enough room to see all of it, such were the number of folds in the paper, Ally spread it out as best she could on her lap.

"What is it?" asked Antoine as he leant forward from the now crowded back seat.

"It's a family tree."

"Whose?"

"Nostradamus's," said Ally almost speechless.

"Dear Lord, so it is."

"And at the bottom," she continued, "someone has circled a name in red ink. Bernard didn't want us to discover the painting, he wanted us to discover this."

"Whose name is circled?"

"Mario Peruzzi," replied Ally. "Mean anything to you?"

"Nothing at all."

Gabriel turned the keys in the ignition and gave the little car a dose of petrol via the accelerator pedal to resuscitate it back to life. "So who's this Nostradamus bloke anyway?"

- Chapter 23 -

Killer Queen

"Your majesty I have received a letter."

"And?" replied the Queen dismissively. There was a time and place for matters of state and the middle of a lavish court festival wasn't one of them.

"Forgive me, but I believe you will find it most illuminating," said Michel de l'Hôpital, holding the letter in his hand to make the point more firmly.

"More interesting than ballet, music and dance," replied Catherine. "Monsieur l'Hôpital, maybe you should relax a while. Take a drink from one of our lovely topless ladies."

The Queen's festivals were more than just celebrations. They were strategic messages sent to rivals, both at home and abroad. When other nations strongly believed that the French state had been bankrupted by years of poorly fought wars, the Queen would prove to the contrary by throwing ever more eccentric gatherings. The fact that these were almost always funded by bank loans didn't really seem to matter.

These were political as much as general affairs of revelry. While the men of the court were distracted by the many outlandish gimmicks such as the topless waitresses, and had their glasses constantly topped up with strong alcohol, she would infiltrate their conversations and gain the advantage. It was the only way she could do it. Men weren't comfortable with a woman in power and Catherine was in the most powerful position of all.

These parties also allowed an outlet for one of her other passions, the arts. The renaissance that Francis, her father-in-law, had stimulated more than two decades ago was now being championed by her. The best architects had been engaged to continue the development of her palace in Fontainebleau, she'd introduced ballet as an art form, and continued to build on the old King's huge library collection. Her husband's meagre passions had been women and warfare; she would be famous for culture and learning.

"Your majesty, I'm a little too old for that type of excitement," replied l'Hôpital, shielding his eyes from the debauchery.

"Who is the letter from?" asked the Queen faking interest.

"A man by the name of Philibert Lesage."

"Never heard of him."

"Neither had I until I received information from an ally I trust in the South. But the letter says he has important information for you."

"About what exactly?"

"The religious disagreements."

"What expertise does he have on that subject?"

"It says he fought at the Battle of St. Quentin and has trained under the tutelage of Monsieur Nostradamus. It also states he's been operating inside the Protestant community and understands their intentions."

"Then is he a soldier or a seer?"

"Neither. Apparently he's a doctor."

"I don't really need another doctor or another seer. One of each is more than enough," replied Catherine.

"But your majesty, perhaps it might be prudent to hear what he has to say?"

The din of the festival made it difficult for Michel to hear himself think, let alone conduct a meaningful conversation. In every corner of the room actors in fantastical costumes, that resembled all kinds of mythical beasts and characters, were interacting with the guests through forms of entertainment as diverse as mime and juggling. Dancers weaved their way through the crowd, often teasing guests with their provocative moves. Musicians battled for dominance over the airwaves, and lutes and harps clashed with trumpets and recorders in a cacophony.

In the middle of all of this revellers scoffed all manner of delicacies, flirted with the women hired solely for their entertainment, and broke into song at the drop of a hat. Everyone who was anyone was in attendance. Freeloaders the lot of them, but as they'd eventually be responsible for raising the taxes needed to pay for it, they might as well push themselves to excess. Even the young King was up after his bedtime to watch how things should be done, all part of the education his mother designed for him.

"Fine, I will see him, but if I am unimpressed I will be forced to have him put to death," she replied unemotionally.

"Yes, your majesty. I'll go and get him."

"Not now!"

"But he's already here. He was most determined to see you tonight. Apparently he's travelled all the way from Marseille."

"Then maybe he should have thought about making an appointment first. Why is it so urgent anyway?"

"I believe he also has important information about your son."

"My son?"

"Yes, a prophecy about the King in fact."

Catherine loved a good prophecy, a great deal more than she did her own son in truth. Prophecies had an almost mystical quality. They could be ridiculous, inspiring, powerful and insightful, but they were always interesting. If there was a prophecy about her son she must hear it and speak to the one brave enough to commit it to paper.

"In that case you'd better go get him," said Catherine suddenly more engaged. "And while you're at it, bring my advisors, Montmorency and Throckmorton, at the same time."

Philibert was guided into the great ballroom where his senses were so overloaded by what he saw he thought they might all shut down in exhaustion. He'd been to plenty of parties thrown by high society, but this one went so far past extravagance the others were barely visible on the horizon. And here he was again, alone, out of place in a palace, and dressed in clothes made to measure by the finest tailors that Paris had to offer.

White socks ascended to his knees and combined with red hose, fitted with an outrageously large codpiece. As the fashion of the day demanded, a white doublet was worn over the top of his shirt, one sleeve tightly fastened around his wrist while the other was left to hang loose. At the collar a white ruff, a fashion item that Catherine herself had influenced, circled his neck and a dark grey mantle was slung casually over his left shoulder to add some individual flair. All of it was topped off with a ridiculously elaborate gathered hat with a large, speckled feather poking from the top and several jewels sewn into the front. He looked and felt like an idiot, but fitted in with the crowd perfectly.

The unpredictable road of life had led him to this impossible moment. From a position of complete poverty he'd wriggled up the social ladder through plagues, wars, near scraps and adventure. He'd passed through every major French city, met and conned almost every famous family or church stalwart, witnessed war, escaped prison, started uprisings and learnt how to survive. Only one last massive hurdle to leap. On the other side of the door that led from the ballroom the Queen awaited his entrance.

The Queen.

If only she really knew who she was meeting. The scrawny waif of a boy born to a simple farm labourer who'd spent his entire life up to his knees in manure. In his so far successful attempt to leave history behind him, he'd managed to convince everyone he'd ever met except for Annabelle. She was the only one to see through him. He hoped it wasn't a quality that all females possessed, otherwise this wouldn't just be the biggest moment of his life, it might end up being his last.

The double doors were swung open and Philibert strolled confidently into the elegant lounge where he found two figures sitting comfortably on chaise longues covered in purple velvet. A further man stood uncomfortably inside an unusual metal contraption. A metal band was fastened around his waist and protruding from that were further bars that stretched over the top of his head and down to his knees. It looked to Phil at least that he'd recently picked a fight with a parrot's cage and had lost, badly.

The Queen was dressed in black, as she so often was, further propagating the notion that she was in league with the supernatural. Unlike her party guests, who used the event as an opportunity to push the boundaries of their own fashion standards, art and decency, she made little effort to fit in with any conventions. The black attire reflected the elaborate façade of grief she wanted to portray. Others would be forced to notice the deep grief she still carried two years on from the passing of husband. She was thin of stature and had eyes that protruded out as if on stalks from an otherwise rather plain face. A steely determination oozed from every gesture and posture she adopted.

"Please ignore Sir Nicholas," she said, referring to the man covered in metal. "He believes someone is trying to assassinate him."

"Right," said Phil, not certain quite how the birdcage get-up was going to protect him other than making any would-be assassin stop and gawp.

"So you are Philibert Lasage."

Phil nodded gracefully.

"And you had the audacity to come here and demand my time?"

"Yes."

Phil placed his hand in his pocket and removed the Montmorency ring, tossing it with a flick of his fingers to Anne, the other occupant on the couch. It landed on his lap jolting him from an open-eyed snooze.

"Well, I never," said Anne, "I had it on me all the time. Strange how things turn up like that."

"Constable, this man had your ring," said the Queen, pointing at Phil.

"What did you say?" said Anne, shuffling along the couch to get closer to his Queen.

"HE HAD YOUR RING."

"You!" said Anne. "I remember you. You're that doctor! Papadopoulos. Why, I should cut out your gizzard right here."

"Papadopoulos?" said Catherine with a furrowed brow.

"Yes, it's a small town just outside Saint Quentin," whispered Phil.

"What did he say?"

"Never heard of it," replied the Queen. "It's irrelevant anyway. Why are you in possession of the Constable's ring?"

Then Philibert did something he was unaccustomed to. He spoke the truth. It was a significant gamble, but weeks of planning and testing each possible scenario had convinced Phil and Chambard that the only possible route to success was the truth, the whole truth and nothing but the truth…up to a point. The Queen was known to have no love for the country's peasants, but she did recognise spirit. She herself had fought against the male-dominated world order to prove that she, a woman, could outdo the endeavours of men. Phil's story exhibited the same struggle with similar hurdles.

Phil summarised his history from Aix through St. Quentin to Marseille and everything in between without making mention to any of the scams he'd conducted on people unquestionably known to Catherine. He purposely focused most of his tale on his time with Nostradamus, his teachings and Phil's own natural ability at writing accurate prophecies.

"That's quite some story," she said after patiently letting him tell it.

"You couldn't make it up," said Phil.

"Well, you could."

"Majesty, this man is a thief and an imposter. He should be executed immediately," demanded Anne, advancing on Phil with a small but sharp dagger in his hand.

"Sit down," snapped the Queen.

Anne had been one of her husband's and father-in-law's choices as advisor and she only maintained his role because too many others were decidedly less loyal and more dangerous than he was.

"The Constable does make a valid argument, though. Why shouldn't I have you immediately dragged from my presence so they can separate your head from your body in an entertaining way?"

"Because I have seen what comes next?" said Phil calmly.

"Is it the sight of a gleaming blade crashing down on your throat?" replied Catherine menacingly.

"No. It's the sight of the gleaming blades of rebellion crashing down on your throne."

"I don't believe you."

"That's your choice, my majesty. Time will judge which of us is right."

"How do you know this?"

"Because I have spent time in the Huguenot camp and have witnessed their plans. Bloodshed is on the horizon unless you stamp your authority down on it now," said Phil.

"Nostradamus is my seer and, even though he is wrong as often as he is right, I still believe in his work. I could just ask for his opinion and have you killed for the fun of it."

"You could, if you can find him and then get a semblance of sense out of him. I'm surprised you're so fond of him. Didn't he predict that your husband would have a long and healthy life several months before he died."

The Queen's emblem, which adorned the walls of the room as well as the two shields above the fireplace, depicted a broken lance under a banner that read 'hence my tears, hence my sorrow'.

"Yes," she said joyfully, clearly much less in sorrow than her emblem suggested. "It did me more favours than it did Monsieur Nostradamus, I gather."

"But I am not him. You can't afford to ignore what I have to say," teased Phil, desperate to find the fear inside her that would set the con in motion.

Queen Catherine was fascinated by astrology and astronomy in equal measure and had an insatiable thirst for self-development. She also had a deeply superstitious nature. Not all superstitions were stupid. Not walking under ladders was symbolic of the path convicts took to the gallows, spilling salt was bad luck because it was rare and expensive, and it made perfect sense in religious circles that the number thirteen was best avoided. There were some, however, that plainly weren't sensible.

There appears no obvious reason why the shoes of horses are lucky. In a horse race all horses wear shoes, but how many fall over? Plenty. That doesn't sound very lucky.

And yet how often does the horse in your local field win the lottery? Never. At least the horse only had to give up a shoe. The poor rabbit had to lose the whole foot, and no rabbit that suffers such a curse will ever agree it was very lucky for them. Then there's the practice of 'touching on wood', which is only slightly weirder when people use someone's head as a substitute for wood. Wood isn't often confused with foreheads in other situations. If a landscape gardener runs out of wood when constructing a garden deck he doesn't round up random passers-by and nail-gun their heads to the beams instead.

It didn't matter if they were stupid or sensible because Catherine believed them all. And the one she believed in more than any other was not to reject a prophecy when it's being offered to you for free.

"I can afford to ignore you if I choose to. How confident are you in this prophecy of yours?"

"Unlike Michel, I don't make mistakes," replied Phil boldly.

"Excuse me," said Nicholas Throckmorton gingerly from behind his own personal mobile prison cell. "Can you tell me if the end is nigh?"

"Oh yes."

"And is it?"

"I couldn't possibly say," teased Phil. "It depends how long away you think nigh is?"

"Now," replied Nicholas. "It's always now!"

"Whatever you want to believe," replied Phil.

"I tire of this nonsense!" exclaimed Catherine. "Constable, take him away and torture him cruelly until he turns a lovely shade of blue."

"Which one of them?" asked Anne, uncertain which of Phil or Nicholas she most wanted punished.

"Him," said Catherine, pointing at Philibert. "He's clearly a fraud."

"With pleasure!" said Anne de Montmorency.

"WAIT!" shouted Phil. "Let me prove I'm the real deal. I have seen what will become of your son the King."

With a mighty crash a side door was kicked in and a young boy in full evening wear stormed into the room like he owned the place. Which, as it happened, he did. A face of pale thunder, he picked up an expensive-looking china ornament of a woman nursing a dog and threw it at the fireplace where it shattered beyond repair. Further priceless artefacts were purposely tipped from their position until he felt he'd gained their full and proper attention.

"Mother, the milk has made me emotional!" he said, stamping his feet petulantly.

"Not now, dear, Mummy's working."

"MILK!"

"Ok, my sweetheart. Calm down. Do you want cow or human?" answered the Queen.

"Peacock!"

"Nicholas, please attend to the King's wishes," the Queen demanded of her aide, clearly in no mood to challenge her child's boisterous behaviour.

"Um…I don't believe you can milk a peacock, your majesty. They generally not equipped for it."

"Look, if the King wants peacock milk he must have peacock milk," she said with a glare that wasn't even partly in jest.

Nicholas shuffled off towards the exit frequently snagging his protective metal cage on long, flowing curtains or frames of doors.

"Anything else, my dear?" she said to Charles.

"Yes. I want to invade Luxembourg."

"What, now?"

"Immediately!"

"My darling, the peace treaty took a very long time to negotiate, it would seem a shame to break it to acquire a densely wooded forest little bigger than the royal gardens."

"I don't care. I can do what I want. I am King. Get me Luxembourg without delay."

"We'll talk about it in the morning," replied Catherine.

"Who is this man?" said Charles, pointing aggressively at Philibert.

"State business."

"I don't like him. He has a woman's beard."

"That's enough, Charles, go to bed at once or I will not sanction your executions for a week!"

"How dare you threaten me, hag! One day you will do as I tell you. And if you don't, I will marry you off to some ghastly old widower in a horrible place like Wales."

"Yes, dear, of course you will. Constable, please escort my son back to his quarters."

"Don't touch me!" shouted the King before Anne could take him by the hand. "You smell of cheese, old man."

Soon the noise of distant tantrums receded and it was overtaken again by the din of the party next door. Now Phil was alone with the Queen and their dealings were poised on the edge of a knife.

"Lovely boy," said Philibert. "Full on, though."

"It is no concern of yours. One day he will be King and we will all have to do as he says."

"I'm sure peacocks everywhere will rejoice the day."

"His choices are his."

"I understood he was ill, your majesty."

"You know nothing of it."

"Not true. I know he suffers from mood swings that often place him and others in danger."

"How do you know this?"

"I know many things. It must worry you that he might not be able to carry out his royal duties in the manner you expect?"

"What do you know exactly?"

"I know it will have consequences to the Crown unless you act, my lady. I have already foreseen it. His behaviour, and your management of it, will impact the course of this religious discord. Let me show you what I can do. Then you can benefit from my vast insights in the future."

The bait was on the hook. It would be consumed by the next bite or it would swallow him. The Queen considered his proposition for a moment. It was a no-lose situation. If he failed she could work his death into one of her next operas, and if he succeeded she would understand more than her enemies.

"Very well. Write me a prophecy. If it doesn't come true within a week I will have you executed. But I won't just chop off your head like everyone else, I'll find a really long and painful way of doing it. Do you understand?"

"Yes."

"What are you waiting for, then? Go write," she said, wondering why he was still standing in front of her.

"I already have."

"Oh. Then show it to me."

Phil produced a small roll of paper from the inside of his mantle and bowed as he placed it in her hands. Catherine unrolled the scroll and read the information it contained. Once she'd processed it calmly she rose from her seat, walked to the raging fire in the hearth and threw the paper carefully into the flames.

"You now have my attention," she said, turning to Philibert.

- Chapter 24 -

In Pursuit of Madness

Jacques de Saluces and his goons waited in shadows as Philibert left the palace of Hôtel des Tournelles. To his great relief he'd left by his own free will and with all his faculties fully functional, thereby proving to his captors that he was every bit the spy Michel had said he was. Now came the debrief that Jacques had already declared before the visit would happen immediately. Their destination for this was a property owned by Louis de Bourbon, Prince of Condé, one of the Protestant ringleaders.

Whatever intelligence Phil had gathered would be vital to establishing the Catholics' next move, and Jacques would be the hero of the hour for passing it on. Or at least he would, if Phil had gathered anything interesting. Or anything at all for that matter. When entering an interrogation, 'nothing' was a pretty poor starting position, particularly when the other party had interesting ways of making you run much faster than the human body was normally capable. If he didn't want branded skin with permanently burnt scar tattoos he definitely needed to have something.

"Tell us all you know," demanded Jacques angrily the moment they set foot in the building.

"Hold on a second. Where are your manners? Aren't you meant to take my cloak from me, offer me a drink and engage in some hearty yet pointless chit-chat?"

"No. I think you're confusing me with someone who cares. Tell me now."

"Ok, the Queen has very exotic parties," replied Philibert, stalling as much as possible to gather his thoughts and invent the 'something' that might delay his inevitable beating. He failed.

The back of Jacques' hand struck Phil's cheek with force, knocking him clean off his feet. Jacques may not have been blessed in the thinking department, but he more than made up for it in physical presence. A giant of a man for the age, measuring in at around six feet, his arms were thick with hair and even thicker with muscle fibres. The first strike was merely a warning shot. He was capable and willing to inflict much more pain and Phil knew it. Jacques grabbed him by the ruff and dragged him up the stairs. A door jumped out of the way in fear of its hinges as Jacques thundered towards it. Finally Phil was deposited into the corner of the room with a simple flick of the wrist.

"If you speak out of turn again, traitor, I will punish you further, and next time you may not find it quite so easy to talk."

"Noted," said Phil, caressing the life back into his face.

"I'll ask you again. What are the Queen's intentions?"

Phil had no idea. At no point in their brief conversation had religion put in an appearance. It hadn't been important because Phil was setting up another part of his plan and his brain didn't have the capacity for more than one concept. Every stage would have to be tackled step by step. This was the next one and it had consumed very little of his attention. It didn't matter that Phil would have to get out of it by telling Jacques a lie, as long as he had enough time and opportunity to influence it suitably so it didn't end up being one.

"She's in a conciliatory mood," guessed Phil taking a lead out of Nostradamus's playbook by being as ambiguous as possible.

"How?"

"She will attempt to bring both sides together to agree how each should tolerate the other's faith."

"When will this occur?"

"It has not been agreed, but I'll know within a week," said Phil.

In a week either he'd be sawn into chunks and deposited in various parts of Paris or he'd successfully gained the Queen's trust. In attempting to achieve the latter, and this new lie, he'd have to convince Catherine of a new course of action through another suitably crafted prophecy. One step at a time.

"Why will it take a week?" demanded Jacques.

"Apparently she's got a hair appointment."

The other cheek received a smack and brought both sides of his face into harmony.

"You think you're so clever, don't you? The imposter who, like a wisp of smoke, can pass effortlessly through places that remain impassable to others. A master of disguises, here today and gone tomorrow. Well, I see through your disguise, Philibert. If you are lying to me, I'll be forced to remove your innards and wear them as a scarf."

"I'll never understand Renaissance fashion," replied Phil, quite unflustered by the physical and verbal intimidation. Threats of death and torture were not a new phenomenon in a world where presently more people wanted him dead than those who didn't.

Jacques raised his hand for another strike.

"Do you know a lie when you see one?" said Philibert to delay the punch. "Because a lie can be many things. To some a lie can be as believable as the truth, if they really want it to be. Sometimes a lie can lead in unexpected directions that may possibly be more advantageous than the truth. A lie is a perception of the facts as they are presented. I am the master of lies, Jacques, and you will never know if I'm telling you one or not until it's much too late."

Lies come in many forms. There's a huge variety on the spectrum between truth and untruth. Fibs, white, black half, exaggeration, subterfuge, bluff, memory hole, fake news all have a unique colour between black and white. The opposite of a lie is not always the truth, and the absence of truth does not always constitute a lie. Those who proclaim that they never tell lies are lying with the very statement because to humans lying is as natural as breathing. People lie to protect themselves, to gain advantage and to inflate their egos. But lying is not always a negative act. It can be used legitimately to avoid hurting someone's feelings or reducing pain.

So should all lies be treated equally?

If a lie is created with the right intentions, is the person who tells it sinister? Phil told lies as much as the next man. He was just better at it. Phil's lies were different because he fully intended to manipulate events so that in the end they turned out to be true. Is that still a lie? It's a matter of opinion. There was no malice in Phil's deceit because his objectives were clear. Make life better for himself whilst reducing the impact on others, except for those that did not deserve the relief.

"A lie is a lie," replied Jacques, angrily reinforcing the righteousness that all blue bloods carried deep in their DNA. The rich were right and the poor were liars. End of story. "Take him back to his quarters and keep guard over the door."

Two men of dubious genetic integrity each grabbed an arm and dragged Philibert carelessly down the corridor. It wasn't far. His room was next door, presumably to allow for his speedy retrieval and ability for others to eavesdrop. Inside, Chambard waited patiently for his return.

"You ok?" asked Chambard, while showing little other signs of concern.

"Fine. Been busy?"

"Not really. I've just spent the last four hours counting to myself," said Chambard.

"Counting?"

"Yeah. Couldn't think of anything else to do so thought I'd see how far I could get."

"How far?"

"Seventy-nine."

"And that took you four hours?" said Phil removing himself from the spot in the middle of the floor where he'd been dumped.

"No. That only took five minutes. I spent the rest of the time trying to remember what came next."

"It's quatre-vingts," replied Philibert.

"Four-twenty?" said Chambard. "That's mental."

"Oh, that's nothing. Just wait until you get a little further, it'll mess with your mind. Ninety-seven is four-twenty seventeen."

"Who the hell came up with that system?" replied Chambard. "Were they at the absinthe?"

"No idea. Just one of those oddities of history. I'm sure in the future someone will realise the stupidity of it and make changes."

"How did it go with the Queen?" said Chambard, mocking a little bow.

"I have a week."

"Did she buy it, then?"

"Time will tell."

"What prophecy did you give her?"

From the top of his head, Phil retold the prophecy he'd presented to the Queen no less than two hours ago.

Paris cowers under dark winter clouds
Screams of panic, fists of fury and the satanic babble
The madness of a royal child will change the nobles' mood
And only her medicine will cure the Saints of Germany

"How did you come up with that?"

"Well, Venus is in conjunction with Mars and it suggests, if you look at the events from thirteen-fifty-seven, that solar flares will increase the atmospheric pressure on earth. This will in turn impact on the level of complex molecules in the air, which, if you believe the studies of the notorious physician Jean Ruel, will greatly affect those with fragile mental states like the young King."

"Will it!?" said a highly gullible Chambard, deeply impressed by Phil's explanation.

"No idea...I made it up."

"Right...it was very convincing, though."

"That's good," he smiled, "it's kind of my job."

"But what does it mean?" asked Chambard more seriously.

"It means the already crazy Charles is about to advance up the madness scale from doolally to not allowed sharp objects."

"That's where I come in, isn't it?"

"Yep."

"You have a plan, then?"

"Of course."

"It's not going to be easy, this one. I mean we're stuck in here, aren't we?"

"That's true, but we've got out of more difficult situations than this. Let's use the old sacks in the bed routine," said Phil.

"Then out through the window," nodded Chambard in agreement.

"Exactly. The prophecy shouldn't take too long to pull off but it'll need to be done at night. Should be back before anyone notices we're gone."

"Ok, when?"

"Tomorrow night," replied Phil assertively.

"What do we need?"

IN PURSUIT OF MADNESS

"A small bag of gunpowder, a wooden box, two guards' uniforms, a long ball of string and someone who's excellent at gossip.

*****

Other than the two cronies stationed just behind their door, often heard snoring to expose their ineffectiveness, security around the house was limited. Jacques and his cohorts had much more to occupy themselves than chaperoning prisoners. They had an ulterior motive for being in Paris. Each night they congregated in the room next door to Phil's to discuss matters of the day and put alternative plans in place in case the Queen's attitude remained conciliatory. They didn't want tolerance of the religions, they wanted dominance of it. Calvinism, the new Protestant code, was the future.

Annabelle was never party to these debates. In fact she was never party to any conversations at all. Her existence in this strange city was one of abject loneliness. No friends here to confide in, or release the tight noose of isolation. While others planned their own exciting adventures, she was left to idle away the day with needlework, piano practice or reading. This wasn't the life she pined for. Her eyes had been opened to the world's suffering and it had impressed upon her a need for action. It was impossible for her to contribute to that while she remained married to Jacques, whose only interest in her was in bed or in public. It was time to join the ranks of the era's other notable women who were making their mark.

As Phil and Chambard descended through their window and out into the chilly night air she ventured up to the first floor to eavesdrop on muffled conversations leaking through the door from Jacques and his men. Ear pressed up to the wood to decipher as much detail as possible, she followed that evening's debate.

"He said the Queen was in a conciliatory mood," laughed the unmistakable voice of Jacques. "Let's see how long that lasts."

"Do you still intend to go through with it, then?" said another voice whose owner Annabelle couldn't place.

"Yes. Every good monarch needs a war, it's only this one isn't marching over the borders. And Catherine is getting a war whether she wants one or not."

"How will it be triggered?"

"There will need to be a flashpoint. A confrontation between the leaders of both faiths. On the Catholic side the Guise brothers are probably the most volatile and least tolerant. If they were to, let's say, accidentally discover…" The room giggled like schoolchildren. "…A Protestant service in progress I'm sure it would send them into a violent retribution."

"But what if the Queen gives permission for such religious freedom? You did say she's being conciliatory."

"What if she does? We will build the bonfire of war, but the Catholics will light it. It will trigger an unstoppable chain of events that will set each side off against each other. There must be fatalities, lots of them, and it must be easy for each side to blame the other. What we are planning is the first spark that will light the great fire of religious war. A war that we will win."

"But sir, surely this is madness. We will turn people against us and lose any goodwill that we've earned."

"I have no interest in goodwill. The Catholics have had their turn. Those corrupt bastards in Rome have ruled over faith for more than a thousand years and look what good it has done us. Corruption, conflict, cruelty and now it's time for change."

A series of drink-fuelled yelps of agreement echoed around the room and forced the single naysayer into silence.

"When will this flashpoint occur?" said a third voice.

"Very soon. When the Guises return to Paris from their homestead in the early spring next year, then we will strike. I've even identified the perfect location."

"Where?"

Before Annabelle heard the answer footsteps approached the door. She turned and fled for fear of being discovered. In the comfort of her own living quarters she considered the impact of what she'd heard. Peace had been a rarity in her short life. There were already enough wars around Europe without the need to construct one between their own people whatever their religion. As the only person with any knowledge of this deception, she set to work on a plan to stop it.

*****

Getting inside the grounds of the Palace was easy. For professionals like Philibert and Chambard it was no harder than opening the door to your own home. It was a well-rehearsed trick. Chambard would approach one of the guards at the front gate pretending to be a distressed local or lost traveller, while Phil would come up behind them and strike a blow to the head. Once dragged away and tied up, uniforms could be borrowed and 'voilà' you were on the Queen's payroll. No one wore security badges or name cards. Uniforms were all you needed to fit in.

Phil's plan had two stages. The first was to carry out an act designed purely to increase the already erratic behaviour of the young King. The second was to ensure as many of the royal court, most of whom were tucked up in bed, witnessed it with their own eyes. That way the most loose-lipped amongst them would spread the message within their circles of influence and the King's reputation would be broken irreparably.

To achieve the first stage they needed to scare the crap out of Charles without being noticed. Phil had already completed the necessary reconnaissance during yesterday's visit, even though he wasn't aware of it at the time. He'd identified the best entrance into the castle, knew where the private quarters were and what security was in place. Very few guards protected the royal family who believed that any dangers were likely to come from external rather than internal threats. If there was no army at the door people slept peacefully.

They moved swiftly through the corridors unchallenged, just two regular guards going about their normal business. They easily obtained the location of the King's chamber by asking one of their 'colleagues' for directions. They justified this unusual question by confessing that they'd not been to this palace before, which wasn't that unusual given how many homes the royal family owned. Once they were in the corridor outside the King's door the two took stock.

"Why am I doing this again?" asked Chambard.

"Because the boy knows what I look like. I have a woman's beard apparently."

"He's right."

"Never mind."

"You know what to do?" asked Philibert.

"Yes. I sneak in without waking him and place this strange box under the bed. What did you call it again?"

"A firework," replied Philibert.

"Right. So, I put the firework under the bed and light the slow fuse and then come back out pronto."

"Exactly, but you must retreat quietly or we'll give the game away. I expect there will be a bit of a delay as the fuse reaches the wood. That way we'll be nowhere near it when it goes off."

"Won't it blow up the bed?"

"No. I've only put a tiny amount of gunpowder inside. It'll just make a really loud bang, scare the wits out of the King and send him into a fit of panic. At least that's what

I'm hoping. Right, in you go. Quiet now, his nurse sleeps in the room attached to his. I'll keep watch."

*****

Sir Nicholas Throckmorton never slept particularly peacefully. But tonight he woke with a jolt sweating heavily. His dreams had always troubled him. Most of them had a habit of picturing scenes of terror, mostly involving him. Biblical ones were very popular. A recurring one involved a small pack of demons poking him with sticks while he rotated over an open fire and they made vigorous accusations about his parentage.

But tonight's dream was a little closer to home.

It had involved the young King rampaging through the palace, screaming obscenities, destroying prized art collections and repeatedly punching his young sister in the face. It was clear, in the dream at least, that Charles had totally lost control of his mind and could no longer function normally. 'But what could have triggered him into it?' everyone in the dream was asking. It was at that moment Nicholas woke up.

Of all the personal qualities that people recognised in Nicholas, one was stronger than all others: paranoia. If they gave out awards for it he'd have so many acceptance speeches he'd run out of people to thank. Whether in his waking moments or unconscious ones the fear of impending doom consumed fifty per cent of his attention. The other half was taken up with schemes to avoid it.

One of these elaborate tactics was always to do whatever you were told to do. Not doing so was the equivalent of accepting you'd wake up in the morning somewhere underwater covered in rocks and with your ankles tied to your ears. Of course that probably wasn't the likely outcome, but paranoia doesn't do 'best-case' scenarios. Failure in normal situations didn't have such terrifying outcomes. Imagine if a wife or husband threatened the other with execution just because they'd forgotten to wash the dishes or walk the dog. Now there are laws against such things. But there wasn't in the Middle Ages, which meant paranoia forced you to do as instructed.

Even the impossible.

And by doing so he'd lied to the Queen.

It wasn't really peacock milk. How could it be? He'd called it peacock milk because no one in history, including the King, had actually seen it before or knew how it tasted. To escape the possibility of a watery grave with only cod for company, Nicholas had invented one. The exact recipe was hard to remember as he'd got carried away, adding ingredients like an experimental chef. The recipe definitely started with cow's milk and was finished with a garnish of the little mushrooms he'd found growing in the meadow near the cows.

*****

"And he definitely didn't wake up?" enquired Phil.

"Not a peep. Quiet as a mouse, like he wasn't even there. What now?"

"We silently make our escape and act like we really do work here. I think we have about five minutes before it goes off."

They descended the stairs from the first floor, walking abreast and looking nerveless. They were used to blending in. Their heart rates were normal and not a bead of sweat was present on either of them. The nearer they advanced on the ballroom, the more an unexpected noise grew in volume. It was difficult to understand why there was such a commotion at this hour of the morning, particularly considering it was a Sunday and there was no party tonight. They shuffled calmly towards the door to the sitting room which had been flung open.

The contents of the room were in chaos. Many of the priceless paintings had been dislodged from their hooks, every porcelain vase had been smashed, a clock lay on the floor spewing its springs into the air, and a chaise longue had been upended. Somewhere, hidden in the midst of this destruction, echoed the familiar sound of a fist hitting flesh followed immediately by muffled whimpering.

"Chambard, was the King definitely in bed?"

"Yeah, I think so. I didn't stop to read him a lullaby or anything. Why you asking?"

"Because I think he's in the middle of that," said Phil, pointing into the room.

Through an entrance on the other side of the room a number of adults dressed in bedclothes rushed in looking horrified. Sir Nicholas whose sense of paranoia had already pictured it, was the first on the scene.

"Piggy tail!" screamed Charles. "I saw a pig's tail coming out of her nightdress. And two little pixies in her hair. They taunt me."

"Mamma!" cried the young girl.

Nicholas rushed forward to grab hold of the boy's fists before he could inflict more punishment on his sister.

"Ah, the little milkman!" screamed Charles, desperately trying to free himself. "May the Devil scorch your behind with handfuls of fiery hedgehogs."

It wasn't long before the room was a veritable crowd of people who'd been woken from their slumbers by the noisy racket and had been forced to seek out its source. They would all witness the deeds or aftermath of the King's anarchy, which only ceased with the arrival of the distraught Queen.

"I think that's probably done it," whispered Phil.

"I'd say so," replied Chambard. "I don't really understand what's happened, though."

"Retreat now, understand later."

Heart rates a little speedier than normal, they turned on their heels and jogged as swiftly and quietly as they could from the castle via the nearest exit. Once they were in the safety of the palace grounds they slumped against one of the outer walls to give Chambard a chance to give his aging body a breather.

"That's the second time," said Chambard.

"I know," replied Phil, equally perplexed.

"If you were a woman they'd have burnt you by now. It's proper dark, this."

"Don't look at me. I'm not trying to do it. I broke most of Michel's rules and it's still happening. What more can I say? Fluke?"

"I think we're way past fluke, Philibert. I think you might have an actual gift."

"Don't be ridiculous, we don't believe in such stupidity. We never have. We get by with self-discipline, not some unexplained magic."

"I know, but how else would you explain it?"

Their conversation was violently interrupted by a large explosion from the tower above them. Instinctively they covered their ears, crouched like a golfer had just shouted fore in their direction. Pieces of rubble splattered the ground, narrowly missing them, before a fully intact four-poster bed landed on the lawn with a thud.

"I might have overdone the gunpowder," said Phil, straightening up.

"It's a good job you can predict the future, because you're shit at faking it."

*****

They returned to the relative safety of the house in the early hours of the morning by shimmying up the side of the house in the same manner as they'd left it a few hours before. Chambard struggled, both his extra years and extra weight combining to cause his face to go red and his body to shake. He hit the floor of the bedroom in a heap of human exertion.

"I'm getting too old for this," he puffed.

"I know. You should retire," replied Phil with a cheeky grin. "Hopefully that day is coming for both of us."

"I may not see it. I felt it tonight, more than ever before. It's hard to explain. It feels like a shroud is pushing down on my body as if it can no longer hold my soul in place."

"You'll be fine, it's just the exertion of tonight."

"No Phil, I'm in my sixties. I can't go on forever."

On the table in the middle of the room was a letter that had not been there when they left. Someone had been in their room. Philibert unfolded it and read the elegantly written message.

"What's that?" asked Chambard.

"It's from Annabelle. I think she's a planning something stupid."

- Chapter 25 -

End of the Line

What began as a restrained and disciplined panic was evolving into something much more lawless. Initially people's reaction to the special measures implemented across Europe was one of resigned acceptance. Stay indoors, ignore other people, hunker down and wait for it to all blow over was how they'd interpreted the message. And this collective behaviour was working well almost everywhere.

Everywhere except France.

The French don't follow rules. They make their own depending on what has annoyed them most on any particular day. Which could be literally anything. The price of cabbages, the enforcement of a tax to support the protection of cute, fluffy animals, the speed on motorways, the number of times they were legally allowed to shrug, car indicator lights, how much fish they could catch, boomerangs, gravity, the consistency of whipping cream, and queues containing more than two people. It's hard to say where this national culture for rebellion came from, but the people of Marseille five hundred years ago might have offered an explanation.

The mood in France was changing because normal life was being messed with, and change was just not an acceptable premise. The supermarkets weren't being restocked sufficiently, and unlike the people of the United Kingdom, where every family of four now had more milk than their fridge could physically hold, they hadn't panic-shopped to quite the same degree. Bins weren't being collected, hospitals were cancelling all but the most critical operations and the police were absent because they were stuck on cordons rather than protecting shops and homes.

It only took one person to break the rules before everyone followed suit like a pack of lemmings attending a free bar. Ghostly streets made way for burning cars and masked vigilantes. Looting was widespread and crimes of all types and severity had become more popular than reality television. Most of these temporary felons, crossing casually to the wrong side of the line hoping no one noticed, justified their actions by claiming they only robbed essential items they needed to survive.

Closed-circuit television proved otherwise.

One in two robberies involved the stealing of flat-screen televisions, one in three targets were high-end jewellery shops, and one in ten thefts hit car dealerships. And the culprits of these crimes weren't just youths looking to climb through a window of opportunity that the police had opened wide before they'd left town permanently. Little old ladies with false hips were seen ram-raiding shopping centres in disposable sports cars, children as young as ten were wielding semi-automatic rifles, and gangs of middle-class mothers, brandishing baseball bats and wearing face masks, were roaming the streets generally tidying up the mess.

Buildings were set alight for the sheer fun of it, gangs patrolled their own sectors of cities like Gallic mafia families, and the police did nothing but watch from their cordons as a new genre of mass entertainment was created. They weren't that bothered. They only had one order to follow. As long as these people were kept inside the city they couldn't spread the virus. Whether anything of the city or its inhabitants survived afterwards was debatable. But then again this was the actual apocalypse, so no one would survive long enough to care.

END OF THE LINE

None of this behaviour would have been possible without a catalyst. It's not enough to have a culture of people with a propensity to break rules. Lots of people, for example, secretly held the belief that homeless people were feckless layabouts with only themselves to blame who blighted the streets and should be removed, or even better, lined up and shot. However extreme this notion might be, generally people withheld these views because of a complex set of social rules and the very good chance of being categorised as a heartless bastard. Most kept these views, and others they held about people of colour, men with Rottweilers and those afflicted with ginger hair, largely to themselves. Until someone or something made it acceptable to voice them. And when someone made racism, or looting acceptable, the floodgates opened.

The Oblivion Doctrine was the catalyst.

Anytime the authorities tried to calm the public, the Oblivion Doctrine would pop up in news feeds and mailing lists to offer the opposite opinion. After all, this was their apocalypse. No government was going to spoil it. Bird flu might be the compound that drained the life from people by mobbing their senses and squeezing the nutrients they needed to survive out of their bodies, but the Oblivion Doctrine provided the soundtrack, the documentaries and the official merchandise. The only question was whether they themselves understood the price of wiping out humanity.

*****

It was agreed unanimously that the safest place for their retreat was the caravan. It might be small, cramped and in desperate need of a damn good clean, but it was, at least for now, far enough away from danger. Limonest was a small provincial town of mostly rural folk. The flu might be wreaking havoc just fifteen kilometres away but it had not yet arrived here. Nor had the fear and panic that went with it. The town hadn't completely avoided the looting and crime, but there were more attractive targets to pillage than the spoilt ready meals of three obvious misfits living in a small, sheltered wood just off the main road.

In the vast pantheon of disappointing car journeys it seemed almost impossible that the journey back from Mâcon could be worse than the one out. But it was, on several levels. The long pieces of splintered wood, that once held together a humongous and valuable piece of Renaissance art, made a tremendously irritating rattling noise, and because most of it trailed out of the opened boot, the bitter winds penetrated the car and pummelled its passengers. Gabriel's driving had got worse, although neither Ally nor Antoine could identify where she was hiding the vodka which she was clearly using to top up her mood. And while on the way out no other drivers had challenged the Renault's erratic dominance of the roads, now a venerable collection of locals thought they were auditioning for the next *Mad Max* film.

To avoid the dystopian chaos that was the A6 between junctions twenty and twenty-two, they made a hasty detour via the smaller national roads which gave Gabriel a much larger pallet of objects to aim for. Lime trees, bollards, roundabouts, soon to be deceased pedestrians and rogue pets all served to add some extra excitement to a day that would last long in the memory.

Back in the relative sanctum of the knackered caravan, mugs of hot drinks prescribed and administered to settle head and heart, they sat around the small retractable table to analyse the family tree that had been concealed behind the picture frame.

"Do you think Bernie wanted you to find this?" said Gabriel, fiddling with the paper in a rather irritating way that showed a lack of respect to the clearly sizeable amount of work that had gone into it.

Family trees were hard to construct even with the benefit of computer archiving, the internet and family insight. Going back fifty years wasn't such a problem because most of the people who featured were likely to be still alive. Going back a hundred years was also fairly straightforward given the desire of every First World country to document people like a sinister stocktake. But, unless you hit a line of royalty in a family tree, going back further than that was almost impossible. Paper records had a habit of being lost or burnt or simply never existed in the first place. Yet Bernard had managed to track Nostradamus's tree from the roots of the famous seer right up to the present-day branches in every detail.

"Bernard always had a purpose. He certainly meant for us to find the family tree," replied Ally. "The real question is why?"

"It has something to do with the coffer," said Antoine confidently. "Bernard knew what was in the coffer and wanted to keep it out of the wrong hands. After they tried to steal it from me, but realised it was already gone, I imagine they traced it back to Bernard. I bet whoever killed him now has it. And we must get it back."

"But we don't know who they are."

"We do now. It's clear to me that Bernard had a suspect in mind. The man circled right here in red ink." He placed his finger over the name of Mario Peruzzi the fifteen times great-grandson of Michel Nostradamus.

"I think that's a reasonable hypothesis," replied Ally.

"But why hide it in the painting?" said Gabriel, twiddling her hair. "Why not leave it inside a bin or keep it in a high-security bank vault?"

"Or put it in an envelope, add a stamp and send it in the post? That's an ancient way of sending physical documents to each other, Gabriel," she added sarcastically.

"Maybe he was trying to be more dramatic?" offered Antoine who was clearly unconvinced by his own answer.

"The painting has more to do with this," said Ally. "The two are connected. I don't think it's a coincidence that the painting left to me, and not Antoine, contains a reference to a piece of jewellery that you own. Bernard is placing you and Mario in the same puzzle."

"More than that," said Antoine. "Him, me...and you."

"I know," said Ally not fully understanding why that might be. "He believes that I can solve it."

"And can you?" asked Gabriel.

"Not without help," she replied uncharacteristically. She hated to accept or ask for it, but collectively they had more chance of success together.

"Was that difficult?" asked Antoine.

"Very."

"Give it time, it'll get easier. Let's consider all the evidence. The coffer was living in my basement for four hundred years, and along with it the locket was also in my family's possession. Based on that, it would seem appropriate to assume that my ancestors were in some way connected with Nostradamus himself."

"I'd go further than that," added Ally. "I think maybe one of the people in the painting was the real author of the prophecy."

"Which one?" said Gabriel.

"That's just it, we've no way of knowing for sure. Our only lead is Mario Peruzzi. If he has the coffer then he has the secrets it contains."

"But why would Mario want to kill someone to retrieve something that once belonged to a distant relative of his?" asked Antoine.

"How do you feel about your ancestors, Antoine?"

"Proud, in general. I know they were active in supporting those that were not as fortunate as themselves."

"And how would you feel if someone uncovered some dark secret that destroyed that legacy?"

"I'm not sure really, it would probably change how I viewed myself. What are you implying?" said Antoine scratching a patch of scalp that his white hair was unable to cover.

"A theory, that's all. The only item that Bernard didn't buy from you was the book. And in that book is probably one of the most accurate passages that Nostradamus ever wrote…"

"But you say he didn't…"

"Correct. But do you see anyone else in the world disputing it? I mean they've already nicknamed N1G13 the Nostradamus flu. That prophecy was the perfect weapon for securing Nostradamus's legacy so why would you want to hide it? Then the question remains, what else was inside the coffer? What if those contents were less than complimentary about his work?"

"But that would mean this Mario character knew they existed all along, otherwise why would he go to such lengths to steal them?"

"Must have," said Gabriel trying her best to follow, but not altogether succeeding.

"Look at the family tree again," said Ally, having already used her highly honed research skills to make the conclusion she was leading them to. "What do you notice about all the people at the bottom of the tree?"

Antoine took a long, hard look at the document again as Gabriel stared vacantly at the mirror down the other end of the caravan. What was the point wasting valuable brainpower, when he worked it out she'd find out anyway?

"They're all dead," replied Antoine. "Apart from one."

"Exactly. Mario isn't just one of Nostradamus's descendants, he's the only descendant."

"Our trail points to Mario Peruzzi, then."

"Great!" exclaimed Gabriel. "Call the police, they can deal with it. Then both of you can go back to whatever it is that you do, and I can return to the important work of building my tree house to escape the angry mobs of zombies that will soon be marauding through the streets of Limonest."

"You know the virus only kills people, right? It doesn't also bring them back from the dead. Viruses don't do that, they're not Netflix writers," said Ally disdainfully.

"Plus the police are a little busy, what with all the looting and social disorder," added Antoine correctly.

"What then?" asked Gabriel.

"We have to find out where and who Mario is. We need the internet," added Antoine.

"I already tried that in the car on my phone," replied Ally. "Mario's a ghost. There's not a single piece of information about anyone with that name."

"That's impossible," said Gabriel.

Only members of isolated tribes living deep in the Amazon rainforest, who wore clothes made from feathers, hunted exotically coloured amphibians with small, blunt sticks and still prayed to the big yellowy thing in the sky, didn't have an online footprint. If you weren't one of those it was impossible not to have one. Yet here was an individual who was effectively invisible to the vast expanse of the worldwide web.

"It's not impossible," huffed Ally.

"I'm telling you it is! Give me the name of someone you think can't be found anywhere on the internet," said Gabriel perked up by the inclusion of the modern world into the conversation.

"Ok. My dad, Horace Oldfield. He's never touched a computer in his life."

"Pass me your phone," said Gabriel, hand outstretched.

She went to work. It didn't take long. Watching her work was no less captivating than watching a skilled craftsman blowing glass or a surgeon conducting a successful lobotomy.

"There you go," she said defiantly after no more than a five minutes. "Horace Oldfield, eighty-six years of age, widower, one child, which is you of course, lives in Blackburn, retired carpenter and rather fond of Turkish Delight."

"Jesus! How did you do that?" said Ally with a newfound respect for her.

"Oh it's easy if you know how. I got his photo from the care home's website and used that to scan for all other visual references of him. Got some more information by hacking a couple of government agencies."

"I'm impressed, and slightly worried," said Antoine.

"Well, that wasn't where I got most of the info from."

"Where, then?" asked Antoine.

"He's on Facebook and Snapchat," she added matter-of-factly.

"Bullshit!" exclaimed Ally, grabbing her phone back. "He'd think Snapchat was the noise a crocodile makes before it eats you. Oh…right…so he really is. They must have run a class at the home."

"Looks like your dad is more down with the kids than you are," replied Gabriel, intentionally trying to rile her.

"Gabriel, before you became a prepper?" asked Antoine, "what was your job exactly?"

"Computer programmer…and IT ninja," she replied, adding a bit of spice in case this might turn out to be a job interview.

"So, if you can find all that information about Horace, could you also find Mario?"

"Of course. There's a reason you can't find any information on him, but it's not just because you don't have the talent," she said without flinching. "The real reason is because he's working hard not to be found."

"Then what are you waiting for, find him."

"It'll cost…"

END OF THE LINE

"Another ten thousand euros," replied Antoine before Gabriel could even offer her starting price.

"I'm sure this isn't good for her," added Ally.

- Chapter 26 -

The Royal Seer

Every now and then a set of seemingly impossible combinations will come together to beat the odds. Down the years hundreds of people have won bets on unlikely sporting outcomes, but it would be false to say that they predicted them. Most of these punters didn't believe in their wildest dreams that the result would actually happen, they just hoped it would. However, the seemingly impossible occurs with frequent regularity.

Statisticians, a breed of people who shrivel up at the slightest contact with sunlight and own exceedingly boring haircuts, would be the first to pour scorn on people's claims of such things being coincidences. If two strangers met at a party and quickly identified they had the same birthday they'd quickly label it a rarity. Until the numbers men point out that the chances of it happening are more likely than it not happening. In a room of seventy-five people there's a ninety-nine percent chance of this eventuality. What might seem rare is in fact almost guaranteed.

Accurately predicting one event might not be quite the fluke that it first appears. But doing it twice, that was starting to look like skill.

The odds of being struck by lightning once are about twelve thousand to one. It's possible to dramatically increase these odds by walking out in a storm wearing inappropriate footwear and waving a pole vaulting stick in the air. The likelihood of being hit twice in a lifetime, though, are closer to one in a million. It does happen. But no one who's survived both events curses their luck. They're quite convinced that they've angered the cosmic energy in some way.

Philibert had now correctly predicted two events that he'd been quite prepared to falsify. In his attempts to con people into believing he was a powerful force in the world of future telling, he'd inadvertently done just that. The day after the incident with the King, the Queen had summoned Phil to see her. And this time there was no entourage to accompany him.

On arriving at the palace he was shepherded through a series of magnificently decorated reception rooms, each one suffocated by a collection of priceless objects inside their colourful walls. Decadence also oozed through the architraves and upholstery in a vulgar attempt to prove the royal family's wealth and class. Phil was torn between disgust and jealousy. Although he appreciated the hours of artistry and craft that had been poured into creating such wonderful pieces, he couldn't escape his anger that each one had been paid for by money that might be better spent on simpler pleasures, such as food and warmth for citizens whom the royals were supposed to protect.

Catherine stood alone on the terrace, covered in cosy layers and gazing out over vast gardens currently hibernating under winter's duvet. Phil bowed out of habit, even though she had her head turned away from him. He moved forward so he was standing next to her, but not close enough for it to feel uncomfortable. Her expression had a more fragile quality than it had done at their last meeting when circumstances were different.

"Do you know how it feels to be an outsider?" she said solemnly.

"I do, your majesty," he replied without an ounce of irony.

"When I first married my husband, Henry, I was a stranger here. I'd never even been to Paris before and all of a sudden it was my home. No one cared how I was feeling. I was simply here because I was a princess and the prince needed an heir. Not a wife, that was an inconvenience for the real need, a legitimate heir."

"And you provided him with many, your majesty."

"Eventually yes. But at first I was unable to bear him one," she said, her voice trembling under the emotion. It was rare for her to let her real self sneak out from behind her tightly fitting mask, and she only did so with those she trusted. "We tried of course, when the King wasn't in the arms of his mistress. Do you know what I had to do?"

"No."

"Everything," she snapped. "Doctors suggested all manner of untested therapies to boost the chances of conception. They made me drink mule's urine and told me to place antlers on my 'source of life' in a ridiculous attempt to improve my fertility. But no children. When his brother died suddenly and he ascended to the throne they even suggested that I be replaced. Can you imagine how that feels?"

"Lonely," replied Philibert.

"And through all of this personal embarrassment the main cause for my situation turned out to be an abnormality with him."

Philibert listened intently, and just a little awkwardly, as the Queen talked about her late husband's tackle.

"These are the great lengths I have been through to have my children and I will do everything in my power to protect them and their legacy, do you understand?"

"Yes, of course."

"My forced alienation made me determined to succeed where lesser men had failed, and how do they reward me? They call me a witch," she said, turning to face her subject, a tear in her eye. "Yet you, Philibert Lesage, who clearly possesses great affinity with the dark arts, they call you a prophet. How can that be fair?"

"It isn't, your majesty. The world isn't."

"Your prophecy about the King has come to pass," she said casually.

"I wasn't aware," he lied.

"Word for word."

"Really? Because even I was slightly uncertain about the part about German saints," he replied.

"That was the really impressive part. I had already decided to gather the nobles together next month at Saint-Germain here in Paris to heal the wounds of division. Very few others knew of this decision. Now that the discontent over the King's behaviour is growing, I must stamp my authority over the nobles even more. But I cannot foresee their reactions."

Phil knew that was where he came in.

"I am appointing you my Royal Seer," said Catherine.

"I am flattered, your majesty, but I'm not really in the market for a…"

"You're not being asked, Lesage. You either accept the position with honour or lose your head with trauma."

Phil hadn't predicted this, which was annoying, really, given his recent successes. He'd never wanted a permanent arrangement within the court, only to use it to remove himself from the clutches of Claude and his family. Now they both had control over him, and control was something he cherished above all other privileges.

"Then I cordially accept," replied Phil.

"Good. Now tell me what I need to know."

The letter from Annabelle was brief and lacked detail, but it was enough to make some predictions of what might happen. Whatever Catherine agreed between the two sides of nobles during the Edict of Saint-Germain it might not survive what was being planned in a month or so from now. But even Philibert couldn't predict where it would happen. He told Catherine as much as he knew, dispensing with any need to hide it within the text of a quatrain. She took note of the potential disruption to her plans and advised Phil to keep her briefed on any further information. Whatever involvement Annabelle was planning to have, Philibert would have to beat her to it.

*****

It was a day of many firsts for Annabelle. The first time she'd worn male clothes. She wasn't a fan. The leggings were so tight they cut off the blood flow to the crotch area, presumably, she thought, in the vain attempt to enlarge everything. It was the first time she'd ridden a horse unaccompanied. Ladies didn't ride alone. They couldn't be trusted with anything as complicated as making a large mammal move in the right direction. She knew how to ride of course. It wasn't skill that stopped her, it was invariably men.

It was also the first time that she'd stolen a horse, although she liked to think of it as an unapproved lease. After adding a few hundred miles on the clock she was definitely planning to return it in reasonable working order sometime in the near future. And the first time she'd been to the town of Vassy, although nothing identified it as such, to her it was just another town called poverty. It must be a town of significance because it was here that Jacques had unknowingly led her. The location that she'd failed to hear from his conversation.

Always riding far enough behind, to avoid her husband or any of his men noticing her following them, it had taken three days of hard riding to reach the town. Whatever Jacques was planning it was serious enough to require the entire company, which meant leaving her alone. She was glad of it, too. It allowed her the ideal circumstances to ensure she wasn't missed.

Not long after arriving, Jacques and his group had slipped into town to blend in with the locals, dispensing with their normal clothing and dressing as commoners. Intrigued by this, Annabelle tied up her borrowed horse and did her best to follow them.

Vassy had few sights of merit. A few peasants rolled around in the mud engaged in a fierce argument over a woman called Nelly. An inn was on fire, although it didn't seem to be halting normal business, as everyone continued enjoying the hospitality without being overly distracted. Even though it was late winter most patrons sat outside on benches, the inside being a little too toasty.

Annabelle wondered why this town was even known by the nobles, let alone a place of interest. After searching the streets for most of the morning she noticed that a large number of people were moving stealthily in one direction. She followed them to the outskirts of the town where they entered a huge barn. It looked very much like any other barn. Wooden structure, surrounded by livestock, simple farming equipment leaning idly against the sides. But once she'd ventured inside she knew the structure was doubling as a church.

It wasn't much of a church. Location was one of the downsides of being a Protestant, something Annabelle knew only too well. The Catholics had spent centuries building mighty monoliths in which to praise their idea of God. There was plenty of choice, too. Every city, town and village had their own version, the scale of the effort to build it often in stark contrast to the limited size of its likely congregation. But this was not true for the new religious doctrine. If you were Protestant anywhere would do, and in Vassy this was it.

By lunchtime around six hundred worshippers had gathered secretly in this simple place of prayer in the knowledge that no rules had been broken. The recent Edict of Saint-Germain, although not yet ratified by Parliament, had clearly stated that all religions had the right to practise freely, as long as they did so in rural locations and not to the detriment of the other. This rule only applied to them of course: the Catholics could keep doing whatever they wanted to. But at least it was a start, a compromise that finally gave legitimacy to their faith even if it wasn't altogether equitable. Perhaps the fated war against each side might yet be averted.

Not wanting to draw attention to herself, she stood at the back of the barn and watched the service commence. There were hymns, prayers and Bible readings, just like a Catholic service with only one crucial difference. There was a lot less doom. The Catholics needed a big, healthy dollop of the stuff and usually still went back for seconds. Almost anything a member of the congregation had done since the previous Sunday was likely to be doomworthy. Ploughed the wrong field, doom. Wore the wrong-coloured hat, doom. Exhaled noisily in church, doom. Complained of a headache, doom. Smiled at someone kindly, doom. Woke up next to three random naked women having drunk nineteen bottles of wine the night before…actually that was doom in both religions.

Midway through the service, as the pastor was giving his address, a loud thump bellowed through the wood of the closed barn door. It was largely ignored until several more fists rained down upon it, furiously seeking attention. Finally, after none of the six hundred people seemed eager to open it, someone on the outside took it upon themselves to force it open. Annabelle watched from the shadows as two dozen heavily armed men appeared at the doorway behind a skinny man dressed from head to foot in black other than the single white feather that poked through his hat. He puffed out his chest and stroked his wispy blonde goatee beard before addressing the congregation, who did their best to crane their necks around to see him.

"Not much of a church, is it?" he said, kicking the straw under his feet. "To think that you would give up the one true faith in order to praise our Lord in a barn only suitable for swine. Is that how you would offer Him reverence? Come to our church, pray for God's grace and honour Him in the shit and dust," he said in mock announcement.

"We have done nothing wrong, and you are not welcome here, Catholic," said the pastor in the loudest booming voice he could muster.

Francis, the Duke of Guise, chuckled to himself. He despised anyone who had succumbed to the Calvinist brainwashing that had kidnapped their minds from the one true religion. But other than taunts there was little he could do. Unless he was given cause to do so, he would have to leave them be at the behest of the Queen's decision to allow the sacrilegious Edict of Saint-Germain.

"You are right, my blasphemous friend. You have broken no laws. But everything you do here is wrong. I ride to Paris, and when I get there I will impress upon Her Majesty her own misguidance and lack of judgement. And if she does not bow to this pressure I will take all action necessary to wipe this phoney religion from the fields and," he chuckled again, "barns of France."

As his small band of soldiers turned to leave a man stood up in the crowd defiantly. It was Jacques and he was holding a large stone in his hand. Annabelle knew that this was the flashpoint he'd been planning. There was no way she could get close enough, quick enough to stop him. Everyone watched helplessly as he wound up his right arm to launch the rock in the direction of the Duke. But before he released it someone caught hold of his wrist. It was Philibert.

A minor and rather one-sided fight broke out in the middle of the congregation as Philibert tried vainly to wrestle the rock from the hand of his enemy. Jacques' greater strength prevailed and Phil was knocked to the ground. His attempt to foil the plan had failed and he was forced to witness the rock, hurled with great precision, strike Francis Guise on the back of the neck. The Duke was immediately knocked to the floor in a state of semi-consciousness, blood gushing from the wound. His band of soldiers drew their swords and bows to defend their leader. And everyone knows that the best form of defence is attack.

The first arrow struck an elderly gentleman in the chest and like a Mexican wave the panic spread from the back of the church to the front. The crowd of worshippers were totally defenceless: they'd come for communion not confrontation. More arrows pierced flesh and bone as the people tried desperately to locate a protected space or alternative exit. There were none. The only way out was through the flying arrows and shiny blades, and the only safe place was to cower behind another body.

Annabelle's concern rested with only one of these people. She scurried around the side of the chaos so she could cut in through the crowd to find the place where Jacques and Philibert had fought. Bodies fell in her path as they were struck by projectiles that whizzed through the air. An arrow struck a barrel just as she ducked in behind it. It wobbled precariously in the wood and she instinctively pulled it out to use as a meagre weapon if she had to protect herself. Within the mass of bodies, some alive and some dead or close to it, Jacques had Philibert pinned to the floor with a massive hand on his throat. No con or prophecy would extricate him from this.

"What more proof do I need?" growled Jacques as Phil desperately struggled to release himself from the stronger man's grip. "A Catholic spy just as Nostradamus said."

"No. I'm not even religious, I just didn't want to see these innocent people killed in cold blood," he replied through broken gulps of air as the breath was squeezed from his airways.

"This is war, my friend, that's what they're supposed to do. Now you will join them and the good news is it'll look like it was done by your own people. It'll be on Guise's head, not mine."

Jacques raised his hunting knife with his free hand, poised to strike the fatal blow. "Any final words, traitor?"

"Yes," Phil gasped, "I think your wife wants you."

"What?"

He followed Phil's eyes through the commotion and came face to face with a figure kneeling in the sawdust behind him.

"Hello, Jacques."

A million emotions flooded through her in a fraction of a second. All the times he'd hurt her physically and emotionally. The way he'd destroyed her confidence and made her feel small. All the times he'd summoned her, dragged her, beat her, abused her and humiliated her were all rolled up into one single compulsion. Annabelle thrust the point of the arrow into his eye. Jacques fell to the floor and immediately released his grip from Phil's neck as he lay motionless on the ground.

"Annabelle," said Philibert, trying to break concentration, transfixed on the scene she'd created.

"I've…killed…him," she mumbled.

"No more than he deserved."

"Help me," she trembled. "I don't know what to do."

"We need to get out of here before we end up joining him," Philibert said assertively as the arrows continued to rain down around them. "Come on, I know a way."

On their bellies they scrambled through upturned benches and passed wounded victims. All around them the sound of battle ensued, even though there was only one side fighting. Terrible, ear-splitting screams echoed around the high-vaulted roof unable to escape, much like their owners. When they reached one side of the structure Phil searched around for the route out. A broken panel had been his means of entry and he hoped it would offer the same ease of exit. It did.

On the other side of the barn there was an odd sense of tranquillity as if the massacre inside had occurred in another dimension entirely. Still they moved a good distance away in case Guise's men decided to spread their menace further. How many had been killed in the melee was unclear. But when you had a motivated foe, a cul-de-sac and limited resistance, it was safe to assume that dozens would have fallen.

"Looks like Jacques has his war," said Phil. "Even if he won't be there to witness it. Are you ok?"

"I'm not sure," replied Annabelle, her exposed skin paler than normal.

"It's over for you now. He can't hurt you anymore."

"No, it isn't over. There will be others. Father will not accept a daughter out of wedlock: he'll soon have me hitched again, you'll see. I can't go back, Phil, let me stay here with you."

"You must. I can't hide you here. Go back to Marseille, tell your father that Jacques was killed here. When the time is right I'll come for you, I promise."

"Really? You'd do that for me."

"Yes. But only once everything is in place and we can be together without interference."

"What about Chambard?"

"I don't really think he fancies you," said Phil with a chuckle.

Under the enormity of the last hour she just about managed to force a smile as she looked around surprised to see that Chambard was nowhere to be seen. "Where is he?"

"He wasn't up to the journey. Not fit enough. I have to accept that Chambard's time is coming to an end and I need to prepare myself for a life without him. I need a replacement. Want to apply?"

- Chapter 27 -

The Search for Mario

Most people only understand a tiny proportion of the equipment they use every day. How many people knew how a TV works? Not many. How much of the average computer do people actually use? Ten or twenty percent maximum. It was the same with the internet. The vast majority didn't even know what it was capable of, let alone use its full capacity. Banking, shopping, locations on maps, funny pictures of cats and naughty videos were easy enough to find. But what if someone wanted more from it?

Then they'd need someone who was under thirty.

That subgroup of humanity haven't developed their capabilities with technology over an extended time because the internet was always there. As familiar in everyday of life as the air that flows through lungs. And it's not just what they had available to them that changed. The way they used it changed, too. Take instruction manuals, for example. Not the online videos you see of some hairy-arsed electrician from Hartlepool showing you the correct method for wiring a plug. I mean the paper instructions. When was the last time anyone saw a millennial reading one of those?

Never.

They didn't do it that way. They didn't need to because they learnt in a way that appeared to involve magic, intuition and a heavy dose of self-confidence. At least that's how it looked if you were someone of Ally Oldfield's age. They can't explain how this is possible, and will only gawp at you insultingly if you even mentioned it. They just can, and everyone born before nineteen-ninety needs to get over it. End of. It's no wonder the rest of society looked at them like aliens. Imagine what it'll be like when their children grow up.

While the rest of us struggled to remember a simple eight-digit password that we only set last Wednesday, they attacked an online problem with the same ease that a football player attacks an open goal. And all they needed was WI-FI, a smartphone and a power source. Take those away from them and they were about as useful as a plastic saucepan.

Over the last hour, Gabriel's attention seemed unbreakable. Quite unlike the attitude they'd witnessed over the rest of the day, when the smallest stimulus would distract her into daydreams, now you could set a grenade off and she wouldn't have flinched. The other two sat quietly drinking cups of tea, having received plenty of scalding from the computer expert when they'd casually enquired what exactly she was doing. This wasn't their world. They just had to wait and hope that behind all the furious finger-tapping, Gabriel was in fact searching for Mario and not playing Angry Birds.

"Got him!" she said with a little bounce in the air and a fist pump with the invisible man.

"Excellent," said Antoine. "Well done. How did you do it?"

"Do you really want me to explain it?" replied Gabriel in a horribly disdainful tone that indicated she could but he probably wouldn't understand.

"Yes, I'm big on learning, even if I am this old."

"Right," she sighed. "Well, I started off by accessing the dark web, then I angulated the peer-to-peer networks, datamined a few server directories, thunked and phished for a while to extrapolate some of the Linux interfaces…"

"You're right," replied Antoine, struggling to understand even a single word of it. "I don't really need to know."

"Thought not."

"So who is Mario?" asked Ally.

"He's a genius," replied Gabriel, "but as I found him that makes me one, too."

"I'm sure you are, and modest, too. Why is he a genius?"

"You said he was a ghost, right, and I said he was trying not to be found," reminded Gabriel slowly. "Well, they're both true. Mario Peruzzi is responsible for the most secretive organisation in the world. Mario is the Oblivion Doctrine."

"Are you sure?"

"Definitely. Once I'd made the link, and fought through about twenty encrypted firewalls, by the way, I tracked his IP address and they connect the two of them together."

"IP address…Immediate Postal Address?" said Antoine naïvely.

"Internet Protocol. But in effect it works the same way as your house address for your online presence."

"Do you know where he is, then?"

"Yes and no."

"How does that work?" said Ally.

"The IP address doesn't tell me exactly where he is because you can move around with a phone and your IP address moves with you. I can use it to narrow Mario to one place, though."

"Where?"

"Marseille."

"Jesus. Only five million people across a massive city, then. Shall we just pop down there now and start a door-to-door search, if we can avoid the ram-raiders, burning cars and squeeze past the police cordons of course? I can't think of a more efficient way of catching N1G13, can you, Antoine?"

"I never suggested that," replied Gabriel, looking a little hurt at the accusation after all the hard work she'd put in.

"What do you suggest, then? Something technological no doubt."

"Duh, of course. I thought you were smart," replied Gabriel, accentuating every word in a childish manner.

"What a good idea," said Antoine, immediately making the connection. "Now we know Mario is the Oblivion Doctrine we use his own platform to draw him out."

"This will be the same man who's trying to have you killed, is it? I'm not sure I want to tell him where we are, actually," replied Ally.

There was undoubtedly an element of risk involved in making contact with the Oblivion Doctrine, but there wasn't another obvious way of getting to him. Gabriel had done all she could, and that was more than anyone had expected. If they wanted to know what Mario knew it seemed the only option.

"We have to," said Antoine more forcefully than normal. "Don't you see? All the dots are being connected together and they all point in one direction. The Oblivion Doctrine started all this panic and it looks clear to me why. Mario is doing what Nostradamus never could. Trying to prove how powerful his predecessor was. This is the last step to discovering the answer, Ally. Isn't that what you wanted?"

"I just want to go home. I'm actually tired of all of this nonsense. I want my own bed, new clothes and a nice, easy life," she replied, her normal granite persona showing the first sign of cracking.

"What sort of attitude is that?" said Gabriel unexpectedly. "Nothing is free and easy in this life, you know."

"Apart from thirty thousand euros," replied Ally, making reference to Gabriel's earnings in the last twenty-four hours, which was almost as much as the pittance she earned at the university.

"I'll give it back if it makes you happy. I want to see the end of this story, too, you know."

"That's the spirit," said Antoine.

"You don't really want the money back, do you?" she whispered a little too loudly for it to be officially defined as a whisper.

"Of course not," replied Antoine. "You've earned it."

"Ok. Fine," huffed Ally. "Let's make contact, but don't say I didn't warn you when we all end up with bullets in our heads. I don't think Mario is going to roll over and let us tickle his belly, you know."

"Maybe not, so we'll need to be prepared for it. Good job we have one of the best preppers in the world with us," he said, winking at Gabriel.

"Have we!? I didn't know you were a prepper, Ms. Oldfield," replied Gabriel gormlessly.

Antoine's head sank. It was quite an impressive skill to flip-flop between genius and idiot as quickly as Gabriel did. He wondered whether she might have some undiagnosed attention deficit disorder, or whether in fact it was just because he didn't spend a lot of time with her generation. If neither of these were true then it certainly proved that intelligent people were just as gullible as idiots.

"Let's get on the line, then, and post something to him," instructed Antoine, changing the subject to hide her embarrassment.

"What should I post? Smiley-faced emoji, a pair of eyes and a finger pointing out of the screen?"

"I think we've evolved enough as a species to demonstrate the use of actual words," replied Ally.

"What about a prophecy, that will get his attention, don't you think?" said Antoine.

"I'm not sure there's an emoji for that," replied Gabriel.

"No, but we do have one of the world's leading medieval language experts with us."

Gabriel didn't have the first idea who he was referring to and continued to download a new app for unusual emojis onto Ally's phone without her knowledge.

"What do you say, Dr. Oldfield? Can you do it?"

"Of course I can do it. Pass me that notepad and a pen."

Ally worked for several minutes crafting a passage that was accurate to the style of Nostradamus's time, incisive enough for Mario to know what they meant while keeping within her own interpretation of Michel's rules. When she was happy with it, Gabriel logged onto one of the Oblivion Doctrine's message boards and started to type it into the phone with the hashtag Mario. She added a nice smiley face for good measure without telling the others. Some habits were hard to break.

Dark secrets will lie hidden under ancient oak
Withered branches on the tree of deceit point to 'our lady'
And the sunrise will bring a doctrine to its knees
At the hands of angels and demons the hammer will fall. ☺

"I don't understand it," said Gabriel, pausing before sending the message just in case Ally had made a mistake.

"Are you a professor of medieval languages?"

"No."

"There's your answer, then."

"I understand most of it," said Antoine. "But what's the hammer about?"

"That's actually the bit I got," replied Gabriel. "Clearly we're going in armed, then. Can't we use something a bit sharper, though, like a flick knife or some nunchucks?"

"No, it's not a video game. We can't just respawn if it all goes wrong. The meaning of the name Mario comes from the word hammer, so it's a metaphor for how we intend to bring him down."

"Right," replied Gabriel. "I still think we need weapons."

Once Ally had taken Gabriel through the whole quatrain in the simplest language and speed she could muster, finally the send button was pressed and the prophecy was fired off into cyberspace. All they could do now was charge their coffee mugs and wait.

*****

It didn't take long for their message to get traffic. Dozens of anonymous weirdos had already commented on the meaning of their prophecy. One even asked them on a date. But worryingly Mario's response to their prophecy didn't come through the forums on the Oblivion Doctrine website, it came as a text message from an unknown number. Not even Gabriel had any plausible explanation as to how that was possible. They'd posted under a false name and they didn't need to provide contact details to access the site. Unlike an IP address, a mobile phone was traceable, if you had the equipment to do it.

Something told them that the Oblivion Doctrine did. The text message read simply, 'I'm sending the chopper. Bring the painting.'

They didn't know when the chopper would arrive but they did know they had to come up with a plan, and fast. It seemed likely, given his potential use of cameras and other technology, that Mario knew about all three of them, so there was little point splitting up. As Ally suggested possible scenarios that might keep them safe, Antoine continued to show no anxiety whatsoever.

"It will be alright," he repeated a number of times.

"You don't know that, do you? They've already tried to kill you once. They might try again."

"Not now that we know who they are."

"Surely that makes it even more likely."

"A chopper," muttered Gabriel. "Is that a baddie with blades on his hands and feet. He was in a Bond film."

"No," said Ally. "Gabriel, let me know when you're ready to rejoin the real world, the one with adults in it."

"I think if they wanted us dead they would have already done it," added Antoine passively.

"Then what do they want from us?"

"They want the painting, but more than that, I think."

"I don't get why they want the painting," said Gabriel. "I mean it's alright, nothing special. Do you think Mario is an art dealer?"

"No!" replied Ally and Antoine together.

"I suspect if they want the painting and us, they seek the same thing that we do. Answers."

- Chapter 28 -

Fifteen-Sixty-Three

It was a big day for Jean de Cavigny. It always was when you got to meet a hero. He shuddered at the thought of being face to face with the man who'd inspired him. But what would he say when he got there? What if he said something stupid under the pressure of trying to impress him. After all, he had form. It wouldn't be the first time he'd reverted to first-class gobbledygook after being starstruck. Last year after meeting the legendary poet, Pierre de Ronsard, he inexplicably broke into a monologue about gussets.

And what if his hero wasn't the unblemished idol he'd built him up to be? The only impression of the man had come from his writing. The man behind those words might be an incredible bore who couldn't hold down an intelligent conversation. Perhaps he had a horrible lisp that made him sound like a buffoon. Maybe he'd act like one of those people his father once told him about, locked up in that special place where patients were fed through funnels and wrapped in cushions for their own protection. The pressure was building uncontrollably. Nerves gave way to paranoia, and panic barged up behind them brandishing the next ticket. Jean sucked as much air into his body as possible, ran his free hand through his long, flowing hair and pushed the tavern doors open.

Rolls of papers clutched under one arm, he walked as confidently as his trembling knees allowed. The raucous noise he'd heard while standing out on the dark street was evacuated by utter silence. Eyes bore imaginary holes in the back of his head, dice stopped dead in mid-toss, and a variety of criminal activities were speedily removed from view. Taverns were an alternative. A substitute for a place of worship, when God had decided not to listen, an oasis of light relief from the drudgery of everyday life, and a place that acted as an alternative to abiding by laws of the land.

If skulduggery was likely anywhere, it was likely here. Men gambled on the outcome of dice or card games, barmaids picked up a little extra income working in the world's oldest profession, while thieves and rogues plotted their next score. The proprietor was no less culpable. If it happened within these walls he was certainly aware of it, and most likely in on the deal. It was impossible to keep the place afloat without embracing criminality. It was the only way of paying the extortionate level of tax duties the Crown levied on alcohol. At least that was the defence the landlord always gave to justify it. Anyone whose face looked unfamiliar might just be working for the state. Which made most taverns a locals-only sort of place and if you weren't in the club, as Jean was discovering, the hospitality was less than cordial.

Undeterred, he scanned the occupants at each table. It was a busy evening and most of the tables were taken. Surely he'd recognise his hero, though, wouldn't he? But what if he didn't? After all, he'd only ever seen an oil painting of him and artists were almost as corruptible as tavern owners. If you paid them a few extra francs they'd often paint out certain flaws. It wasn't unheard of for an artist to completely reconstruct someone's face in the pursuit of a customer's vanity. Jean recently saw a painting of Michelangelo that had a passing resemblance to Hercules. What if his hero wasn't tall with a neatly trimmed, white beard and a slightly receding hairline. What if in reality he was a dumpy, disfigured muscle-man who wore an eyepatch, just like the man on his left stabbing a knife into the table and growling in his general direction.

Panic appeared at the front desk, pointing excitedly at its ticket number. Jean metaphorically ripped it up and refused admission.

There on the other side of the crowded bar, at a table by the fire, his hero scribbled furiously into a book. Physically at least he was exactly as he'd been depicted in his painting. To avoid the searing heat of the other patrons' displeasure at his existence he hastened his pace to join him. Standing next to the free chair he waited patiently for the request to sit. None came. Even heroes can be rude.

"Monsieur Nostradamus," Jean stated quietly, simultaneously attempting to both gain his attention and not disturb him at the same time.

"Finally!" replied Nostradamus joyously, immediately looking up. "I knew it would happen eventually."

"Um…what would?" asked Jean.

"The general public recognising who I am. I'm guessing you wanted an autographed quatrain, didn't you, you little scamp?"

"But sir, I'm not the general public. I'm meant to be here."

"Rubbish. I don't know who you are, so you must be common."

"No, I'm here for the interview, you do remember, don't you, sir?"

"Damn it!" cried Michel, immediately turning his attention back to his book and pointing at the seat opposite. "Sit."

Complete silence followed. Was this some horrendous interview technique designed to disable him? If it was, it was working brilliantly. Jean fiddled with his papers as the inner disbelief of his very presence here inflated internally and destabilised his conscious attempts not to talk bullshit. It burst.

"Lovely weather we're having. I mean, if you like torrential rain, that is. Good for ducks, I guess. I wonder if it'll clear up by the weekend. Be a shame if the Sabbath is a wash-out. Although I guess you could tell me that," he said, laughing nervously. "What with you being a great forecaster of the future. Maybe it's already in one of your quatrains, let me have a look…"

"I think even the most opportunistic interpreter would struggle to find this weekend's weather forecast in one of my prophecies," replied Michel with a withering scowl.

"Suppose so. But what about Century three, Quatrain eighty-five: you predicted clouds in that one."

"Yes, I did. Clouds of lobsters, locusts and gnats."

"The lobster clouds have always confused me."

"Do you know all of my quatrains?" asked Nostradamus.

"Every single one."

"Really! I'm impressed. And who are you exactly?"

Jean rose from his seat and conducted a pathetically over-elaborate bow, further propagating the tavern's collective desire to stab him to death before he left the building. "Jean de Cavigny, at your service."

"And you've come for an interview," mumbled Michel, wondering whether this naïve young man had accidentally slipped through the net of their recruitment process.

"Yes. Here are my credentials," he said, placing a roll of paper on the table.

It was the most pristine example of paper Michel had ever witnessed. Firstly it was white and most paper was beige with signs of flame damage. Secondly it was written with curiously intricate fonts of differing sizes and styles. It had been crafted so carefully it must have taken the author weeks. Thirdly it contained words like 'self-starter,' 'team player,' 'entrepreneurial' and 'results driven' in a rather self-indulgent opening paragraph. Michel was searching for a secretary not a luminary.

"I only need someone to do my admin," said Michel abruptly.

"Yes, sir, I know."

"But that's not you, is it?"

"Really?" replied Jean crestfallen. "Why do you think that?"

"Let me explain. How does a degree in ancient Greek from the College Royal in Paris help me manage my filing or written correspondence?"

"Are any of your letters written in ancient Greek?" asked Jean desperately.

"Nope. They're not even written in modern Greek."

"Oh. Well, I have many other attributes that I think you might find useful," said Jean, nodding towards the paper.

"Are you referring to your recent article on the mating habits of butterflies?"

"Probably not."

"Or the fact that you state here that you can play lute to grade six?"

"Music is soothing, sir, I could play it in the background to make the atmosphere more inspiring."

"No," replied Michel curtly. "Do you have any skills as a secretary? Are you good at proofreading? Skilled at filing? Good with diary management?"

Jean's chin dropped down onto his chest. "No, not really."

"Then why are you wasting my time?"

"Because I want to work for you, Monsieur Nostradamus. I'm desperate to learn the ways of the prognosticator. I have been inspired by the great prophets of our time: you, Jean Froissart, Philibert Lesage…"

"Who?"

"Surely you've heard of Froissart?"

"Obviously. The other one."

"Philibert Lesage. You mean you're not aware of his work?"

"No, I'm not."

"Oh you should, the man's a genius. Everyone in Paris knows who he is. He can't walk the streets without a stranger recognising him. He started working for the Queen about a year ago. Apparently he originally came from these parts. They say he's the most accurate prophet who's ever lived."

"Bastard!" said Nostradamus, smashing both fists on the table.

"I might not be right for the job, sir, but I hardly think that language is fair. I do have feelings, you know."

"Not you. Philibert."

"You do know him, then."

"Oh, I know him. And it's about time he and I had a little chat."

"You'll need a month, sir, he's still in Paris."

Michel had barely thought about Philibert over the last eighteen months. The last he'd heard, Claude had shipped him off to Paris on his own suggestion. He'd not expected him to last the year. But not only had he survived, he also appeared to be gaining notoriety using the skills that Michel himself had taught him. It would not stand. He'd been very clear about his offer to train Phil. He was under no circumstances allowed to be better at it than him. How this fraud had managed to do so didn't matter. No one was going to put him in the shade.

"Jean, do you own a horse?"

"Yes, of course."

"Then why on earth didn't you include it on here?" replied Michel, stubbing his finger on the page. "I mean that changes everything. You're exactly what I'm looking for."

"Really…because I own a horse," replied Jean, a little annoyed he'd gone to so much trouble writing up his credentials in so much detail and with so much effort.

"You're hired."

"Wow, that's amazing! I won't let you down, you'll see. What time do I start in the morning?"

"Morning? No, you start immediately."

"Now?"

"Oh yes."

"But we haven't agreed a salary yet. And what about healthcare, insurance…"

"I'll pay you two francs a week. If you get sick you'll probably die like everyone else, and you don't need insurance because I predict the future. You can have a free copy of each of my almanacs and my personal access key to the cosmic energy. Take it or leave it."

"The horse needs new shoes."

"Done."

Michel found the cleanest piece of blank paper from his pile, although it was still many shades of beige away from Jean's gleaming résumé, and started to craft a letter. Once it was finished he sealed it with candle wax and handed it to his new employee.

"Ride back to Paris immediately. Take this to Her Majesty The Queen. Then return here for your next duties."

"But sir, I just arrived here from Paris," sighed Jean. "Couldn't I get some food and rest first?"

"Jean, everyone within these four walls other than me wants you dead: do you really want to risk it?"

Jean scanned the patrons to see that many were sharpening blades or pointing aggressively at him. "See you in a couple of months, then."

*****

Much had happened in fifteen sixty-three. After Vassy, Annabelle had returned to Marseille to attend to her late husband's funeral in the full, but undisclosed, knowledge that she'd been responsible for his death. Back in her home town, Claude had soon seen to it that she was walking down the aisle with husband number two before she hit twenty-five.

The massacre at Vassy had indeed been the flashpoint that Jacques de Saluces hoped for, even if it hadn't panned out quite the way he'd expected. The events of that March day, fifteen-sixty-two, had forced the Guise brothers, never shy in their support of the Catholic mantra, to adopt a more militant set of tactics. Further flashpoints developed into scuffles, which developed into brawls and, without anyone blowing a trumpet, full-scale religious war.

Louis Bourbon, Prince of Condé, and unelected leader of the Protestant cause, mustered his support and successfully seized the city of Orléans. Buoyed by his achievements, bullish groups of Protestants sprang up all over France to capture the strategically important towns of Angers, Tours and finally Lyon. The sides clashed in significant battles at Orléans, Rouen and Dreux.

Anne de Montmorency once again donned his armour, keen not to miss an opportunity to further blot his abysmal military record. True to form, the now sixty-seven-year-old Constable was yet again captured during the disastrous Battle of Dreux. But the Catholics weren't the only ones to suffer setbacks. When one of the Guise brothers was assassinated in the first months of the new year the Queen was forced to negotiate a truce through the Edict of Amboise.

One of the biggest changes that year happened in August when Charles was declared the legal monarch. Still only thirteen, Charles had been kept well away from matters of state since the infamous attack on his sister and the widespread discontent that had festered amongst the nobility as a result. But in a very different climate it was actually the nobility who held the key to his reinstatement. Each side in the war felt they would gain more power from the young impressionable King Charles than they ever would from the more conciliatory Queen Catherine.

As all these events unfolded through the year, one person penetrated them all. Philibert had predicted the outcome. What began as the occasional input at the Queen's request migrated to the role of full-time advisor. If the Queen wanted to know what Italy would do in the spring, they called for Phil. If the Queen wanted to know which nobles were on side, out they wheeled him. If the Queen wanted to decide who to execute, particularly if Phil didn't want it to be him, there he was ringing the doorbell of the palace first thing in the morning. There wasn't a single aspect of the day-to-day running of the country that hadn't been put before his consideration.

And frankly, he was getting sick of it.

In many respects he was as much a prisoner now as he had been when he was officially in one. There was a little more space, better breakfasts and a lot less lice, but ultimately he was trapped in employment with no notice period. People like Philibert didn't get jobs, they were unemployable. Yet he'd done such a good job of convincing the Queen of his talents she couldn't rule effectively without him. So reliant on him was she that Philibert and his assistant, as the Queen liked to call Chambard, had been relocated to the Palace of Fontainebleau, her personal and official new residence. Always close at hand in an emergency, all she needed to do was ring his bell.

Oh that ruddy bell!

Ten times a day that bell rang, only ceasing when he left his quarters to retreat from it. Over the years he'd built up a strong resentment towards the way the rich and powerful treated the commoners of this land, and here he was advising them how to do it more efficiently. There had to be a way out. He'd got himself into this mess and he would have to get himself out of it. That was his real job, after all.

There was a time, early on in his role as official Royal Seer, when Philibert would actually consider what to write in his predictions. He would even replicate the conditions and approach that Michel had taught him, to increase the chances that cosmic energy might lend a hand here and there. Not anymore. Now the requests for, and outcomes of, his prophecies were so regular, certain and predictable he'd lowered himself to writing the first thing that popped into his head. Sometimes he purposely wrote total rubbish in the hope that his unbreakable run of form might desert him.

It never did.

For his own amusement he'd written a rather explicit prophecy about the Duke of Guise, whom he'd never forgiven for his actions in Vassy. The verse suggested that Guise would be discovered in a well-known brothel wearing woman's clothes and in the company of three women scantily dressed as clowns. It was hard to say whether Phil or Guise were more shocked when it turned out to be true. Unsurprisingly, Francis of Guise was not seen in the royal court much after that, deciding his talents were better employed elsewhere.

It was clear that sending Chambard out to give his predictions a little helping nudge was unlikely to alter the outcome. What was the point? They all ended up coming true anyway. What's more, Chambard was no longer strong enough to wrestle boar or run around castles avoiding exploding beds. His health had faded rapidly over the past twelve months and the cause of his ailments were very simple. Age.

Old Father Time had finally caught up with the great wanderer. It was hard to say how old he was exactly because even he didn't know what year he was born. There were no documents concerning his birthdate, place or parents, a common fact for those born into poverty. Half of them died before they got off zero, so why waste the paper. For as long as Chambard could recall he'd fended for himself. Most people thought he was sixty, but it's very possible he was even older than Anne de Montmorency.

His old friend's slow degradation, and the return of Annabelle to the south, had punished him with a loneliness he'd not experienced since the death of his family. He missed Annabelle more than he'd expected. Her bravery at Vassy had saved his life and latterly helped him to understand that the love she had for him was no fool's crush. It ran deeper, and not just in her. It welled in his heart also. Absence had only strengthened those feelings. Love, though, shared a room with guilt. Guilt that the repercussions on her own life because of her actions would be significant and harsh. A debt that must be repaid.

The last significant event of fifteen sixty-three was the arrival in Fontainebleau of a letter in the hands of a young scholar called Jean de Cavigny.

The bell rang once more. Two minutes later he was trotting down the corridors to see what she wanted this time.

"Philibert, I require your counsel," she demanded in a tone that suggested she knew how much power she had over him.

"I live to serve you as always," he replied cordially.

"I want to take the court on a tour of the country to heal the divisions that are all too evident between our people. I want the King to see his domain and build trust with his people."

"Do you think that is wise? Even here, protected by the court, the King is a handful."

"Silence! Know your place in matters concerning my children."

This abruptness of tone was not new to Philibert. It was a common occurrence that had slowly escalated over the months as his service was taken for granted. The novelty of his talents had worn off and now his input was controlled with the same ruthless efficiency as the military or tax collection.

"Why have you called me here, your majesty?"

"Because I want your opinion."

"I can easily write you a prophecy," he replied, knowing full well he kept about half a dozen about his person at any one time like discarded jokes from Christmas crackers. He had a tendency to deal them out at royal gatherings to impress the guests.

"That won't be necessary. I only want your opinion."

"I think there is good logic in your decision," he replied, not in the least bit interested whether there was a grand tour or not.

"Good. He thinks so as well," added the Queen tapping the letter on her lap.

"Who does?"

"Nostradamus."

"What's he got to do with it? I thought I was the Royal Seer?"

"You are, but I still value his input. His letter clearly states that he has seen visions of the tour and its potential success."

"Good for him."

"There was something else he was adamant about, though."

"Oh, he's always adamant, he struggles with any other pose."

"He said you must accompany the party and Marseille must be one of our first stops. We leave in a week."

The Queen left, followed as always by her other advisors, including Nicholas Throckmorton who'd taken to carrying a Bible with him at all times. Sometimes without warning he'd kneel and shout a Psalm before making the sign of the cross three times in the air. Phil wondered if this had anything to do with the prophecy he'd given him suggesting that God was considering purging all first-born children who had moustaches and were called Nicholas.

Philibert ambled dejectedly back to his quarters where Chambard was laid up in bed, bored and welcoming the end of his days.

"I can't stay like this," said Chambard as Phil shut the door and slumped into the seat by the window thoroughly exhausted by the hours spent each day crafting history from his own imagination.

"Feeling any better?"

"No. My legs hurt, my arms hurt, my butt's fallen asleep again and my brain wants to attack my body with a scythe, but it can't convince any of my limbs to join in because they're all knackered. This is no life. I'm a wanderer who hasn't wandered in months. Can't you do something?"

"Like what?"

"Push me off a cliff."

"It's pretty flat around Paris."

"Um…any plague kicking around at the moment?"

"There's a bit in Limoges. But that's in the wrong direction."

"Wrong direction for what?"

Philibert summarised the Queen's plans for a royal tour that they were soon to be a part of.

"I'm done with this," said Phil with a sigh. "This is not what we planned. We're meant to trick people for our benefit not theirs. I have to find a way out of it."

"Any ideas."

"Yes, I think so."

"A mark?"

"Yes."

"Who?"

"Nostradamus."

"Really. Why him?"

"Because he's the reason we're in Paris in the first place. And he's the reason we're going back on this ridiculous tour. Which means it must be benefiting him in some way. Plus he's a charlatan and I want everyone to see it for themselves."

"But how does that remove you from the Queen's service?"

"You'll see. If my plan works, I think I can win Annabelle's hand, crush Michel's image and get the sack all in one con. But it means I need your help one more time."

"I can't do much."

"I don't need you to move. Just write."

"Write what?"

"A prophecy."

"But that's your job."

"Oh, we're both going to write one."

"I think my mind might be on the way out. I'm sure you just said both of us?"

"Yes, I did. The problem with my prophecies is they always come true, and for this con we need one that doesn't. The only way to convince a mark is to entice them with their strongest desires, you taught me that. So what does Michel want most in the world?"

"Fame and legacy."

"Exactly. So we need him to think that we're giving it to him. And the way we do that is by breaking all three rules."

- Chapter 29 -

The Royal Tour

If a mentally fragile thirteen-year-old boy with too much power is allowed to organise anything more complicated than to run his own bath, it's bound to happen. And from the moment that Catherine relented to Charles's pressure to organise the tour, the wheels started to come off. And boy were there a lot of wheels.

Down the ages a grand tour was the rite of passage trod by upper-class youths and inquisitive scholars in order for them to 'find themselves'. Often all they found was syphilis and an allergic reaction to olives, but they still went in their droves. These trips were usually solitary affairs involving no more than the individual in question and possibly a mentor, who acted as a cultural and geographical guide.

They tended to lack solid planning, as it generally took away from the principle of searching. If you knew what you were looking for and where it was, there wasn't much point going out in the first place. It was almost impossible to know when someone had 'found themselves', in the same way that it's difficult to locate an object you've lost but haven't actually ever seen. It's not like virginity, there weren't rules to prove that it had happened.

And there was another significant reason why it wasn't like someone losing their virginity. Grand tours might last for years. Even if you were lucky enough to 'find yourself', the length of the trip might be extended unexpectedly by not actually knowing where you were, or a sudden lack of funds to find out. There were no traveller's cheques, cashpoints or credit cards to swiftly lift you out of financial crisis. Gaining more funds meant writing a letter, if you could find a postal service in whatever godforsaken backwater you were in. Failing that you were expected to take up some bohemian profession like painting to pay your way. Even better still you could arrange a quick marriage to some wealthy local woman.

But Charles wasn't planning this type of tour.

The one he demanded was a little more excessive and a lot less uncertain. And his ability to demand taxes from anyone he met en route meant he wasn't likely to run out of money anytime soon. But to call this a tour at all was misleading. It was better described as a city on wheels.

Not all the King's decisions on who joined it were misguided. It was wisdom to include a battalion of soldiers to protect them on the road for what would last two years. The council, who were responsible for overseeing all aspects of the country's welfare, would have to join him for continuity. And servants of course would be needed to tend to the royal family much as they would at one of the palaces. Hairdressers, cooks, squires, maids and courtiers were all forced to tell their families they were popping out for a while and it was best not to wait up for the next, say, twenty-four months.

Others decisions the King made were much less sane. There would be servants on tour whose only job would be to carry a tapestry or piece of furniture the length and breadth of France. This was fine if your piece of furniture was a lightweight ornament that could be neatly wrapped in cloth and placed in a sack. Not so good if you had to carry the wardrobe.

Taking a leaf out of his mother's addiction for a good knees-up, all of the usual entertainers were also in tow. The eighty or so naked ladies, known locally as the flying squad, the musicians, the singers, the actors, the mask makers, the triumphant arch carriers, and the man that came to every party, even though no one claimed to know who he was.

Oh, and the dwarves.

Nine of them in fact travelling in their very own miniature coach.

In total the population of the grand tour that left Paris in January of fifteen sixty-four was made up of fifteen thousand souls. Keeping track of them all was a nightmare. Particularly the dwarves who constantly got left behind. In the midst of this hoard of extravagance were Phil and Chambard. Chambard, almost completely bedridden by his ailments, travelled in his own private coach equipped with its own bed and creature comforts. It was quite a change compared to the journey they'd experienced to get to Paris in the first place. Phil rode out in front of the coach at the head of the procession, never far from the Queen. Thankfully the bell was one of the few possessions the family had left behind.

The tour travelled south from Fontainebleau and every time it reached a major town, which was at least twice a week, a great party was organised to celebrate the tour's arrival. Locals were forced to wear fake smiles and applaud the King's coach as it passed by their impoverished existence. There was no begging or charity sought. Such notions had been banned by the authorities and would be met by fierce reprisals if any were witnessed. This was a celebration of the King's ascension and a way of reconnecting the monarch to his people. The rich ones at least.

Party after party, department to department, the swarm of people crept on like a malignant cancer. Hangovers were cured by sleeping on the journey, which was fine for anyone not carrying a wardrobe. This pattern seemed to continue endlessly until one summer's day the convoy invaded Provence.

"Chambard, wake up," said Phil, gently nudging the horizontal lump that consumed most of the coach. "We're here."

"Urgh...and I'm still here, too. Come on, God, I'm easy pickings," he sighed from under the sheets.

"It's home!" exclaimed Phil.

"There's no such place."

"There is for me."

Twenty years had passed since he'd last set eyes on the ancient Roman walls of the city and the purple hue of the lavender bushes that cut a path like a silk scarf along the roadsides. The fragrant smell triggered a deep emotion inside him and unexpected tears welled in his eyes. They were passing into Aix, a city that was much transformed from the dark, spectral one he remembered. Children chased each other in and out of the spaces between their carts, playing merrily, oblivious to the bodies that Phil had once seen on these very streets. It was a city reborn, full of vigour and life. The memories may never die but the people at least lived on.

"I never thought I'd see it again," said Phil. "Not like this anyway."

"Life and death are not separate forces, you know," said Chambard, squirming to sit up for the first time in weeks and take in the scene. "Maybe you should stay."

"No. I couldn't do that, it would be like admitting failure. I wandered from this city for a reason."

"Maybe it was so you might wander back," replied Chambard prophetically. "Every journey has to have a destination."

"Yours didn't."

"Then don't make that mistake, Philibert. The only reason I didn't stop was because I never found a reason to. But I think you have. You can con everyone, apart from yourself."

THE ROYAL TOUR

The main section of the tour, which housed the most important members, disconnected from the rest and delved further into the city. They came to a stop in the centre next to the Cathedral whose bells were once again chiming happily in the tall bell tower. The Italian fountains frothed vigorously as if the clear fresh water had been responsible for cleansing the horrors from its own skin. Phil was keen to explore, to remember a more innocent time when his parents would send him down to the market to buy bread for dinner. To discover the streets where he'd play-fight with his younger siblings. To smell the cooked meats wafting from the windows of the inn on the corner. The inn right across the street from him now. The one with the elderly, white-haired gentleman outside currently waving at him.

'Oh. This might get awkward,' he thought.

Standing in his most colourful clothes, designed both to stand out to the royal family and equally to overshadow anyone else's attempts to do so, was Michel Nostradamus. Phil wondered how many in their tour would know who he was and how long it would take before he got tired of posing in that unique way of his when he had to tell them.

"I'll be back a minute," said Phil, stepping off the cart and down onto the cobbles. He strolled casually forward to greet his old mentor, uncertain quite what welcome he might expect.

"Philibert Montmorency, or is it Lesage?" said Michel without offering a handshake or friendly pat on the shoulder. "You have been busy."

"Shall we get a drink?" said Philibert.

"I think you owe me that much at the very least."

They settled in the corner of the inn, far from others but near the window to allow the light, sunny air to purify the otherwise obnoxious odours of a place frequented by filth of all kinds. The shabby barman, seemingly one of those who knew Michel's face, brought two goblets to the table that contained what might be excused for beer, but might equally pass as medieval disinfectant.

"Are you well?" asked Philibert casually, as if nothing had happened in the intervening two years since their last meeting.

"How do you do it?"

"I'm not with you."

"How do you make them all come true. Your so-called prophecies."

"Honestly. I don't know."

"You're a conman, that's how you do it."

"No, I was a conman, now I am the Royal Seer."

"Don't make me laugh. You're no seer. You have been fabricating history so that it appears your foretelling is accurate."

"You're right, I did at first. But then I found there was no need."

"Prove it."

"How?"

"If it's not an illusion, prove how powerful you are right now. Predict something."

"About what?"

"The next ten minutes."

"I'd have to break your rules, though, wouldn't I!?"

"Sod the rules. Do it!"

"This is ridiculous, no one can be that accurate."

"Most of us can't, but you've already broken all the rules. I know your game. I have swum in the cosmic pool and all you did was pee in it."

"A cosmic pool now, that's new."

"Come on, show me."

"Fine, if you must embarrass yourself. In the next ten minutes a man will threaten your life."

"Is that man you, Phil?"

"No. I'm no murderer. I'm a pacifist. The man who I speak of will have three front teeth and will carry a small sack in his left hand."

"Right. We'll see, won't we?"

"We're just going to wait, are we?"

"Yes."

Michel was noticeably fidgety in his seat, constantly shifting his weight to find the right position. His limbs creaked with every movement and the old man held his right wrist with the palm of his other hand, massaging it back into life.

"You're looking old," said Philibert darkly. "Not long left now."

"Is that another prediction or a question?"

"Six months at the most if you ask me, and what then, Michel? How will you control your legacy when you are no longer here to influence it?"

"I have friends, family, and my new secretary Jean who will see to it that people remember me long into the future."

"But why do you need to. You'll be dead."

"Because what I do is real."

"No. You're the fraud, Michel, with all your cosmic nonsense. What you write is a confidence trick against the weak and uneducated. And soon I will show them."

"It'll be too late. Plans are already in place to protect my legacy. There's nothing you can do about it."

"So why am I here?"

"Because I need something that you have."

"What?"

"Your prophecies of course. The next ten minutes will prove whether or not you are as good as they say you are. While we wait, I want you to write me another. A proper one. A prophecy of such extraordinary implications that it will carry my name forever."

"And if I refuse?"

"Then I will tell everyone who you really are. I have the power to reach every corner of this country. In a couple of weeks the name of Philibert Lesage will be on the lips of every one of your victims. You'll be hunted in every town and village from Caen to Cannes. A ghost no more."

"My people are all ghosts. The powerful are blinkered from them and another will soon take my place."

"Maybe, but you will lose everything in the process."

"I already have."

"Not yet. What about the young woman? Annabelle, wasn't it? Don't you desire to start a life with her now that she has returned a widow from Paris?"

Michel spoke the truth. Philibert had run so far and so fast a stitch was forming in his soul. Maybe it was time to stop. Time to build a new life. But there was only one way that could be achieved with Annabelle, and the window of opportunity sat in front of him.

"Ok. You win. I do have a prophecy you might be interested in."

Philibert pulled out the small, wooden box that Michel had given him all those years before, and removed what he needed. Once he'd written out the quatrain he handed it across the table.

"But this breaks the third rule!" replied Michel in shock.

"Yes, it does. Scares you, does it?"

"Not particularly. The events you speak of will not happen for five hundred years. The end is hardly nigh, is it?"

"No, but think how long you will remain in the public conscience as they wait on tenterhooks to see if the great Nostradamus was right all along."

"You're sure about this?"

"Never more so. Do you know how many of my predictions have come true? All but that very first one I wrote in prison with you."

"Oh yes the famous canoe prediction. Not your finest hour. But this, this is extraordinary. There's only one part I don't understand. Who are these mountain men that you refer to?" said Michel, pointing to the last line of the prophecy.

"Oh come on, Michel," he replied with a smirk, "You said it yourself, it's for scholars to interpret meaning, not for the prophet himself."

"It isn't enough."

"What do you mean?"

"I need more than one. I need all of them. I once told you that if you became better at predicting than me, I would unveil you as the imposter that you are."

"You also told me to make something of myself and I have."

"At my expense. It won't stand."

"What if I promised not to write anymore."

"It's not enough. I need you to work for me."

"No. I'm done with employment and bells and routines and my mind being squeezed dry every three hours for the next piece of insight. All of which was your fault in the first place, by the way. Why did you tell Claude that I was working for the Queen?"

"I didn't tell him that. I predicted it. Looks like I got it right, too."

Phil got up angrily from the table, making its legs scrape the floor. Was that true? Was his destiny in the hands of this vain arse-kisser who was about as connected to the cosmic energy as a horse was connected to God. He'd heard enough, he'd take his chances and accept whatever Michel felt compelled to do. As he marched away from the table, Michel attempted to stop him by sticking his leg out to trip him up. Phil gently hopped over it, but the man coming in the other direction didn't.

To protect the small bag of coins that he carried in his arms the man didn't stop his fall and his face took the full impact with the floor, dislodging several teeth on the bloodstained wood. Phil watched as the man pulled himself up.

"Stupid old idiot, I'm going to kill you!" he shouted, grinning manically and revealing only three teeth still attached to his gums.

- Chapter 30 -

Home to Roost

Michel utilised all of his wit and skill in an attempt to extricate himself from the awkward situation in the inn. Luckily when that failed, Jean was close at hand to rescue him. The ultimate cost was a larger bag of coins and an agreement never to show his face in this part of town again. But that didn't matter. It had all been worth it. Phil had proven his talent irrefutably, and there was no question now that the prophecy that broke all the rules was legitimate.

"Jean, I need you to ride to Lyon at once. Take this," he said, handing him the prophecy he'd taken from Phil. "I need them to include it in my most recent edition of 'Les Prophéties.' Bring the first copy back to me as soon as you can."

"Yes, of course. Is it a good one?"

"My best yet. It's the most important quatrain I've ever written, which is why I want it included in the preface of the next book. It must stand out and be remembered by all who read it."

"Consider it done. And where will I find you on my return?"

"I'm heading to Marseille. Meet me there. Hide the book inside my oak coffer if I am not around."

"What will you be doing?"

"I'll be gathering a few people to destroy a legacy."

*****

Two weeks after its visit to Aix, the front of the tour trundled into Marseille. The back of the tour arrived three days later. This was the southernmost limit of the King's influence and from here the company would travel west along the coast before turning north just before it hit the Spanish border. Six months had already passed since that January morning in Paris when this whole procession set off, and they weren't even halfway. In that time three wardrobe carriers had perished, and the wardrobe had only been opened once. And that was only because the dwarves were playing hide-and-seek.

Philibert approached Marseille with a sense of foreboding. Two years ago he'd arrived in total anonymity. He returned as one of the most famous figures in the whole of France. In the intervening years the Queen's Seer had been an unavoidable presence in court and there wasn't a noble or lord he'd not been introduced to. They'd always looked him up and down suspiciously, as if there was something familiar about him. Which wasn't surprising as most of them had been victims in the last decade, even if their memories didn't place the current name or outfit. Phil and Chambard's predicament had stemmed from their last visit to Marseille, so it was fitting the end would come there, for both of them.

There was only one dignitary in the city worthy enough to host the King, and only one place where it would happen. For the second time in his life Maubert Tower loomed over him. Much had changed since then, but it was likely that Claude's opinion of him wasn't one of them. Had Annabelle told her father about the events at Vassy and his role as the Queen's seer? Did Claude still believe that Phil was working for both sides. Fortunately he didn't have to immediately deal with the answers: Claude was not in town. According to whispers amongst the council leaders, he'd been delayed at his Castle of Cadarache due to ill health. The party would be greeted by his daughter instead.

The Queen's inner circle, which included the King, Anne, Throckmorton, Phil and Chambard, carried in a chair like an Indian prince, approached the steps of the tower where they were greeted by a fanfare of trumpets, huge flags running down the stone walls and a crowd of excited well-wishers. At the top stood Annabelle looking radiant in a long, flowing green dress and hair intricately coiffured into a bun. A man stood on her left-hand side.

"What a dump!" shouted Charles, purposefully as loud as he could. He wasn't one for sugar-coating what he thought.

"Welcome Your Highness," said the man standing next to Annabelle, in a deep, booming voice that was heard across much of the city. "I'm Georges de Clermont d'Amboise, and this is my wife Annabelle. The master of the house offers his sincere apologies for not greeting you in person."

"Don't care who you are!" ranted Charles petulantly.

At thirteen he'd spent a significant portion of his life meeting people he didn't like very much and he was bored of it. Even the nobles were paupers to him, no different from the pathetic plebs who lined the streets looking hungry and ill. There were none who matched him for divinity and power. Everyone else was insignificant.

"Manners, Charles. These are your loyal subjects and you need their support," whispered Catherine to remind him of his responsibilities.

"I won't do it again."

"You must."

"It's degrading. Instead let's have them all executed so we can melt down their jewellery and make a massive monument in the shape of a harp!"

"Charles, the speech."

"Urghhh. Fine. But it's the last time. My noble subjects, the King offers you his good tidings," rambled Charles monotonally in a way that suggested it had been well rehearsed. "In these times of great upheaval I seek to heal divisions, build alliances and honour those who fight for their King and Country. I offer my counsel and am honoured to be in your company."

"A fine sentiment, your majesty. We welcome you as our honoured guest," replied Georges. "Are there any provisions or luxuries that might make your stay more comfortable?"

"Yes," said Charles with a grin. "I want two dozen swans, a miniature trebuchet and something I can throw daggers at, preferably someone poor."

"I'm sure it can be arranged, Your Highness. We would also like to pay tribute to this momentous occasion by having the council sit for a painting by the renowned artist François Clouet."

"Swans first, painting later."

The King marched up the stairs unwilling to continue the daily charade of being nice to people. The rest of the company followed subserviently behind. Phil held back so that he had the opportunity to get Annabelle's attention, but by the time he got there she'd already been led away by her new husband.

That evening, after another meal fit for a king, the company were led into the round banquet hall and carefully positioned on furniture strategically placed in front of an easel. Behind it a bohemian-looking gentleman stood next to an enormous canvas which he'd already started working on. Once everyone was in place Clouet painted at a speed that looked impossible for such a weak-armed pensioner. It was an arduous experience for everyone. Throckmorton was forced to part with his ever more elaborate protective clothing, designed to withstand all manner of threats to life. He replaced it with a propensity to sweat through every available pore.

Charles's boredom elevated itself into anger within minutes. The lurchers that had been placed for artistic effect on either side of him had a mild disposition until he'd jabbed them with a concealed fork. But even after that they still moved less than the young King, who would wander off regularly, often flicking a rude gesture or simply shouting 'King' loudly and pointing at himself. Chambard and Anne, who were of a similar age, struggled just to stay upright. To overcome this, Chambard was held up from behind by a squire out of eyesight. Every minute or so the frail wanderer would mumble, 'Kill me,' from the corner of his mouth and then pretend it wasn't him. By the end of the day it wasn't, as the sentiment was also being muttered by the exhausted squire.

Worse was yet to come.

The painting wasn't a quick job. It would take more than one sitting to capture the detail and subtle nuisances that the artist required. Every evening for a week the collective repositioned themselves in exactly the same place, often checking the painting itself to remember what posture they'd adopted previously. The frowns grew with every passing moment. At the end of each session Philibert tried to engage with Annabelle, and on the seventh and final evening he managed it.

"Was this your idea?" he whispered from the corner of his mouth.

"No, it was Father's and he's not even going to be in it."

"Smart move."

There was one question he wanted to ask above all others, but felt incapable of forming it. In substitution he resorted to the awkwardness he'd used with her at their very first meeting.

"I've always liked that locket," he said, pointing at the chain around her neck. "Is it a ram or a sheep, though?

Real craftsmanship, that. In all my travels I have never seen anything with quite such beauty. Well, apart from…"

"I know what you are thinking, Phil," she interrupted before he could finish his sentence. "You mustn't worry about me. Georges is a fine man who treats me with dignity and love. It is best this way. I must settle down and comply with my father's expectations. My life's purpose."

"But do you love him?"

"Why is my love important? It will not heal the world's wounds. It will not overcome war or death. It will not transcend what cannot be allowed. So it matters not. It is my place and I must be thankful for it."

"That's not the Annabelle that I know. You're a rebel, and the world needs more of them."

"What can I do?"

"You can do whatever you choose, just look at me."

"Phil, however much you try, whatever skills you learn, it's impossible to be someone that you are not. None of us can defeat the established hierarchy."

"But I don't want to be someone else. I want to be someone better. None of us can change the road on which fate has placed us…but we can decide which steps to take."

"I'm sorry, Philibert, I can't take those steps with you," she said, a single tear weaving its way down her pale cheek. She lingered for a moment in his gaze before gliding serenely away to her chamber.

Phil's chin dropped to his chest. The fight was up. Nothing left to cling onto. Time to call it a day. In the corner of his eye Chambard was flummoxed on a chair panting from the pointless exertion of posing for a painting that no one would ever know he was in. He held up a hand and beckoned him over.

"Not the answer you hoped for?" he said as Phil flopped on the ground beside him.

"No."

"It was just a fool's dream, Philibert," he croaked. "Some things are just not to be."

"Maybe."

"It's been a good ride these past few years. I've tried to guide you as best I could, to teach you lessons of survival and how to stay ahead. But there was one lesson I hope you've learnt above all others."

"Never give up, until there's nothing left to give."

"Exactly. So are you ready?"

"Yes. You?"

"I've been ready for months. I can't cling to this broken body until my mind decides to release it. I've been in control of my life for as long as I can remember, I'm not going to stop now."

"I can't ask this of you," Philibert sobbed. These tears were not for Annabelle, they came from a source much closer to home.

"You're not asking me. I am offering. In fact, I am demanding it. I have done much for you and asked for little in return. This you must do for me," said Chambard fighting to summon the energy to complete the words.

"I have lost enough. I can't lose you, too."

"Do not feel sad, my friend. It's what we both want. Our freedom relies on it. Everything is in place."

"Not everything," replied Phil. "Do you think he will come?"

"He'll come, and then he and a few others will get what's coming to them. Eventually at least."

Phil stretched out an arm and held Chambard's hand in his. The tough skin felt like an old saddle, split and worn. Old, white scars ran across his fingers like dried-up tributaries of a once magnificent river.

"How can you do what's needed in this state?" said Phil. "It'll take strength and mobility to get into position. Not to mention speed. We'll get maybe thirty seconds at most."

"Don't worry. I know people here that I can rely on. They will help me. The plan is already in motion."

"I'm not sure I'm ready."

"Of course you are. You're about to become a legend, just like I said you would. Everything I have taught you, all the scrapes we have escaped from, and all the moments we have shared have prepared you for it. I'm going to miss it."

"Well, we have lived impossible lives."

"And you still have another to live. Spare a moment to remember me somehow, won't you?"

"Oh, don't worry, I will. The name Chambard will live on somehow."

"Go. We will see each other only once more before the end."

*****

Phil had a difficult night's sleep. Brain activity crowded his ability to shut down. Each new synaptic impulse fought to scramble the last. Over and over these threads kept a 'no entry' sign up to the bliss of slumber where nothing but imagination or the blank nothingness could affect him. But his mind was right to be agitated. The interconnectivity of his actions was about to come to a head. Was he ready? Had he foreseen every possible scenario? Had he judged it just right?

If sleep had been difficult, it was nothing compared to the challenge of waking up. It hadn't been natural. The sunlight hadn't crept in through the window to bathe his body back into consciousness. No loving partner had leant tenderly across his body to kiss him back to life. The start to his morning involved half a dozen guards shouting commands and pointing swords in his face.

"I'm guessing Michel is here, then?" said Philibert expectantly.

"Get up!" barked the closest guard.

"Can I get out of my nightgown first?"

"No."

"Whatever turns you on, weirdo!"

To the guard's surprise, and against what they had been told, the prisoner made no attempts to resist arrest. They took no chances. His hands were tied behind his back, and with a guard positioned on all sides he was led down through the levels of the tower. In the banquet hall where they'd spent so much time posing for their portrait, the Queen's company were waiting for him. The Queen sat stony-faced in the middle of the throng. The King paced manically, as if rage would burst out the moment his feet came to rest. There were other faces in the crowd that Philibert recognised, but they certainly weren't part of the royal tour.

The Marquis of Calais brandished a heavy mace which he thumped regularly down onto his other palm. It had been six years since he'd threatened to kill Phil: clearly time had not softened his perspective. Next to him was Jean Goujon, the famous Renaissance architect. Phil once convinced him to employ them as stonemasons whilst they stole a valuable jewelled cup from the Holy Roman Emperor. The list of victims increased every time he turned his head a fraction. They encircled him like a three-dimensional art exhibition of offences, a timeline of his chequered career. And they were all here for one thing. Justice.

The convincer had worked. It wasn't the exact response he'd expected from Michel but the outcome would be the same nonetheless. Only one friendly face cut through the angry melee. Watching nervously from the side of this pop-up court was Annabelle. The baying crowd, each desperate to extract their own personal justice from Philibert, were subdued by the entry of the Queen's soldiers and two elderly men. Michel and Claude.

"Just as I predicted, your majesty," said Michel, grinning from ear to ear. "This man is a fraud. These are just some of the victims of his crimes."

"But he has done much for this country, for me," replied the Queen, torn between her personal need and a responsibility to do what was right.

"This man is not a doctor, or a lord, or a soldier, or an architect, or a prophet as he has led us to believe. He is nothing but a simple street rat who has played us all for fools," said Claude.

"But he has great gifts."

"Only lies, deceit and the means to manipulate the outcome," insisted Michel, accentuating a tone of self-importance. "True foresight ebbs from study and research, not from fortunate guesswork."

"Every one of these people can tell a story of his deception," said Claude. "They have all been wronged or robbed and it must not stand."

"What do you have to say for yourself?" said Catherine.

"It's true. I am guilty as charged. I have scammed and stolen from all of these people. Apart from that man there, I've never seen him before."

"How dare you deny it," said the old man with the scraggly beard. "Your majesty, this man stole my canoe and hid it in the bushes."

"I'm pretty sure that wasn't me, actually," replied Phil, considering if it was at all possible that prophecy number one had been true all along.

"What made you do it?" asked a disappointed Catherine.

"What did you expect?"

"Expect?"

"You may rule, my Queen, but you are not wise. The vast majority of your subjects are slaves to your oppression. Their endless suffering helps to build your magnificent palaces and fund your ridiculous lifestyle. And there is only so much they can take. One day they will rise up and burn it down. I am but the first pebble to be dropped in your serene pool of power. But the ripple will multiply. It will not be the last."

"You talk of treason."

"No, I speak of rebellion. It may not happen in your lifetime or mine, but it will happen. After all, as you said yourself, I have a gift for these things."

"He's a traitor!" shouted Michel clutching his arm as the blood pressure squeezed through his veins.

"And what would you have me do?" she said to him angrily. "It is not your place to offer me counsel or make decisions."

"No, Mother," said Charles who was still pacing up and down in front of Philibert, delighted to have this one chance to exert his power. "It's mine."

- Chapter 31 -

Finding the Queen

Given the secretive circumstances of the text message it was hard not to imagine that the helicopter would look like one straight out of a Bond film. It would be an imposing black monster with devious contraptions of death bolted to every available panel, while the interior would conceal a band of highly trained killers with curious names like 'Mr. Thrash', 'Colonel Socrates' and 'Dead Before We Land'. The reality was far less sinister and a little disappointing.

A blue and white helicopter landed in the adjacent field a couple of hours after they'd been told to expect it. The only occupant was the pilot, who stood patiently next to the machine and waited for them to come to him. When they'd heard the distant hum of blades come to a halt the three gathered the painting and a few other items they'd discussed might be of use and squelched through the mud towards it.

The pilot was the least likely looking movie villain you could employ. Firstly his name was Julian, not a name that Hollywood would get excited about at any movie pitch. People called Julian worked in florist shops or plied their trade as self-employed dog groomers. No one wanted to see a Julian hurling a hand grenade at a bunch of innocent bystanders while shouting lurid obscenities. Action movies might stretch believability but that would just be plain silly.

This particular Julian was from Canada, had excellent manners and greeted them with a soft handshake and some gentle words of reassurance. It was clear from the pensive expressions on his passengers' faces that none of them had ever travelled in this way before and they might appreciate a short briefing on the important safety features.

Only when they were comfortably secured on-board did the machine rise gently from within the surrounding trees like a hummingbird hovering for nectar. Ally was the least nervous about the experience, although it might be put into context with the terror of being a passenger in Gabriel's car. After that everything was easy. By contrast, Gabriel was in bits, howling hysterically every time the helicopter made a gentle movement or produced a new noise. After the initial strangeness wore off they settled more comfortably and distracted themselves by watching the world by night zooming past them.

It was quite some view, too.

Lights like little fireflies shimmered over the landscape. Columns of acrid smoke rose from the cities as unknown buildings were slowly choked by flames. Flashing blue lights mapped out the edge of urban areas while the rest of the land was cloaked in an eerie darkness. This was the anarchic world the Oblivion Doctrine had created in just a few weeks with the help of a natural flu strain and some good, old-fashioned fake news. Soon they might find out why.

After two hours of flight the stark view, repeated over every major metropolis, became more vivid as they descended closer to the land. It wasn't Marseille's distant burning heart that they were aiming for, but somewhere more tranquil on the edge of it. The helicopter came to rest gently on a manicured lawn of an old château.

The outside of the building was gently lit to create the impression that it was more than might be first perceived. Cream-coloured turrets with slate hats guarded each corner, while a collection of red-framed windows blinked from behind their shutters. It was an elegant rather than ostentatious structure, that nonetheless was still full of mystery.

As the violent noise of propeller blades faded from their ears they were assisted onto the grass. Gabriel practically leapt from her seat as if there had been pins in it. She made a little whooping sound as her fancy wellington boots hit the safety of land. Antoine and Ally were left to lift the rolled-up painting and small rucksack they'd brought with them.

Outside the chopper they were greeted by a woman holding a clipboard. Her black hair had been suffocated by a strong dose of thick gel which was entirely in keeping with the rest of her immaculately slick persona. From her black heels to her creaseless suit everything about her shouted precise.

"Cynthia van Straffen," she pronounced in welcome, shaking them all vigorously by the hand. "I am Mr. Peruzzi's personal assistant: he's been expecting you."

"I think we can dispense with the Bond clichés from here on in," said Ally gruffly, barging past the taller woman and setting off in the direction of the house.

"Ms. Oldfield, if you wouldn't mind waiting for the rest of us," said Cynthia.

She stopped dead in her tracks. It wasn't a surprise they knew who she was. But how much did they know about her? Maybe it was time to lower the assertive bolshiness until she had more to work from.

Cynthia strolled up the garden path like a catwalk model, which wasn't easy in the current light and with heels that were longer than most women's shoe size. She led them through the front door and into an entrance hall where a roaring fire was consuming huge logs with a crackle. Other than the floating embers dancing in the air there was no other obvious activity. For such a large property they'd expected to find more people either living here or supporting whoever did.

"Does Mario live here alone?" asked Antoine, wiping his feet on the mat. Friend or foe, you always had to remember your manners.

"Mr. Peruzzi is still a bachelor. Other than a couple of loyal employees he lives alone. The two of you can go straight in," she said, pointing to a door to the right of the entrance hall. "I'm afraid you'll have to stay here."

"Me," said Gabriel, looking crestfallen.

"Yes. He doesn't know who you are yet and is deeply suspicious of those he cannot judge."

"But he doesn't know us either," said Ally indignantly.

"More than you know," replied Cynthia.

"Stay here, my dear," replied Antoine to Gabriel. "I'm sure you'll be quite safe."

"What about us?" whispered Ally as they made their way towards the door. "How safe are we?"

Antoine knocked firmly and after a brief pause was invited to enter by a softly spoken voice on the other side.

The lounge was adorned with an eclectic collection of furniture arranged in a horseshoe formation around a low table that was camouflaged by a black silk tablecloth. Beautifully carved wooden panels featured on every wall and the entire ceiling space was covered by intricate murals in colourful hues. Sitting casually in the chair on the other side of the horseshoe directly behind the coffee table was Mario.

Above all else he looked normal. At least normal in the context of what their imaginations had considered he might look like. There was little mystery to him now. A skinny man, probably in his early fifties, with a fair face and carefully regimented hair. His brown leather jacket sat comfortably on his shoulders, partially concealing a simple white T-shirt underneath.

"Welcome," he said as if greeting friends. "Please, make yourself comfortable."

They did as requested. Any nerves or anxiety that had been whizzing through their minds prior to the helicopter ride were washed away by this apparently harmless-looking individual.

"Is that it?" asked Mario, pointing at the long roll of canvas that Antoine and Ally had propped up against a sofa.

"Yes."

"Can I see it?"

"Hold on a moment," replied Ally, starting to mistrust the calmness of the situation given everything she'd been through over the last few days. "Why should we show you anything after what you have put us through?"

"And what is that exactly, Ms. Oldfield?" he said calmly.

"Oh, I don't know, how about a burglary, trying to blow us up, and the murder of a fellow scholar for a start?"

"And where is your evidence of my apparent misdemeanours?"

"Evidence?"

"Come on. You know how it works. A woman of your reputation and standing. I have read your books and research papers, Ally. They are extremely impressive. I know the lengths you go to in order to obtain certainty. You're a researcher as much as a professor of languages. Would your opinion of me pass your own rigorous standards? Would you publish what you believe, in the certainty of your sources?"

"No," she replied meekly.

He was right. There was no evidence of any of her assumptions to the guilt she'd already judged him on. How could she so easily have overlooked it? How could she get caught up in what normal people did? Believe in something without a shred of proof. She sat back in her chair feeling small and foolish.

"The painting, Monsieur Palomer."

"How do you know who I am?"

"All will become clear."

Antoine stood up and laid the painting down at the back of the room which was the least cluttered space available for such a large object. To the best of his ability he rolled it open on the floor. All three got up to assess it once more.

"Magnificent piece, isn't it?" said Mario. "And quite unique."

"Why unique?" asked Ally.

"Because it's the only known painting of Philibert Lesage."

"Who?" asked Antoine.

"This man here," said Mario, pointing to one of the figures behind the Queen. "Philibert is the man responsible for the prophecy."

"He wrote the prophecy!" said Ally. "How do you know this?"

"Because this is my painting. It has been handed down through my family ever since it was bought by Nostradamus's grandson."

"Your painting!" said Antoine. "Then how did Bernard have it?"

"Because I traded it with him in return for something more important."

"The coffer."

"Ha ha, no of course not." Mario laughed loudly. "Please sit down: there is much to discuss."

As they returned to their seats Ally's head was spinning. She couldn't be sure that anything she'd believed in over the last week was true. She was being told the answers she wanted about the prophecy but considered them with a hefty pinch of salt.

"When Nostradamus passed away in fifteen sixty-five he passed a message to his son César from his deathbed," explained Mario. "Cesar was only about ten at the time, but his father insisted that the message be passed from father to son until the right time arrived. The story Michel told was of a young man he'd once trained to predict the future, and how that man, Philibert Lesage, had written a powerful prediction that the world would end. Nostradamus confessed to taking this prophecy from Lesage and passing it off as his own. But the only copy that existed had been stolen from him."

"So you accept that Michel didn't write the prophecy," said Ally defiantly.

"Oh yes, there's no question of that."

"So why are you using the Oblivion Doctrine to suggest that he did?"

"Because Michel's message to his son was clear. Philibert Lesage was an imposter and his memory must be erased from history. And the only way to do that was to ensure that mankind believed the prophecy was by Nostradamus."

"At what price," said Antoine. "Have you been outside? Have you seen the destruction that you have helped create?"

"No. I'm a recluse, I haven't left this building for a decade."

"Then maybe you should take a stroll."

"The price, as you put it, is well worth paying. A little chaos amongst weak-minded idiots in return for the protection of a legend. All people will perish eventually, but he will live on. Ally knows what I mean: you have no love for the general public either as I understand."

"Maybe not, but I have no desire to see them obliterate themselves because of your greed."

"Greed? I'm not in this for money. You academics always get confused by reality. The world does not run on money or oil as you believe. Those commodities do not break economies or bring down governments. Human beings have been powered by the same fuel since Moses came off his mountain. Fear is what really drives our world. And people trust fear. They crave it. It excites them. It motivates them to reach out to faith, to personal freedoms or more physiological urges like survival. All animals are raised on a respect for fear, and without it we are nothing but machines. The Oblivion Doctrine simply gives the people what they want, so they are distracted from what they have."

"And when does it stop? When the mobs break down your own gates and razes your house to the ground, or when you get bored of playing games with your online toys?" asked Ally.

"No. It stops when I have answered my own questions. That's why I have allowed you to come here."

"Which brings us to our own questions," said Antoine. "How did you know that the book was in my basement?"

"I didn't. Cesar knew from his father that the prophecy predicted that the end would come in the second millennium, so for the last decade I have had people searching for it. I even wrote to you to ask for assistance, Ms. Oldfield, although you never replied. Bernard Baptiste was the only one who did. He was the one who noticed the link in the painting which eventually led him to finding it."

"And you killed him because you wanted the coffer," she replied, unable to resist the accusations again.

"The coffer? Ms. Oldfield, I don't think you've been paying attention."

"How dare you! I have a massive IQ and more doctorates than most Oxford dons, of course I've been paying attention."

"It's interesting how the most intelligent people are always the most susceptible." Mario reached inside his leather jacket and removed a deck of playing cards. He took three cards from the deck: the queen of hearts, the seven of spades and the two of diamonds, and laid them face up on the tablecloth. "Dr. Oldfield, do you know how to find the queen?"

"What are you doing?"

"Showing you how the game works. Now keep your eye on the queen."

He turned the cards over and gently mixed them around into different positions before turning to Antoine first.

"Antoine, you know where the queen is, don't you?"

"Yes. It's in the middle."

"Very good. I see there's no fooling you. Your turn, Ally."

He turned the cards over again and moved them around much more quickly. Even so Ally was certain she knew which card was the queen. Mario stopped and moved his hands over the cards before nodding at her for an answer.

"It's the one on the left," she replied with a tired and frustrated tone.

"You're absolutely sure. You don't want to change your mind."

"What I want is for the world to go back to normal. And that is something you can deliver."

"Ok. I'll tell you what. If you find the queen, I will stop the world from burning. You can't say fairer than that, can you?"

"And if I don't."

"Then I won't. Come on, play. Pick a card, just one," replied Mario, losing his temper a little for the first time.

"I said the card on the left, you ridiculous man."

Mario turned the back of the red speckled card over to reveal the two of diamonds. Ally's mouth dropped. She was convinced she'd followed it as accurately as Antoine had.

"It looks to me that you haven't been paying as much attention as you thought. There's a reason Antoine picked the right card. He's played this game before. Tell me, Ally, what does this coffer you seek look like exactly?"

"It's black and made of oak."

"That's a very loose description. It sounds to me like it comes from someone who hasn't actually seen it."

"I haven't."

"What about a photograph? Surely he had one of those," said Mario, pointing at Antoine, whose expression was suddenly very sheepish.

"No."

"Yet you, a woman of enormous reputation for precision and certainty, still believed unwaveringly that the coffer was in Antoine's basement."

"Yes, because I saw the mess in the basement after someone tried to steal it, so it must have been there."

"And what do you believe happened to it?"

"He sold it to Bernard."

"And when you went to find it, was there any trace of it amongst poor old Bernard's possessions?"

"No."

"And do you know why that was? Why in fact he hadn't left it to you with the painting if it was so important?"

"Stop playing games with me."

"Sometimes it's very hard to find the queen, if someone doesn't want you to see it."

"So where is the coffer, if it even exists?"

"Oh it exists. It's where it has been for hundreds of years."

Mario pulled the black tablecloth off like a magician at a tea party to reveal an ancient black coffer underneath.

"You weren't looking for the coffer, Ally. Antoine was."

Chapter 32

Don't Blink

There hadn't been a good execution in Marseille for ages. Claude had a reputation as a compassionate man who liked to find alternative ways for people to rectify their crimes that didn't involve so much mess. But he did make the odd exception and the people loved him for it.

The last one people talked fondly about was the execution of Benoit the forger. It was notable for several reasons. Firstly, not all executions were conducted in the same way. There were many ways of wiping out life and the choice depended on the manner of the crime. Poisoners were boiled to death, thieves were subjected to the breaking wheel, and those found guilty of sodomy were impaled on long spikes, which probably wasn't very appropriate. In the case of Benoit, the punishment was to be hung, drawn and quartered.

And then there was the second reason for its notoriety. It took ages. Two days, in fact. The four horses, tethered to each of his limbs, apparently weren't on message. They decided they didn't want to pull at the same time, only managing to drag poor Benoit for an unexpected tour of the city in surprising directions. Most people didn't have the attention span for it. They popped in and out to see how it was progressing, only to find poor Benoit still had some life left in him. When the end did finally come there was almost no crowd left at all. Not unlike today the masses wanted entertainment, they just didn't want to wait for it.

Execution days were more popular than Christmas. Mainly because on execution days you were allowed to enjoy yourself without the prerequisite of enduring the mind-numbing ramblings of a stuck-up priest who, even on this of all days, wanted to promote doom. And like Christmas, executions were very much family affairs. Mothers packed a lunch, gathered their children and joined the queue as early as possible to secure the best view.

And the demand for this execution was unprecedented. It always was when it involved one of their own. No one really cared if some wayward noble got what was coming to him. But they'd watch this one with a twisted sense of admiration and disappointment. At least until the blood poured out and they were faced with the reality of their own miserable lives.

The night before, the stage had been set and the gallows had been constructed. It had a prominent position in the middle of the main square to allow as many visitors as possible to appreciate the warning, in case any of them were planning on being the future ripples that Phil had warned of. The important guests, including the royal party, would watch events unfold from the windows and balconies of houses that circle the plaza. Not only was this the best view, it also kept them distant from all the poor people. Nostradamus was one of the lucky few to receive an invite. From his lofty vantage point he would witness the end of his only real challenger, and once that formality was complete he could die peacefully in the knowledge that his legacy was secure.

*****

Annabelle searched everywhere for it. She looked in the small chest by the side of her bed where it normally lived. But no sign of it. She checked her jewellery box next to the mirror, not there either. She looked under her pillow in case she'd forgotten to remove it and it had slipped off while she'd slept. No trace. She asked her husband, but he hadn't seen it either. It couldn't be lost: after all she was always so careful with it. But that didn't explain where it was now. It wasn't easy to lose after all. Only one had ever been made and its uniqueness meant no one could mistake it for their own.

She sat down on the bed and forced her brain to retrace her steps. She'd worn it for a week while posing for the painting, that much she was sure of. After Philibert's arrest she recalled placing it back where it lived. The chest was locked and only her closest family knew what lay inside. Its emotional value to her was significant. Her mother had presented it to her on her eighteenth birthday, but it wasn't a new piece. It had been in the Savoie family for years, handed down from mother to daughter. But more importantly than that, Philibert had complimented her on it and she desperately wanted to wear it for him. One last silent chance to show him how she truly felt.

There was no more time. She had to get ready, locket or not. In an hour from now a trapdoor would open and the man she loved would hang. It would bring an end to the impossible dream of lasting happiness. Unless someone could do something to stop it.

And that was another reason for wanting to wear it.

The symbolism of the locket was not lost on her. In a biblical context the ram was in tune with the mentality of the people that lived in the city. It represented determination. A willingness to overcome the odds and stand tall. Yet that determination and courage had deserted her when she most needed it. A regret she would bear for the rest of her life.

But the Bible wasn't the only place where you might find a ram. It could also be found in Aries, the first sign of the zodiac. She knew that much. But not what it symbolised. Maybe he could answer that question.

*****

The atmosphere in the square was rising. Hordes of bedraggled figures jostled for the best positions down on the ground below the balconies that surrounded the square. An ironic cheer went up every time someone ventured onto the platform sometimes to check the noose or ensure everything was in order. The occasional piece of mouldy fruit would fly out of the crowd prematurely. It was no surprise that the poor went hungry when the short supply of food they did have was thrown at corpses.

Annabelle moved into position on the balcony next to Nostradamus. Her father sat in the seat next to him. As he beckoned for someone to pull a chair out for her, he noticed the gravity of her expression.

"My child. Do not mourn those who have themselves to blame. At the end, all of us must justify ourselves in the eyes of God. I think it might take Philibert longer than most. He's not worthy of your sadness."

"He is worthy," she whispered. "Father, you are a man of kind heart and strong will, you have the power to stop this. Does it make us stronger to punish those weaker than ourselves, who were not granted the same chances as we were?"

"I can't stop it. This is the King's order and he wants to set an example to others. It's just the way of things."

"Your father is right," said Nostradamus desperately trying to keep a straight face. "Philibert knew the costs. I tried to encourage him to go another route, but alas, he did not listen."

"You gave him no choice."

"I gave him what he asked for. I taught him to read the cosmic energy and he repaid me by making me look like a fool."

"Well, what do you expect from an Aries?" said Annabelle.

"Very good. I see you have been paying attention. Those born under the sign of the ram have always been independent, committed and determined to win. Philibert showed all of those traits in life. But he never fully embraced the Aries motto."

"There's a motto?"

"Yes. When you know yourself you are empowered. When you accept yourself you are invincible."

Annabelle reflected on the words and smiled. "But I think he has accepted it."

"A little late, don't you think?"

A roar went up as a bedraggled jailor wandered onto the stage and milked his fifteen minutes of fame. Like a warm-up act to the main event, he encouraged the crowd to practise the noises and hand gestures that were appropriate for each stage. The first was a loud boo that they delivered impeccably as Phil was led out onto the stage, thankfully no longer in bedclothes. Philibert had requested simple garments to mimic what thousands of others were wearing around him. Simple leggings and a rough tunic ill-fitting and littered with holes. With the midday sun on his face he walked out with his hands tied in front of him. Even from this distance, Annabelle could see that he was smiling and making every effort to glance around in all directions to ensure everyone saw who he was.

When the crowd's collective voice and patience had run dry he was positioned in the middle of the stage directly underneath the noose. The masked executioner read out a proclamation of crimes, each one greeted with more cheers and the occasional fruity projectile. The list was so long that it took almost fifteen minutes to read, although it was merely a fraction of the actual crimes he was responsible for. When the list came to an end the executioner breathed a sigh of relief; for one last time Philibert aimed his gaze purposefully to where Annabelle was positioned.

Or was he staring at Michel? She couldn't be certain.

The sun shimmered off something silver worn around his neck, but disappeared as an old sack was roughly dumped over his head, extinguishing his view of the world. The noose followed immediately after and Annabelle turned away.

The door to their balcony suddenly burst open and a red-faced young man flew in hysterically. "SIR!"

"Not now, Jean," said Michel, unmoved by the distraction. Whatever it was it could surely wait another five minutes while he enjoyed the show.

"But sir…"

"I'm sure it can wait."

"It really can't! If Philibert dies it might be lost forever."

"What are you talking about?"

"The coffer. It's not there anymore!"

"What? Please tell me you didn't put the book in there yet."

Jean nodded. "Yes. As you instructed me, too, only three days ago."

"But where is it?"

"Stolen. The thief even left a note," said Jean, passing Michel a scrap of paper that read, 'the real prophecy dies with me'.

No one liked being conned. It created a horrible abyss in your stomach. A menagerie of emotions were simultaneously triggered as they attempted to identify which one of them was responsible for blindly walking into the trap. Pride, vengeance, jealousy, stupidity and greed were all prime suspects. Michel blamed all of them, as well as Jean, Phil and the world in general. While he had sought to limit Philibert's reputation he was unwittingly helping it along. If the coffer had been stolen three days ago then it had happened before Michel had introduced Philibert to his past. Which meant Phil was expecting him to do just that. In fact he'd orchestrated it to fulfil his own plans. But was he really willing to die for it?

"Stop the execution!" shouted Michel at the top of his voice, drawing the crowd's attention away from the platform and up to the balcony. On hearing the surprise request, King Charles leant over the barrier.

"Carry on, executioner, or I will be forced to throw fruit at you." The young King turned to his mother. "Wood's a fruit, right?"

Michel limped out of the room, bounced down the stairs ungainly and burst out into the onlookers. He pushed his way past burly men brandishing turnips, dishevelled women in strong voice and puny children hurling grapes at each other. Focused on only one outcome, he even ignored the occasional comment of 'who's that?' as he barged his way closer to the stage. Metres from it a loud bang echoed off the walls of the buildings as the wooden trapdoor opened and a limp body was left dangling from the rope.

"No!"

The crowd sprang to their feet and in the surge forward Michel's frail body was buffered to the ground.

In a vain attempt to avoid being trampled to death he squirmed in between stomping feet as his face was squashed into mud. From that position he was unable to see what happened next, but he certainly heard it. There was an almighty snap as the rope sheared in two and Philibert's body fell limply through the hole and into a void under the stage.

Pandemonium broke out. The crowd became unruly as they bemoaned their lack of satisfaction. The King angrily lobbed blocks of wood, most of which hit the crowd. Throckmorton gave a quiet little fist pump in celebration that someone else had beaten the odds and proved it was possible to cheat death, even when fate had demanded it. Anne heard nothing, but that was quite normal. And the Queen simply leant back in her chair bored by the barbarity of the baying mob. Annabelle watched like a hawk for the slightest sign of the unusual.

The crowd weren't robbed of their bloodthirst for long. As soon as the executioner realised that his subject had fallen into the hole, he was soon clambering down into the stage to recover him. Two minutes later a new rope was being attached to the gallows and the noose was repositioned on the unresponsive masked body. Take two. The trapdoor fell and once again the body swung above the floor. A loud sigh of relief seeped out of the corpse as life was finally extinguished.

Michel brushed himself down and watched the final moments of Phil's life being squeezed out of him. The location of the coffer would die with him. As he turned away from the scene almost ashamed at his part in it, he overheard a conversation between two old-timers who had managed to get a prime position at the front of the crowd.

"I'm telling you something's not right," said the first through gums that had long forgotten what teeth felt like.

"But you're never happy, are you?" replied the second. "You always complain. Not enough blood. Too much blood. Not enough screaming. Too much screaming. Should have used an axe…"

"You have to watch the establishment. Always trying to fool us, that's all I'm saying."

"It's always a conspiracy with you."

"Use your eyes. I'm telling you that Philibert Lesage was taller than that a minute ago."

"It's normal. Bodies do that."

"Do what?"

"They appear shorter after a hanging."

"Bollocks. Surely the stretching makes them longer, not shorter."

"It's a mystery but true. I blame witches. I've seen a couple today, I reckon."

"And you say I'm always the sceptic. Look," said the man pointing to the corpse rocking gently in the air. "Tell me that's not a pot belly."

*****

There was much on Michel's mind as he and Jean de Cavigny returned home to Salon, a day's ride north of Marseille. The grand tour had departed for its next destination, Phil's body had been buried in an unmarked grave, and there were no clues to the coffer's whereabouts. Its contents were much more than a collection of Michel's work, they charted his own personal history. Mementoes from some of his assignments, his favourite pen, a medicine cabinet full of his experimental therapies, a cookbook, and many other items of sentimental value. And now, like Phil, they were gone.

In Salon the two men received a warmer welcome than they felt worthy of. People in the streets called out his name and waved in appreciation of their favourite local celebrity. It was the adulation the rest of France had not yet mirrored. At home Michel's wife, cradling his youngest child, and the rest of his band of children rallied around him, excited to learn of his latest adventure. Unknown to them it would be his last. Age had crept up on him almost unnoticed to diminish the mental and physical strength he'd once taken for granted. When the energy of the spirit leaves, it doesn't take the body long to notice. What life was left in him he would spend here on simpler pleasures amongst his family. It would be up to others to decide what marks he left on history.

"There was a man here to see you," said his wife casually.

"Right," he replied completely lacking interest.

"He had a delivery for you."

"A delivery. I wasn't expecting anything. Show me."

She took him into the house and pointed at a black, oak coffer in the middle of the room.

"What did he look like?"

"I'd say late-thirties, dark, frizzy hair, fair skin. Was kind of cunning-looking," she replied.

"Oh, he's certainly that."

"The coffer," said Jean peering over his boss's shoulder. "It's a miracle."

"Don't be foolish. Even prophets don't believe in miracles. Everything happens for a reason, you should know that from what I have taught you."

"But why did he send it back?"

"To prove he could."

Michel opened the door at the front and took a cursory glance at the contents. Almost everything was where he expected it to be, apart from one item.

"Why only take the book?" said Jean.

"Because now it has my name on it."

"But you can just send another version to the printer, can't you? You remember how the prophecy went, right?"

"There's no point. It's not genuine, I'm afraid. It was never meant to be. One day, far in the future, it will destroy me. Unless someone can steal it back."

- Chapter 33 -

The Truth

"Liar!" barked Ally, slapping Antoine fiercely across his face. "You've used me."

"Don't take it too hard, Ally, conning others is in his genes," replied Mario.

"It's not what you think!" exclaimed Antoine calmly. "I'm on your side."

"Of course you are," replied Ally sarcastically. "Why did you do it?"

"I know you don't trust me, but I can explain, just not right now. Believe me when I say it had to happen this way, there was no choice."

"I don't believe anything you say. You've dragged me on a wild goose chase, and Gabriel for that matter."

"Is that the young woman out in my entrance hall?" asked Mario, considering his third guest for the first time.

"Yes," replied Ally. "It's part of some sick game."

"It's not a game. We both want the same thing. We both want to stop the chaos."

"By creating more of it!"

"No. I have the answer to stop it, but it had to be like this."

"What, by staging the whole thing?"

"I think it's about time you told the truth," added Mario, intrigued as to why Antoine had gone to such extreme lengths to place all of them here at this time.

"Mario isn't the only one who has received guidance from the past. The discovery of the book was a genuine surprise to me, but since I was a very young boy my parents had told me about the prophecy and what to do when it began. To my surprise it arrived in the shape of Bernard Baptiste."

"I'm starting to feel sorry for him," replied Ally.

"About a month ago, Baptiste came to my home. I didn't know who he was until that morning. He didn't say why, but it's obvious to me now that he was looking for the book. I certainly wasn't the only one in the town he'd visited. He'd been to all the houses in my area dating back to Nostradamus's time, and he must have concluded that the book was hidden somewhere in one of them. When he saw the picture in the hallway of my wife wearing the locket, the same one he must have seen in your painting, then he knew he'd found the right place. I thought it was ludicrous at first when he suggested there was a book hidden somewhere in my house, but he was so convinced he offered to pay for a survey to see if it could be found. That's when they discovered the secret wall in the basement and the book inside a commode."

"Not a coffer, then."

"No, which was most disappointing because the legend passed down through my ancestors was of a coffer and nothing about a book at all."

"So why did you need me?" asked Ally.

"Because I knew Bernard was working for someone and if I wanted to work out who, I needed someone who understood how Nostradamus worked. Don't forget at that stage I didn't know the prophecy was a fake."

"But why burgle yourself and destroy your own car? Oh my God, you killed a policeman!"

"No, I didn't. It was all staged, I'm afraid."

"Staged! Why?"

"Because I knew when I first met you at the Basilique that I couldn't tell you what I knew, you wouldn't have believed me. You made it abundantly clear that prophecies never came true. I knew then that I'd have to convince you to trust me. And it worked. After the explosion you believed what I told you. The explosion acted as the perfect distraction. The policemen were both actors and the body on the step was a dummy."

"It's a bit extreme, isn't it?" replied Ally. "You could have just asked me nicely."

"And what would your response have been?"

"Something about sex and travel more than likely."

"Oh, that's very good," chuckled Mario, a mere interested bystander to their tiff.

"Exactly, so my approach worked as planned. You accompanied me and helped me get to this point."

"And Gabriel, why her?"

"A lucky coincidence. It was only after we met her when I realised I didn't need to keep trying to make anything happen anymore. It would happen anyway."

"What would happen?"

"This. Some outcomes are just written in the stars," replied Antoine. "Call it cosmic energy."

"You're mental. Prophecies never, I repeat never, come true."

"We'll see, won't we?"

"Once this is done I'm taking out a restraining order against you."

"Very well."

"And Bernard, what happened to him?" asked Ally.

"I don't know," replied Antoine. "But I would never kill anyone."

"He had plans of his own," said Mario. "I became suspicious that he was trying to identify the last descendants of Nostradamus, and if he succeeded he might accidentally stumble upon the true identity of the Oblivion Doctrine. I couldn't let that happen."

"Then you did kill him!" exclaimed Ally.

"That was not a confession. You still have no evidence to prove it. The flu would have taken him anyway, like it will everyone else. He just got a head start."

"One day you'll pay for your crimes," replied Ally, pointing a finger at him. Her anger was bursting through the surface. Everyone in the room had played her and it hadn't been a pleasant experience. Now that she'd finally heard the truth, all that was left was to find some way of revealing it to the world.

"I doubt it. You've seen the world burning, Antoine's revelation doesn't change anything. It doesn't matter who wrote the prophecy because people believe in the Oblivion Doctrine. Nostradamus's legacy is secure and I'm making more money than Amazon. There's nothing you can do to stop it."

"Just watch me!" said Ally defiantly.

"I'm afraid you won't be leaving this room."

Mario delivered the threat with an almost effortless calm. However harmless he might look, they were sure he meant every word, even if his means were unclear. This man had single-handedly organised Armageddon, two more casualties wouldn't give him a sleepless night.

"Mario, before you silence us, as I'm sure you're planning to, there's one thing I need to ask you," asked Antoine.

"Go ahead. I've waited a decade for a descendant of Philibert Lesage to beg me for their life."

"Oh, I'm not going to beg for anything," said Antoine, calmly rising to his feet. "All around you people are dying from N_1G_{13}, but you don't seem concerned about catching it. Why not?"

"Because I'm a recluse. The virus travels through the air and the only employees I have here are tested daily."

"But you've not checked us, have you?"

"No, but fortunately I'm a brilliant internet hacker and it's not hard for me to access the files of a simple solicitor's firm like Lamy & Veron's."

Antoine paced around the back of the sofa pretending to take in the view through the window while collecting his thoughts. As he slowly circled the horseshoe he reached inside the pocket of his beige jacket. Antoine's movement took him behind Mario and out of his eyesight.

"But what if we had the virus in a different form?"

"What?!"

Antoine jabbed a small syringe in the back of Mario's neck and pushed down on the plunger. In shock the victim leapt in the air, holding the back of his neck with the palm of his hand. There was no blood, but if he was able to bend his head far enough around he would have seen a small pinprick.

"What have you done?" screamed Mario.

"I've injected you with a concentrated dose of N_1G_{13}. Probably strong enough to kill you in the next hour, unless you do as I say."

"Where did you get that!" demanded Ally who'd scurried to the back of the room uncertain as to his state of mind and next action.

"When we first met, Ally, I told you I was once a pharmacist. But I'm not any old pharmacist. My company still owns a laboratory, which the government recently requisitioned from me. In order to find a cure for N_1G_{13}, every lab has been given samples of the virus to work on. It wasn't difficult to get one."

"You're a fool, Palomer," laughed Mario, slumped in his chair. "Just like your ancestors. Now that I have the virus it will quickly spread to you. There's no stopping it. You'll die, too."

"Oh, I beg to differ," replied Antoine. "We're not just here to pull down the Oblivion Doctrine."

"We're not?" said Ally.

"No. You see the prophecy in the book is a fake."

"We know that already. I told you that weeks ago. He says this Lesage character wrote it," she said, pointing at Mario.

"Lesage did write prophecies. Just not that one. It's a hoax, a fraud, a con. Created to fool people, many by Nostradamus himself, into believing that Lesage wrote it. And it was designed for this very moment."

Mario slumped to the floor, his brow thick with sweat and his body shaking violently as the extreme dose of flu overcame his immune system.

"If you want to live, Mario, you must give me the coffer."

"Why?" he spluttered.

"Because inside it your ancestor unwittingly produced a cure."

"How do you know this?" replied Ally.

"No time to explain," replied Antoine, riffling through the contents of the coffer to Mario's pathetic requests to stop. "Go find Gabriel and take this with you."

He passed her a fragile book opened at a specific page. On it were the details of a recipe whose base ingredients were out-of-date oranges, water, a squeeze of lemon, and sugar.

"It looks like a recipe for marmalade."

"Yes, but it's a very special one with additional antibodies."

"And what do you want me to do with it?"

"Tell Gabriel to find his servers and post it online. Then email it to my lab so they can start to mass-produce it."

"What about me?" murmured Mario.

"You'll have to hope they work fast."

Out in the hallway, Ally found Cynthia unconscious on the hall tiles and Gabriel sitting quietly humming to herself.

"What happened here?!"

"Oh, I punched her," replied Gabriel, calmly snapping out of her daydream and back to reality.

"Why?"

"She looked at me funny."

"Describe funny?"

Gabriel made an almost imperceptible change to her own expression. "Like that."

"Remind me never to piss you off. Come on, we need to find a way to get this online."

It wasn't long before Gabriel had located Mario's computer and had hacked in to act on his behalf. The speed and accuracy of how she worked was breath-taking as always. Ally could barely see her hands moving. And whilst Gabriel's fingers moved with incredible speed, the rest of her body was decidedly sloth-like in its lack of urgency.

Within an hour the message boards, blogs and website banners were all primed with details of the remedy and it wasn't long before the internet community were jumping on-board to spread the message. Antoine's laboratory signalled their receipt of the formula and set to work trying to find as many mouldy oranges they could lay their hands on.

- Chapter 34 -

The Longest Con

Death comes to us all, but the impact mostly affects the living. The deceased rarely complain. Living in the shadow of grief changes your outlook on life, until it's your own turn to walk that same path. One death is hard enough to deal with, but several at once was even worse. Annabelle had had enough this year to last a lifetime. By the end of fifteen sixty-five her father, Claude, had passed away peacefully. Her brothers, of course, shouldered much of the responsibilities for the administration of his affairs, but she bore the emotional impact.

Only months later Nostradamus had also shaken off his mortal coil, although she would not mourn his passing to the same extent. And at the age of only twenty-six she'd just buried her second husband, Georges. It wasn't true to say that she truly loved him, but unlike Jacques, he was no monster. There was at least an affection and some mutual understanding that made their relationship benign at worst and at best occasionally enjoyable. The mysterious circumstances of his passing had shocked everyone. And passing was the right description. Neither Georges's boat nor body were ever found from the excursion he'd taken along the coast to Spain, in extremely calm conditions.

At least her father couldn't marry her off again. She was too old now anyway. Who wanted a middle-aged widow with two husbands under her belt and a body that was beyond its best-before date when it came to childbirth? Maybe she'd get a cat. Dabble in some witchcraft and live out the stereotype no doubt others were already creating for her.

She excused herself from the wake and retired to her chamber, dragging her long, black funeral dress across the cold, sharp steps.

Above all else she wished for the pain of loss to ease, and allow a semblance of normality to make a welcomed return. It wouldn't be anytime soon, she thought. This year of grief had been layered on top of the greatest loss of all. The biggest void in her heart was for the one person she'd loved above all others, whose passing just over a year ago had stripped away her vitality and one last chance to lead a life of purpose.

As she approached her chamber on the top floor of the tower she noticed that the door was ajar and the light from the fire no longer shone through it. From the crack between door and wall she could see that the curtains had been pulled shut and the room had been plunged into almost perfect darkness, quite unlike the way it had been left. Someone had been here. No, someone was here. A shadowy figure sat in a chair by the window.

An involuntarily scream escaped her mouth and her body froze. "Guards!"

"They'll come. Give them a few minutes," said the man. "Those stairs are a killer."

"What do you want?"

"I wanted to pay my respects."

"The funeral is downstairs, maybe you took a wrong turn."

"It's easy to do."

"That way," she pointed.

"I wanted to pay my respects to you, not a corpse. I'm sorry to hear of your loss," replied the man solemnly. "I didn't hate him even half as much as the first one."

As her eyes became more accustomed to the lack of light she did her best to identify the imposter. A wide-brimmed hat concealed most of his features and his body was sheathed in black.

"Who are you?"

"I'm a no one. The real question is who do you want to be?"

"That's no concern of yours," she said nervously.

"Oh, but it is. You see you're being given one last chance to answer before the guards try to remove me."

"I thought I knew once, but I lost the courage."

"It wasn't the only thing you lost."

The man held his clenched fist out in front of him so it was bathed in the slightest slither of moonlight that was desperately trying to infiltrate the room. The plan worked perfectly. The moon glinted off a cluster of pearls that dangled from a fine silver chain.

"My locket. How did you get it?"

"I took it from the chest, of course. I almost took it the very first time we met. The pendant now holds something of great importance. What say we take it with us?"

*****

The trip was only meant to last a weekend, but in reality she'd been in France for more than a month. It was quite some field trip. A week on from the experiences at Mario's the world was taking its first gentle steps towards normality. If that was at all possible. Once the messages about the Nostradamus cure had saturated the public consciousness and the scientists had quickly perfected the production, batches of it were being delivered to every corner of the globe. Orange prices went through the roof.

Rather than pull the Oblivion Doctrine down completely, Gabriel had reprogrammed it to show a recurring story detailing the work that Nostradamus had been least proud of that had also been concealed within the coffer. Not everyone accepted it. After all, some people avoid the truth at all costs. But enough people got bored of seeing the same story rotating over and over for the Oblivion Doctrine's popularity to sink to obscurity in a matter of days. The Oblivion Doctrine's work had once gone viral but there was always a cure for everything.

Gabriel's skills were soon in high demand. Not from the prepper community, who were mostly still underground and unaware of recent developments, but as a freelance internet security expert. She bought an extremely expensive new car and still drove like an idiot.

Mario received the remedy before N_1G_{13} took his life. Arrest followed soon after for the murder of Bernard Baptiste. In the months to come the prosecutors revealed the extent of Mario's activities through the Oblivion Doctrine. It included various lobbying groups, e-commerce sites and even pharmaceuticals. Antoine was not the only person who had access to a laboratory. The connections would soon produce the evidence needed to secure a conviction.

Flu cases decreased as fast as they'd risen and the restrictions on public movement were lifted. Ally could finally book her flight home. Antoine offered to drop her at the airport. She accepted. It wasn't because they'd settled their differences, she'd never forgive him for the lies he'd told her. But her curiosity and need for answers had still not been quenched. There were explanations he owed her.

"What time is your flight?" said Antoine as he accompanied her into the airport's departure area.

"It's meant to be eleven-thirty, but it's a low-cost carrier so it could be anytime this week," she replied bitterly.

There was an awkward silence as the two stood in front of the boarding gates trying to decide how their parting should be managed. Antoine went first.

"Ally, I know the last few weeks haven't been a great experience for you, but I just wanted to say that I enjoyed spending the time with you. You really should let people in more."

"What's the point? Just as you proved, people always end up being a disappointment."

"I really am sorry. What happened was entirely necessary even if it wasn't comfortable."

"Why? What possible benefit came from lying?"

"The lie was necessary for the prophecy to come to fruition without anyone manipulating it. There was too much at stake."

"But the prophecy didn't come true, did it? The end of the world wasn't nigh after all."

"No, and that's mostly thanks to you."

"Blah, what did I do? Gabriel had more involvement than I did."

"It would have been impossible without both of you."

"Before I leave, explain one thing to me?" asked Ally politely. "Why would Lesage go to all that trouble pretending that he wrote the prophecy?"

"Do you still believe that no prophecies are accurate?"

"Yes, of course. This episode proves it completely."

"Well, I think Philibert Lesage did believe in them. Which is why he tricked Nostradamus into believing that his prophecies were superior. That way he wouldn't notice if Philibert gave him a fake."

"Then if it was a fake who wrote the one in the book?"

"I'm not sure we'll ever know who," said Antoine, reaching into his pocket and pulling out a small, wrapped box. "I want you to have this."

"What is it?"

"Open it. That's the point of covering it in paper!"

The box had been beautifully wrapped with silver paper and a small gold bow. She untied it and slowly removed a box from the shiny paper. Inside the box the ram locket stared back at her.

"I can't accept this."

"You've earned it."

"But it's part of your heritage. You must pass it on to the next in line."

"There isn't anyone. It would die with me. Anyway, I think it belongs to a woman not a man. I used to sit for hours after my wife died just staring at it, as if her life was concealed somewhere in its surface. It was only after that when I realised its significance."

"I can't take it."

"You must."

Antoine adjusted his hat and turned without further comment, leaving Ally alone in the middle of Lyon Airport holding the locket on her palm. She placed it in her handbag. After the rigmarole of check-in, airport security and an hour watching hopefully for the flight number to finally reveal its gate number, finally she settled into her seat on the plane.

Her thoughts settled on home. She missed her little cottage, the peace, the quiet and even, to her surprise, the people she worked with. Maybe they weren't so bad after all. They were trying to do their best, even if their brainpower couldn't keep up with hers. It wasn't a surprise that none of them had contacted her over the last month. No one had wondered about her welfare, but then again nor had she about theirs. Maybe if she made the first move it might draw people closer to her, rather than push them further away. She reached inside her handbag to find her phone and text one of them, but her fingers rested on the small, square box.

She lifted it out to take a second look. As she rotated the locket in her fingers she noticed a little clasp on the bottom edge. It was firmly lodged shut but with a little effort and the assistance of a hairpin she managed to force it open. There was a small cavity inside where a lady might conceal a small ring or perhaps in later periods a treasured photograph. Now, though, the locket contained something much more interesting. A beige scrap of paper folded over many times. This wasn't new paper, she knew that. The fibres were rough and the surface uneven as a result of it being made by hand rather than by a machine.

She unfolded it carefully. Written in a clear, flowing handwriting were four lines, a signature and a date.

When the Baptist of Mâcon learns the secrets of Oblivion
And the Angel Gabriel prepares for the end,
Tirelessly plough old fields to discover man's demise
The black, oak coffer and Michel's oranges will cure all.

Philibert Lesage, 1563

THE END

Read more Dr. Ally Oldfield in
'Last of the Mountain Men'

Sign up to the newsletter
www.tonymoyle.com/contact/

Printed in Great Britain
by Amazon